W9-ACZ-127

MAGNOLIA DRIVE

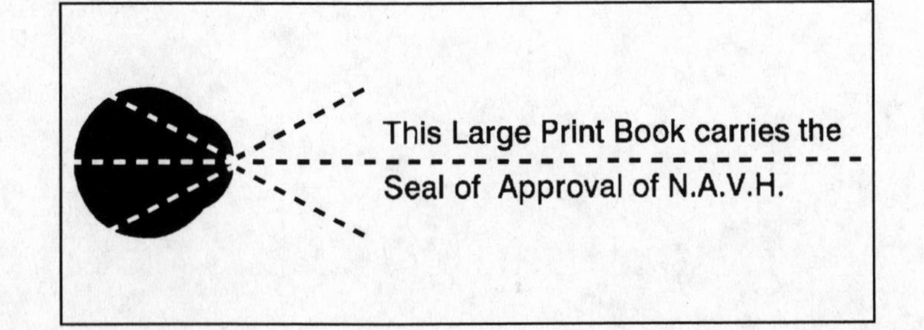
This Large Print Book carries the
Seal of Approval of N.A.V.H.

A CAVANAUGH ISLAND NOVEL

MAGNOLIA DRIVE

ROCHELLE ALERS

THORNDIKE PRESS
A part of Gale, Cengage Learning

Farmington Hills, Mich • San Francisco • New York • Waterville, Maine
Meriden, Conn • Mason, Ohio • Chicago

Thorndike Press, a part of Gale, Cengage Learning.

Thorndike Press® Large Print African-American.
The text of this Large Print edition is unabridged.
Other aspects of the book may vary from the original edition.
Set in 16 pt. Plantin.

LIBRARY OF CONGRESS CATALOGING-IN-PUBLICATION DATA

Alers, Rochelle.
Magnolia Drive / Rochelle Alers. — Large print edition.
pages cm. — (A Cavanaugh Island novel ; 4) (Thorndike Press large print African-American)
ISBN 978-1-4104-7411-7 (hardcover) — ISBN 1-4104-7411-9 (hardcover)
1. Actresses—Fiction. 2. Motion picture producers and directors—Fiction. 3. African Americans—Fiction. 4. Large type books. I. Title.
PS3551.L3477M34 2014
813'.54—dc23 2014031975

Published in 2014 by arrangement with Grand Central Publishing, a division of Hachette Book Group, Inc.

Printed in Mexico
1 2 3 4 5 6 7 18 17 16 15 14

To my granddaughter
Nadia G. Gonzalez

Children's children are a crown to the aged, and parents are the pride of their children.

Proverbs 17:6

Chapter One

Francine Tanner downshifted, decelerating to less than ten miles an hour as the rain came down in torrents, obstructing her view. The rising wind blew the precipitation sideways. The wipers were at the highest speed, yet did little to sluice the water off the Corvette's windshield fast enough. She maneuvered along Sanctuary Cove's Main Street before turning off onto Moss Alley and parking behind the Beauty Box; she turned off the wipers and then the engine of the low-slung sports car. It'd been raining for nearly a week and she, like everyone else who lived along South Carolina's Sea Islands, wondered when they would ever see the sun again.

Pulling the hood of her raincoat over her head, she sprinted through puddles in the parking lot to the rear of the full-service salon and day spa. It took several attempts before she was able to unlock the door. Her mother had had the locksmith change the cylinder, yet it still jammed. She made a mental note to have him replace the entire lock. Pushing open the steel door, she flipped on the light switches and within seconds recessed and track lights illuminated the newly renovated salon like brilliant summer sunlight.

Francine had come in an hour before the salon opened for business to take down Christmas decorations and pack them away until the next season. After hanging up her raincoat in the employee lounge, she slipped out of her wet running shoes and turned on the satellite radio to one of her favorite stations. Hip-hop blared through the speakers concealed throughout ceiling panels.

She took a quick glimpse at her reflection along the wall of mirrors. A profusion of dark red curls framed her face, falling to her shoulders; it wasn't the first time she realized she'd been so busy styling the hair of the salon's customers that she'd neglected the most important person in her life: Francine Dinah Tanner.

Although she normally didn't make New Year's resolutions, she resolved she would dedicate this year to herself at the same time she pulled her hair off her face, securing it in an elastic band. Several wayward curls escaped the band, grazing her ears and the nape of her neck.

She needed a new look and definitely a new attitude but didn't want to think about all the things she had to do to change her life as she pushed her sock-covered feet into a pair of leather clogs and walked to the front of the shop to check the voice mail. Five days a week Francine helped her mother manage the salon, cut and style hair, and occasionally fill in for the manicurist and/or aesthetician whenever they were backed up. The other two days were now spent helping her grandmother adjust to moving from her Charleston condo to living under the same roof with her son, daughter-in-law, and granddaughter.

Eighty-one-year-old Dinah Donovan Tanner had protested loudly when her son insisted she give up living independently and move into a wing of his house on Cavanaugh Island. Frank Tanner had installed an elevator so his mother wouldn't have to navigate the staircase, converted the west wing to include a bedroom suite with an adjoining bath outfitted for a senior, a living/dining room with a sitting area, and a state-of-the-art kitchen. Once the octogenarian saw her new apartment she reluctantly agreed to move to Sanctuary Cove.

Even if Grandma Dinah had initially pouted like a surly adolescent, Francine secretly applauded her father's decision to take control of his mother's life because it meant she didn't have to drive to Charleston to see to her grandmother's physical and emotional well-being. And most nights she ate dinner with her. Dinah, who'd lived up to her reputation as one of the best cooks in the Lowcountry, had settled into a more laid-back life on the island, grinning nonstop because she got to see her only grandchild every day.

Now that her best friend, Morgan Dane Shaw, was married, they had curtailed their early morning bicycle outings from five days a week, weather permitting, to one or two. She and Morgan had been high school outsiders and had never cultivated close relationships with the other students living in Charleston or on Cavanaugh Island. Even when both left the island to attend out-of-state colleges they never lost contact with each other. She missed hanging out with her friend, but she was glad that Morgan had found her happily ever after with Nathaniel Shaw.

Pencil in hand, Francine activated the voice mail feature and jotted down appointments in the book spread out on the reception desk. There were messages from regulars who wanted a myriad of services. Then she went completely still when she heard the last two messages. The nail technician and one of the stylists had called to say they were experiencing flulike symptoms.

Two weeks after Thanksgiving influenza had swept across the island like wildfire. Hardly anyone was left unscathed. Classroom attendance in the schools in the island's three towns — Sanctuary Cove, Haven Creek, and Angels Landing — was drastically reduced when students, faculty, and staff alike succumbed to the virus. The local health department had declared a health emergency, forcing the schools' superintendent to issue an order to close the schools four days before the onset of the Christmas recess. Under another set of circumstances students would've applauded extending the holiday recess, but most were too sick to celebrate.

The waiting room in Dr. Asa Monroe's medical practice had been standing room only. The island's resident doctor sent his patients home to limit the spread of the virus and made house calls instead. Dinah refused to let Dr. Monroe give her a flu shot, declaring she didn't like doctors or needles, opting instead to take an herbal concoction guaranteed to offset the symptoms of colds and flu. The elderly woman declared proudly that she was healthier than many half her age because of the herbal remedies that had been passed down through generations of Donovan women. Francine and her parents took the shot and were fortunate enough to avoid the full effect of chills, fever, and general lethargy. However, her mother, Mavis Tanner, like most of the merchants in the Cove, closed the Beauty Box for a week because of a rash of cancellations. She'd used the time to have repairs made to the adjacent space that was now the Butterfly Garden Day Spa.

Francine disassembled the lifelike artificial tree, putting it and the ornaments in a large duffel bag on wheels. Coming in early had its advantages. She could listen to her favorite stations on the radio before some of the elderly customers gave her the stink eye about her taste in music. They'd grumbled constantly to Mavis until Francine told her mother she wouldn't be opposed to listening to a station featuring songs spanning the sixties, seventies, and sometimes the eighties because she'd grown up listening to the music from her parents' youth.

She'd just wheeled the duffel into the storeroom when the rear door opened and her mother walked in. "We're down two this morning, Mama."

"Who are they?" Mavis asked as she hung her jacket on the wall hook.

"Candace and Danita have come down with the flu. Don't worry, I'll cover for both," Francine volunteered.

She watched as Mavis shook the moisture from her shoulder-length twists. Physically she and her mother were complete opposites. Mavis, petite with a dark complexion, claimed the distinctive broad features of her Gullah ancestry, while Francine had inherited her paternal grandmother's fair complexion, red hair, and freckles. However, the special gift she'd been born with to discern the spirit had come from her maternal grandmother.

Mavis slipped into a black smock with her name and *Beauty Box* embroidered in white lettering over her heart. "How many customers does Candace have?"

Francine put on her own smock. "Three. She has two cuts and a color. We can't afford to turn anyone away after losing a week's receipts."

"We're going to fare a lot better than some of the other shop owners who rely on folks coming in from the mainland to keep them out of the red until the spring and summer."

The Beauty Box, the only salon on the island, boasted a thriving year-round business because many residents didn't want to drive or take the ferry into Charleston to get their hair and nails done, while most mom-and-pop stores in the Cove and the Creek weren't as fortunate. They relied on an influx of tourists during the spring and summer months to sample the cuisine, buy local handicrafts, and tour the antebellum mansions and plantations.

"You're right," Francine agreed. She stared at Mavis as she took a large envelope filled with cash out of her tote. Although the salon accepted credit card payments, some of their customers still preferred using cash. "You're past due for a rinse, Mama." The neatly twisted hair was liberally streaked with gray.

Mavis's dark brown eyes met a pair of shimmering emerald green. "Your mama is fifty-nine. And that means I'm old enough to have gray hair *and* at least *one* grandbaby."

Francine rolled her eyes. "Please, let's not start in on grandbabies again, Mama. You don't hear Grandma Dinah talking about becoming a great-grandmother."

"That's because she's already a grandmother," Mavis countered. "Adding *great* to *grandmother* is just a formality. I'm the only woman in the Chamber of Commerce's Ladies Auxiliary who's not a grandmother and that is something Linda Hawkins is quick to bring up every chance she gets."

"That's because she's still pissed off that you took Daddy from her."

Mavis glared at Francine. "I didn't take him from her because she couldn't lose something she never had."

"That's not what she tells anyone who will stand still long enough for her to bad-mouth you."

"And you know I don't entertain gossip *or* lies."

"I know and so does everyone on Cavanaugh Island," she mumbled under her breath at the same time she took the envelope from her mother. "I'll put this in the cash register for you."

She did not have to be reminded of her mother's pet peeve; beauty salons were usually breeding grounds for salacious gossip, and because of this Mavis had a hard and fast rule that if any of her employees were caught gossiping with the customers or repeating something they'd overheard it would be grounds for immediate dismissal. Mavis ran her business with the precision of a Marine Corps drill sergeant much to the satisfaction of those who frequented the salon. If someone had an appointment for two, then they were guaranteed to be sitting in a chair at that time or within fifteen minutes.

Francine knew if she didn't put some distance, if only temporarily, between herself and her mother, Mavis would invariably bring up the topic of her not dating some of the men who'd expressed an interest in her. Although Mavis claimed she didn't entertain gossip Francine knew she'd overheard talk about her daughter being linked with David Sullivan.

The attractive Charleston-based attorney had become a very eligible bachelor once his girlfriend ended their five-year relationship because of his inability to commit. Although she and David were seen together at the annual Island Fair, she was aware their friendship would never become more than that. David was a wonderful catch but not for her. Francine knew her mother's wish to become a grandmother was overshadowed by her need to see her daughter married to someone with whom she could spend the rest of her life.

When she married Aiden Fox, Francine believed it would be forever. But, sadly, her fairy-tale marriage didn't end with a happily ever after. Deceit and mistrust had reared its ugly head once she realized the man who'd declared his undying love had only used her to further his acting career. What had shocked her more than Aiden's duplicity was that she hadn't seen it coming. Although she could see someone else's future in her visions, she could not do the same with her own. She still believed in love and happily ever after, although it appeared to have passed her by. She wanted all of the things she and her best friend, Morgan, had talked about when they were teenage girls. They'd wanted to fall in love and marry men who would love and protect them, who'd become the fathers of their children, and with whom they would grow old together. She hadn't given up on love, and she was still hopeful she would be given a second chance at finding her own happiness.

Tapping buttons, she entered the passcode on the electronic cash register, placing the bills in the drawer and then closing it. Staring through the front door's beveled glass, Francine smiled when she saw pinpoints of sunlight coming through watery clouds. The downpour was letting up. Maybe with the sun her mood would improve. Last night she'd had a vision wherein she heard angry voices; the sound grew louder, reverberating in her head. She then saw gaping mouths from which spewed expletives and threats. What she couldn't see were the faces of the people in her vision. She knew it was in Sanctuary Cove because she recognized the marble statue of patriot militiaman General Francis Marion atop a stallion in the town square. The vision had vanished quickly, but the uneasiness that had gripped her persisted. This was the second time the vision had come to her. The first was on Christmas Eve, when she'd returned from Charleston after a day of last-minute shopping, and Francine hadn't thought much of it until now.

She made a mental note to talk to her mother about it. Mavis, who'd grown up with her own mother talking about dreams and visions, had taught Francine how to interpret her visions, but this one puzzled even her. It was on a rare occasion that she didn't or couldn't see the faces of the people in the images and because of that it was more than disturbing. Who, or what, she mused, had set neighbors against one another?

Francine was six when she realized she was different from other children. A week before she was to enter the first grade she could describe what the school's new first grade teacher looked like. When Francine recounted the frightening incident to Mavis she reassured her that Francine had been born with a special gift just like her grandmother, but that the gift would have to remain the family's secret. The second vision didn't appear until she turned ten, and then they became more frequent as she grew older. Morgan was the only person aside from her family that knew she had psychic abilities.

Francine unlocked the front door and turned over the sign to indicate the Beauty Box was open for business. Francine returned to the lounge and found Brooke Harrison, the shampoo girl, and Taryn Brown, the aesthetician-masseuse, brewing coffee and setting out an assortment of sweet breads from the Muffin Corner for the staff. The space contained a utility kitchen with a microwave, cappuccino-espresso machine, refrigerator-freezer, half bath, and a table with seating for six as well as a seating arrangement to accommodate eight. It was where the employees came to relax between customers and take their meals. A cleaning service came in twice a week to keep the salon and spa spotless.

Mavis spared no expense when it came to creating a relaxing environment for her customers and employees.

"The coffee smells wonderful," Francine said as she tuned the radio to a cool jazz station. Brooke smiled and the skin around her robin's-egg-blue eyes crinkled with the gesture. They teased each other, saying they were sisters from different mothers, because both had red curly hair.

"It's a hazelnut blend."

Brooke, a recent cosmetology graduate, had offered to assume the responsibility for brewing coffee. She still worked part-time as a Starbucks barista. "Candace and Danita have called in sick, so we're going to be a little tight today," Francine informed the two women.

"Do I have any cancellations?" Taryn asked Francine.

"No. You're good." Taryn, who'd worked at a spa in Atlanta for more than fifteen years but wanted a more laid-back setting, had applied for the position of masseuse when she'd read that the Beauty Box had expanded to include a day spa. Offering spa services had attributed to a steady increase in the salon's overall profit margin.

The chime on the front door echoed and Francine went to greet their first client of the day.

Keaton Grace knew he couldn't meet with his attorney and business manager looking like the Wolfman. He hadn't shaved in more than two weeks and hadn't cut his hair in four. He'd spoken to Devon Gilmore, who'd arranged to meet him in Sanctuary Cove so he could sign the necessary documents to dissolve the partnership between him and his investment banker slash brother-in-law. At forty-one, he now wanted complete control of his projects: writing, directing, and producing. The dissolution had caused a rift between Keaton and his sister Liana, but he was willing to risk their close relationship in order to control his own destiny.

Opening the binder on the boardinghouse's bedside table with listings of shops and services on Cavanaugh Island, he perused it. Reading the advertisement for the Beauty Box, he noted the hours of operation. He smiled. They welcomed walk-ins and that was exactly what he was going to be this afternoon.

Keaton had spent the past week cloistered in his suite at the Cove Inn because of the rainy weather. He'd ordered room service instead of eating with the other boarders because he'd found himself in the zone when revising a script. His first visit to Cavanaugh Island had been last summer, to survey the region. At that time he'd checked in at a Charleston hotel and drove to the island under the guise of tourist when in reality he was looking to purchase property.

Cavanaugh Island was one of the many Sea Islands ranging from South Carolina to Florida that Keaton had explored. Either the price of an acre of land on some of the better known islands like Hilton Head, Myrtle Beach, and Jekyll was exorbitant or the zoning laws wouldn't permit him to erect a movie studio, or both.

Once he'd found the perfect property on Cavanaugh Island, he knew this time he intended to stay. Keaton had arranged a proxy purchase of a twelve-acre lot with an abandoned farmhouse because he'd been unable to leave Los Angeles. He was involved in wrapping an independent film that was already well over the initial budget and it was important that he remain on the West Coast to complete the project. He planned to live in the renovated farmhouse and utilize ten of the twelve acres to build a studio and soundstage for Grace Lowcountry Productions. Thankfully Sanctuary Cove's zoning laws did not have the restrictions he'd encountered on many of the other islands.

Living at the Cove Inn suited Keaton's daily needs. His furnished suite had a private bath, minibar, TV, and radio, and his laundry was done on the premises. He'd had little contact with the other boarders because he coveted his time. Relocating from Los Angeles to the small island off the coast of South Carolina was definitely a culture shock. He didn't have to deal with traffic jams, bright lights, smog, and wailing sirens. And then there was nightlife. It was virtually nonexistent. The exception was the Happy Hour, a nightclub in Haven Creek. The quietness and slower pace were things he hadn't known before and had come to look forward to. It was as if everything around him was slower, serene, and at times it appeared surreal.

Pulling on a bright yellow slicker over his sweatshirt and jeans, he picked up his keys and left the suite, closing the self-locking door behind him. Taking the back staircase, Keaton walked to the parking area. The cars and SUVs in the lot bore license plates from as far away as Michigan. His BMW sedan with Pennsylvania plates was parked between two minivans from Illinois.

Snowbirds. He'd discovered many of those at the boardinghouse were spending their winter in South Carolina to escape the snow and frigid northern temperatures. If they thought him a snowbird Keaton wasn't about to correct their perception. He'd come from L.A. to Sanctuary Cove via New York and Pittsburgh, which many of his family members still called home. In his heart he was still a son of the Steel City and a rabid Steelers' fan. He'd joked to a reporter during an interview that if stabbed he wouldn't bleed red but black and gold.

The rain had slackened to a drizzle and after starting up the engine he turned the wipers to the lowest setting. Although he'd heard some people complain about the incessant rain, he didn't mind the inclement weather. Keaton discovered years ago that he did his best work with the sound of rain hitting the windows; he'd always found it soothing. It was akin to being in a cocoon where he was able to shut out reality to escape into a world of his own choosing.

He'd also noticed there were no posted speed limits, traffic lights, or stop signs on the island, prompting him to drive slower than twenty miles per hour when he saw other motorists driving slowly, as if they didn't have a care in the world. The adjustment hadn't been easy after years of zipping along California's freeways. However, the topography was something he never wanted to get used to. The primordial swamps and forests teeming with indigenous wildlife, ancient oak trees draped in Spanish moss, the fanlike fronds of palmetto trees, the stretch of beach and the ocean were unlike anyplace he'd ever lived. The rain had stopped completely when Keaton entered the business district and maneuvered into an area behind rows of stores that had been set aside for parking.

Leaving his slicker in the car, he set out on foot for a leisurely walk along Main Street, while glancing into the quaint shops so integral to the viability of everyone living and working in the small town. Shopkeepers were cleaning plate-glass windows and sweeping up the palmetto leaves littering the gutter. Keaton smiled. It was as if the island were waking up from a weeklong slumber. He noticed the woman in the Parlor Bookstore placing a sign in the window indicating a 15 percent discount on best sellers, and a couple of doors down a man in the Muffin Corner was filling a showcase with trays of muffins and doughnuts. His stroll ended when he pushed open the beveled glass door to the Beauty Box.

When he saw the woman at the reception desk, a line from one of his favorite films popped into his head: *Of all the gin joints in all the towns in all the world, she walks into mine.* But he wasn't the Humphrey Bogart character referring to Ingrid Bergman, and the Beauty Box wasn't Rick's Café from *Casablanca.* What were the odds he would walk into a hair salon in a town on a remote sea island and come face-to-face with Francine Tanner?

Dark red curly hair framed a face he could never forget. The last time he'd seen her she'd been on an off-Broadway stage basking in thunderous applause as she took an infinite number of curtain calls. He'd been living in New York City, working as a scriptwriter for an Emmy Award–winning daytime drama, while completing a graduate degree in theater at New York University. When not working or studying he'd spent all of his free time going to Broadway and off-Broadway plays or catering parties.

When he went to see the play in which she'd played one of the lead characters, Keaton had sat close enough to the stage to see the vibrant color of her emerald-green eyes. He knew it was rude, but he couldn't pull his gaze away from her beautiful face. What, he mused, was she doing in Sanctuary Cove? And why was she working in a hair salon?

"May I help you, sir?"

Her beautifully modulated voice, with traces of a Southern drawl, shattered Keaton's reverie. "I don't have an appointment, but I'd like a haircut and a shave."

Francine smiled. "You don't need an appointment. Please, Mr. . . ."

"It's just Keaton," he supplied.

"Mr. Keaton, please have a seat in the second chair."

"No. Keaton's the first name," he corrected in a quiet voice.

He sat where she'd directed him, the salon's sleek black-and-white color scheme reminding him of the upscale establishments in tony New York and L.A. neighborhoods. The mirrored walls, track lighting, white marble floor, and soft jazz were sophisticated as well as inviting. Keaton's eyes met Francine's in the mirror when she draped a black cape around his neck and over his shoulders and chest. The scent of her intoxicating perfume wafted to his nostrils, and he thought the scent perfect for her.

"How short do you want it?" she asked, running a wide-tooth comb through tightly curling hair sprinkled with flecks of gray.

Keaton couldn't stop the smile finding its way over his features. "I want it cropped close to my scalp."

Francine rested her hands on his shoulders over the cape. "I'm going to analyze a few strands before I cut it. After the cut I'll wash your hair and condition your scalp because it looks a little dry. I'd like to warn you that you'll have to sit with a plastic cap on your head while I shave you. Do you have a problem with that?"

Smiling and exhibiting a mouth filled with straight white teeth, Keaton shook his head. "I don't think so."

A slight flush suffused Francine's face. "I said that because there are some men who don't want to be seen sitting in a salon wearing a plastic cap."

He smothered a chuckle. "I'm not one of those men." And he wasn't. If there were two things Keaton was secure about it was his masculinity and his work.

Settling back in the chair, he succumbed to the touch of the woman who had him intrigued the second he recognized her. Rather than stare at her, he closed his eyes and crossed his arms over his chest under the cape. Keaton remembered Francine's performance in the off-Broadway play *Sisters;* he had been profoundly disappointed when she hadn't been nominated for an Obie. Years later he'd recalled her acting ability when he wrote a script with her in mind. He contacted her agent, who told him she'd left the business. The news stunned Keaton, because he didn't want to believe someone of her incomparable talent would walk away from a career to which she'd been born. He opened his eyes when someone tapped his shoulder.

"You're new around here, aren't you?"

Keaton stared at an elderly woman with white hair set on a profusion of tiny multicolored plastic rollers. She stared back at him over a pair of half-glasses, dark eyes in an equally dark face narrowing slightly. There was something about her face that reminded him of his grandmother, but knew his prissy relative would never be so forward as to approach a stranger to ask a question without first being introduced.

"Yes, I am."

"Are you keeping company with anyone?"

Francine returned from the back, where she'd analyzed several strands of Keaton's hair. She knew he wanted it cropped, but she had to cut it short enough for the strands to lay flat. Her steps slowed when she saw Bernice Wagner engaged in conversation with him. She didn't want Keaton, as a first-time customer, to get the wrong impression about her mother's establishment. Miss Bernice, a former seamstress, had been an incurable gossip for as long as Francine could remember. There was never a time she came into the salon that Miss Bernice didn't start up a conversation with someone. And there were a few times when she'd become embroiled in a verbal confrontation and ended it only before it escalated into something short of a physical altercation.

"Miss Bernice, let me check and see if you're dry."

"There's no need to check," the older woman snapped angrily. "I was under that dryer so long it's a wonder I didn't smell my hair burning."

Affecting a smile she didn't feel at that moment, Francine counted slowly to five. She loved doing hair, but there were times when the folks who came into the Beauty Box tested her patience and she had to bite her tongue to keep from trading barbs with them.

"If you're dry then it's time for you to be combed out." She beckoned to Brooke. "Please come and comb out Miss Bernice."

"Not her, Red. You know your mother always combs me out," Miss Bernice said loudly.

Francine gave her a saccharine smile. "Do you mind if Brooke takes out your rollers?"

"Yes, I do mind. She can wash my hair, but I draw the line when it comes to setting and combing me out."

Cupping her elbow, she led the recalcitrant woman to Mavis's chair. "Please sit down and my mother will comb you out as soon as she finishes in the back." Her mother was busy mixing colors for a customer who'd wanted to lighten her hair to conceal the gray.

"If you say so," Miss Bernice said loudly. "What I cain't understand is why Alice Parker thinks she's going to be a better mayor than Spencer White," she said loudly when a customer walked in wearing a campaign button. "She and her husband look like dem Ken and Barbie baby dolls. Ain't dat enough one of dem is a politician?" she asked, lapsing into dialect. "Why cain't she stay home and raise her babies instead of runnin' round trying to git votes."

"Quit jawing, Bernice," admonished a woman who'd just sat down to wait for her hair to be blown out. "If it hadn't been for Congressman Parker we wouldn't have the newly paved road between the Cove and Landing."

Francine agreed, but held her tongue.

Before the road was built the residents of Sanctuary Cove had to take the ferry to the causeway, then the rutted, unpaved road connecting Haven Creek to Angels Landing. Few were brave enough to navigate the swamp, quicksand, alligators, and poisonous snakes on foot or in a vehicle, which made travel very difficult.

Bernice pushed out her lips. "I ain't saying her husband didn't do good, but why does she want to pit folks against each other by running agin Mayor White?"

Francine wanted to tell Miss Bernice that becoming mayor wasn't the same as being confirmed to the Supreme Court. It wasn't a lifelong position. And Spencer White had become complacent when it came to a number of issues affecting the Cove. Alice Parker's decision to challenge him in the upcoming election was certain to light a fire under the popular politician with matinee-idol looks. Alice had come out the front-runner in a special fall election to have her name placed on the ballot in order to oppose the incumbent mayor. Francine thought it would be nice for the Cove to have its first female mayor.

She managed to ignore her mother's client, who continued to engage the other customers in conversation as she picked up a pair of clippers and began cutting Keaton's hair. As a trained actress she'd learned to hide her innermost feelings behind a façade of indifference. Although she wasn't as blunt or prying as Miss Bernice, she wanted to know what had brought the incredibly handsome man in her chair to Sanctuary Cove.

The first thing she'd noticed about Keaton when he'd walked in was his height and broad shoulders. She'd estimated he stood several inches above six feet and his sweatshirt and relaxed jeans did little to camouflage a toned, slender body. His dark olive complexion, high cheekbones, lean jaw, and large, deep-set dark brown eyes made for an arresting *and* unforgettable face. When asked if he was new to the Cove, he'd said yes and Francine wondered if he meant new as in visiting the island or if he'd come to spend the winter.

Forcing her thoughts back to her task, she cut his hair, clumps falling to the cape around his shoulders and onto the floor. Once Francine had given up her acting career she'd returned to Sanctuary Cove and enrolled in cosmetology school. There weren't many employment opportunities on the island for a former actress but working with her mother at the Beauty Box had become a perfect fit.

She passed all of the courses and with a license in hand she worked as a floater at the salon, filling in as a shampoo girl and manicurist. It wasn't long before she could roller set faster than any of the other stylists, and like her mother, she excelled in cutting all types of hair.

If she'd felt she was born to act, Francine discovered doing hair was more than a satisfying substitute for what had been a lifelong dream. For as long as she could remember there'd been two barbershops in the Cove, but now there was only one. In order to take in the overflow she decided to go to barber school. The old-timers still frequented the barbershop on the side street between an auto body shop and shoemaker, while many of the younger men frequented the salon. Besides haircuts and hot towel shaves they also requested manicures, pedicures, and eyebrow waxing. Once Mavis opened the day spa, men and women lined up to make appointments for facials and massages. During prom season the Beauty Box offered student specials. There were also packages for brides, grooms, and wedding parties.

Francine picked up a blow-dryer and blew the remaining hair off the cape. "Is it short enough?" His cropped hair lay close to his scalp.

Keaton's eyes met hers in the mirror. He nodded. "It's perfect."

"Come with me and someone will shampoo you."

"You're not going to do it?"

"No. We have a shampoo person."

There came a pregnant pause as they stared at each other. "Okay," he conceded.

Francine didn't realize she'd exhaled a breath until Keaton rose to tower above her. She didn't want a replay with Keaton of what she'd just had with Miss Bernice. Customers who insisted on having one particular stylist do their hair occasionally caused problems when the stylist was either out sick or on vacation. Despite her worry, she couldn't help her excitement at the possibility of seeing Keaton again. She glanced up at him and realized it wasn't often that she had to look up at a man. He was a full head taller than she was. Standing five-eight in bare feet, and at least three or four inches taller in heels, made her height somewhat intimidating for some men.

Even in high school, Francine had been taller than many of the boys. She and Morgan had become best friends because both were tall and had been rail thin. It wasn't until just before they left the island to attend college that their bodies had begun to fill out. And with her red hair and freckles, Francine had become the brunt of more jokes than she cared to remember. She was Red to everyone but family members and Morgan. She escorted Keaton to the shampoo area, instructing Brooke which shampoo and conditioner to use.

After his wash and treatment, the next thirty-five minutes were spent with Francine shaving Keaton. She skillfully wielded the sharpened straight razor while struggling not to react to the warmth of his body and cologne. Each time their gazes met she felt as if someone had punched her in her midsection, causing a shortness of breath. The beard had concealed attractive slashes along his lean jaw and strong square chin. After Brooke rinsed out the conditioner, Francine applied a light hairdressing, plucked a few stray silky eyebrow hairs, and gently massaged a moisturizer on Keaton's smooth face before realizing everyone in the shop had been watching her.

There were audible sighs and she overheard someone mumble Keaton made Denzel Washington look hideous. Murmurs of agreement and protests followed the declaration. Francine hid a smile when she escorted him to the reception desk to total his bill.

Reaching into the back pocket of his jeans, Keaton took out a credit card case. "I'd like to make an appointment for a haircut in two weeks."

She took the card, glancing at his name, swiped it, and then handed him the card and a copy of his receipt. "We're closed on Sundays and Mondays, so you'll have to tell me when you'd like to come in." He moved closer, his breath sweeping over her ear when he leaned in to peruse the appointment book.

"Make it two weeks from today. Ten o'clock is good."

Francine penciled him under her name at ten. "Thank you for patronizing the Beauty Box and I'll see you in two weeks."

Keaton reached into his pocket again, this time taking out a money clip and a business card. "I'd like you to have dinner with me later this evening. That is, if you're not busy. You can reach me at the number on the card." He paused. "By the way, I'm staying at the Cove Inn, Miss Tanner."

Francine was too stunned to reply when he pushed the card and a bill into the pocket of her smock. Her first name was on her smock, but how did he know her last name? "I can't," she whispered once she recovered her voice.

"You can't or you don't want to?"

"You must be mistaken, Mr. Grace. I'm not who you think I am."

"You're wrong, Francine Tanner. I know exactly who you are."

"But I don't know you," she countered.

He leaned closer. "Have dinner with me and you'll have the opportunity to get to know everything you need to know about me."

Francine knew she couldn't continue to carry on a conversation with the arrogant man without someone eavesdropping. As it was, customers were craning their necks to overhear what they were talking about. "It can't be tonight."

"When if not tonight?" he questioned.

A shiver of annoyance swept over her. If or when she met with Keaton Grace he would quickly learn that she wasn't someone who reacted positively to being pressured. That was something her ex-husband had had to learn the hard way.

"I'll call you."

The slight frown between Keaton's eyes disappeared. "Thank you, Francine."

Much to her chagrin she gave him a warm smile. "You're welcome, Keaton." He inclined his head.

A woman pushed up her dryer, her gaze fixed on Keaton's retreating back. "Damn!" she whispered. "Where did he come from?"

The woman sitting next to her shook her head. "I don't know, but I'd sure like to sop that up with a biscuit."

Francine successfully hid a smile when the women exchanged fist bumps. She wanted to agree with them but kept her opinion to herself. Keaton was gorgeous. She had to give it to him. There was no doubt he was subtle, waiting until it was time to settle his bill before asking her out. She knew she should've been flattered, but she wasn't about to date a perfect stranger, even one as handsome and charming as Keaton.

Reaching into her pocket she took out the card and the money. Her eyes widened. He'd given her a fifty-dollar tip. Was he a generous tipper or trying to get her to go out with him?

Her gaze lingered on the business card. Keaton U. Grace was an independent filmmaker. The card bore a Los Angeles post office box and e-mail address, and a telephone number. What, she mused, was he doing in Sanctuary Cove? Did he plan to use the island as a backdrop or locale for a film? And how long did he plan to stay? There were so many questions she wanted answers to, which made her more than curious about the filmmaker — curious enough to consider setting aside time to listen to what he had to say.

However, meeting with Keaton would have to wait until after she and Morgan co-hosted a baby shower for Kara Hamilton, the current owner of Angels Landing Plantation. She wasn't as close to Kara as Morgan was, but when her best friend asked for her help she hadn't hesitated. They'd also enlisted the assistance of Jeffrey Hamilton, the island's sheriff, to take his wife away for a couple of days so they could finalize what they hoped would be a surprise for her. All of the invitees were sworn to secrecy, but Francine knew secrets on the island were like the mythical unicorn. And because they didn't exist, she and Morgan knew it was their sole reason for keeping the gathering small and very intimate.

The door opened and Trina Caine bumped into Keaton, her arms going around his waist in an attempt to keep her balance. Trina's eyes grew wider when she stared up at him. "Well, hello there," she crooned.

Francine watched Keaton smile, and then

reach around his waist in an attempt to extricate himself from her arms. "I'm sorry, miss."

However, Trina was not to be denied when she held on to his hands. As a teenager she'd earned the reputation as a flirt, and it had continued into adulthood. Twice divorced, she'd made it known that she was on the prowl for her third husband, and there was never a time when she wasn't seen wearing an outfit that was at least one size too small for her voluptuous body.

"Where are you going so fast, handsome?"

Francine had had enough. "Trina, stop harassing my customer, or you can go to Charleston to get your hair done." Trina dropped her arms and Keaton gave Francine a look of gratitude before he walked out.

Trina pulled down the hem of her spandex top. Large eyes framed with thick false lashes fluttered wildly. "I was just teasing him, Red."

Francine leaned in close. "The next time you act up like that you'll be banned from coming into the Beauty Box."

"You tell her, Red," shouted a woman close enough to overhear her admonishment. "What is wrong with you, Trina?" she continued. "I'm certain if your grandmomma, God bless the dead, were here she would skin you alive if she saw you hanging on that young man like some strumpet."

Trina stood up straight, resting her hands on her ample hips. "Well, for your information, my grandmomma ain't here, so there."

"Didn't anyone teach you not to sass your elders?" Mavis asked. She'd returned in time to hear Trina insult a woman old enough to be her mother.

Lowering her eyes, Trina managed to look contrite. "I'm sorry."

A frown marred Mavis's smooth forehead. "Don't apologize to me, but to Miss Chloe."

"I'm sorry, Miss Chloe." The other woman nodded.

Mavis's frown disappeared. "Trina, please sit down and someone will be with you directly."

Francine shook her head in amazement. It was just another day at the Beauty Box.

Chapter Two

Francine climbed the porch stairs to Morgan's house, peering through the screen door. She caught a glimpse of the Russian Blue cat before it scurried from view. They were like oil and water. Francine wasn't fond of cats and Rasputin knew it. She thought them too quiet and finicky. She tried the doorknob and, finding it unlocked, opened the door.

"Morgan. It's Fran!" she shouted.

People who'd grown up on the island usually left their doors unlocked during the day, locking them once the sun set or before retiring for bed. The ritual was no one ever entered someone's home without announcing one's self. And if you didn't get a response, then you wouldn't go any farther than the front porch or the parlor.

She knew her friend was home because the lights were on and her Cadillac Escalade was parked under the carport in front of her husband's truck. Nathaniel Shaw appeared before she could ring the doorbell. "Come on in, Red. Morgan's in the solarium." He held the door open, dipped his head, and kissed her cheek.

Walking into the parlor, Francine glanced around at the exquisite furnishings. She knew if she ever had her own home she wanted Morgan to decorate it. Her friend had helped her when she decided to redecorate her apartment. Directing her attention to Nate, she gave him a warm smile. There had been a time when every girl at their high school clamored to get the honor student to notice them. Tall, dark, and extremely handsome, his aloofness had set him apart from the other single men on the island. However, he was unable to resist Morgan's charm and wit once they'd begun working together on the Angels Landing Plantation restoration project.

"How's business?"

Shaw & Sons Woodworking was legendary in crafting the most exquisite furniture in the Lowcountry. Nate's father had gone into semiretirement; Nate was a master carpenter and he and his younger brother Bryce had carried on the family business. Nate, like many high school graduates, had left the island to attend college. It had taken him twenty years to find his way back home to a woman who'd been secretly in love with him for more than half her life. His decision to move back to Cavanaugh Island had changed him and he'd confessed to Francine that being married to Morgan made every day seem like Christmas.

A warm smile lit up Nate's light brown eyes. "It's real good." He picked up a set of keys from a small sweetgrass basket on a low table. "I'm going out for a while so you ladies can finish your planning. I told Morgan to text me if she needs me to pick up something she's forgotten."

Francine waited for Nate to close the doors behind him, and then made her way to the rear of the one-story house and into the solarium. Walls of one-way glass brought the outdoors in, while providing ultimate privacy from anyone looking into the room from the outside. Morgan sat on the natural sisal rug with a pile of small decorative gift bags, stuffing them with pastel tissue paper.

Marriage definitely agreed with Morgan because she was glowing. Her hair had grown out to chin length. Her sable-brown complexion was flawless and her dimpled cheeks were rounder, fuller. Francine had been maid of honor at Morgan and Nate's October wedding, and while Morgan insisted she wanted to wait two years before starting a family, it was more than obvious to Francine that the newlywed had scrapped her plan to delay motherhood.

Morgan had set up M. Dane Architect and Interior Design after she was commissioned to oversee the restoration of Angels Landing Plantation. Her business had grown since then and she now had Abram Daniels, a full-time interior decorator, to assist her. Once Abram became a partner, Morgan changed the company's name to Dane and Daniels Architecture and Interior Design.

The solarium was the perfect space in which to hold the shower. Morgan had decorated the room with a white wrought-iron daybed, a white wicker love seat, and a chaise with floral-patterned cushions. A rack with a dozen padded folding chairs was pushed against the wall. The royal blue, yellow, and bright green glazed pots overflowing with ferns, flowers, and palms positioned in front of an indoor waterfall filled with rocks and stalks of bamboo resembled a lush oasis.

Sitting on the floor opposite her friend, Francine picked up a sterling baby rattle paperweight engraved with the date of the shower, placed it into a felt sack and then the shopping bag, and tied the handles with lime-green and lemon-yellow curling ribbon. She and Morgan had spent hours going through catalogs before deciding on the paperweights as shower favors.

"Have you told Nate?"

Morgan's hands stilled. "What are you talking about?" she asked, giving Francine a direct stare.

Francine held the architect's gaze. "Have you told your husband that he's going to be a father?"

"How long have you known, Fran?"

"I knew even before you began dating Nate that you were going to marry him and that you weren't going to wait two years before starting a family."

Lowering her head, Morgan stared at the diamond eternity band on her left hand. "Why didn't you tell me?"

"I know you don't like it when I tell you about my visions, and I'd promised myself I'd stay out of your personal business."

"What if you see trouble for me?"

Francine patted Morgan's hand. "I would never keep that from you."

Morgan tucked her hair behind her ears. "I know I talked about waiting a couple of years before having a baby, but then I thought about Nate and what he went through with his ex-wife. She chose her career over motherhood and I was doing the same. The difference is I love Nate and he loves me, and because of that I know for certain that I'll be able to balance being a wife, a mother, and having a career."

"Are you having this baby for Nate or for you?"

"I'm having it for *us,* Fran. I've been in love with Nate for so long that it feels as if I've been married for years instead of three months. I used to dream about marrying him and having his babies. How many girls do ou know who are blessed enough to realize their teenage dream?"

Francine smiled. "You're the only one I know, Mo."

"What about you, Fran?" Morgan asked after a comfortable silence. "When are you going to open up enough to let a man love you the way you deserve to be loved?"

Morgan had just asked her a question Francine had asked herself over and over since her divorce. She was realistic enough to acknowledge she wasn't the first woman with a duplicitous husband and she definitely wouldn't be the last. What hurt her more than Aiden using her to advance his career was his justification in asking for a divorce: *As much as I've tried, I can't bring myself to love you. You're a woman men can sleep with but should never marry. In other words, you're a good lay but that's it.* It'd taken years for Francine to stop reliving his painful declaration and believe that she was more than worthy of becoming a man's wife, worthy enough to be loved.

However, she'd given up the notion of finding love on Cavanaugh Island. Many of the boys she'd grown up with had moved away and those who'd stayed were either married or divorced. The ones who were divorced or confirmed bachelors were like her because they were still carrying around a boatload of emotional baggage.

David Sullivan was a prime example of this. Although David lived in Charleston, he still had familial ties to Cavanaugh Island. He had dated an oral surgeon for five years without committing to a future together. Then, when Petra decided to end their relationship, he complained that he'd been blindsided because he'd planned to propose. Francine was forthcoming when she told David it shouldn't have taken him five years to realize the woman he'd dated and slept with was remarkable enough to become Mrs. David Sullivan.

She smiled. "I'm open. It's just that I haven't met the right man. When are you due?" she asked, shifting the conversation away from her.

"The first week in September, and I don't want to think about going through my last trimester in the summer heat. Nate plans to add a second floor to the house because I want another bedroom for the nursery."

"When?"

"He wants to begin next week. He's already bought the supplies and hired a crew."

"How long will it take?"

"Nate claims it shouldn't take any more than a month. I told him I wanted at least three bedrooms and another bathroom in the larger one."

"Where are you going to stay during the renovations?" Francine asked. Working alone, it had taken Nate more than six months to put up a barn with the family workshop on the first floor and an apartment on the upper level after he'd returned to Haven Creek. He'd given his brother and sister-in-law the apartment as a wedding gift several months before he married Morgan.

Morgan emitted a soft sigh. "We're going to stay with his sister and her family. Rasputin mated with Sharon's cat, and she's carrying her first litter. Patches is a beautiful Snowshoe so I'm certain her babies are going to be beautiful, too." She paused. "Do you want one of the kittens?"

Francine cut her eyes at her friend. "You know cats and I don't get along. I prefer dogs."

"I like dogs, too, but cats are more independent. You don't have to walk them, or give them constant attention. The only thing you have to do is give them food and water, change their litter box, and they're nice and content. Speaking of litter boxes, Nate is going to take Rasputin over to Sharon's tomorrow and leave him there until after I give birth. My doctor cautioned me about changing the litter box because it may be harmful to the baby. Even though we'll be living there while the addition is put on the house I won't have to change the box." Morgan held up a hand when Francine opened her mouth. "Promise me you won't reject my offer until you see the kittens."

Biting on her lower lip, she nodded. Both Rasputin and Patches claimed pedigree status, and that meant their kittens would also be pedigree. Having a cat as a pet was better for her than a dog because of the hours she spent at the salon. Maybe she would accept one of the kittens because it would become a companion for her grandmother, who definitely was a cat fancier.

Francine thought about the rash of recent pregnancies. Last summer Morgan's sister, Rachel, had given birth to twin boys. Stacy, Nate's sister-in-law, was also pregnant, Kara was due to give birth within two weeks, and now Morgan.

"Do you plan to take off after you have the baby?"

Morgan nodded. "Yes. At least for three months."

"What about babysitting, Mo?"

"Rachel claims she loves being a stay-at-home mom, so taking care of another baby plus her three kids will just add to the insanity."

"Have you told Nate about the baby?" she asked Morgan again.

"Yes, but I asked him not to say anything until after the shower. Tomorrow's going to be Kara's special day and I don't want anything to detract from that."

"I know I sound like a reporter interviewing you, but how did he take the news?"

Morgan's dimples deepened like thumbprints when she smiled. "Believe it or not, my macho husband cried."

Francine's jaw dropped. "No!"

"Yes! Please don't let it out that I told you."

She pantomimed zipping her lips. "You'll

never hear it from me. I checked with the florist and they know to deliver the flowers and balloons by ten. Is that too early for you?"

"No. I'm usually up early."

Francine checked her watch. "Dawn called to say her train was delayed an hour, so I'll hang out here until it's time to head out to the station."

Dawn Ramsey, Kara's former New York City roommate, had a fear of flying and preferred taking the train from New York to Charleston for the weekend. Francine had volunteered to pick her up from the Amtrak station and drive her to the same hotel where Kara's parents were staying. The Newells, who'd driven from Little Rock, planned to extend their stay to await the arrival of their first grandchild.

"Are we all right with the food?" Morgan questioned.

"When I spoke to Otis he told me he has another party tomorrow night and doesn't have anyone available to make a delivery. I told him I would pick up the trays if he can get the waiters to put them in my car."

"Will you be able to fit everything in the trunk of your Corvette?"

"I'm certain they can. Nate can bring the trays in once I get here."

She and Morgan had decided to order from Jack's Fish House because they were local and known for serving some of the best cuisine in the Lowcountry. Even her overly critical Grandma Dinah claimed Otis and Luvina Jackson's chitterlings, fried green tomatoes, and red beans and rice with spicy sausage were beyond exceptional. They'd also decided to place an order for an assortment of mini desserts from the Muffin Corner, the island's only bakeshop.

On a scale of one to ten, Francine's cooking skills hovered around a two. If she didn't eat with her parents or her grandmother, then she was more than content to reheat the leftovers they always put aside for her. Even when she was married, she and Aiden either ate out or ordered in.

Morgan counted on her fingers. "Food, flowers, balloons, and gift bags. I've washed the china, crystal, and silver, so all I have to do is set the table and put out the warming racks. Why do I think I'm forgetting something?"

Francine went through the checklist in her head. Everyone would eat in the formal dining room before processing into the solarium, where Kara would open her gifts. Invitations had been sent to Kara's parents; Dawn, her former roommate; Willie and Iris

Todd, Angels Landing Plantation's groundskeeper and housekeeper; Jeff's grandmother Corrine Hamilton; and his cousin David Sullivan.

"I think we've covered everything. I'm only working a half day tomorrow at the salon, so if there's anything you need me to do, then call or text me."

"You've done enough, Fran. I told Nate to hang around tomorrow in case I need him to do something."

Francine and Morgan finished filling the gift bags, and then went into the dining room to set the table. She gave her best friend a thumbs-up when she backed her red Corvette out of the driveway and drove in the direction of the causeway. Turning the radio up, Francine sang along with the all-music station in order to keep her mind off Keaton Grace. *I know exactly who you are.* His words were branded on her brain. He may believe he knew her, but nothing could be further from the truth. That was something he would discover once they sat down to talk.

Right now, all she could think about was her best friend becoming a mother. When they were younger, she and Morgan had talked about falling in love, marrying the men who would love them selfishly, and becoming mothers. Now that it had happened for Morgan, Francine wondered if it would ever happen for herself. She still hadn't given up on love.

Keaton sat across the table from Devon Gilmore in Jack's Fish House going over the partnership dissolution she'd drafted for his approval and signature. He'd come to Jack's during his first visit to the island and decided it was the best place to eat dinner while conducting business. The restaurant was noisy, but not so much so he couldn't carry on a normal conversation.

His head popped up, glaring at his attorney as if she'd taken leave of her senses. "You want him to pay me one hundred thousand dollars for breach of contract?"

A sweep of lashes concealed Devon's wide-set hazel eyes when she stared at a copy of the same document she'd given Keaton. "Financially he reneged on the last project. I could've charged him ten times that amount, but figured because he's your brother-in-law I'd give him a break."

He watched numbly as she flipped several strands of straightened hair over the shoulder of her suit jacket. Smiling, she picked up a glass of sweet tea and took a sip. Devon was beautiful, cutthroat, and brilliant, and the latter was the reason he'd hired her to represent him. They were also very good friends. They met at New York University when he was taking graduate courses and Devon was a first-year law student. He'd lost track of the number of times they would run into each other at the same coffee shops or occasionally at off-campus mixers. When Devon accused him of stalking her he finally introduced himself. Keaton was used to seeing her seduce men whenever she stared up at them through her lashes before parting full lips and playing with her hair. And for a reason he couldn't fathom he'd found himself immune to her unblemished mocha complexion and curvaceous petite body. "No, Devon. I'm not going to take food out of the mouths of my niece and nephew or their college fund, even if Hollis did stiff me on the last project. Dissolving our business relationship should be enough." He didn't want his lawyer involved in his personal family dynamics; his sister had stopped talking to him once he'd disclosed that he and her husband were parting ways, and Keaton definitely didn't want to compound the alienation by suing his brother-in-law.

Devon reached for the page, tore it in half, and then did the same with the page in her copy. "I'll go along with whatever you want."

"I want out and nothing else. It's enough . . ." His words trailed off. From where he sat he could see Francine as she walked into the restaurant. And if it hadn't been for her hair color he wouldn't have recognized her. A smooth hairstyle, parted off-center and barely brushing her shoulders, had replaced the tousled curls. He was close enough to see the light cover of makeup that enhanced her eyes and mouth, and Keaton couldn't take his eyes off the chocolate-brown body-hugging dress accentuating every curve of her slender frame. His gaze was drawn to a pair of long legs that seemed to go on forever in a pair of stiletto leopard-print booties.

"You really shock me, Keaton. I didn't know you were into redheads," Devon teased, grinning from ear to ear.

"I know her."

Devon leaned over the table. "How *well* do you know her?"

Keaton continued to stare at Francine. "I should've said that I recognize her."

"It's been a while since I've seen you *this* interested in a woman."

His gaze swung back to his attorney. "How often do you see me with women?"

Devon sat up straight. "Probably not often enough. At least not since you broke up with that uptight bank auditor."

Devon was wrong about Lisa's being uptight. He'd dated the three-time-married CPA because she was straightforward, wasn't into playing head games, and was okay with having a casual relationship. "Is there anything else in this document I should be aware of before I sign it?" he asked, deftly changing the topic of conversation. Reaching into the breast pocket of his jacket, he took out a pen.

Devon flipped through several pages. "No. The rest is self-explanatory."

"To whom, Devon? It may be self-explanatory to you, but I don't want Hollis to sue me because of some legalese technicality."

"If he decides to sue you, then I'll represent you pro bono."

Keaton leaned closer. "I don't want him to sue me at all. As it is my sister isn't talking to me and that means I'm cut off from my niece and nephew. And my parents, who're trying not to take sides, are barely speaking to me. This isn't just about business, Devon. It's about family."

Devon smiled. "Trust me, Keaton. He's not going to sue you."

Unscrewing the cap to the pen, he scrawled his signature across the last page.

It was apparent his legal counsel was a lot more confident than he felt at the moment. His decision to dissolve his professional partnership with Hollis wasn't an easy one. If it hadn't been for his brother-in-law, Keaton wouldn't have had the financial backing he needed for his first film. Things had worked well between them until Hollis demanded more creative control, while Keaton was quick to remind him that he was the creative partner. Hollis conceded, but with each subsequent project he would again ingratiate himself only to be told to back off or stand down. Their working relationship ended when Hollis refused to release the funds needed to complete an independent film Keaton wanted to submit to the Sundance Film Festival.

Gathering the pages, he handed them to Devon. "That should do it."

She nodded. "As soon as I get back to my office I'll make the corrections and overnight it to your brother-in-law." She slipped the document into a leather portfolio, and then glanced at her watch. "I think I have enough time to eat before I catch my flight."

Devon had told Keaton that she had a reservation to take a red-eye out of Charleston for Newport News, Virginia, instead of returning to New York. "You can always stay over and catch a flight in the morning."

She affected a sexy moue. "I can't. I'm scheduled to meet someone early tomorrow morning."

A hint of a smile softened his firm mouth. "That means I'll have to cancel the room I reserved for you at the Cove Inn."

Leaning back in her chair, she gave him a long, penetrating stare. "Living here has changed you, Keaton."

"Why do you say that?"

"Just look at you. Whenever I came to see you in L.A. we always ate at three- or four-star restaurants, not in a family-friendly one like Jack's Fish House. Instead of a tailored suit you're now wearing a leather jacket, a pullover, and jeans. You look like you did when we met in grad school."

"That's when we were both struggling students, stretching dollars and pinching pennies to make ends meet."

"I was the struggling student, Keaton. All you had to do was call your father and he would send you money to cover your rent and other living expenses. It was very different for me because I've always been on my own."

Reaching across the table, Keaton covered Devon's hand with his. He wanted to tell her that his father had stopped sending him money once he earned his undergraduate degree but decided not to. "You can't dwell on the past. Don't think of where you've come from but where you are now. You're an incredible attorney, Devon. You've worked deals for me that would've been impossible for a lawyer with less tenacity."

"That's because as a female entertainment attorney I'm forced to swim with sharks and piranhas in three-thousand-dollar suits who are masquerading as gentlemen. You're the only client of mine who's also a friend."

He gave her fingers a gentle squeeze before releasing them. "That's good to know."

"How long do you expect to stay at the Cove Inn?" she asked.

"Probably another two months. I'm really anxious for the contractor to finish renovating the house so I can move in."

Devon exhaled an audible breath. "Will you hire a new housekeeper?"

"No. Mrs. Miller is prepared to move from L.A. as soon as the house is finished."

Devon frowned. "The woman hates me."

"Mrs. Miller doesn't hate you," Keaton countered. "We just happen to look out for each other."

A slight frown marred Devon's smooth forehead. "What's the connection?"

"The connection is she's a very trusted employee. She says I remind her of her son." Keaton smiled when Devon grunted under her breath.

As soon as the renovations for the farmhouse were completed Keaton would arrange for Susie Miller to settle into her own suite of rooms in one of three guesthouses that would be erected on the property. His housekeeper would occupy one and the production company's full-time permanent employees the other. His initial encounter with Mrs. Miller had begun with her panhandling behind the building that housed the office he'd rented to produce his films. When his office manager talked about having her arrested for vagrancy he intervened. He discovered she wasn't homeless, but was experiencing reoccurring panic attacks after she'd lost her son to a drug overdose and then her grandson to gang violence all in the same year.

Susie had admitted she had been fired as a sales clerk because she feared getting out of bed. Keaton instructed his office manager to add Susie to their maintenance staff. She'd proved to be an exemplary employee and two years later he asked her to become his live-in housekeeper.

Unlike some men, he'd never flaunted his

affairs, rarely entertaining women at his home. The few who were lucky enough to cross the threshold had to contend with Mrs. Miller. Keaton had been forthcoming with his housekeeper when he told her about Jade, his ex-girlfriend, and the older woman's *Don't worry, Keaton, I have your back* translated into "I'm going to look out for you." Twenty years her junior, he'd become the son she'd lost to the streets.

Devon picked up a menu, studying the selections. "I can't decide what to order."

Keaton wanted to ask her who or what was in Newport News that had her rushing back there, but didn't. He studied the menu even though he knew what he wanted to order. His perusal was interrupted when a piercing whistle rose above the babble in the restaurant. "You're looking real pretty, Red," a man called out.

Francine, who'd followed two waiters carrying covered aluminum trays, blushed to the roots of her hairline. Keaton wanted to give her a standing ovation when she tilted her chin and continued to walk. At the last possible moment her eyes met his before she disappeared from his line of vision.

"Hello? Earth to Keaton? Looks like someone has caught your interest," Devon said, before laughing and taking a sip of her drink. Keaton cleared his throat before forcing his eyes away from Francine.

"She's an actress. I saw her perform in an off-Broadway play years ago."

"She's very pretty."

He nodded in agreement. "That she is, but I'm not interested in her in the way you might think. I was involved with an actress when I worked as an assistant director on my first film. She took her own life and I swore an oath I would never become involved with anyone in the business."

Devon's eyes were as large as silver dollars. "Why didn't you tell me about this before? What happened, Keaton?"

"I missed all of the signs. Jade had been emotionally unstable for a long time, until it was too late. It'd begun with mood swings vacillating between euphoric highs and moody lows. She wanted marriage and a baby and when I told her I wasn't ready for either at that time in my life she would lapse into crying jags that went on for days. I suggested she seek professional help, which she refused. I issued a final ultimatum: go to a psychiatrist or our relationship was over. She chose to end it by swallowing a bottle of sleeping pills. Jade's mother accused me of taking advantage of her daughter's fragile mental state, but investigators for the studio uncovered documentation that as an adolescent she'd been confined to a mental hospital for several months because she'd attempted to take her life after a breakup with her boyfriend. Studio suits paid the late actress's mother a large sum after she signed a nondisclosure agreement never to connect me with her daughter's death."

It'd been the first and the last time he'd dated an actress assigned to any of the films in which he'd been involved. Jade's death had affected him more than he'd wanted to admit. It wasn't that he had been in love with her, but he had liked her and enjoyed her company. When she wasn't in a funk she was upbeat and lots of fun. He'd thought of her as an extremely talented small-town girl with big-city dreams of making it in Hollywood. Unfortunately, all of her dreams died with her.

Devon blew out her cheeks. "I'm sorry I asked."

He gave her a half smile. "Now you know." Raising his hand, he signaled a waiter closer. "We're ready to order now." Devon gave him her selections, changing her mind twice about whether she wanted gumbo or conch stew. She finally settled on the stew with a side dish of collard greens, while he ordered oxtails in gravy and white rice.

Waiting until the young man walked away, Devon smiled at her client. "I hope the food is good here."

"I've eaten here before and it's excellent."

"They need to add sushi to the menu."

Keaton laughed under his breath. "I doubt if that will ever happen. The next time you come down I'll arrange for us to eat in Charleston, where you can order sushi."

Devon shook her head. "That's okay. Cavanaugh Island is a nice place to visit, but I doubt whether I'd want to come here too often."

"What's the matter, counselor? Is it too quiet for you?"

"It's too quiet *and* too slow for this Big Apple sister. However, I'm willing to come back to see your house once it's renovated."

Keaton smiled. He welcomed the solitude and slower pace after spending nearly fifteen years off and on in the City of Angels. Although born and raised in Pittsburgh and having attended college in New York City, he still thought of himself as a country boy. He never felt more carefree than he did each summer when he visited his relatives' small farm in rural Tennessee. He woke early and when not working on a project he went to bed early. Drugs, frat parties, and clubbing were never a part of his social repertoire.

While in college, going to plays and viewing films had taken up all of his free time.

"The next time you come down I should be able to put you up in one of the guest-houses instead of a hotel."

Devon's smile was dazzling. "Now I know I have to come back, just to see your house when it's done," she said.

All conversation ceased when the waiter returned, setting down a plate of fluffy, buttery biscuits. Keaton knew his dining partner was as intrigued by Francine as he was with the former actress. However, his interest in her had nothing to do with romance. He'd learned his lesson well after his involvement with another actress.

Their entrées arrived quickly and Keaton gave Devon a thumbs-up when she asked if he was enjoying his oxtails. Not only was he enjoying his meal but also the casual, laid-back, family-style restaurant. All of the mounted televisions were muted, while diners craned their necks to see what the wait-staff carried in trays balanced on their shoulders, and the various mouth-watering aromas wafting throughout the restaurant always made it difficult for him to choose his meal. That's when he decided to systematically order a new dish each time he visited Jack's.

Keaton became suddenly alert when he heard someone at a nearby table mention Francine's name, referring to her as Red. Some of the customers in the Beauty Box had called her that. It was probably a childhood nickname that had carried over into adulthood. The locals called her Red but he knew her as Francine Tanner, actress extraordinaire. It'd been more than twenty-four hours since he'd given her his business card, and he hoped she would call him before he was scheduled to return to the salon for his next haircut.

Devon finished eating and Keaton settled the bill, then drove her back to Charleston in time for her flight to Virginia. Waiting until she disappeared into the terminal, he maneuvered away from the curbside. During the drive back to Cavanaugh Island he realized the document Devon would send to his brother-in-law would end what had become a contentious business relationship. It was time he began anew in a new state, a new house, and eventually a new film studio. He also thought about Francine and what she could mean to his life both professionally and personally.

Chapter Three

Francine turned off onto the road leading to Morgan's house. The uneasiness she felt when leaving Jack's Fish House had vanished. Nothing could've prepared her for what had just occurred in Jack's. Although her dress revealed more skin than her jeans, tees, and/or summer sundresses, she hadn't expected the wolf whistle or catcall from the man who'd teased her relentlessly when they were in high school. While everyone called her Red, Leon James referred to her as Little Orphan Annie. She hadn't responded when she wanted to call him a pig with no home training, because young boys on the island were lectured about disrespecting a woman in public. It was apparent Leon and a few of the other male students ignored their parents' teaching when their teasing made her high school experience one she wanted to forget.

She'd be the first to acknowledge she

didn't wear body-hugging attire or four-inch heels unless she went to the Happy Hour. She'd frequented the club in Haven Creek less than a half-dozen times since its opening, and always with Morgan. It wasn't often she got the chance to dress up, but when she did she always felt ultrafeminine wearing a slinky dress and stilettos. Working five days a week in clogs and a smock did not leave Francine feeling very glamorous. She put all of her energy into improving her regular customers' appearance, while she barely wore makeup or styled her hair in anything other than a mass of curls. When her mother trimmed her hair and blew it out earlier that afternoon it was the first step in fulfilling her New Year's resolution to take time focusing on her.

What had unnerved her was the expression on Keaton Grace's face when she walked by. Even from a distance she saw unadulterated lust in his eyes. At that moment she felt sorry for the woman sitting with him. He was gawking at her when he should've been paying attention to his dining partner. She still hadn't decided whether to call Keaton or not, but if she did it was only to uncover what he knew about her.

Maneuvering around to the rear of the house, Francine parked the Corvette next to David's Lexus. Seeing his sedan and Nate's SUV under the carport meant they'd picked up all the guests. She and Morgan had insisted everyone arrive before six thirty. Jeff had confirmed he would bring Kara at seven thirty. The sheriff had told his pregnant wife that Morgan and Nate had invited them to dinner.

She opened the back door, walking into the kitchen. Nate stood next to Morgan, watching as she filled a platter with hors d'oeuvres. Both wore white shirts and black slacks. "Nate, could you please get the food out of the trunk of my car? I left it open for you."

Nate turned around. "Of course. You look real nice, Red," he said, smiling.

Pinpoints of heat pricked her cheeks. She didn't know why, but she always felt uncomfortable whenever men complimented her. "Thank you." Perhaps it had something to do with being teased so much about her hair when she was younger.

Resting her hip against the countertop, Morgan nodded slowly. "You do look incredible, Fran. Are you certain you don't have a date later on tonight?"

Francine rolled her eyes upward. "Yeah, right," she drawled facetiously. "You know I'm not seeing anyone."

"Well, you should."

"You know how I feel about men from Cavanaugh Island."

"Yes, I know we made a pact when we were in high school that we would never marry a boy from here, but that's exactly what I did."

She moved closer to Morgan. "That's because Nate never teased or bullied us."

"What are you two whispering about?"

Francine turned to find David watching them. She hadn't heard him when he entered the kitchen. The always dapper conservative attorney wore a dark blue tailored suit that he'd paired with a pale blue pinstriped shirt, a navy-and-white-striped silk tie, and imported wing tips. His deep-set dark eyes grew wider as her gaze was drawn to the slight cleft in his firm chin. Once the word was out that David had split with his longtime girlfriend, women went after him like a swarm of hornets, and Francine knew he would make a wonderful catch for some woman when he finally recovered from his breakup.

"It's only girl talk," Francine said. When he didn't respond, she added, "What's the matter, counselor? Cat got your tongue?" she teased, grinning from ear to ear.

David recovered quickly. "You clean up

nicely, Francine."

Francine wondered if she'd been such a hot mess that putting on a dress and heels had transformed her into a ravishing princess. She affected a slight curtsy while smiling sweetly.

"Thank you."

Nate returned to the kitchen, carrying three covered trays stacked on one another. "David, could you please get the last two trays from Red's car?"

Francine picked up the platter filled with sushi; an assortment of filo tartlets stuffed with shredded spicy chicken, smoked salmon, or shrimp; deviled eggs; and tempura. "Where do you want this?" she asked Morgan, who'd tried unsuccessfully to hide a yawn.

"You can take it into the parlor. You'll find plates, forks, and napkins on one of the tables. Everyone's here except Kara and Jeff. I figured folks need something to nibble on until we sit down to eat. I know when we talked about what to serve we'd decided against serving appetizers, but once we get everyone settled it'll probably be around eight."

Francine wagged a finger at Morgan. "You've done enough. Sit and relax." She winked at her. "I'll be right back."

She didn't want to tell her friend that she looked as if she hadn't had enough sleep. Her eyelids were drooping and there was a slight puffiness under her eyes. She wasn't certain if Morgan had gotten up early to make the hors d'oeuvres or if being pregnant was sapping her energy. Without warning, the vision of Morgan holding a baby wrapped in a pink blanket came to her. If the spirit was right, then she knew Morgan and Nate were going to have a daughter.

Even though she was a failure as a cook, Francine was the complete opposite when it came to being a hostess. As a child she'd watched intently whenever her mother made preparations to entertain her husband's business associates. The formal dining room table was set with heirloom tablecloths, crystal, silver, and china. Mavis would order fresh flowers from the local florist for the centerpiece, while Francine had been recruited to make the place cards because she'd learned calligraphy in her art class.

Her mother would spend days making up the menu, revising it over and over. Mavis had inherited her culinary skills from her mother, who'd been employed as a cook by a wealthy Charleston family. Mavis would become the consummate hostess, making everyone feel at ease when she welcomed them with a warm smile and a practiced charm that restaurateur Frank Tanner couldn't resist.

She walked into the parlor, setting the platter down on a table, and then greeted each of the invitees with a hug or kiss on the cheek. Corrine Hamilton, Jeff's grandmother, ran a hand over Francine's hair. "You look lovely, Red."

Francine blushed. She'd grown tired of telling people that her name was Francine until she was forced to accept the nickname. "Thank you, Miss Corrine."

Corrine pressed her mouth to Francine's ear. "Don't you think it's time you find a nice young man to marry, like Kara and Morgan?" Tall and ramrod-straight, the seventy-something former teacher and principal had announced she couldn't wait to become a great-grandmother.

"It'll happen when the time is right, Miss Corrine." She motioned for Willie and Iris Todd not to get up. "Please sit down, Mr. Willie, and you, too, Miss Iris. I'll bring you both a plate."

Dawn popped up. "I'll help you serve, Francine. I heard what Miss Corrine said to you," she whispered as they stood at the table filling plates with hors d'oeuvres from the platter. "She asked me the same thing last night."

Francine gave the professional dancer a sidelong glance. Using a pair of tongs she gently lifted a deviled egg and several sushi rolls, placing them on a plate. A natural blonde with sky-blue eyes, Dawn had given up a career as a dancer to teach young children because of bouts of stage fright.

"What did you tell her?" she asked sotto voce.

"I told her I wasn't looking, but if and when the right man comes along I'll know it."

Francine bumped fists with Dawn. She hadn't set a deadline for marriage because she'd been there, done that. Only Morgan, who'd stood in as her bridesmaid and witness, her grandmother, and her parents knew she'd married. As up-and-coming actors, she and Aiden knew they were more marketable if they were single and had agreed not to disclose their marital status. They'd dated, married, lived together, and then divorced all in secret.

After passing around plates to the assembled, she signaled for silence when the sound of an approaching car could be heard through the partially opened door. Morgan had drawn the shades in the parlor to conceal the occupants waiting to surprise Kara.

The seconds became minutes as everyone waited for Jeff to announce himself. Morgan stood off to the side, camera in hand, while Nate opened the door. Kara's shocked expression was frozen in time with guests' cameras and camera phones. Francine and Morgan shared a knowing smile. They'd accomplished the impossible. They'd managed to keep the baby shower a secret.

It was minutes before midnight when Francine returned home, removing her shoes as she climbed the staircase to her apartment at the easterly side of the house. There was never a question of not moving back into the house where she'd grown up. The year she'd celebrated her thirteenth birthday, her parents had expanded her bedroom, adding an additional bedroom and bathroom, kitchen, and a living/dining area. Once word got out that she had her own apartment within the expansive five-thousand-square-foot Colonial, Francine was forced to endure spiteful jealous remarks from girls and snide overtures from boys asking if they could sleep over.

Walking on bare feet, she made her way into the bathroom, undressed, removed her makeup, and took a quick shower. Dressed in a cotton nightgown, she adjusted the thermostat in her bedroom, crawled into bed, and reached for the switch on the lamp on the bedside table. Francine's hand halted when she saw the business card Keaton had given her. Picking up the card, she brushed a forefinger over the raised lettering. At that moment she decided not to call but e-mail him.

Throwing back the sheet and blanket, she got out of bed and retrieved the laptop resting on the window-seat cushion. Her fingers were poised on the keyboard as she waited for the computer to boot up. She typed in Keaton's e-mail address and *Meeting* in the subject line, and outlined when and where they were to meet. Francine ended the message with the number to her cell for his reply. Logging off, she shut down the computer, went back to bed, and fell asleep within minutes of her head touching the pillow.

Keaton sat on the veranda outside his suite taking in the view while thoroughly enjoying his second cup of coffee that morning. It was the first day in a week that he'd awoken to clear skies without the prediction of rain. The cool wind blowing off the ocean raised goose bumps on his exposed upper body yet he was loath to get up and go back inside the bedroom to put on a shirt. Inhaling a lungful of salt air, he closed his eyes and smiled. When he'd checked his smartphone earlier that morning he discovered the e-mail from Francine. She'd agreed to meet him, but on her terms. What Francine didn't know was that Keaton was willing to agree to anything she wanted if only she would accept his offer to appear in his next film. He opened his eyes, reached for his cell phone, which was resting on a wrought-iron table, and punched in the programmed number he'd gotten from her e-mail. Her phone rang twice before there was a connection.

"Hello."

"Good morning, Francine. I hope I'm not calling too early."

"Not at all," came her reply. "I've been up for hours. I take it you saw my e-mail." There was a hint of laughter in her dulcet voice.

"I did, and I want to thank you for getting back to me. You're going to have to let me know which restaurant you want to go to in Charleston, so I can make a reservation." Francine had indicated she was available Monday and that she didn't want to get together on Cavanaugh Island.

"You choose the restaurant," she said.

"Are you familiar with the Charleston Grill?"

"Yes."

"Have you ever eaten there?"

"No," Francine said, "but I've heard the food is very good."

Keaton wanted to tell her the food was excellent and the service at the hotel impeccable. "Then it's a go?"

Her sultry laugh came through the earpiece. "Yes, it is."

"I'll make a reservation for seven. How do I get to your house to pick you up?"

He listened intently while she gave him directions to Magnolia Drive. It was the second time in a matter of days he was shocked to find his life linked to Francine's. The farmhouse currently undergoing renovations was less than a quarter of a mile from Magnolia Drive. "I guess that does it. I'll pick you up at six fifteen." Taking the causeway and barring delays, he estimated it would take less than a half hour to make it to the hotel located in Charleston's Market area.

Keaton ended the call, grinning like a Cheshire cat. He could not have written a better script. He'd come to Cavanaugh Island to set up a production company, had run into Francine Tanner, and now planned to share dinner with her where he would outline his intent to cast her in a movie that was certain to make her a much-talked-about actress.

And it wasn't the first time he'd applauded himself for making the decision to sever his business relationship with his brother-in-law after he'd secured a financial backer for his modestly budgeted films. Once he'd agreed to put up half the money for each of the films the private banker agreed to put up the other half, leaving Keaton with complete creative control when it came to casting, editing, and final production. They'd also agreed to split the profits: 49 percent for the banker and 51 percent for Keaton.

Scrolling through his phone's directory, Keaton tapped the button for the hotel where he'd stayed when he'd first come to the island to set up Grace Lowcountry Productions. It took less than a minute to make the reservation for the following evening. Pushing off the chair, Keaton left the veranda, closed the French doors, and flopped down on the bed. Cradling his head on folded arms, he stared up at the ceiling. Events in his life came to him like frames of film. He'd had disappointment, a few failures, but those were overshadowed by unexpected successes beyond his imagination. When he enrolled in college as a film student his long-term goal was to set up his own production company, and within a year it would become a reality.

Francine sat at the table in her grandmother's breakfast nook, staring back at the elderly woman who'd set down her teacup when Francine answered her cell phone. She knew Dinah eschewed the tiny phones and Francine had made it a practice not to bring it with her whenever they ate together.

"I had to take that call, Grandma."

Green eyes that had dulled slightly with advancing age pinned Francine to her seat when Dinah glared at her over a pair of glasses that had slid down the narrow bridge of her nose. "Who is he?"

Picking up her fork, Francine speared a piece of melon, putting it into her mouth. "It's not a date, Grandma," she said after chewing and swallowing. Since her grandmother had come to live with her she'd altered her Sunday routine. Instead of sleeping in and attending the eleven o'clock service at Abundant Life Church, Francine had promised Dinah she'd accompany her to the one scheduled for eight.

Dinah's eyes narrowed as she studied her granddaughter. "I didn't ask you if it was a date."

"His name is Keaton Grace. And he's an independent filmmaker."

Slumping back in her chair, the older woman lifted finely arched eyebrows. Dinah's once fiery red hair had lightened, making it appear more strawberry blond than silver. Delicate blue veins were clearly visible under skin that had become more translucent as she aged. Black-and-white photographs of Dinah as a young woman had captured her stunning beauty as she stared into the camera lens. It'd been her outgoing personality, practiced Southern charm, and gift for conversation that had attracted the attention of a man who owned prime real estate in downtown Charleston. She'd succeeded where so many other women had failed when she married John Tanner in what had been touted as the wedding of the season.

"How did you meet him?" Dinah asked.

Dabbing the corners of her mouth with a napkin, Francine folded it, placing it beside her plate. "He came into the salon the other day for a cut and shave. Even though I didn't recognize him, he knew who I was."

"He wants you in one of his films." It

wasn't a question but a statement.

Francine shook her head. "I'm not certain what he wants."

"If you don't know, then why are you meeting him, Francine?"

Reaching for the china teapot sitting on a decorative trivet, Francine refilled her cup. "More tea, Grandma?"

"No thank you. Back to your Mr. Grace. Why have you agreed to meet with him?" Dinah repeated.

Francine wanted to tell her grandmother Keaton wasn't her Mr. Grace but a Beauty Box customer. "Maybe I'm curious because he says he knows me. I did research him on the Internet."

"What did you find?"

"He's directed and produced three films, one for which he won a Spirit Award."

Dinah patted her coiffed short hair. "He must be good."

"Whether he is or not, I don't intend to return to acting. I'm going to be polite, hear him out, and then tell him thanks, but no thanks. I'm not interested in resuming my acting career."

"You could do that without going out with him," Dinah insisted. "Unless there is something you're not telling me, grandbaby girl."

A hint of a smile played at the corners of Francine's mouth. Although her grandmother claimed she wasn't psychic she felt Dinah wasn't being completely truthful, and she wondered if she'd picked up on something that Francine hadn't been able to discern.

"It appears as if he's going to become a regular at the Beauty Box."

"So, he's staying here?"

Francine nodded. "I believe he's here for the winter season."

"Where's he staying?"

"The Cove Inn. And please don't ask me if he's married because when I saw him last night at Jack's Fish House, he was with a woman."

A becoming blush darkened Dinah's face as she averted her gaze. "You know I don't like it when you do that."

"Do what, Grandma?"

"Read my mind."

Throwing back her head, Francine laughed. "You know I can't read minds. It's just that I knew what you were going to say next. I'm surprised you didn't ask me his age."

"Well . . . how old is he?"

Cocking her head to the side, Francine pushed out her lips. "The information I gleaned from the Internet says he's forty. Is there anything else you want to know?"

"Yes. How was the baby shower?"

Francine was relieved Dinah had changed the topic of conversation. "It was wonderful. Kara was really surprised, and that's a feat unto itself because no one let the cat out of the bag."

Dinah pressed her thin lips together. "That's because most of the folks weren't from here but out of town, and those who live here know how to keep their mouths."

"You're right about that."

Francine stood up and cleared the table. Her father had returned from a business trip Saturday afternoon, announcing loudly that he was going to sleep in for the rest of the weekend. And that meant she wouldn't get to see her mother until Tuesday when the Beauty Box opened. Mavis was very concerned about her husband's health after he'd collapsed from dehydration during a franchise business convention in Las Vegas. He'd had to be hospitalized for several days before he was able to return home.

Her father had played professional football for five years, but was forced to retire when he injured his knee. His backup plan included going into business for himself when he purchased his first fast-food franchise.

One became two and eventually five. He owned two in Charleston, one in Summerville, another in Beaufort, and had recently opened one in Conway.

"She got some wonderful gifts." As she rinsed the dishes and stacked them in the dishwasher, Francine gave her grandmother an update about the gathering. Dinner had become a festive leisurely affair as everyone ate their fill. Jeff had revealed that Kara was having a boy and they'd decided to name him Austin Taylor Hamilton. Austin Newell was the man who'd raised Kara from birth and Taylor Patton had been her biological father. It wasn't until the reading of Taylor Patton's will that everyone on the island was made aware that the confirmed bachelor had a secret love child.

Once dinner was over, everyone went into the solarium, where Kara opened her gifts. Morgan had given her a hand-quilted crib blanket she bought from a craft shop in the Creek and a gift certificate for a day of beauty at the Beauty Box. Morgan had also purchased a layette, and Nate had taken time from his busy schedule to make a cradle. The Newells had given their daughter a gift certificate for nursery furniture. David had admitted he didn't know anything about buying baby clothes so he'd given Kara a gift certificate for a year's supply of disposable diapers. Mrs. Todd's gift was a pair of hand-knitted sweaters and matching caps in soft pastel green and yellow. Dawn, the prospective godmother, had given Kara and Jeff an exquisite christening gown and matching hat.

Francine had become a spectator, watching the interaction between Morgan and Nate and Jeff and Kara. It was obvious the two couples were very much in love whenever they exchanged glances. She'd tried remembering if Aiden had ever looked at her like that — even when he'd pretended to love her.

She didn't blame her ex-husband as much as she did herself for their sham of a marriage. During a whirlwind six-week courtship, he took advantage of her naïveté to convince her to marry him, assuming she would support him financially until he got his big break. Their divorce was quick and uncomplicated. They didn't have children, so there wasn't the issue of custody or child support, and no prenup or division of assets because Francine had relied on her parents for financial support.

She'd tried to move on but insecurities dogged her emotionally and she had stopped going to the auditions her agent had set up for her. One morning she woke up and called her agent to tell her she was quitting the business. A month later, she handed over the keys to the apartment to the building manager, rented a car, loaded her luggage in the trunk, and drove back to Cavanaugh Island. Francine had never looked back and never regretted walking away from her childhood dream.

At this point in her life Francine wasn't entirely certain what she wanted for her future. She knew she would eventually own and manage the Beauty Box, but deep inside she wanted more than that. What she didn't want to acknowledge was that, although surrounded by a loving family and friends, she felt something was missing. And if she were truly honest she would've admitted she envied her best friend. Morgan had what every woman wanted: a loving husband and eventually a family of her own.

She knew nothing about Keaton other than what she'd gleaned from the Internet, but she felt a ripple of excitement whenever she thought about going out with him.

Chapter Four

Keaton forced himself to drive slower, aware it would take time before he reprogrammed his brain not to drive above the unofficial twenty miles an hour speed limit. Minutes before leaving the Cove, he had received a text from Devon confirming she'd mailed the dissolution agreement to his brother-in-law and now all he had to do was wait for the fallout.

When he'd first come to Cavanaugh Island he realized the three towns were unlike neighborhoods in suburbs where the socio-economic strata were determined by income levels. Here, it was the size of the parcel and the upkeep of the home that had become the indicator of the owner's income. As he turned onto Magnolia Drive the sweep of his headlights illuminated several Lowcountry-style homes erected off the ground with wraparound porches; a few modern ranch-style homes; a two-story

Spanish-inspired stucco with a tiled roof; and, at the end of the road, a three-story Colonial with a circular driveway. Lanterns flanking the double doors, a fixture suspended under the portico, and strategically placed inground lighting illuminated the structure Francine Tanner called home. He pulled up ahead of a fire-engine-red Corvette, shutting off the engine and alighting from his vehicle at the same time the front door opened.

Keaton hadn't realized he'd been holding his breath until tightness in his chest forced him to exhale. Light spilling from within the magnificent structure bathed Francine in gold. It was as if he'd stepped back in time, standing on his feet in the theater as Francine stood onstage under the spotlights with the play's cast members as they took their bows to thunderous applause.

Her provocative attire from Saturday had been replaced with a pair of dark slacks, a white man-tailored shirt, and black patent leather pumps. A slow smile spread over his features. Each time he saw her she looked different. However, a single word came to mind: *sexy*. Even with her tousled hair when working at the salon he'd detected an innocent sexiness about her. The figure-hugging dress she wore when she'd strutted out of Jack's revealed and concealed at the same time. And now, even seemingly buttoned up, she still exuded an air of feminine sensuality. The screenplay he'd written with her in mind was about a woman who undergoes a transformation inwardly and outwardly after her husband is murdered. She starts out timid and introverted but is forced to come out of her cocoon to assume control of the company he'd built from the ground up when a rival company attempts a takeover.

Running her hand over the nape of her neck, Francine smiled up at him. "I see you managed to find my street."

Keaton returned her smile. "I did notice quite a few Magnolias: Court, Lane, Street, and, of course, Drive."

Francine opened the door wider. "Please come in. This section of the Cove was once known as the Magnolias because someone planted hundreds of magnolia trees. Once the roads were paved, the town planners decided to give each street its distinctive designation."

Keaton nodded like a bobblehead doll. His gaze was riveted on the entryway, which opened out into an expansive living room with spectacular staircases suspended over an archway and branching off in different directions. The staircases reminded him of outstretched arms ready to greet and embrace visitors. A trio of runners on the gleaming parquet floor mirrored the symmetry of the stairs, indicating different directions one could take. He saw the house in the same manner through which he stared through a camera lens. It was a movie set.

"Your house is magnificent."

Francine picked up a suit jacket, slipping her arms into it. "I'll be certain to let my mother know you like it. She's quite proud of her home."

"You don't live here?" She met his stunned gaze, the skin fanning out around her brilliant eyes when she laughed.

"I do live here, but I have my own apartment in the east wing. If we weren't pressed for time I'd give you a tour."

"Perhaps the next time — that is, if you decide to invite me back."

"Perhaps," she repeated, picking up a set of keys and a black patent leather clutch from a straight-back chair covered in embroidered silk. "I'm ready whenever you are."

Waiting until she closed and locked the door, Keaton rested a hand at her waist, escorting her to the passenger side of his

SUV and assisting her up. He rounded the vehicle, getting in beside her. The scent of her perfume wafted to his nose when he leaned to his right to fasten his seat belt. It wasn't the same fragrance she'd worn at the salon.

"You're wearing Samsara."

Francine met his eyes as he punched the Start Engine button. "Does my perfume bother you?"

Shifting into gear, he drove back the way he'd come. "Not in the least. In fact I like it. I find it sophisticated and sensual. I'm familiar with different perfumes and cologne because my sister is a perfumer."

"She sells perfume?"

Keaton chuckled softly. "No. She creates fragrances for celebrities."

"That must be exciting."

"It sounds exciting, but for Liana it becomes an exercise in patience. She has a sign written in Latin at her lab that translates into leaving one's ego at the door, but that doesn't seem to make a difference for some of her customers, even if they can read the language. There was a female performer who will remain nameless that demanded Liana have a certain type of mineral water on hand for her to drink along with a bouquet of two dozen white roses for inspiration."

"Did she comply?"

"No."

"What happened?" Francine asked.

"Miss Diva pouted for a few minutes, but when she realized Liana wasn't going to send someone out for her water or flowers she sat down to inhale the scent strips from the different blends. I'm certain you've met fellow actors who'd become intoxicated on fame."

There came a noticeable silence before Francine said, "I had the misfortune of meeting more than I care to remember."

Keaton heard something in her voice indicating she wasn't ready to talk about her former career. He decided to change the subject. "How long have you lived on Cavanaugh Island?"

Francine was certain Keaton could hear her sigh of relief. She was under the impression he wanted to talk about his upcoming film, not her past involvement in the industry. "I've lived here all of my life. The exception is when I went to college and . . ."

"And when you appeared off-Broadway," he added when she didn't finish her sentence.

"Yes."

"Are your folks from here?"

Francine stared through the windshield as the landscape whizzed by. He was driving much too fast. "You're going to have to slow down before you're stopped for speeding."

He took a quick glance at the speedometer. "I'm only going thirty-five and we're the only ones on the road."

"Thirty-five is fifteen miles too fast. The first time you're stopped for speeding you'll have to pay a fine. The second infraction is an even bigger fine, along with your vehicle being impounded."

Keaton whistled softly as he eased off the gas pedal. "That's excessive." He told her about a young woman he'd seen on the side of the road who had been stopped by an island police officer and that she'd been crying.

"If she was crying then that probably meant it wasn't her first offense. We have strict rules, but they've made the island safer. We have an occasional DWI or DUI but we've never had a vehicular hit-and-run on Cavanaugh Island. And please don't try to pass a stopped school bus, because you'll have to spend a week in the local jail."

"Da-am-mn!" He'd drawn out the word in three distinct syllables. "Other than the stringent vehicular laws, Cavanaugh Island seems like a wonderful place to live."

"It is," Francine confirmed.

"How long have your people lived here?"

She smiled when he said *people.* It was typical Southern vernacular. "My mother's people came from Africa in chains and they have been here for hundreds of years. The Gullahs were able to retain much of their African customs, traditions, and superstitions because of the Sea Islands' isolation from the mainland. Daddy's folks came from England to South Carolina during the French and Indian War as indentured servants. They have a checkered past because there were brothers and cousins who fought on opposing sides during the War for Independence and the Civil War. The Tories who supported the British crown either went back to England or fled to Canada."

"What happened to those who decided to fight for the North after the Civil War ended?" Keaton asked.

"They came back to Charleston. They were luckier than many Confederate soldiers who'd lost everything, because they'd befriended the son of a New York banker who gave them the loan they needed to set up a dry goods store. A few of them had children with ex–slave women, and in succeeding generations some of those who were mixed race were able to pass into the white race. My paternal great-grandmother was a quadroon."

"So you're half Gullah."

Francine shook her head. "Not half. I'm all Gullah. One drop of Gullah blood means you're Gullah."

"I'm certain if someone wrote a book about your family it would make for fascinating reading."

Francine laughed. "I'm certain it would. There's nothing juicier than opening the door to expose family secrets."

"Are you speaking from experience?" he teased.

"No!"

"Milady, thou dost protest too much," Keaton accused in a clipped British accent.

"I think not, milord," she countered as if she were a Cockney tavern maid.

Without warning, both broke into hysterical laughter as Francine touched the corners of her eyes with a fingertip to stem tears before they fell and ruined her makeup. The fact that Keaton had made her laugh was definitely a plus. It'd been a very long time since a man had been able to make her do that.

"You have the face of a lady and the body

of a serving wench," Keaton continued, not breaking character.

Resting her right hand over her heart, Francine closed her eyes. "You wound me, milord, for can't you see I'm a lady?"

Keaton accelerated as he entered the causeway. "Aye, me lovely. A lady best served wearing silk and fine lace instead of scullery rags."

Her gaze lingered on his well-defined masculine profile. "Are you certain you didn't take acting courses? Because your accent is spot-on."

"As a theater student I had my share of drama courses," he said, chuckling softly. "It also comes from being behind the camera. You'd be surprised what you see and hear that stays with you even after you wrap the project."

"You're very good," she complimented, switching fluidly into Cockney again.

Francine and Keaton continued their impromptu role-playing until he turned off onto King Street and maneuvered into an area set aside for hotel parking. She waited inside the SUV as he got out and slipped into the jacket to his dark gray suit. If she had to describe Keaton in one word it would be *delicious*. The white shirt with French cuffs, silver monogrammed cuff links, gray-and-white silk tie, and shiny black slip-ons bespoke big-city sophistication.

It'd taken several outfit changes before she'd decided on the wool gabardine suit and three-inch pumps. After all, she was going out to dinner and not to a club where skimpy attire was the norm. And she didn't want Keaton to get the impression she was trying to seduce him because that wasn't even remotely her intent. Despite his not wearing a wedding band he still could be married. Francine had caught a quick glimpse of the woman sitting with him at Jack's and it was apparent she was totally enthralled with her dining partner.

Keaton came around and opened the door for her, holding her hand in a firm grip as he helped her down. Whoever the woman was who claimed him as her own was very, *very* lucky. She could count on one hand the number of men who elected to hold doors, pull out chairs, or assist a woman getting into and out of a car. She'd grown up watching her father pull out a chair for her mother whenever they sat down to eat and she expected no less from the men she'd met. When she asked him about the ritual Frank admitted growing up and watching his father do the same for his mother.

A slight shiver eddied over Francine when Keaton took her hand, and it had nothing to do with the cooler nighttime temperature. The warmth and strength in his fingers reminded her of what she'd been missing. Her grandmother had insisted her meeting with Keaton was a date, while she'd vehemently denied it. But walking alongside him holding hands did feel like being on a date. They walked into the elegant hotel and then the restaurant. Keaton opened the door, standing aside to let her enter before him. The maître d' approached them, smiling.

"Good evening, Mr. Grace. Welcome back to the Charleston Place Hotel. Your table is ready, sir."

Keaton shook hands with the fastidious man in a black suit, surreptitiously pressing a bill to his palm. "Thank you."

Once they were seated in the beautifully appointed restaurant, Francine stared across the table at Keaton. The table was set with a damask cloth, a crystal bud vase with a moth orchid, and a matching votive with a flickering candle. A trio playing soft jazz provided the perfect backdrop for a night of romantic dining.

"How often do you come here?" She'd

asked the question because the waitstaff had greeted him with obvious familiarity.

He pulled down his shirt cuffs and she spied the embroidered monogram on the left one. "I stayed here when I was looking to buy property in the area."

She went completely still. "Did you, Keaton?"

The light from the candle on the table irradiated the gold undertones in his complexion. "Did I what?"

"Buy property."

He smiled, revealing his beautiful straight white teeth. "Yes."

"Where?" At that moment Francine had become her grandmother, asking question after question.

"In Sanctuary Cove. I bought the abandoned farmhouse and land between the salt marsh and Intracoastal Waterway."

Her jaw dropped slightly as she met his eyes. If Keaton owned that land, then that meant he lived a short distance from the Magnolias. "The house and the land on which it sits has been abandoned for years."

"So you're familiar with it?" he asked.

She nodded. "It belonged to the Webbers. They came from a long line of rice farmers and were growing Carolina gold up until the Second World War. My grandmother told me three of the Webber boys joined the army after the bombing of Pearl Harbor and when they returned after the war they married local girls and then moved away. That left Walter and his wife, Kate, and their youngest son, who was born with a number of deformities. Grandma Dinah said he looked like the French impressionist painter Toulouse-Lautrec and was a mathematical genius. Unfortunately he didn't live to celebrate his thirtieth birthday. However, his parents lived well into their nineties. Their surviving children and grandchildren came back to bury them, but refused to stay, so the land went into receivership."

Keaton was impressed with Francine's wealth of knowledge about the island and its inhabitants. "Now I own the house and the land," he said proudly.

"Are you aware that the house needs a lot of work?"

He nodded. "Yes, I know. An architect has drawn up plans to gut the interior and start over. The structure and foundation are sound, so renovating the interior shouldn't take as long as building it from the ground up."

"Do you plan to expand it?"

Spreading his left hand out on the pristine

white tablecloth, he stared at his fingers for several seconds. The original plans called for four bedrooms, and that was more than enough for his needs. "No. I'm just going to add a screened-in back porch for cross ventilation; other than that I like the original design. I'll probably put in a flower garden and a patio with an outdoor kitchen, but I still haven't decided whether I want a gazebo."

A beat passed. "What does your wife want?" Francine asked.

He went completely still. "I wouldn't know because I don't have a wife, girlfriend, or children. The woman you saw me with at Jack's is my attorney. Her name is Devon Gilmore." He knew Francine was embarrassed when a blush darkened her fair complexion. His gaze was drawn to the sprinkling of freckles over her delicate nose that makeup couldn't conceal.

"Why would you need an outside kitchen if you don't have a family?"

"Do I have to have a family to cook in- or outside?"

Her flush deepened. "I wasn't presuming you couldn't cook —"

"How about you, Francine?" he asked, interrupting her. "Do you cook?" The sweep hand on his watch made a full revolution as he waited for her answer. "You don't."

She shook her head. "I don't."

"If you don't cook, then who feeds you?"

Staring at him through her lashes, Francine said, "My grandmother and occasionally my mother."

Resting an elbow on the table, Keaton anchored a fist under his chin. "Your grandmother cooks for her grandbaby," he teased. "What's going to happen when you have kids? Who's going to cook for them?"

"Their grandmother, of course."

He shook his head slowly. "There's going to come a time when you're going to have to break the cycle."

"Maybe by the time I decide to have children I'll sign up for cooking lessons."

"Instead of taking lessons, why don't you have your grandma teach you?"

"You don't know my grandmother. She won't allow anyone to cook in her kitchen."

"Oops." Keaton hesitated, remembering what Francine had said about having her own apartment. "What if she teaches you using the kitchen in your apartment?"

"That's not going to work. Grandma will only cook in her own kitchen. She says her kitchen is filled with good karma, and that's why her dishes are so spectacular."

A slight frown creased Keaton's forehead.

"That sounds like a lot of hocus-pocus, mumbo-jumbo nonsense."

Francine pulled her lower lip between her teeth. "It's about superstition. I told you folks down here still hold on to their superstitions, even though you think of it as mumbo jumbo."

He blinked once. "But . . . but your grandmother isn't Gullah."

"Please don't let her hear you say that. Her mother was a quadroon and that one-quarter black ancestry is Gullah."

He inclined his head. "I stand corrected."

Francine flashed a wide grin. "Apology accepted." Her smile faded as she angled her head. "Who taught you to cook?"

"I come from a family of restaurateurs. My dad's mother started out making boxed lunches for factory workers to supplement her income and support her four children after her husband died. She expanded her kitchen and when word got out that Sadie Grace made the best fried chicken in the county people started placing orders. When my father was old enough he helped her cook. He went to culinary school, where he met my mother. They married a week after graduating and he relocated Sadie Grace from his momma's kitchen to a free-standing building not far from the interstate.

Once I was tall enough to look over the grill I began working in my parents' restaurant on weekends during the school year. After I left Pittsburgh to enroll in college, my uncles opened Sadie Grace II in Mount Lebanon."

"I noticed you have Pennsylvania plates on your truck. Should I assume you're a Steelers fan?"

"Wh-a-a-t," Keaton drawled. "If you stab me I'll bleed black and gold." Without warning he gyrated and launched into Wiz Khalifa's "Black and Yellow."

Francine clapped a hand over her mouth to stifle the laughter bubbling up from her throat. At that moment she wished she could be anywhere but in the upscale restaurant so she could laugh in abandon. There was no doubt Keaton was a rabid sports fan. "You are hilarious. You missed your calling, Keaton. You really should be in front of the camera instead of behind it."

Reaching across the table, he captured her hands, tightening his hold when she tried escaping his firm grip. "I have a confession to make."

"What is it?"

"I've been carrying on an affair with the Steelers for more than half my life," he admitted without even a hint of pretense. "One year my father bought season tickets and he gave me an early birthday present when I accompanied him to every home game. My mother wasn't too happy because then she had to deal with the highs and lows of not only her husband but also her son whenever the Steelers won or lost."

A mysterious smile flitted over Francine's parted lips. "My father was drafted by the Steelers back in the day. He was forced to retire after five years because of a serious knee injury."

Keaton released her hands and waved away the sommelier who had approached their table. "Please don't tell me your father is Frank 'the Tank' Tanner."

She closed her eyes for several seconds. "Daddy stopped playing the year I was born, so the only memories I have of him playing ball come from old photographs. I still can't wrap my head around seeing him carrying that much weight. Once he retired he hired a nutritionist and went on a diet. He told me it took more than a year to lose fifty pounds, and thankfully he's kept it off all these years."

"The Tank was my dad's hero."

"Daddy still has a collection of old jerseys my mother keeps threatening to throw out.

Would you like one for your father?"

Keaton bowed his head. "Bless you, my child." His head popped up as he gave Francine a sheepish look. "Do you think he'll autograph it?"

"You can ask him. Daddy is away at least four days a week on business, but he's always home on weekends. If you're not doing anything Sunday, then I'd like to invite you to dinner, where you can meet him in person."

Keaton pumped his right fist. "Tell me the time and I'll be there."

"We usually eat around four. Do you have any food allergies?"

"No."

She smiled. "Good."

"Are you cooking?"

Francine narrowed her eyes at him. "That's not funny."

"What's not funny is you depending on others to feed you."

She wanted to tell Keaton that it wasn't the first time someone had talked about her inability to cook. She hadn't had to learn when she'd had people who were willing to make certain she didn't miss a meal. Francine wanted to tell Keaton she wasn't completely undomesticated. She could do her own laundry, iron, and clean.

"Would you cook for me if I asked you?"

There came a swollen pause as he stared at her. "I would, but only with the proviso you allow me to teach you how to prepare breakfast, a light lunch, and at least one or two complete dinners."

Crossing her arms under her breasts, she returned his stare. "What do you want in exchange?"

"What makes you think I'd want something from you?"

Being married to Aiden had taught her not to trust men. "I really have to give it to you, Keaton. You're ingenious. You wine and dine me at one of Charleston's best restaurants, and then offer to teach me to cook in lieu of my having to audition on your casting couch."

Francine was right about his wanting her to audition for a role in his upcoming film, but wrong about attempting to seduce her. "Is that what you really believe?" he asked her.

"Why else would you invite me to dinner, Keaton?"

"Maybe it's because I like you."

Her eyelids fluttered wildly. "I told you before I don't know you."

"And that's why I wanted you to have dinner with me, so we can get to know each other."

Francine kept silent, but the look on her face told Keaton she didn't believe a word he'd said.

Chapter Five

Keaton counted slowly, hoping it would give him time to diffuse his rising temper. He didn't know if Francine had had to audition on some casting agent's couch to get the supporting role in *Sisters,* but she was mistaken if he wanted to use the excuse of giving her cooking lessons in exchange for accepting his offer for her to star in one of his films.

"Please don't tell me that's how you got the role of Abigail in *Sisters.*" He knew he'd struck a nerve when she glared at him.

"Of course not! For your information I happened to have been the wrong gender."

He didn't visibly react to this disclosure. Keaton was more than familiar with the agent who'd cast Francine in the play, but not the man's sexual proclivity. He exhaled an audible breath. "My bad. I asked you to have dinner with me because you claim you know nothing about me, and I told you I'll give you the opportunity to get to know everything you need to know about me." He held up a hand when she opened her mouth. "Please don't say anything until you hear me out. I'm planning to put up a movie studio on the property. It will include a soundstage and set decorations for interior shots. There are places on Cavanaugh Island that look like Florida, California, or even the Caribbean I can use for exterior shots. Charleston is perfect as the quintessential Southern city and set designers can replicate most of the country's major cities using special effects along with digital imagery.

"And my offer to teach you to cook has nothing to do with strong-arming you or even going as far as attempting to seduce you. I've made it a practice not to get involved with actresses working in my films. I'm not going to lie and say I wasn't disappointed when you told me you wouldn't star in my movie, and that means I'll just have to suck it up and move on. I want you to know that I wrote a script with you in mind when I returned to New York to enroll in a graduate program at NYU Tisch School of the Arts after seeing your performance in *Sisters*. I saw the play twice because I believed you were a fluke. But after the second time I realized your performance was nothing short of brilliance."

Spots of color dotted her cheeks with his compliment. "Thank you."

"There's no need to thank me. You're an incredible actress."

"Former actress," she corrected. "I gave up life on the stage eight years ago, and I vowed never to return."

Keaton wanted to know what or who'd forced her to abandon what could've become a career of long duration. She gave him a prolonged stare, her bright green eyes darkening noticeably. He wondered if Francine knew how strikingly exotic she was. There was something about her palomino-gold skin, burnished red hair, and catlike eyes that made him want to drown in the emerald pools. He'd convinced himself that he didn't have any romantic notions when it came to her, but after their over-the-top dramatic hamming back and forth during the drive from the island to Charleston he'd gotten to see another side of the actress-turned-hairstylist. What he'd enjoyed most was her spontaneity and the fact that she didn't take herself too seriously.

He'd learned from experience when to choose his battles and he knew he had to retreat. Before he'd walked into the Beauty Box he'd forgotten about Francine Tanner.

However, seeing Francine again had rekindled his interest in the script he'd written expressly for her, forcing him to search through the computer disks he'd brought with him from Los Angeles to load into his laptop. He'd stayed up all night reviewing, editing, and tweaking until he felt comfortable with the revisions. His initial instinct to cast Francine in the lead hadn't changed, but her reluctance to take on the role meant it was time for him to move on and look for another actress.

"I'm disappointed, but I have to respect your decision."

A hint of a smile parted her lips. "Thank you for being so gracious, Keaton."

Picking up the wine list, he studied it, wanting to tell Francine he'd been called a lot of things, but no one had ever said he was gracious, at least not to his face. "I'd like to order a bottle of wine." He looked at her. "Will you share it with me?"

"I will, but only if I don't have to be the designated driver. After two glasses I'm usually three sheets to the wind."

Keaton lifted his eyebrows at her admission. That meant she wasn't much of a drinker. "I'll make certain you get home in one piece." He signaled the sommelier and when the man brought the bottle he'd selected he watched Francine as she sampled the small amount in her glass.

Her expression brightened. "I like it."

He'd ordered the pinot noir, hoping she would like it. Waiting until after their glasses were half filled, he raised his glass, touching it to hers when she repeated the action. "To friendship and the success of Grace Low-country Productions."

"To friendship and award-winning movie-making," Francine said after a pregnant pause. She took a sip, savoring the slightly sweet aromatic wine on her palate before swallowing. She'd never been much of a wine connoisseur, but she knew she could very easily get used to drinking this particular fragrant red wine.

The framed paintings hanging on the dark paneled walls of the Charleston Grill reminded her of the Cove Inn's parlor boardinghouse where the guests lingered over cordials after dinner. Not only did she like the wine but also her dining partner; when they'd walked into the restaurant there weren't more than ten couples. Now it was almost filled to capacity with conservatively dressed couples, groups of men, women, and some with their families.

"Do you want to order an appetizer?" Keaton asked, breaking into her thoughts.

Francine perused the menu featuring dishes listed as pure, lush, cosmopolitan, and Southern. "What do you recommend?"

"The Charleston Grill crab cake with shrimp and tomato dill vinaigrette is delicious. I only say that because I'm partial to Southern cuisine."

"What type of dishes do they serve at Sadie's?"

"The first Sadie's is strictly soul food, and Sadie's II offers continental cuisine."

Francine decided to forgo an appetizer, ordering lamb with spring vegetables, mint chimichurri, and lamb jus. Keaton opted for prime beef tenderloin with a bourguignon sauce and cubed baked potatoes.

Over dinner she couldn't shake the notion that Keaton's moving to Cavanaugh Island to set up a studio was more than a coincidence. That he'd known who she was when she was totally unaware of him. But then she told herself if she had kept up with the film industry she probably would've heard of Keaton Grace. As a Yale drama student Francine read every available trade publication and watched entertainment news religiously. She even went so far as to buy the tabloids. Within some of the misleading headlines there was usually a kernel of truth. After all, it was the *National En-*

quirer that broke the news that Rielle Hunter had had the 2004 Democratic vice presidential candidate John Edwards's baby.

Her gaze landed on a woman at a nearby table. Instead of concentrating on her dinner partner she was staring openly at Keaton. Francine wondered if the woman had recognized him. It was when she saw her run the tip of her tongue over her lips that Francine realized she was witnessing an attempt at blatant seduction. "What was that all about?" Keaton asked.

"What?"

"Don't play innocent, Francine. I saw you glaring at that woman."

She leaned over the table. "It was the death stare, not glaring. The brazen heifer was staring at you and licking her lips as if you were dessert."

Keaton touched his napkin to his mouth. "You really surprise me."

"How?"

"I never figured you for someone who would fight for her man."

"I would never belittle myself physically fighting another woman over some guy. Glaring is not fighting. I only did it because she's rude and totally inconsiderate to her dining partner."

"What if he were your husband?"

"Not even if he were my husband. And you're not my man." She'd enunciated each word.

Attractive lines creased his lean jaw when he smiled. "I am tonight. Whenever I take a woman out I always regard her as my lady and myself as her man."

"Was it the same when you had dinner with your attorney the other night?"

"Of course. Devon and I happen to be good friends."

Her professionally arched eyebrows lifted slightly. She wanted to ask Keaton what he meant by "good friend" but decided to let it drop. "Back to Miss Can't-Keep-Her-Eyes-to-Herself. What would you have done if her man decided to come on to me?"

"I'd invite him to the men's room and jack his ass up."

Her jaw dropped. She didn't know Keaton well. In fact, she didn't know him at all, but she wouldn't have guessed he was prone to violence. "No, you wouldn't."

"Yes, I would, if he disrespected you. Dudes back in Pittsburgh had to learn the hard way never to disrespect my sister."

"What did you do?"

He shook his head. "You don't want to know."

Francine now regarded Keaton in a whole

new light. It was apparent the urbane man with whom she shared a table had some thug in him. "You're right. I don't want to know."

"Are you always this gullible?"

She closed her eyes, biting back laughter. "You are unreal. You definitely missed your calling, Keaton, because you should've become an actor instead of a director."

"I tend to believe most directors are frustrated actors."

"The reverse could be said with the number of actors who've become directors."

"Which ones do you think have successfully made the transition?" he asked.

"With the exception of Robert De Niro, Sean Penn, and Jodie Foster, who are equally proficient at acting and directing, I feel the actors who become directors have found their true niche."

"Which ones are you talking about?"

"When it comes to contemporaries I would say Clint Eastwood, Penny Marshall, Woody Allen, Ron Howard, Ben Affleck, Kevin Costner, and George Clooney. However, my personal favorite would be Orson Welles."

Keaton nodded, smiling. "The man was truly a genius. And I'd have to put Hitchcock in the same category as Welles."

Francine had forgotten her vow to distance herself from any and everything that pertained to acting when she and Keaton discussed their favorite films and actors. He went into detail as to Francis Ford Coppola's directorial insight of the *Godfather* trilogy, then sheepishly admitted he'd earned a second graduate degree from the University of Southern California's School of Cinematic Arts. The master of arts degree in critical studies was a comprehensive curriculum offering courses that analyzed the power and responsibility of American and international film and television. A year later he'd joined the faculty at USC as an assistant professor of critical studies. She'd found herself mesmerized as he analyzed the significance of scenes and dialogue in the *Godfather* films in relation to the world it represented.

"The next time I watch the trilogy I'll try and notice the nuances, keeping in mind the similarities between the Corleones and Borgias," she told him.

"Have you seen the *Borgias* miniseries?"

Francine's emerald-green eyes shimmered like the precious stones they resembled. "But of course. I've watched every episode. I love historical dramas like *The Tudors, Da Vinci's Demons,* and *Copper.*" She didn't tell him that she minored in history.

"I don't have the mind-set to write a historical drama," he admitted.

"What about a period piece like *Daughters of the Dust, Eve's Bayou,* or *Ruby's Bucket of Blood*? The setting could be integral to the plot and characters."

The smile that spread across Keaton's face was one she would remember forever. It began with the parting of his firm lips before spreading to his eyes. Francine didn't have time to react when he held on to her hands, not permitting her to escape his grasp. "Are you a psychic?"

A slight frown furrowed Francine's forehead at the same time a chill washed over her body, bringing goose bumps to her skin. She hadn't wanted to believe Keaton had discovered her gift unless . . . She didn't want to think that perhaps he also was clairvoyant.

"I don't know what you're talking about." Her voice was shaded in neutral tones, giving no indication of her inner turmoil.

"You have to be very intuitive, because that's exactly what I've planned once I begin production sometime late next year. It will be a period piece set here in the Lowcountry."

Inwardly, Francine blew out a breath,

forcing a calmness she didn't feel. She hadn't answered him and for that she was grateful. No one had ever asked her if she had second sight because it was a special gift, and she feared if people knew they would ostracize her even more than they had by teasing her about her looks.

"Have you written the script?"

"No, not yet. I still have a lot of research to do."

"When are you going to complete the research?" she asked.

"Hopefully before the end of the summer. That will allow me time during the fall and winter to finish the script. Next spring I'll advertise for an open casting call, and I estimate we can start shooting around the beginning of November."

"Where are you going to go for your research?"

"I'll probably begin with the Internet, then go to the local library."

"May I make a few suggestions, Keaton?"

"Sure."

"When you go to the Cove's library ask for Hannah Forsyth. She's the head librarian and island historian." Francine didn't tell him that the woman was a notorious gossip or that Hannah may know the written history, while Francine knew more than she needed to know about the unwritten history of Cavanaugh Island. "You can also visit the Parlor Bookstore. Deborah Monroe is the owner. She should be able to give you a listing of books with subjects ranging from Lowcountry food, crafts, customs, and traditions, to how to speak Gullah. Now, if you want to uncover things you won't find in books, then you're going to have to interview the locals. A lot of our history is oral, which means it's passed down through generations by griots."

"Who do you think will give me the most authentic information?"

She smiled. "There's a couple in the Cove and I know of one in the Creek."

His thumbs made circular motions over Francine's fingers. "I need you to help me out."

"Help you out how?" The four words came out slowly.

"I'd like for you to introduce me to the griots."

"That means I'm going to have to ask around about finding someone in the Landing. The only problem is they may not talk openly with you because you're an outsider."

"How much of an outsider can I be if I'm going to live here?"

"Then you're going to have to let them know that. You also have to tell them you're a filmmaker, because there's no such thing as keeping a secret on Cavanaugh Island."

Keaton had solicited her assistance because Francine knew he would be met with resistance from longtime residents who usually viewed strangers with trepidation. However, they welcomed the snowbirds because the additional revenue helped to sustain the small businesses during the winter months.

"Okay. But it can only be when the Beauty Box is closed. If you come to church with me on Sunday I'll introduce you before or after the service. A few may even feel comfortable enough to invite you to Sunday dinner," she teased.

Lifting her hands, Keaton dropped a kiss on the knuckles. "I'll accept their invitation, but only if you accompany me. I'm going to owe you."

"Just be prepared to hand over your firstborn. Gotcha!" she whispered when he let go of her hands and settled back in his chair, seemingly in slow motion.

"I suppose I deserve that," Keaton admitted.

Francine scrunched up her nose. "Yes, you do. No more," she said quickly, placing her hand over her wineglass when Keaton attempted to refill it.

"Do you want dessert?"

Pressing her hands to her belly, Francine shook her head. "No thank you. I can't eat another morsel."

"Would you like coffee or tea?"

"No, please." She didn't tell Keaton that she usually brewed a single cup of decaf coffee before retiring for bed. She'd found the warm brew was the perfect sleep aid. She waited while Keaton settled the bill, scrawling his signature across the credit card receipt.

Keaton suggested she wait inside the restaurant while he brought his car around to the front of the hotel. The 38° readout on the sign above a nearby bank building was a constant reminder it was winter. Although she'd spent three years at Yale as a drama major Francine never got used to Connecticut's long, frigid winters. After graduating she'd elected to continue to live in the northeast when she moved to New York. Francine loved living in Manhattan because she'd discovered she never wanted to go to sleep. Even at three in the morning she could find someplace to eat, and during the summer months she found herself mingling with the massive crowds in either

Times Square or Greenwich Village. During the summer she got by on an average of four hours of sleep a night because it was as if the bright lights were calling her name. The city had become a magical place where everything she wanted or needed was seemingly at her fingertips. As much as she would openly admit she was content to live on Cavanaugh Island, she did occasionally miss the late nights and big city lights.

She hadn't fit the stereotype of the struggling actor waiting for his or her big break or that plum role that would make casting agents or movie producers take notice. When she'd made the decision to become an actor Francine knew it would be an upward climb no matter how talented she'd believed she was. She was realistic enough to accept that she was one of hundreds that would audition for a role, no matter how big or small.

The hotel doorman opened the door for her when Keaton got out of the BMW, striding toward her. He removed his suit jacket and placed it around her shoulders. "I turned on the heat, but it's going to take a few minutes before the truck warms up."

Francine inhaled the scent of the cologne clinging to the fabric of the jacket as Keaton cupped her elbow when she stepped up into the idling vehicle and secured her seat belt. Warm air feathered over her face as she reclined against the leather seat.

Keaton fastened his seat belt, then rested a hand over her knee, squeezing it gently. "Are you okay?"

She closed her eyes. "I'm good, Keaton."

"Sit back and relax; I'll take the longer route back if you want to take a nap."

Keaton couldn't believe he'd hit the proverbial jackpot when he walked into the Beauty Box and saw Francine Tanner standing there. At first he'd thought he was either hallucinating or he'd conjured her up. But the instant she'd opened her mouth he knew she was the same actress with whom he'd become enthralled due to her flawless performance of a woman who'd done everything to be accepted by her half sisters who hadn't known of her existence until after the death of their father. Not only hadn't she looked like them, but the woman who'd been their father's secret lover had been extremely wealthy. Abigail, Francine's character, had grown up spoiled, pampered, and indulged, while her sisters lived in public housing, where the sounds of gunfire and drug dealing were a daily and accepted occurrence.

Despite her rejecting his offer to star in one of his films, Keaton felt all wasn't lost. Francine had become the perfect vehicle through which he would glean enough research for a future project. As a pragmatist, he always dealt with what was real. Even his scripts dealt with real-life issues. Most were resolved, but his signature was to leave some unresolved issues at the end of the film because of the character's unwillingness or inability to overcome them. And although he wasn't superstitious, he knew relocating to Cavanaugh Island was unconsciously based on a film he'd seen the year he celebrated his eighteenth birthday.

He'd always been a movie buff, but when he saw *Daughters of the Dust,* an independent film written, directed, and produced by Julie Dash in 1991, he knew that was what he wanted to do. The film was touted as the first feature directed by an African American woman distributed theatrically in the United States.

It was another twenty years before he recalled the images of the iconic film when he'd attended a party given by an A-list actress. One of her guests was a tarot card reader and he had his cards read for the first time. The hair had stood up on the back of his neck when the woman told him that he was going to move across the country to a place that would completely change his life. His skepticism must have shown when she told him the spirit had never lied to her. She then put aside the deck of cards, took his hand, and read his palm. When she mentioned the movie directed by a woman about people living on an island in the South, Keaton knew she was referring to *Daughters of the Dust.* She concluded, saying he had to take control of every aspect of his career or he was going to lose everything he'd worked for.

Her prediction, which had lingered around the fringes of his mind, came back to haunt him six months later when his brother-in-law insisted he wouldn't release the money needed to produce future films unless he was involved in the creative process. Keaton had sought to compromise with Hollis, who stood firm in his demand. He'd logged thousands of miles flying from L.A. to the Georgia, Florida, and South Carolina Sea Islands, finally selecting the town of Sanctuary Cove on Cavanaugh Island.

He managed to take a lingering look at his passenger when he stopped for a red light. A shaft of light from the dashboard cast soft, flattering shadows over Francine's delicate profile. The tarot card reader had revealed information about his family, finances, and health. When she turned over the card representing love she'd stared at it for at least a full minute, then told him he would never marry or father children if he didn't let go of his past. Keaton knew she was talking about Jade, but the image of her lifeless body when he'd gone to her apartment after her mother called to tell him she couldn't wake her up would stay with him forever.

There were other women after Jade, but none who held his interest long enough to form what he would even consider a friendship. Even his on-again, off-again relationship with Lisa was more platonic than intimate. It was just a hunch, but he knew he could cultivate an easygoing friendship with Francine. The three hours he'd spent with her felt like one.

He flipped his directional signal and turned down the street leading to the causeway, the lights and church steeples of Charleston fading in the rearview mirror. Francine stirred slightly as he entered the town limits for Haven Creek but didn't open her eyes. If it hadn't been for the vehicle's headlights, the glow from a half moon, and light coming from homes in the distance Keaton would've encountered complete darkness.

Francine opened her eyes when Keaton shook her gently. She rolled her head on her neck. "Sorry about that," she apologized. "I must have fallen asleep." Unbuckling the seat belt, she slipped out of his jacket.

Leaning to his right, he pressed a kiss to her hair. "There's no need to apologize. Don't move. I'll help you down."

She anchored her hands on Keaton's shoulders when his hands went around her waist. Her head was level with his as he held her effortlessly, her feet inches off the ground. "You can put me down now."

He complied, one arm going around her waist. "I'll walk you to your door."

"The door to my apartment is on the east side of the house." Francine led the way, Keaton shortening his stride to accommodate her shorter legs. Wrought-iron solar lanterns suspended from stanchions lined the path leading to her apartment. She unlocked and opened the door. A table lamp turned to the lowest setting provided enough light for her to make it up the staircase without falling or bumping into objects.

"Do you ride?" Keaton asked behind her.

She turned around. “What?”

He pointed to the bicycle positioned on a stand in the spacious entryway. “The bike.”

“Yes. Yes, I do. Every day my best friend and I used to ride rain or shine. She just found out she’s pregnant, so she’s going to curtail riding for at least three months.”

“Where do you go when you ride?”

Pressing her back to the open door, Francine tried to make out his expression in the diffused light. “I ride to Haven Creek to meet her, then we ride back to the Cove before she returns to the Creek.”

Keaton leaned against the door next to her, their shoulders touching. “Do you drive?”

“Yes. The red Corvette parked out front is mine.”

His eyebrows lifted. “It’s nice.”

“It’s fast, but I rarely get the chance to take it out on the highway and let it fly.”

Pushing his hands into the pockets of his trousers, Keaton crossed his feet at the ankles. “So, the pretty lady has a lead foot.”

“Yup. But only once I leave the island.”

“You don’t date.” His question was a statement.

Francine held her breath, and then let it out slowly. “I haven’t dated in a while.”

“How long is a while?”

She didn't want to say it'd been eight years. That was certain to make her sound like a loser. Then she thought about going to the Island Fair with David last summer. It wasn't an actual date but he had asked her to accompany him. "Six months. The last time I went on a date was last July."

"That is a while."

She chewed her lower lip. "I don't want you to feel sorry for me, Keaton. I —"

"Why should I feel sorry for you?" he said, interrupting her. "If you're not dating anyone, then that has to be by choice because you happen to be blessed with looks and brains. You caused quite a stir when you walked into Jack's wearing that dress. Most of the men had their tongues hanging out and I was no exception."

Francine couldn't help the rush of heat that traveled through her. But she had to ignore his remark about gawking at her. He'd made it known that whatever they would share would be strictly business. Pushing off the door, she rested a hand over his chest. "I want to thank you for dinner, your engaging conversation, and your witty performance."

Keaton covered her hand with his. "It's I who should be thanking you." He gave her fingers a gentle squeeze. "I'd like to do this again."

Francine lowered her gaze, her heart rate kicking into a higher gear. In high school she hadn't been able to get a date even if her parents would have paid a boy to take her out. Things changed slightly when she enrolled in college because the male students were more mature, while a few were forthcoming when they told her they wanted to sleep with her. It wasn't until she enrolled in a master drama class and met Aiden that she experienced what it meant to have a passionate relationship for the first time. Fast-forward to age thirty-three and a man who'd recently moved to Cavanaugh Island had asked to take her out.

Keaton embodied everything she'd dreamed about in a man. He was respectful, well mannered, intelligent, erudite, and solvent. He also wasn't a baby daddy, which meant she wouldn't have to deal with baby mama drama. "So would I," she whispered.

Lowering his head, Keaton pressed his mouth to her hair. "Is there a reason you insisted we not be seen together on the island?"

"I only said that to keep down the gossip. If we'd eaten at Jack's tonight it would be all over the island before the sun came up tomorrow that Frank and Mavis Tanner's girl is dating a snowbird staying at the inn."

He laughed softly. "You should know people are going to talk and put their spin on whatever they want. You have to learn to ignore the gossips."

"You can do that when you live in a city like New York or L.A., but it's very different here because everyone knows each other."

Vertical lines appeared between Keaton's eyes in a frown. "If you're ashamed to be seen with me on the island then —"

"I'm not ashamed," Francine said quickly, cutting him off. "I'm just warning you about the fallout if we do go out together."

"Why don't you let me worry about that?"

Francine knew she had to let go of the emotional baggage she'd carried for far too long. Keaton was asking to take her out, not marry her. She also had to remember he wasn't Aiden, a scrub looking for a woman to take care of him.

"Okay."

"Okay what, Francine?"

"I'll go out with you."

He chuckled, the sound rumbling in his chest. "That wasn't so hard, was it?"

Her laughter joined his. "No, it wasn't." Going on tiptoe, she kissed his cheek. "Good night and thank you again for dinner. I have to get to bed before midnight because I'm going to need at least seven hours of sleep in order to deal with the folks who come into the salon tomorrow."

"Is it always like that? The back and forth between customers?"

"Yes."

"How do you stand it?"

"I've learned to tune them out."

"Good for you." Keaton pressed a kiss to her forehead. "Good night, beautiful. I'll call you in a couple of days."

He was there, and then he was gone, Francine closing and locking the door behind Keaton. Tossing her keys on the table, she slipped out of her shoes, leaving them on the doormat, and climbed the staircase. She didn't want to read more into Keaton's wanting to take her out than it presented. It was apparent he'd enjoyed her company as much as she'd enjoyed his.

Stepping off the last stair, she touched the switch, turning off the recessed lights at her end of the hallway. The lights at the west wing illuminated the staircase and recently installed elevator outside her grandmother's apartment.

Walking into her apartment, Francine made her way through the living/dining area and into her bedroom. While most thirty-something women would've loathed moving back home to live with their parents, it was the complete opposite for Francine. She had her own entrance, while her mother and father respected her privacy. Mavis never came to see her unless calling first to question whether she was indisposed. When she'd questioned her mother as to why she'd called her, Mavis claimed it was about respect. Although she was her daughter, Mavis had to respect her as an adult.

Francine loved her mother and they had become even closer since they'd begun working together, but she knew nothing would make Mavis happier than becoming a grandmother. Francine didn't like being an only child because she'd felt pressured to grant her mother's wish. The one time she'd talked about adopting a child Mavis couldn't stop grinning.

Adoption still was an option for Francine. She'd admitted to Morgan that there were too many babies and children languishing in foster homes waiting for someone to make them a part of a permanent family. She would celebrate her thirty-fourth birthday on St. Patrick's Day and with each passing birthday she was reminded that her biological clock was winding down. Walking on bare feet, she went into the adjoining bathroom to remove her makeup and take a shower. Crawling into bed, she pulled the sheet, lightweight blanket, and comforter up and over her shoulders. She tossed restlessly, her mind filled with thoughts of Keaton. There was something about him that made her fantasize about a future with him. It was more than a half hour till she finally fell asleep.

Chapter Six

Francine got up feeling more tired than she did before she'd gone to bed. She woke up twice during the night, tossing restlessly until falling back to sleep. What nagged at her was that she hadn't been dreaming, so she was in a quandary as to why she hadn't slept soundly.

She walked into the first-floor stainless-steel gourmet kitchen, stopping short when she saw her parents and grandmother sitting in the breakfast nook. When Mavis met with the contractor to renovate the space on the second floor for her mother-in-law's apartment she had him update the main kitchen. Her father was the first to notice her.

"Come and join us, Frannie."

She approached her father, throwing her arms around his neck, and kissed his clean-shaven cheek. Born Francis Daniel Tanner, he'd shortened his first name to Frank. He would turn sixty this coming summer, but looked at least a decade younger. His reddish hair was now completely gray, and a pair of large gray-green eyes, surrounded by minute lines, were his most striking feature. Standing six feet in bare feet, he tipped the scales at an even two hundred pounds. He told anyone who stood still long enough to listen that his two greatest accomplishments were becoming a father and keeping off the fifty pounds he'd lost after his football playing days.

"Good morning, Daddy. I thought you'd be on the road by now," she said, before kissing her mother and grandmother. Frank was a hands-on franchise owner. He'd made it a practice to visit each of his restaurants every week. None of the managers knew the day or time when he would show up, forcing them to make certain everything passed Frank's white-glove test.

"I decided to stick close to home this week."

Mavis cut her eyes at her husband. "That's because I told him it's time he stop traipsing up and down the road so much. His restaurants are not going to fall apart if he's not there every week."

Patting his wife's hand, Frank gave her a sidelong glance. "You know you want me home because you think I'm cheating on you."

"Daddy!"

"Francis!"

Francine and Dinah had spoken at the same time. "Now, you know Mama doesn't have a jealous bone in her body," Francine said, while glaring at her father.

Mavis sucked her teeth loudly. "If you didn't cheat on me when you played pro ball, you're not going to cheat now — *old man.*"

Francine knew her parents had lived in separate states when he played for the Steelers. Mavis stayed with her in-laws in Charleston during the football season, and then moved back to the Cove with her husband once it ended. Unlike some of his teammates, Frank rented a furnished apartment in Pittsburgh instead of buying a house, mailed his paychecks home, and called his wife every night.

She picked up a plate and walked over to the chafing dishes, lifting the covers to find silver dollar buckwheat pancakes, slices of crisp bacon, sausage links, home fries, and scrambled eggs. Picking up a pair of tongs, she placed two pancakes, a slice of bacon, and a sausage link on the plate. Returning to the table, she sat down next to her grandmother.

Mavis stared at her plate. "Do you want me to cook a couple of eggs for you?"

Francine shook her head. "No thank you." She preferred her eggs prepared over easy to scrambled.

"If you learned to cook, then you could make your own eggs," Frank mumbled under his breath.

Her hand halted pouring juice into the glass at her place setting. "I'm going to take cooking lessons."

"From whom?" Dinah questioned, staring at her granddaughter over her glasses.

"Keaton has promised to teach me."

"Who's Keaton?" the other two at the table asked in unison.

Francine didn't know whether she'd spoken too soon, but now that his name was out she knew she had to explain his existence. "He's the man I went out with last night. He comes from a family of chefs, so when I told him I didn't know how to cook he offered to teach me. In my kitchen, of course," she added, staring directly at her grandmother.

Dinah affected a smug expression. "I guess that means your date went well."

Francine rolled her eyes upward. "It

wasn't a date, Grandma Dinah." Her gaze swept around the table as she took a sip of freshly squeezed orange juice. She knew her mother would never question her about Keaton, but her father wasn't as easygoing as his wife when it came to protecting his daughter's emotional stability. And knowing this, Francine never told her father that Aiden had used her financially to advance his career. That had remained her and Morgan's secret. In between bites of food she told her family about what had transpired between her and Keaton.

"So, he plans on setting up a movie studio here in the Cove?" Mavis asked.

"I think it's a wonderful idea," Frank said before Francine could answer her mother's question. "Think of the revenue it would bring to the island. He could hire locals as extras, pay shopkeepers to use their stores and other folks who are willing to open their homes for interior shots. Moviemaking isn't just Hollywood anymore. It's Vancouver, Chicago, New York City, and Pittsburgh. And now it can be Cavanaugh Island."

Francine raised her glass in a toast to her father. "Spoken like the businessman that you are."

Mavis dropped an arm over Frank's shoulders. "I never thought of it in that way. I keep thinking that folks don't want their laid-back lifestyle disrupted by having movie people hanging out here."

Suddenly Francine felt the need to defend Keaton. "Independent films are very different from the big budget blockbusters produced by major studios. They don't take as long to shoot because funding is limited and they're always concerned with running out of money."

"How long is not long?" Dinah questioned.

"Many times they can be completed in under a month. And because their budgets are minuscule when compared to the big box office films, the producer will hire unknowns, or if the script is good enough they'll be able to entice an A-list actor to work for scale."

Mavis traced the design on the handle of her fork. "What's your involvement in all of this?"

Francine knew her mother was concerned with her leaving the Beauty Box. "I promised Keaton I would introduce him to some folks so he can research the Gullah culture for a script he wants to write. I told him I have no intention of resuming my acting career."

"Is he okay with that?" Mavis asked.

"I didn't give him a choice, Mama."

Mavis glanced up at her daughter. "Did you tell him that because you believe I can't run the salon by myself?"

"Please stop being melodramatic, Mama," she chided. "I love doing hair and you know it. Where else can I work and be entertained by a shop full of comedians every day?"

"You ain't lying," Mavis drawled, smiling.

Francine stood up, stacking dishes. "Speaking of doing hair. It's time I head over to the salon. Mrs. Harris is coming in at eight thirty, because she has to be at the airport at eleven."

Frank waved to her. "Put those dishes down, Frannie. I'll take care of them." He kissed Mavis's twisted hair. "You girls go to work. Mama and I have to decide what kind of trouble we're going to get into today."

Francine clapped a hand over her mouth. "I forgot to tell you that I invited Keaton to come here for Sunday dinner."

Frank squinted at her. "Are you cooking?"

"Very funny, Daddy."

"I'll cook," Dinah volunteered, "but you're going to have to eat upstairs. I don't know why I have a dining room if I never use it."

Mavis smiled. "Should I bring anything, Grandma Dinah?"

"You can make dessert."

"And there's something else I should tell you, Daddy. Keaton is a serious Steelers fan. He says his father used to go to see you play. I told him you still have a few jerseys from back in the day. Could you please autograph one for his father?"

"Sure. What's his father's name?"

She winced. "I didn't ask him. But his last name is Grace."

Frank's expression changed, becoming one of confusion. "Why does that name sound so familiar?"

"Keaton's father owns and runs a restaurant in Pittsburg called Sadie Grace."

"Oh she-e-e-at," Frank drawled. "I know exactly who he is! His name is Scott, but everyone called him Scotty." He wasn't able to hide the excitement in his voice. "I used to go to Sadie's at least three times a week. Most of the team would go there and order everything on the menu. We'd call Scotty in advance to let him know we were coming, and he'd shut down the place, with the ruse that he was hosting a private party. Our rationale was that we had to maintain our weight, but in reality it was because they served the best fried chicken, mac and cheese, collard greens, and peach cobbler this side of the Mississippi. I'd go back to my apartment, too full to move, fall across the bed, and sleep like a newborn."

Mavis shook her head. "That's why you came home after the season looking like a blimp."

"Don't hate, honey. I may have been a little round, but I did come home one of those seasons with a Super Bowl ring."

"Mama said you were fat," Francine chimed in, winking at her father. She'd been born the year her father retired.

Frank rose to his feet. "Your mama sometimes tends to stretch the truth."

"You *were* fat," Dinah said, deadpan.

He patted his flat belly. "That was then, and this is now. Just last night Mavis told me I was the sexiest man alive."

Francine covered her ears with her hands. "That's a little too much information for the breakfast table." She wondered if she were married would she and her husband still make love at sixty. She lowered her hands. "Come on, Mama, let's get outta here."

"You're going to have to forgive your father," Mavis whispered as she and Francine left the kitchen. "There are times when he's a little bit too frisky and loose with the tongue."

Looping her arm through Mavis's, Francine pulled her closer. "I think it's wonderful that you and Daddy still make love after forty years of marriage."

"What about you, Francine? You know I worry about you being alone so much. I thought when David Sullivan asked you to go to the Island Fair with him the two of you would hit it off."

"David's not my type, Mama. He's too buttoned up. I think *intense* would be a good word to describe him."

"Maybe it's because he's a lawyer."

"Mama, please. I know lawyers who know how to have fun without being so serious."

"You're probably the one who can change him."

Francine stopped at the foot of one of the staircases leading to the second floor. "I don't want to change anyone, because that's not who they are, no more than I'd want someone to change who I am. What you see is what you get. Either they take it, or they can leave it."

"I know it didn't work out between you and Aiden, but you can't let him stop you from finding love again."

Closing her eyes for several seconds, she blew out her cheeks. "I'm not like some women, who join online dating websites or troll clubs looking for a man. When the time is right someone will come into my life because he's supposed to be there." She hugged her mother, seeing the unshed moisture shimmering in her eyes. She knew Mavis worried about her because she was an only child and if she and Frank passed away she would be left alone.

"If I'm not married by the time I turn thirty-five I'm going to start the process of adopting a child."

Blinking back tears, Mavis nodded. "That sounds doable."

"Your car or mine?"

"Mine, of course," Mavis said. "I'm too old to try and sit that low in your car. Not with my bad back."

"I have to get my tote, then I'll meet you outside."

Mavis was sitting behind the wheel of the Lexus SUV that was a fortieth wedding anniversary gift from Frank when Francine slipped onto the passenger seat next to her. The drive from Magnolia Drive to the parking lot behind Moss Alley was accomplished in exactly seven minutes. It was a crisp January morning that called for a wool jacket or lightweight coat. The sun was bright, but the breeze coming off the water made it chilly.

The lock proved resistant as Francine jiggled it vigorously. "Mama, you're going to have to replace the entire lock," she said in exasperation. After a few more jiggles, it opened. She watched as Mavis reached into her tote for her cell phone, then scrolled through the directory and tapped the number for the local locksmith. Her mother left a message on his voice mail to come and replace the lock.

The two women went through the motions of turning on lights and readying the salon for business. Francine checked the voice mail, while Mavis put up a pot of coffee for the staff. The smell of brewing coffee filled the employee lounge when Mabel Kelly tapped on the front door. She had brought a tray of muffins and sweet breads from the Muffin Corner. One by one the staff arrived, hanging out in the lounge, eating and drinking, until Mavis informed them the first customer had arrived.

The morning passed quickly for Francine. She had two scheduled men's haircuts, one shave, and one walk-in for a haircut. She had retreated to the lounge to sit and wait for her next customer when her cell phone vibrated in the pocket of her smock.

She stared, reading the text message from Morgan: *Kara had a boy — 7 lbs. 7 oz. — 21 inches. Mom and baby doing well. She says the baby looks like Jeff, who is over the moon*

☺. Francine pumped her fist. She and Morgan had debated when to hold the baby shower, and it was better they'd decided sooner rather than later. She decided to wait at least a week before visiting Kara to catch a glimpse of the newest Cavanaugh Island resident.

A rush of emotion overwhelmed Francine at the same time tears pricked the back of her eyelids. All of her girlfriends were in motherhood mode, while she was left wishing for something that was just out of her grasp. Pity quickly became anger once she realized she'd let someone else define who she was. It had been eight years since Aiden had spoken those hateful words and like a fool she'd believed him. She shook her head. No more feeling sorry for herself. She was worthy of being loved and maybe it took going out with Keaton to make her realize she could enjoy a man's company as much as he enjoyed hers.

It was Thursday, the salon's late night, when Francine lay on a recliner watching the local news. Her six o'clock was running late. Her cell vibrated. Picking it up, she glanced at the display. "Hello."

"Francine, this is Keaton. I hope I didn't catch you at a bad time."

She smiled. "Your timing is impeccable. I'm taking a break."

"If that's the case, then I'll make this quick. I picked up several books from the bookstore. Mrs. Monroe said if they're not what I need, then I should bring them back. I'm developing a character and I'm stymied because she's into casting spells using roots, candles, and oils. I need clarification on a few things."

"Mark the pages that need clarification and drop the book off for me at my apartment. I'll look them over later on tonight," she said.

"How much longer will you be there?"

Francine estimated how long it would take for her to complete a cut and blowout. "Until about eight thirty."

"Thanks, doll. Then I'll see you around nine."

"I'll leave the side door unlocked. My apartment is at the top of the stairs on the right."

She ended the call, staring at the phone. Francine realized the more involved she became with Keaton the more she would be pulled back into the theater. For her, theater wasn't just about performing onstage or in front of a camera. It went beyond that. It was researching and developing, and breathing life into the character, working closely with the director to interpret the playwright's or screenwriter's script. Keaton wrote, directed, and produced his own films, which probably made him his own harshest critic.

Francine still hadn't figured out whether it was coincidence or predestination that their paths would cross. She understood his rationale for putting down roots on Cavanaugh Island and she was no longer bothered by the fact he'd recognized her when she hadn't known who he was. However, she was still attempting to process the connection between their fathers. Even with her psychic ability she would've never predicted her father would be on a first name basis with Keaton's father.

She'd attempted to concentrate on Keaton when she lay in bed at night, waiting for a vision that would reveal why their paths had crossed. But it was as if a dark shade had been pulled down, not permitting her to see her future and his future. She'd always found it eerie that she could see what was going to happen in someone else's life, but never her own.

Brooke stuck her head in the doorway. "Francine, your six o'clock is here."

She smiled at the shampoo girl. "Thanks."

Pushing off the recliner, she returned to the salon floor to take care of her last customer for the day.

Keaton parked his truck only a few feet from the door leading to Francine's apartment. Most of the windows in the house were dark and there were no cars parked along the driveway. It was still early by L.A. and New York City standards, but here on Cavanaugh Island everything seemed to go into sleep mode with the setting sun. Even the boarders at the Cove Inn who usually gathered in the parlor after dinner to chat over cordials retreated to their respective rooms and suites sometime between eight thirty and nine.

After living in three cosmopolitan cities, and now in Sanctuary Cove, Keaton realized he'd never fit well with the large, bustling metropolises. He'd come to welcome the slower pace, with no one seeming anxious or stressed to get where they needed to go. Francine had warned him of driving too fast and each time he got behind the wheel he made certain not to exceed the island's unofficial speed limit.

Reaching for the shopping bags on the passenger seat, he got out and walked to the door. As promised, she'd left it unlocked. Setting down the bags, he took off his running shoes, leaving them on the mat next to a smaller pair. His sock-covered feet were silent as he climbed the carpeted staircase. Light spilled out into the hallway from the open doorway to Francine's apartment. The odor of burning wood wafted to his nose and when he walked into the living room he saw the source of the scent. A fire flickered behind the decorative screen from the fireplace built into a wall made entirely of brick. Recessed lights reflected off the gleaming black concert piano set on the exquisite herringbone-patterned parquet floor.

His gaze swept over the furnishings in the living/dining area. Constructed without walls, the space gave the appearance it was larger than it actually was. Either Francine had a gift for decorating or she'd commissioned a professional to furnish her apartment. The sofa, chairs, tables, and fabrics were all in keeping with the warmer, semitropical Lowcountry climate. She'd used a light palette on the seat cushions with splashes of green, royal blue, and bright yellow in throw pillows. An off-white cushioned window seat stamped with palmetto leaves spanning a quartet of tall windows beckoned one to come and sit a while.

He hadn't taken more than a half-dozen

steps when she came into his line of vision. His reaction to seeing her damp hair framing her scrubbed, lightly freckled face and the white tank top molded to her firm breasts was like a punch to the gut. Bare feet with toes painted a deep rose-pink peeked out from under the hem of a pair of light blue cotton lounging pants. He marveled that she could appear so innocent and yet wanton at the same time. His gaze followed hers; she was staring at his feet.

"You didn't have to take your shoes off."

He lifted his shoulders. "I saw yours on the mat." Keaton handed Francine the shopping bags.

"I wear those whenever I go biking. I leave them downstairs because I don't want to track mud on the staircase. Come on back to the kitchen with me."

He followed her through the living/dining room and into an eat-in kitchen. "The book is in the small bag and the larger one has a little something for you."

She smiled at him over a bare shoulder. "You didn't have to bring anything for me."

"Yes, I did. I was raised never to come to someone's house empty-handed. By the way, your place is beautiful."

"Thank you. However, I can't take credit for decorating it. My best friend, Morgan, is responsible for everything you see."

"Is he local? I'm asking because I'm going to need a decorator once my home is ready." Keaton had stopped by the construction site earlier that morning. All of the spaces were framed and Sheetrock had been installed in three of the proposed four bedrooms. The head of the construction crew reported if they stayed on schedule, Keaton could expect to take up residence by the middle of March.

"Morgan Dane is a *she* and the Cove's architect. You've probably passed her shop. It's Dane and Daniels Architecture and Interior Design. Abram Daniels is her interior decorator."

"I have," he confirmed. He remembered peering through the plate-glass window of the design firm. "When I contact her should I say you referred me?"

"A little name-dropping can't hurt. Please sit down." Francine pointed to one of the stools at the cooking island.

Keaton glanced around the stark-white kitchen with black appliances. The space was spotless. "I could do some real serious cooking in here."

She set the bags down on the black granite countertop. "Well, you'll get your wish once we begin my lessons."

"Do you have a cleaning service?"

"I don't cook, but I can clean and do my own laundry."

He watched as she emptied the bag with a bottle of wine and the cellophane-wrapped bouquet of flowers. Her lips parted slightly as their eyes met. "Thank you. I'll save the wine for my first completed dinner." She gave him a hopeful expression. "Please don't start me off with a recipe that requires more than seven ingredients."

"I was thinking about linguine with clam sauce."

"Red or white?" Francine asked.

"Whatever you prefer."

"I'm kind of partial to white. The first time I ate it was in a tiny restaurant in New York City's Little Italy and I couldn't stop raving about it."

Keaton angled his head, smiling. "I also prefer white. You'll have to put together a side salad, plus make your salad dressing."

"That sounds complicated, Keaton."

"What does?"

"Making my own dressing. Why can't I use storebought?"

Propping his arms on the countertop, Keaton wondered why Francine had chosen not to learn to cook for herself, especially since her mother and grandmother could.

Most girls he'd grown up with were at least able to cook pasta, even if the sauce came from a jar they'd bought at the supermarket. There were simple dishes she could put together that required one pot. Chili, pot roast with vegetables, and baked chicken called for very few ingredients and didn't require close monitoring.

"Store-bought dressings are loaded with calories and preservatives. To make it from scratch you'll need oil, vinegar, herbs, and spices."

She looked at him from under her lashes. "Are you going to be one of those chefs who scream when the student makes a mistake?"

"First of all, I'm not a chef. And second, I don't yell. Not even on the set."

"So I'm dealing with Mr. Laid-back?" she said teasingly.

Keaton laughed under his breath. He wasn't as laidback as he was controlled. He'd always felt yelling and screaming at someone, especially if he was in charge, was a sign of insecurity. There was never a reason or need for intimidation. He'd always believed he could catch more flies with honey than with vinegar.

"The only thing I'm going to say is I'll never raise my voice to you."

Francine cradled the bouquet to her chest,

inhaling their fragrance. "These peonies are gorgeous. Excuse me while I put them in water."

She opened a cabinet under the countertop, retrieving a faceted cut crystal vase. Filling it with water from one of the twin sinks, Francine methodically arranged the flowers with the greens and baby's breath. Standing back, she admired her handiwork, then set the vase on the table with seating for four positioned near a window.

"Was this apartment here when your parents moved in?" Keaton asked Francine when she returned to the cooking island and sat down opposite him.

"No. When they bought this place it was so rundown Daddy claims it should've been demolished by a wrecking ball."

"What happened?"

"After talking to the architect he realized its historical significance and decided it would be better to renovate it."

"How long did it take?"

"Almost two years. My parents were high school sweethearts. They eloped a day after graduating, much to the disapproval of my maternal grandparents. My mother is the youngest of four. She came along when her mother was close to fifty. What Grandma Emmajean believed was menopause had become a change-of-life baby. With her older siblings already out of the house and married with their own families, Mama was left to care for her elderly parents.

"She compromised and instead of going away to college she went locally, while Daddy enrolled in Notre Dame on a full athletic and academic scholarship. The year Daddy was drafted by the Steelers my mother's father passed away. Grandma Emmajean followed a year later. Folks claimed she died of a broken heart. My parents lived apart whenever my father played ball. Once Mama discovered she was pregnant, she stayed with her in-laws in Charleston, but only during football season."

Keaton listened intently when Francine told him how her parents lived in the house where her mother had been raised until their new home in the Magnolias was refurbished. The grand house had belonged to several generations of cotton brokers who lost their fortune following the 1929 market crash. Subsequent owners made repairs but none had the resources to restore the house to its original grandeur.

Frank had invested his football earnings in a fast-food franchise. Two years later he purchased a second, eventually becoming the owner of five. The year she celebrated her thirteenth birthday Frank gave Francine a gift usually reserved for adults — her own living quarters. The walls in adjoining bedrooms on the second floor were removed to create a two-bedroom apartment.

"Weren't you rather young to have your own place?" he asked.

"Not really," she said, smiling. "Remember, I was still living under my parents' roof. It was their way of forcing me to become independent. I had to keep it clean and I wasn't allowed to have boys over, even with my parents in the house. The second bedroom was for my girlfriends whenever I had a sleepover. When the kids at school found out I had my own apartment my life became a living hell."

"Haters?" he asked.

Francine nodded. "And then some. It was bad enough they made fun of my red hair and freckles, but knowing I had an apartment took the rag off the bush."

Throwing back his head, Keaton laughed. "I haven't heard that phrase in years." He sobered quickly. "Did you have a lot of sleepovers?"

"Yes, but only with Morgan. We were high school outsiders."

He leaned over the countertop. "But look at you and Morgan now. Both of you are successful businesswomen." Keaton wanted to remind Francine that if she hadn't given up acting she probably would've become an award-winning stage or screen actress. She was just that good.

A hint of a smile parted Francine's lips. "I guess you can say the local gals have done all right for themselves."

"The local gal I'm looking at is more than all right." A flush of color suffused her face and Keaton knew Francine was uncomfortable with the compliment. He'd believed she would be more secure since she used to perform in front of live audiences.

She blinked. "You're flirting with me."

He smiled. "Guilty as charged. Does it surprise you that I am?"

"I don't know."

"What don't you know?" he asked.

Francine averted her gaze, staring over Keaton's shoulder. He was a very attractive man. Whether wearing a tailored suit or a sweater and jeans he exuded a masculine sensuality that was almost palpable.

"I was always shy when it came to boys because I was often the brunt of their immature jokes. Not only did they make fun of my hair and freckles, it was also my height and weight. They called me Little

Orphan Annie, Carrot Top, and Bean Pole. One boy came up to me and asked why I had *fly shit* on my face. When I told him they were freckles, he laughed, saying that's what his mother called freckles. People talk about bullying as if it's something new. There have always been bullies, but nowadays it appears more pervasive because kids are using cyberspace to spew their venom." She paused. "It was worse for Morgan and me because we didn't have brothers to protect us."

"Why didn't you tell your father?"

Francine gave Keaton a look that spoke volumes. "So he'd end up serving time for killing some kid? My father is extremely overprotective when it comes to me. It wasn't easy, but I managed to survive. I joined the drama club and while onstage I didn't have to be Francine Dinah Tanner, but Maggie from *Cat on a Hot Tin Roof* or Stella in *A Streetcar Named Desire.* Once I realized I'd been bitten by the acting bug I asked my mother if I could take acting lessons. Four days a week she drove me to Charleston to study with a woman who ran a theater company until I was old enough to get a driver's license. I learned to play the piano, sing, dance, and perform in musical theater numbers.

"After enrolling at a local college, accelerating and graduating in three years instead of four, I applied to the Yale School of Drama. I celebrated for days after I received my acceptance letter. Those were the best three years of my life, and with a graduate degree in fine arts to my credit I headed straight for New York City."

"Were you the quintessential struggling actress waiting for her big break?" Keaton questioned.

Francine shook her head. "Quite the contrary. My father sent me a check every month to cover the rent on my Upper West Side apartment and all ancillary expenses. Not having to worry where my next dollar was coming from left me better prepared for auditions. I attended an open casting call for *Sisters* and was lucky enough to be called back twice. The third time was the charm." She flashed a wry smile. "Even though I got rave reviews I became a one-hit wonder. Once the play closed I couldn't get another role. I did a few commercials, because redheads are usually given priority status. After a while I gave up and moved back here." She couldn't tell Keaton that her so-called fairy-tale marriage had ended and as Aiden's star rose hers had fallen.

"So you became a hairstylist."

She nodded. "Yes."

"Why a stylist?"

"Why not? I love doing hair. And working alongside my mother is a plus. She may run the Beauty Box like a marine drill sergeant but the system she's set up works. Even after she retires I don't plan to change anything."

"Do you like styling hair as much as you did acting?"

"Better." Instead of interacting with a live audience she interacted with her customers, who were also people she'd known all her life. "Do you have a nut allergy?" she asked, deftly changing the subject.

He sat up straight. "No. Why?"

Slipping off the stool Francine walked over to the kitchen table, picking up an airtight container. "My mother made an assortment of tartlets for dessert I'd like to share with you." She placed three tartlets, one of each variety, on a plate and set it down in front of Keaton. Mavis had added strawberry cheesecake and caramelized lemon to her traditional pecan tartlets. "Would you like coffee?"

"Yes, please. I'll brew it," he volunteered, getting to his feet.

Keaton brewed two cups of coffee from the single cup coffeemaker, while Francine set out a tiny cup of cream and sugar along with napkins and spoons. "Do you ever eat in front of the fire?"

She went still. "No. But I do picnic on the beach in front of a fire. Does that count?"

"Nah." Carrying the coffee mugs, he walked out of the kitchen, leaving her to follow.

Francine felt an emotion she hadn't experienced in a while. It was a nervous excitement because Keaton was the first man she'd invited to her apartment. Although being around him elicited a feeling of being slightly breathless, he still made her feel very safe. Maybe it had something to do with his laid-back personality.

Instinct told her she had nothing to fear from Keaton; however, she wasn't as certain about herself, because she feared liking him too much.

Chapter Seven

Francine couldn't believe she was sitting on the floor between Keaton's outstretched legs staring at the smoldering embers, while taking sips of coffee. "I didn't realize you were a slacker," she teased.

"What are you talking about?"

"I asked you to come here because I thought you wanted to talk about your research."

Keaton pressed a kiss to her curls. "Maybe we can discuss it Saturday night."

"What's happening Saturday night?"

Taking the cup from her hand, he placed it on a coaster, then eased her back until she lay atop him, her buttocks pressed to his groin. "If you're not busy I'd like to take you to a show at the Creek's movie house. After that we can go to the mainland and talk over cups of lattes or cappuccino."

Francine bit back a smile. She couldn't remember the last time a man had offered to take her to the movies. And never on Cavanaugh Island. "So you discovered our movie theaters." There was one in the Cove, but most of the films were at least two to three months behind the ones shown in Charleston. The theater in the Creek featured only foreign films and black-and-white movies from the thirties and forties.

"It is one of the reasons I decided to put down roots here." He breathed a kiss against her scalp. "Will you, Miss Tanner, go to the movies with me?"

"I'd like very much to go to the movies with you."

"I like you, Francine."

Francine managed to extricate herself from Keaton's loose embrace enough to turn over and face him. She found herself straddling his lap when he pushed her into a sitting position. Resting her hands on his shoulders, she felt the warmth of his body through his sweater.

"I like you, too, Keaton."

Cradling her face between his hands, his thumbs made circular motions on her cheekbones. "I like your red curls, your freckles, and your incredibly sexy long legs." He pressed a kiss over each eyelid.

Anchoring her arms under his shoulders, Francine lost herself in the strength of his lean body and the scent of his cologne clinging to the fibers of the thick cotton sweater. Keaton liked everything about her that the other men had teased her about for more years than she cared to remember. It had taken time for her to overcome the ridicule and move on. It'd been her ex-husband's deceit that still lingered to the point where she wasn't willing to lower her guard enough to trust a man.

"Do you want me to tell you what I like about you?" she whispered in his ear.

"No. I want you to show me."

She went completely still, certain Keaton could feel her heart beating through her tank top when she felt his erection pulsing under her hips. "I don't like you *that* much, Keaton." Francine watched a myriad of expressions flitter over his handsome features — confusion, shock, and then realization.

"Not that, Francine."

"Not what?"

He angled his head in the endearing gesture she'd come to look for. "No. You're not ready for that and neither am I, even if a particular part of my anatomy says differently. Besides, I don't want to ruin what we have with sex. That's something you can get from any man, and I can get from any woman. What I will take is a kiss." Francine hesitated, then kissed his cheek.

"Nah, nah, nah, baby," Keaton drawled, shaking his head. "That's not a kiss," he said in a flawless Paul Hogan in *Crocodile Dundee* accent. "This is a kiss."

Instead of pulling out a knife as the character had done in the film when confronted by thugs intent on robbing him, Keaton palmed her face, lowered his head, and brushed a light kiss over her mouth, the gesture so tender she could've imagined it. It wasn't a kiss but a caress.

He increased the pressure until her lips parted. Francine inhaled his moist breath, moaning softly when his tongue grazed hers. "I have a confession to make," he whispered.

She closed her eyes as she struggled to slow her accelerated respiration. "What is it?"

"You beguiled me the first time I saw you, and now fast-forward almost ten years and nothing has changed." He lowered his hands and kissed her forehead. "I'd better leave before I embarrass myself. Thanks for the coffee, and please let your mother know her tartlets were delicious."

Now back in control, Francine nodded. "I'll let her know. I'll walk you down so I can lock the door."

It wasn't until she'd locked the door behind Keaton that Francine was able to draw a normal breath. Pressing her back to the door, she closed her eyes, reliving the feel of his mouth on hers. The kiss wasn't as sexual as it was sensual. Francine opened her eyes, smiling. He liked her and she liked him. It was the perfect beginning to an easy and uncomplicated friendship.

Francine felt his breath feather along the column of her neck, then the pleasurable bite of teeth at the base of her throat. She rose off the mattress, writhing on twisted sheets and keening when feelings she'd forgotten surfaced.

His mouth continued its exploration, traveling downward over her breasts, distended nipples, into the dip to her belly button and still lower to her inner thighs. A rush of moisture bathed her core as she attempted to press her knees together to stop the pulsing from growing stronger and stronger with each breath, sweeping her up into a maelstrom of ecstasy and holding her captive.

"Don't stop," she gasped. "Please don't stop," she pleaded over and over. Her plaintive plea became a litany until without warning it ended, her mouth frozen in a silent scream.

Francine woke, sitting up in bed as if

propelled by a bungee cord, the sound of her runaway heartbeat reverberating in her ears. She felt dizzy, lightheaded; the cotton nightgown, soaked with perspiration, molded to her heaving breasts. When she finally focused her eyes she realized she was in her bedroom and that she'd had an erotic dream. She pulled her knees to her chest, holding her legs tightly to still their trembling.

"I don't dream," she whispered in the silent room. "I have visions."

It was a full two minutes before she was able to straighten her legs and fall back to the damp pillow under her shoulders. Francine knew the dream had everything to do with straddling Keaton, feeling his erection, and his kissing her, although she hadn't been able to see the face of her ethereal lover.

She'd dated several men while waiting for her divorce to be finalized, but refused to sleep with any of them, shunning relationships and anything resembling a commitment. She'd found it easy to sidestep their advances, but it'd taken all of her self-control not to beg Keaton to make love to her when he'd kissed her. Even though Francine adamantly claimed she was a former actress, all of her training came into play when she forced herself not to respond to his rapacious mouth and tongue.

Combing her fingers through her mussed hair, she held it off her face. Her mother had never been reticent when it came to talking to her about sex. Two years after she'd returned to the Cove, Mavis had asked if she missed making love with a man. Francine had been forthcoming when she told her mother she didn't, because she hadn't met a man who would make her want to sleep with him.

Now the same couldn't be said for Keaton. They were good together. He made her laugh and she made him laugh. He was creative, smart, *and* perceptive, and had impeccable manners, attributes she hadn't found in the other men from her past. Her life had gone on with an uncomplicated predictability — until now.

After he'd given her his business card she'd gone online to look for films he'd directed. She found one, ordered it, and paid the additional charge to have it shipped overnight.

Francine stayed up well beyond her normal bedtime watching the movie, which was about an artistically gifted sixteen-year-old boy at a crossroads in his life. The lead character was torn between following his older brother, whom he worshipped, into a life of crime that was certain to end with him in prison and/or dead, or accept an offer from a well-known artist to become his apprentice. The heart-wrenching scene in which the character's loyalty is tested moved her to tears when the budding artist demonstrated that blood was thicker than water by walking into a bodega holding a gun, while his older brother stands lookout. He fails to notice the police officer standing in the aisle when he fires point-blank at the store owner. The police officer returns fire, hitting him in the thigh and severing an artery. The robber stumbles out of the store to the sidewalk, falling facedown in the rain, which mingles with his life's blood, flowing into a sewer, while his brother runs away and disappears into the blackness of the night. The final scene showed young girls jumping rope on the same sidewalk where the body had lain days before. The film's message: You live, you die, and life goes on without missing a step. Keaton was the first man since she'd returned to Cavanaugh Island who made her want to take things to the next level.

If her mother were to ask her the same question now she would be forced to admit there was one man she wanted to sleep with if only to relive the passion that made her feel like a complete woman.

She glanced at the clock on the bedside table. It was minutes after four, much too early to get out of bed. Turning over on her side, she pulled the sheet and quilt up over her shoulder and lay quietly until drifting off to sleep. Thankfully there were no disturbing dreams this time around.

Francine was surprised to see Morgan walk into the salon Saturday afternoon. Meeting the eyes of the elderly man sitting in her chair in the mirror, she excused herself. "I'll be right back, Mr. James."

"Take your time, Red."

She approached Morgan. "Did you come in for a trim?" Her friend's hair was beginning to resemble an Afro.

"Not today. I know my hair is a hot mess, but I'm waiting until next week. Actually, I came to see if my best friend wanted to go to lunch with me."

Francine pulled her friend closer to the front door. "Sure. Can you wait for me to finish cutting Mr. James's hair?" The man had lost most of his hair years ago yet came into the salon religiously every week for her to edge up the fringe.

"Of course." Morgan, sitting on a leather

chair in the reception area, flipped through a magazine.

Francine returned to her station, picking up a comb and a pair of scissors to cut away the uneven wisps over the retired plumber's ears. Using a pair of tiny scissors, she clipped the hair growing out of his nose and ears. She enjoyed pampering the older men who sat in her chair because the few that were widowers missed the attention they'd gotten from their late wives. Turning on a blow-dryer, she blew the hair off his face and neck, and then dusted the nape of his neck with a medicated powder to offset razor irritation.

"I'm finished, Mr. James." She unsnapped the cape around his shoulders. "You may pay the receptionist. She knows to give you the senior discount." It had taken a while, but the older customers stopped offering her tips because she refused to take their money. Most, if not all, were on fixed incomes.

Shrugging out of her smock, Francine left the salon floor and entered the lounge. Mavis was in the supply closet mixing hair dyes. "Mama, I'm going out for lunch. I have Miss Sunny at four."

Mavis nodded. "Enjoy."

"Do you want me to bring you anything back?"

"Thanks for asking, but I'm saving my appetite until later. Your father and I are having a date night."

"Good for you." Her parents were having a date night and she was looking forward to her Saturday night date with Keaton.

Francine had noticed the change in her mother's attitude since her husband curtailed his traveling. She smiled a lot more and spent time in the kitchen preparing his favorite dishes. In forty years of marriage there were instances when her parents had spent more time apart than together. They'd attended different colleges, and six months of the year had been devoted to football: training camp, the official season, and post-season play. Since his retiring from the game her father was still away from home when he traveled to check on his restaurants.

Francine brushed her hair, smoothing the flatironed strands into a ponytail and securing it with an elastic band. Reaching for her jacket on the wall hook, she slipped it on and joined Morgan as they walked along Moss Alley to Main Street.

She gave her friend a sidelong glance. "How are you feeling?"

"Hungry twenty-four/seven," Morgan confessed.

Francine and Morgan moved over to the right to let an older couple pass. Afternoon temperatures peaking in the midsixties had brought out pedestrians and motorists alike. The downtown business district was bustling with activity. "What about morning sickness?"

"It comes and goes. I did get to see Kara's baby for a few minutes the day after she came home from the hospital. He's a carbon copy of Jeff except for his eye color."

"Please don't tell me he inherited the Patton gray eyes." Kara was a direct descendant of Shipley Patton, the original owner of Angels Landing. There had been a time when the Pattons had regarded themselves as Cavanaugh Island royalty, refusing to mix outside their privileged social circle, but that changed dramatically once Kara inherited the bulk of Taylor Patton's estate. Many of them were lawyers and had married lawyers or bankers.

"It looks that way."

Francine and Morgan waved to Deborah Monroe, who was standing outside the entrance to the Parlor Bookstore. Deborah, who'd spent her childhood summers in the Cove, returned after the drowning death of her first husband. She was given a second chance at love when she married a widower, Dr. Asa Monroe, who'd become the island's resident doctor. Asa's family practice was located three doors away from his wife's bookstore. Their toddler son was looking forward to celebrating his third birthday.

Francine slowed when she saw Keaton walking in their direction. He was dressed entirely in black: pull-over sweater, jeans, Timberland boots, and a waist-length leather jacket. As he neared, she noticed the stubble on his jaw. Initially she thought he wasn't going to acknowledge her, but she was wrong when he stopped.

His smile was as brilliant as the winter sunshine. "Good afternoon, Francine."

She felt the heat from Morgan's gaze on her face. "Good afternoon. Keaton, this is Morgan Dane. She's the one I told you about decorating your home. Morgan, I'd like you to meet Keaton Grace."

The two exchanged handshakes. "Do you have a business card on you, Mrs. Dane?" he asked.

Morgan unsnapped the small shoulder bag slung across her chest. "Please call me Morgan." She handed him a card. "My partner, Abram, is the interior decorator."

Keaton slipped the card into the pocket of

his jacket. "The renovations to the house won't be completed for at least six to seven weeks."

"That shouldn't be a problem. Do you have the floor plans?" Morgan asked Keaton. He nodded. "We can work from them. It will lessen the time between the delivery of furniture and your moving in."

He flashed his sensual smile again. "I'll get the plans and I'll call Abram to set up an appointment." He took a quick glance at his watch. "I'm sorry to run, but I have an appointment with Hannah Forsyth." Keaton took a step, dipped his head, and kissed Francine's cheek. "I'll call you. It's a pleasure to meet you, Morgan." Francine and Morgan were still standing in the same spot when he continued walking, turning down the street leading to the library.

Morgan looped her arm through Francine's. "I can't believe you've been holding out on me." She held up her free hand. "Don't say anything right now. We'll talk once we get to Jack's."

It was lunchtime and the babble of voices at Jack's Fish House escalated appreciably when diners greeted those with whom they were familiar. A large group of fishermen who'd gone out on the water at sunrise were crowded together, taking up an entire corner in the family-style dining restaurant. The flat-screen televisions with closed captions were tuned to sports, weather, and all-news cable channels. Francine spied an empty table for two not far from the kitchen.

"Do you mind sitting near the kitchen?" she asked Morgan. She practically had to shout to be overheard.

"No!" Morgan shouted back. "If I'd known it was going to be this crowded and noisy I would've called for takeout."

They wove their way through tables, avoiding members of the waitstaff balancing trays on their shoulders. Within minutes of sitting down a waitress came over to take their orders.

"Is that all you're going to eat?" Morgan asked when the young woman left.

Francine had ordered a shrimp grits cake with a lemon sour sauce served on red leaf lettuce and arugula. "I promised my grandmother I would eat with her tonight."

"You must be in hog heaven now that your grandmother lives with you, because all you have to do is walk down the hall to get a meal instead of getting into your car and driving to Charleston."

"Even more rewarding for me than her cooking is seeing my grandma every day. It's like Christmas, New Year's, and the

Fourth of July all rolled into one. I really don't mind being her 'precious grandbaby girl.' "

"That's because your grandma is cool. Speaking of dinner, why don't you come over tomorrow night? Nate and I would love your company."

Francine traced the initials cut into the heart carved into the tabletop. "Can I get a rain check?"

"Sure. When do you want to come?"

"I'll have to let you know."

"Is there something you're not telling me, Fran?"

Francine glanced around her to see if anyone at a nearby table was listening to their conversation. "Keaton and I are having dinner followed by a movie."

Clapping her hand over her mouth, Morgan muffled a scream. "So I was right. I knew there was something going on between you two. Where did you meet him?"

Francine shifted her chair until she and Morgan were sitting side by side. She told her about him coming into the Beauty Box for a haircut and shave. Morgan's jaw dropped when she revealed that he'd recognized her because he'd seen her performance in an off-Broadway play.

"What did he say?"

"He tried to convince me to accept a role in one of his films." She also told her that Keaton had bought the Webber property, where he planned to build a studio on the land.

Resting her elbows on the table, Morgan moved even closer. "What did you tell him?"

She gave her friend an incredulous stare. "I told him no."

"Why did you turn him down, Fran? You're an incredible actress."

"I *was* an actress."

"But you could be one again."

Francine shook her head. "No I can't, because I don't want to."

"This can't be because of Aiden."

"Aiden has nothing to do with my decision." Francine realized she sounded defensive, but didn't care. When she and Aiden broke up she'd tried to pick up the pieces of her life and move on with her career. No matter how many auditions or casting calls she attended it was as if the spark that made her a dynamic actress had gone out. She never flubbed a line, yet she wasn't able to summon the emotion necessary to breathe life into her characters.

Francine knew Morgan had never liked Aiden. After their breakup she'd called him a parasite, user, pimp, and a few other four-letter adjectives. She told her friend she didn't blame her ex as much as she blamed herself. She'd embraced the adage "love is blind" like an addict searching for his next fix.

"How did he take you turning him down?" Morgan asked.

She smiled. "He was very gracious."

Morgan sighed. "Gracious *and* gorgeous. Can you imagine the impact a movie studio will have on this island?"

"Economically it has to be a win-win," Francine answered.

"What type of movies does he make?"

"Mostly films featuring coming-of-age themes. Right now he's researching Cavanaugh Island's history because he wants to set a film here."

Morgan nodded. "So that's why he's meeting with Miss Hannah. I'm willing to bet she'll know his entire life story within a half hour of his sitting down with her. You should've warned him that Miss Hannah is an incorrigible gossip."

Francine giggled. "I decided not to prejudice him. If he survived Hollywood gossip, then he should be able to take on Miss Hannah. He's also offered to cook for me in return for making the connection with Miss Hannah."

Morgan gave her a skeptical look. "He's cooking for you because you promised to help him out? You don't need him to cook for you when your mother and grandmother live in the same house with you." She placed her hand over Francine's. "Talk to me, Fran."

"What do you want me to say? That I'm having an affair with him? I'm sorry to disappoint you but there's nothing going on between me and Keaton."

"Is he married?"

Francine smiled. "No."

"Is he a baby daddy?"

Francine's smile reached her eyes. "No. He's what you would call unencumbered."

"And that means women are going to be on him like white on rice. When was the last time we had an eligible bachelor for women in our age group?"

"We did have Nate before you took him off the market. And don't forget Jeff."

"You're right," Morgan said in agreement.

Francine thought it ironic that Jeff and Nate had grown up on the island; both left to attend college, and then returned after nearly two decades to fall in love and marry. "The pickings have been real sparse for a single woman looking for a husband."

"Do you include yourself in that equation, Fran?"

"No. I told you before I'm not interested in getting married again."

"What about a relationship?" Morgan asked. "Are you opposed to becoming involved with a man without a promise of marriage?"

There were very few secrets Francine kept from her friend, but she didn't want to talk about her connection to Keaton. Everything she'd shared with him was much too new to make any kind of prediction.

"I don't know, Mo," she said instead. "It would be nice to date someone on a regular basis, but if it doesn't happen, then my life isn't going to fall apart." Although Keaton had asked to take her out, that did not translate into an ongoing relationship.

"It's not happening, Fran. You haven't dated anyone since you moved back here."

Francine narrowed her eyes. "That sounds like the pot calling the kettle black. You weren't dating anyone either until you started going out with Nate."

"I have a confession to make," Morgan confided after a dish of fluffy, buttery biscuits was set on the table. "I would've seriously considered dating David, but he was still hung up on his ex. When I saw you with him at the Island Fair I'd hoped you guys would hook up. And you and David were the perfect host and hostess when you put together my surprise birthday party."

Francine had to admit working with David planning the surprise thirty-third birthday party for Morgan was a lot of fun. It was the only time she'd witnessed him completely relaxed. "David is a good guy, but not for me. I told you before I can't deal with an uptight man. I had enough of that with Aiden." Her ex-husband rarely smiled, claiming he had to stay in character. Most of the roles he sought called for the dark, brooding type.

"I would've been uptight, too, if I'd had to share a shoebox-size apartment with three other roommates," Morgan drawled. "You became Aiden's savior once he realized you had a luxury apartment in an Upper West Side brownstone only steps from Central Park. That's when he turned into a predator with you as his prey. He hit the mother lode. It wasn't enough for him to date you. He had to marry you to seal the deal."

Francine made a sucking sound with her tongue and teeth. "Well, the joke was on him, because he never knew my father was supporting me financially. The parasite hadn't believed until it came time for the divorce that I wouldn't have had a penny to my name if Daddy didn't send me monthly checks. Daddy claimed he did it because he'd suspected Aiden married me for money. I wish I'd had a camera phone to take a picture of his face when our lawyers were discussing the division of assets and alimony."

Morgan bit into the biscuit slowly, savoring the taste. "Your father never liked Aiden."

"Word," Francine drawled. When her parents came to visit her in New York they were polite, but very cool toward him. It was as if everyone could see his true colors except her, until it was too late.

"Speaking of single Cavanaugh Island men, there's always Harry Hill Junior."

"I thought you loved me like a sister, Mo."

"I . . . I do," Morgan said between guffaws. "But I couldn't resist that dig."

"Right now Harry Hill Junior is in deep doo-doo. He's under house arrest and wears an electronic ankle monitor. He's facing a rape charge because apparently he impregnated a fourteen-year-old. The police are awaiting the birth of her twins before they can prove paternity."

Morgan looked as if she were going to choke on her biscuit. She took a sip of water. "You're kidding."

"I wish I was, Mo. You know the man is nothing more than what I call a bum bitch. He still lives at home, no doubt still sleeping on his Spider-Man sheets while he runs around making babies with who knows how many women. At last count he's fathered nine kids. Two more will make it eleven." Francine hadn't been able to ignore the gossip swirling around the Beauty Box when the topic of Harry Junior came up. All of the women voiced their opinion of what they wanted to do to him — and none bode well for the serial baby daddy. "If the twins are his, then he's not going to make any more babies where he's going for a very long time."

"Speaking of babies," Morgan continued, "I'd like you to be godmother for my son or daughter. And I'm not going to ask you what I'm having because I want it to be a surprise."

"I wouldn't tell you even if you asked," she teased. She inclined her head. "And I'm honored to be your child's godmother. Have you chosen a godfather?"

"Nate asked his brother almost at the same time Bryce asked Nate if he would be godfather to his baby."

"Do Bryce and Stacy know what they're

having?"

Morgan nodded. "Yes. A boy."

All conversation came to a halt when the waitress set down Francine's shrimp grits cake and Morgan's black-eyed pea soup and side order of turnips and greens over rice on the table.

Chapter Eight

Keaton pounded his fist on the steering wheel after he pulled into an empty parking space behind the Cove Inn. If he hadn't left Francine's apartment he definitely would have embarrassed himself. The first time he saw her he was like a tongue-tied, starstruck adolescent meeting his favorite celebrity. He'd feared looking away because he didn't want to miss a gesture or word of dialogue whenever she was onstage. Only after seeing her performance again did he acknowledge that he was obsessed with Francine Tanner.

The obsession persisted when he wrote the script with the intention of casting her in the lead. It waned only when her agent reported she'd quit the business. But now it was back and this time, stronger than before. His dilemma was learning to make a clear distinction between the former actress and the hairstylist.

Keaton placed a USB voice/audio disk

recorder between himself and Hannah Forsyth. He had wanted to laugh when a clerk escorted him into the woman's office. It was apparent the librarian was stuck in another era, with her oversize red-framed glasses, teased champagne-pink hair, and blood-red lipstick. "I hope you don't mind if I tape our conversation, Mrs. Forsyth."

She waved a hand with nail polish that was an exact match for her lipstick. "Of course not. Red told me you needed an overview of the history of Cavanaugh Island."

There it was again, Keaton thought. Even as an adult Francine couldn't escape her childhood nickname. "*Francine* did tell me that you're the go-to person for historical information." He'd stressed the name. Others may think of her as Red, but for him, the name had begun as an insult and he wouldn't use it. Besides, the name Francine was just as beautiful as the person.

Hannah blinked slowly behind the large lenses before she smiled at him. "You can call me Miss Hannah, son." Her green eyes were the same color as Francine's.

Keaton returned her smile. "Miss Hannah it is."

She laced her fingers together. "Now tell me, Keaton, why is it you want to know about Cavanaugh Island?"

He watched the older woman's expression change from indifference to one that mirrored complete surprise when he told her he'd moved to Cavanaugh Island to live and to set up a movie studio on the old Webber property. "I plan for my first movie to be released under Grace Lowcountry Productions to be filmed here on the island, preferably using the locals as extras. I plan to employ young people wishing to break into the industry. They would be hired as interns to work in every phase of moviemaking."

Hannah patted her lacquered coif. "Is Mayor Spencer White aware that you plan to build a movie studio here in the Cove?"

"I don't believe he is."

"Let me warn you, young man, that you're probably going to get a lot of flak from the mayor because he wants to know about everything going on his town."

His town. The two words resonated with Keaton as he successfully hid his annoyance behind a polite smile. If the mayor was elected, then the town didn't belong to him but its citizens. "I had my attorney research all the statutes on the island, and there is nothing that precludes me from setting up a business enterprise here in the Cove."

Drawn-on reddish-pink eyebrows lifted.

"It appears as if you've done your homework," Hannah said. There was a hint of pride in her voice.

"I never go into anything unless I research it thoroughly. That's why I've come to you, Miss Hannah. I've been told that you are an icon where Lowcountry history is concerned." Keaton gave her his winning smile, watching as a rush of color darkened her pale face with the compliment.

He didn't doubt she was knowledgeable about the island's history, but it was probably the griots, the oral storytellers, who would tell him things that would never appear in books. Just like the skill of weaving sweetgrass was passed down through generations, it would be the same with stories relevant to the Gullah culture. The history of the island was important to Keaton to capture the feel of the locale, but it was the culture of the people that would move the plot forward.

Lacing her fingers together on the conference table in her office, Hannah gave Keaton a lingering stare. "How much time do you have?"

He smiled. "I have as much time as you're willing to allot me."

She pointed to the USB device. "You can

turn on that little gadget whenever you're ready."

Keaton pressed a button, waiting for the blinking red light to turn blue. "I'm ready."

"I don't think I have to tell you about the horrific institution of slavery that was once so pervasive in the South, and that slave labor, cotton, rice, and indigo made immoral men wealthy beyond their wildest dreams. Slaves in the Sea Islands differed from those on the mainland because of their isolation. If they'd lived on the mainland they would have been forced to give up their language, religion, and African customs. They weren't flaunted here, but they weren't eradicated completely because plantation owners didn't live here year-round. Many of them had summer homes in town to escape the swamp fevers brought on by mosquitoes."

"Are you saying the slaves were left unsupervised during this time?"

"They should've been so lucky. The owners had overseers to look after their interests. Overseers were just that. They were hired to make certain everything ran efficiently. Most of them were crueler than the owners. Contrary to what many believe, there were a number of slave revolts throughout the South. History tends to concentrate on Nat

Turner, but there were thousands of Nat Turners who preferred death to captivity. Only they weren't on the same scale or the incidents never made it into the history books. It's been documented that there were approximately sixty thousand escapees. The next time you go to Charleston, take notice of the wrought-iron fences surrounding some of the larger homes. Many of them rise six to eight feet above the street and end with sharp spikes. This was to keep blacks from scaling the walls, while giving the homeowners time to arm themselves. An interesting fact about Charleston is that free men of color didn't live in segregated neighborhoods but alongside their white counterparts."

"Why is Cavanaugh Island divided by towns rather than sections or neighborhoods?" Keaton asked.

"It all goes back to history. Thomas Cavanaugh, a disgraced nobleman who was a distant cousin of a British king, was given a land grant to set up a colony in the Americas. It was apparent he hadn't mended his ways because he got involved in piracy, using this island as home base after plundering British merchant ships moored off the coast. He was caught and impressed into the British navy, forcing him to surrender the land grant. Others came seeking their fortune and were awarded grants because of their loyal service to the crown. The island was divided into three sections — the largest one going to Shipley Patton. He purchased slaves who knew how to drain swamps and divert water for irrigation before he set up a rice plantation. He was already growing cotton on the mainland, but decided Carolina gold, Sea Island cotton, and indigo were much more profitable crops."

Keaton was aware that rice in the Lowcountry was referred to as Carolina gold. "Is there a difference between mainland and Sea Island cotton?"

Hannah smiled. "There's a big difference. Sea Island cotton is Egyptian cotton."

"Which makes it higher quality and more expensive than regular cotton."

"Without a doubt. Patton was an anomaly in his day because all of his skilled laborers were free blacks. He built a grand house and owned the largest plantation, which he called Angels Landing. He learned early on that a freeman was a better worker than one in bondage. They weren't beaten and were paid for their labor. If you want to know the intimate details of the Pattons, then you should speak to the griots. I deal only with what's written, while they have an oral history passed down from great-grandmothers to daughters. What isn't written is talk about Shipley's second wife giving birth to a mixed-race boy she managed to pass off as her husband's. The rumor was she was in love with one of the field slaves and both risked certain death if they were found together."

Keaton was pleased the librarian had given him permission to tape her. The sordid story about a woman cuckolding her husband with a slave and making him raise the resulting child as his own made for an engaging plotline. "Tell me about Haven Creek."

Hannah paused, sighing audibly. "It has a creek running through it, and it became a haven for former slaves who'd left plantations on the mainland after the Civil War, hence its name. It's said the farms on the Creek fed the entire island. The farmers grew vegetables, planted fruit trees, and raised chickens, hogs, and milk cows. There aren't as many farms now, but they still set up their fruit and vegetable stands a couple of days a week, starting in the spring and going throughout the fall harvest. Sanctuary Cove was exactly that. A sanctuary for runaways. There were sea captains who were covert abolitionists. They'd set up an underground railroad system wherein slaves would hide out in the swamps and marshes and wait for a signal when a ship was scheduled to sail north or to Europe with their holds filled with bales of cotton and rice. Again, you'll have to talk to the griots about those who escaped and those who were found and punished for helping them."

"How did life change here once the Civil War ended?"

"Many of the owners abandoned their plantations and those who'd worked the land for nothing claimed their share. They raised their children, attended church services, sent their children to colored schools, and were able to move around despite fear of reprisals. Some left, going north to find jobs or to escape Jim Crow laws, but the majority of them stayed. Over time a few of the old customs faded, yet many still remain. Although most of the young kids don't speak Gullah they still understand what their grandmommas are saying. If you want I can give you some of the names of the griots who still live here."

Keaton turned off the recorder. "Thank you for offering, but Francine has promised to introduce me to them."

Hannah's red lips parted. "Now, that's a

fine young woman." She shook her head. "So much talent going to waste. When we read that she was performing off-Broadway we couldn't stop talking about her. Then" — she snapped her fingers — "it was over and she came back. Folks had a lot to say as to why she came back. Some said she got hooked on drugs, while others claimed they heard she was seeing a married man and his wife threatened to ruin her career if she didn't leave her husband alone."

"What if she decided acting just wasn't for her?" Keaton asked, defending Francine. He didn't want to believe Francine had had a drug problem and he didn't want to think of her having an affair with a married man. Based on what he knew of her, she didn't fit into that category.

"No one works that hard to achieve success, then gives it up because she decides it's not for her. You're in the movie business. Do you know of any actors or actresses who've walked away from success?"

He knew quite a few off the top of his head, yet would not deign to discuss them with the chatty woman. "Is there anything else you feel I should know?" Hannah blinked slowly, reminding Keaton of a heavy-lidded owl behind her glasses.

"We do have an archive section here at

the library. We have a collection of old journals, letters, and diaries from some of the older families that settled here. There are also copies of census records and bills of sale. If you want to see them, then I'll have to contact the archival historian attached to the main library in Charleston. She'll meet with you, answer your questions, and you'll get to see the actual documents. We have a supply of white gloves you'll have to wear when handling them. Let me know where I can reach you and when you're available, and I'll put in a call to her."

Rising to his feet, Keaton took out the case with his business cards, handing one to Hannah. "I'm staying at the Cove Inn, but you can reach me at that number."

Hannah stood up. "It's been a pleasure talking to you."

He inclined his head. "The pleasure has been mine. I'm going to hang out here to see if I can find a few books on the subject."

"We have quite a few in our reference section, but you won't be able to check them out. Have you tried the Parlor Bookstore? Deborah Monroe may also have some in stock."

"I bought what she had."

"The Cove was so lucky when Deborah

moved here. She used to spend the summers in the Cove when her grandmother was alive. It was a crying shame when her husband drowned trying to save a kid who should have been in school when he went swimming. But she was blessed when she fell in love with a snowbird staying at the inn for the winter. He'd left to join Doctors Without Borders when he found out Deborah was pregnant with his baby. When he came back they got married. Having both of them living here is a plus for the island. We get to have a brick and mortar bookstore and a doctor who makes house calls." Hannah made a clucking sound with her tongue and teeth. "Their little boy is such an adorable child. And oh so smart."

Keaton knew it was time to take his leave or he would be subjected to an account of everyone living on the island. Plus, he wanted to talk to Francine about not warning him that the librarian was a gossip — something he abhorred. If the mayor hadn't gotten wind that he planned to build a studio on the Cove he was certain the mayor would know about it before the sun went down.

Forcing a smile he didn't feel, Keaton took a step backward. "Thank you again, Hannah."

"You'll let me know how you make out with the griots."

"Of course."

Keaton left the library, walking back to the Cove Inn. Hannah had given him only a glimpse into the history of the island. However, it was just enough to start his creative juices flowing.

It was a rare occasion that the Beauty Box didn't open or close on time. However, this Saturday everything that could've gone wrong at the salon did. The receptionist had mistakenly booked this week's customers for the following week, resulting in double bookings. It was five fifteen when Francine placed her last customer under the dryer, and she knew it would be impossible to go home, shower, and get dressed before Keaton arrived at seven.

Slipping into the employees' bathroom, she pulled out her cell phone. "Grandma, I need you to do a favor for me," she said when Dinah answered.

"What is it, baby?"

"I'm expecting Keaton to come over at seven, but I won't make it home in time because I just put Cherrie Reynolds under the dryer. I'd like you to leave my door open for him."

"Don't trouble yourself none, Francine. I'll make certain he's comfortable."

"Thanks, Grandma." She called Keaton, leaving a voice mail message that she was running late and that her grandmother would leave the door open for him.

A wave of relief washed over her. She'd tried to convince the court stenographer to cut her near waist-length hair but to no avail. It would take more than an hour for her hair to dry completely, then another forty minutes for a blowout.

Francine used the time to sweep up hair, clean the mirrors, and sort the rollers at her station. One of the rules she'd instituted when she came to work at the Beauty Box was that every stylist was required to clean up her station before going home. She'd told her mother that she didn't want to begin her day sweeping up after the staff.

Her head popped up when the front door opened. She smiled at Alice Parker. Alice, wife of Representative Jason Parker, had thrown her hat into the political ring when she announced her intent to oppose Spencer White in the upcoming local election. The natural blonde flashed her practiced winning smile. The mother of two school-age children looked every bit the politician in a navy-blue wool pantsuit, tailored white shirt, and leather pumps. The semiprecious and precious stones in her American flag lapel pin gave off sparks under the track lights. She was also wearing a campaign button — PARKER FOR PROGRESS superimposed over a palmetto tree — under the flag.

Alice and her husband were opponents of developers looking to buy tracts of land on the Sea Islands to build golf courses, overpriced hotels, and gated communities. Jason, whose roots on Cavanaugh Island could be traced back three hundred years, decided to move back after he married and had children. The Parkers wanted a place with a strong sense of values and history in which to raise their son and daughter. In that instant Francine realized Bernice Wagner had correctly likened Alice to a Barbie doll. The petite, blond, blue-eyed woman with tiny features did resemble a doll.

"Hi, Alice. What can I do for you?"

"I just opened my campaign office in a storefront off Beech Street, and I'd like to know if you would please put one of my campaign posters in your window."

"Of course I will."

Francine and her mother had decided they would support Alice's candidacy for mayor. Alice's political platform included a revitalization of the Cove's downtown business district and community development grants for those living in homes deemed unsafe or not up to code, while the incumbent touted that he was going to let his past record speak for him.

"Thanks, Francine. I'll have someone from my office bring over the posters and a few campaign buttons."

"Please have him bring them before six. After that I'm going to lock the door."

"He's not in the office, so I'll tell him to drop by Tuesday morning."

Francine locked the door behind Alice. She was the only one left in the salon and had no intention of accepting a walk-in. She'd spent the day trying *not* to think about Keaton in an attempt to convince herself he was nothing more than a friend. But the erotic dream was a reminder she wanted him for something more than friendship. It'd been so long since she'd slept with a man.

She now was faced with the decision of should or shouldn't she.

Since declaring their friendship when they first entered high school Francine and Morgan had promised never to keep secrets from each other. They were forthcoming when each lost her virginity, complaining the men weren't worth their giving up their most precious gift. Even when Morgan left the States to study in Europe they continued their close friendship with letters and then e-mails. But her growing feelings for Keaton would remain her secret and hers alone, so she wouldn't keep her promise to her friend. After her failed marriage, she wasn't sure if her heart could take that kind of embarrassment again.

As soon as Keaton stepped off the last stair he saw the woman sitting on the chair beside the table outside Francine's apartment. Light from wall sconces shimmered off her short hair.

"You must be Keaton Grace."

He smiled. The woman had to be Francine's grandmother. Their voices were similar, as were their eyes. She was the picture of elegance, with pearl and diamond studs in her pierced lobes, a matching strand around her neck, and a classic white blouse, black tailored slacks, and a pair of black leather wedge shoes.

"I am."

The woman stood up, tilting her head to stare up at the tall man. "I'm Dinah Tanner, Francine's grandmother. She asked me to open the door for you because she's stuck at the salon." She pointed to the shopping bags he held in each hand. "What do you have there?"

"I told Francine I would cook for her in a couple of days, so I decided to bring over some things and store them in her refrigerator."

"You can put them in my refrigerator. She can get them later."

"If you don't mind, I'll wait in her place."

Dinah narrowed her eyes over her half-glasses in a gesture that reminded him of Francine. "I do mind. Come on, son. I'm not going to bite you. I'm glad you're going to cook for her. That child doesn't eat enough to keep her strength up."

"She starves herself?" he asked Dinah.

"She eats, but never three meals a day. If she eats breakfast, then she'll skip lunch. And if I don't force her to eat dinner she'll skip that too. Now, please follow me."

He had no choice but to follow, staring at her ramrod-straight back. Dinah wasn't tall, but her slender figure made her appear taller. Light from strategically placed sconces glinted off silver hair with streaks of red.

He walked into the older woman's apartment, taking in the foyer in one sweeping glance. Francine may resemble her grandmother physically, but their decorating styles were complete opposites. Francine favored a minimalist style while the opposite with the older woman's American eclectic.

Tables were overflowing with decorative pots of flowering plants and vases of freshly cut flowers. Framed black-and-white photographs of landscapes, the world's capital cities, and children dressed in their country's native customs covered an entire wall.

Dinah led him through a living/dining area with furniture reflecting a vintage mix of romance, warmth, and charm. The grouping of a sofa, love seat, and a club chair, covered with checks and stripes and floral prints, surrounding a low oak table with a stack of books and a crystal bowl filled with tiny seashells evoked a homey feeling.

Keaton was still trying to decide in what style he wanted to decorate his new home. He definitely didn't want the modern furnishings he had in L.A. He detested clutter but didn't quite want minimalism. Maybe after talking to the interior decorator he would be able to combine the two.

"Your home is lovely." Dinah stopped abruptly, almost causing him to bump into her if his reflexes had been slower.

"Thank you. Most of the things you see belonged to my mother and grandmother. I had the chairs reupholstered with fabric that was as close to the original as I could find."

"They are beautiful pieces, Mrs. Tanner."

She wagged a finger at him. "If you're dating my granddaughter, then I want you to call me Miss Dinah."

"Yes, ma'am."

Keaton smothered a smile. It was obvious one person in Francine's family approved of his dating her. Never had he been more honest than when he admitted to Francine that he liked her. It wasn't just her body; it was her sense of humor, quiet Southern charm, and the palpable sexiness he felt whenever they shared the same space. She hadn't lost her Southern drawl completely and every once in a while it would creep into her speech patterns. Kids may have teased her because of her curly red hair but he liked the curls because it made her look as if she'd just been made love to.

As soon as the image of his making love to Francine popped into his head Keaton banished it. That was a subject he didn't want to dwell on because he'd told her sex was something he could get from any woman. What he wanted was to get closer to Francine, to get to know her better. Besides, the island was small and he couldn't risk the chance of ruining his chances with Francine by sleeping around, even though it didn't seem to bother some of the retirees living at the boardinghouse. On several occasions he'd spied a few sneaking in out of one another's rooms. His reaction was either to smile or to pretend he didn't see them. Keaton wasn't one to judge someone's actions — especially if it didn't affect or impact his lifestyle. He'd lived in his gated L.A. suburban community for five years, and during that time had rejected the invitations of his neighbors to attend their pool parties and barbecues. He'd managed to escape the gossip so intrinsic in the entertainment industry by remaining semi-reclusive.

Keaton knew that was realistically impossible in the Cove or in any town on the island with a documented census of less than two thousand permanent residents. If he'd lingered at the library Hannah probably would've given him an account of everyone on Cavanaugh Island, including their birth dates. The fact that she didn't know the reason Francine had given up her acting career was as puzzling to him as it was to others, and he'd begun to wonder if it had been more than disillusionment that made her walk away from the stage when her star was rising.

All thoughts of Francine and her aborted

career vanished when he stood at the entrance to a kitchen any cook or chef, in particular, would covet. The ultramodern stainless steel kitchen reminded him of the one in Sadie Grace's II. Granite countertops, a butcher-block preparation table, rich cherrywood cabinetry, gleaming copperclad pots suspended from racks over the cooktop and grill — everything he'd need to prepare for a dinner party. The refrigerator and freezer were built into a wall. His gaze lingered on a commercial double wall oven before shifting to a microwave, preparation table, twin dishwashers, and utility sinks. Cleanliness must be a Tanner trait because there wasn't a speck of dirt on the spotless stone terra-cotta floor.

"How often do you cook in here, Miss Dinah?"

When she smiled, a network of fine lines deepened around her eyes. "Every day. The only exception is when my daughter-in-law spells me." She pointed to the shopping bags. "They look heavy. Rest them on the bench over there."

Keaton set the recyclable bags on the wrought-iron bench and began emptying them. He removed plastic bags with sweet potatoes, lemons and limes, pears, fresh spinach, containers of fresh berries, romaine lettuce, fresh herbs, frozen green peas, Parmesan and blue cheese, bottles of extra-virgin olive oil and vinegar, bottles of club soda, and a small jar of honey. The local supermarket yielded a cornucopia of fresh fruits, vegetables, and herbs grown on the island. Taking off his jacket, he placed it over the back of the bench.

"What are you planning to make when you cook for her?" Dinah asked, watching as he stored everything on shelves and in drawers of the refrigerator/freezer.

"I figured we'd start with a pear, blue cheese, and pecan salad. Spinach pesto chicken breast with roasted sweet potato wedges and baby peas will be the entrée."

"What are you drinking?"

"It will be a modified virgin mojito. Instead of rum I'm going to use fresh berries along with mint."

Dinah smiled. "That sounds delicious."

Keaton returned her smile. "It is. If you have a pitcher I'll make up a batch so you can sample it."

Dinah's smile grew wider. "Would you mind if I help you? I hate sitting around doing nothing."

Reaching into the bag, he took out a bibbed apron. "You can use this. I don't want you to ruin your blouse."

"I don't need it," she said. "I have my own supply."

Smiling, he nodded. "You begin making the berry fizz by mashing them along with the mint leaves."

Dinah emptied the berries and mint into a colander and rinsed them with a tractable nozzle. "Francine is very lucky."

He gave her sidelong glance. "How's that?"

"She told me you're going to teach her to cook."

"I did promise her."

Dinah rested her hands at her waist over a ruffled apron decorated with red and green apples. "Do you know how long I've tried to get her to let me teach her to cook?"

Keaton shook his head. "How long?"

"Twenty years. Right after her parents set her up in her own apartment I told her if she was going to live quasi-independently, then she would have to learn to cook for herself. But she claimed she never had a reason to since her mother and I cooked for her. Then she went away to college, living and eating on campus. She was so frightfully thin when she moved back here from New York that I thought she was sick. It took about three to four months for her to put back on a fraction of the weight she'd lost. I knew she'd changed when she refused dessert. The only thing she'd eat was something she called s'mores."

Keaton wanted to tell Dinah that perhaps Francine was just naturally slender. He estimated Dinah to be in her eighties and she was still slender herself. "I think she looks nice the way she is."

He found nothing wrong with Francine's body and despite her lean frame, she had curves. Her breasts weren't overly large or small. They were in proportion to her body. And it was her long legs that seemed to go on forever that had garnered his rapt attention when he watched her strut out of Jack's as if she were on a runway. Maybe others found fault in her, but for Keaton she was ideal.

Reaching for the pitcher, he walked over to the refrigerator and filled it with crushed ice from the door. He added a bottle of club soda; the bowl of mulled blueberries, blackberries, and raspberries; mint leaves; sugar; and lime juice to the pitcher and stirred it vigorously. He poured the icy concoction into a glass, handing it to Dinah.

"Let me know if it needs to be sweeter."

She took a sip, a smile spreading across her delicate features. "It's delicious. Light and refreshing. It's the perfect summer beverage."

Keaton poured some into his glass and sampled it. "It is nice."

"Please don't tell me you're starting without me."

He turned to find Francine standing at the entrance to the kitchen and his gaze moved lazily over her body. Fitted jeans revealed her long legs and narrow waist. He hadn't heard her come in. Reaching for another glass, he half filled it with the berry fizz. "Come," he said, extending the glass.

Francine walked into the kitchen, kissing her grandmother's cool cheek, then pressed a kiss to Keaton's clean-shaven jaw. She knew she'd shocked him with the open display of affection when she registered his intake of breath.

When Francine had parked her car next to Keaton's, she'd expected to find him in her grandmother's apartment, but she never would've guessed that he would be preparing food in her kitchen. Dinah had made it known the day she moved in that only she would cook in her kitchen. However, it appeared as if that declaration had been for naught, because Keaton appeared as at home in the space as her grandmother was.

She took the glass from Keaton, their fingers touching. A nervous smile trembled over her lips when she felt a slight shock from the contact. "Thank you." The sweet-tart taste of berries, mint, and lime and the carbonation of the club soda were like a party in her mouth. "Wow! This is really nice." She extended the glass. "May I have a refill please?"

Keaton complied. "Your grandmother has the recipe, so she can make it for you."

Francine peered at him over the rim of the glass. "I think this is something I can make myself. It may take several tries, but I think I'll be able to master it."

Dinah peered over the lenses of her glasses at her granddaughter. "So, it's like that?" she teased. "Now that you have a boyfriend who can cook you're not going to need me to cook for you?"

She couldn't stop the heat creeping up her chest to her face. If Keaton hadn't been there she would've told her grandmother that Keaton wasn't her boyfriend, but a friend. There was definitely a difference between the two. To her, a boyfriend meant something more personal, even intimate. She and Keaton weren't going to make love, they were going to the movies.

"I'd love to stay and chat, but I need to

shower and change."
"Did you eat dinner?" Dinah asked.
"Yes, I did, Grandma." Francine smiled sweetly. "I really have to go or Keaton and I will miss the beginning of the movie."

Chapter Nine

Francine sat with Keaton at a table for two in the crowded Starbucks, taking furtive sips of a mocha Frappuccino. He touched his finger to his upper lip, smiling. Reaching for a napkin, she dabbed it to her mouth.

"You missed it." He took the napkin, gently wiping away the residue of whipped cream.

When Keaton had maneuvered into the parking area behind the Creek Cinema she knew immediately why he'd wanted to go there. The marquee advertised an ongoing retrospective of the late independent director and producer Oscar Micheaux.

Francine stared at Keaton, who was staring back at her. "How many of his films do you own?"

Leaning back in his chair, he angled his head. "How do you do that?" Keaton asked.

"Do what?"

"Read my mind. Are you certain you're

not one of those witches I read about in that book of spells?"

A smile, one Francine definitely did not feel, parted her lips. "I'm definitely not a witch." She wasn't a witch but a psychic. And she didn't and couldn't read minds. What she did read was a person's aura. "It's just that you had this faraway look on your face and I figured you were thinking about Micheaux."

Keaton stared at his cup of coffee. "Oscar Micheaux was born when African Americans had tried to succeed in the film industry dominated by whites. He was regarded as the first major black feature filmmaker. He produced both silent films and talkies. I wish he would've lived long enough to accept the 1986 Golden Jubilee Special Award from the Directors Guild of America so he could have made it to the Hollywood Walk of Fame. I did my first thesis on his film career, and for my second master's I compared him to the African American filmmakers of the second half of the twentieth century."

"How old would he have been in 1986?"

"He was born in 1884, so that would've made him one hundred two."

"Not too many people live to celebrate their one hundredth birthday. However, we have a higher proportion of people on Cavanaugh Island reaching one hundred than those on the mainland because we don't have any industry polluting our air and water."

Keaton shifted his gaze, staring directly at Francine. "I did notice quite a few seniors living on the island. Many of them opt to walk rather than have someone drive them around."

Francine nodded. "My grandmother still drives. Not as much as she used to, but she claims she isn't ready to relinquish her driver's license without a knock-down, drag-out fight."

"She is rather feisty."

"Feisty, belligerent, and downright ornery at times. When she was younger she wanted to be an actress, but her mother threatened to disown her if she even spoke the word in the house."

"So you were the one who realized her dream."

Francine missed the flash of amusement in Keaton's eyes when she nodded to a woman with whom she'd attended high school. "For me it was either acting or teaching high school history."

Keaton went completely still. Nothing moved. Not even his eyes. "You were thinking of becoming a history teacher?"

If his expression hadn't been so unexpected Francine would've laughed at him. "Yes. I majored in theater and minored in American history."

He blinked. "You go on about introducing me to island storytellers and now you tell me this?"

She laughed. "What's the matter?"

"I didn't have to officially interview Hannah Forsyth because she spent almost three hours telling me about the lives of other people who live here."

It was Francine's turn to freeze. "What did she say about me?"

"She said everyone was excited and very proud that one of their own had made it off-Broadway."

"Is that all?"

"She did say you're a very fine young woman. But I didn't need her to tell me that."

Keaton knew he had to be honest with Francine if he hoped to have a relationship with her. First he'd asked for friendship and now he was contemplating a relationship. He'd dated women whose names he couldn't remember and of the few he'd slept with he didn't want to remember. However, he'd never felt as comfortable around them as he did with Francine. He couldn't believe it had been less than two weeks since he'd walked into the Beauty Box for a haircut and shave. Keaton hadn't lied to her when he said he could get sex from any woman and her from any man. He didn't want her to sleep with another man any more than he wanted to sleep with another woman. He wanted to sleep with her because he knew, based on the connection they were building, that their intimacy would bring their relationship to heights he'd never before experienced with another woman.

"She mentioned something about you giving up your acting career."

"I don't know why everyone is fixated on why I needed to change my life. It's *my life,* not theirs, Keaton," she said, stressing the two words.

Shifting his chair closer to hers, Keaton rested his chin on the top of her head. "It's okay, sweetie. People are going talk even if they have nothing to talk about. If they can't get anything on you, then they'll make it up."

"Is that what happened to you? Is that why you decided to leave L.A.?"

A chuckle rumbled deep in his chest. "No, babe. I managed to leave L.A. unscathed."

Easing back, she stared up at him. "How

did you do it?"

Keaton knew if the news of Jade's suicide had been linked to him he probably would've never worked again or would've found it difficult to find another project. While the film had received lukewarm reviews for his inaugural directorial effort, critics still reported that he definitely was a director to watch.

"I realized the moment I sat in a room with the heads of the studio that had produced my first film that everything I said would be captured for posterity by either video cameras or tape recorders. That once I said something I could never retract it, and if I did something my actions would have consequences. It hadn't mattered that the film wasn't going to win any awards. What did matter was that I was a rookie in a game where the media owns you because people were now familiar with my face and name. I managed to distance myself from the Hollywood nightlife, and for me dating anyone in the business was taboo."

"Did you date?"

"Yes, I dated, but only women who were content to stay out of the spotlight."

"What did you do when you were required to attend award ceremonies or walk the red carpet?"

"A few times I took my sister, and my mother accompanied me to Cannes because she wanted to see Europe. That's when the rumors that I might be gay surfaced."

"Did it bother you?" Francine asked.

"Not in the least. My sexual orientation, whether gay or heterosexual, is no one's business but mine."

"You moved to the wrong place if you thought you're going to maintain a modicum of anonymity here."

"No, I didn't, Francine. Folks here may gossip because that is something intrinsic to small towns. What I don't have to concern myself with is someone jumping out from behind parked cars to take my photograph or paparazzi waiting outside my gated community with long-range lenses to monitor my comings and goings. I hope you're not concerned about being seen in public with me —"

"It has nothing to do with me, Keaton." Francine interrupted him. "Being seen with you doesn't bother me."

Keaton's hands moved up to cradle her face. "Does this mean we can now go public with our torrid affair?"

Francine laughed. "I don't know about torrid or an affair, but going to the movies in the Creek is public enough. Do you still plan to go to church with me tomorrow so I can introduce you to some of the island storytellers?"

"I'd like to put that off for a while. Right now I'm going over my taped interview with Miss Hannah. I also wanted to talk to you about roots and spells."

"What about them?" she asked.

"What percentage of folks here still believe in witchcraft and root workers?"

She pulled her lower lip between her teeth. "I don't think I can answer that truthfully, because it would depend on who you talk to, and most people probably wouldn't speak openly about root workers, spiritualists, or conjurers. But I'm certain some of the older folks still hold on to superstitions passed down through generations of Gullah. For example, some believe in hags. There are two types of hags. One is a total spirit, and the other is a slip-skin hag, which is a person, and most likely female, who becomes invisible by shedding her skin and then goes out to raise hell after dark."

Keaton shivered visibly. "I read something in one of the books I bought from the Parlor Bookstore about a man who reported a spirit used him sexually every time he went to sleep. It frightened him so much that he became an insomniac."

A broad smile spread over Francine's features. "That probably was a hag who'd become overly fond of him."

Keaton shook his head. "What I didn't understand was how to get rid of one. Would the man have had to dismantle his house to get rid of her?"

"Some do, but most folks plagued by hags would retain the services of a root worker or doctor for incense, oils, or powders that would prevent the spirit from returning. There are oils and powders that can be used for good as well as evil, so you have to know exactly which kind you need, otherwise the outcome could be terrible."

A beat passed and Keaton found himself spellbound by what he'd just heard. "Tell me about the slip-skin hag."

Propping her elbow on the table, Francine rested her chin on her fist. "The slip-skin hag will get into a house through a chimney or keyhole after dark and always leaves before day-clean, or what is known as daylight. If this hag slips her skin before making her rounds, then it must be located and salted in anticipation of her daylight return. The salt will cut the hag's power and the skin will disappear into thin air, never to return. If you get the chance to visit someone's home and you see salt sprinkled over the doorsill, then you'll know they're keeping away bad spirits."

"Deborah gave me a book on oils, incense, and brews. It will be useful for a few characters I'm developing."

"Male or female?" Francine asked.

"Mother and daughter."

Her eyes sparkled in excitement. "I love it. Talk about keeping it in the family. What are they —" Keaton placed a finger over her parted lips, stopping her words.

His lips soon replaced his finger as he kissed Francine. The press of his mouth on hers reminded her of the gentle brush of a butterfly's wings, eliciting another fluttering. This time it was in her stomach as she struggled to bring her fragile emotions under control.

Breaking away from the kiss, he looked into her eyes. "No more talk about witches and spells, beautiful."

She pantomimed zipping her lips. "Okay. No more questions about the script, but I still want to know more about you. What would you have become if you didn't go into film?" She had to say something, anything, not to think about the kiss that reminded her of what she'd been missing. He'd called her beautiful and Francine wanted to tell Keaton that whenever she was with him she felt beautiful and sexy.

Keaton lifted the broad shoulders under his sweater. "I probably would've been a chef like my parents."

"It's not too late," she teased.

"Oh yes it is. At least for me. I've invested too much time, and now too much money, into becoming a film director and independent producer to walk away before I either succeed or fail. I'm forty-one and I've spent more than half my life taking courses and studying with whom I consider the best professionals in the business to walk away from what has been a lifelong dream."

Her eyes grew wide as she stared directly at Keaton. "We're two different people, Keaton." She knew he was talking about her giving up her acting career.

He returned her angry stare. "I'm glad we're two different people, because I doubt whether I'd be able to abide my female alter ego. Your reason for giving up acting is something you deem personal and I have to respect that."

"But . . . weren't you signifying that —"

"I wasn't signifying anything," Keaton said, cutting her off. "You asked me about giving up making movies to become a chef and I told you why that wasn't possible. And it sounds to me like you still have some unresolved issues on your decision to give up acting."

"Oh, now you're going to psychoanalyze me."

Keaton knew he'd hit a raw nerve with Francine but that was her problem, not his. "I would never presume to analyze you, or for that matter anyone else. Let's not ruin a wonderful evening talking about something we can't or don't want to change. I didn't lie when I told you I liked you, Francine. In fact, I like you more than I intended."

She affected a sexy moue. "How much more, milord?"

This was the Francine Keaton he liked. The Cockney tavern maid was back. "Enough to give up my inheritance as firstborn to take a feisty wench to wife."

"That's too much to sacrifice, milord. How will your wee bairns survive if you have not a farthing to your name?"

He dropped an arm around her shoulders and pressed his mouth to her ear. "I have some land in the Colonies I won with the turn of a card. The bloke who owned it claims the soil is so rich if you drop a seed it will sprout in a fortnight. We can get the ship's captain to marry us before we reach landfall."

Turning her head slightly, Francine's mouth grazed his clean-shaven jaw. "Sorry, milord. I will not lie with thee and then, when we reach the Colonies, allow you to discard me like the contents of a chamber pot for some highborn lady with fancy skirts and a well-turned ankle. If you do not marry me before we board this ship, then begone with you and your fancy talk."

"Wee maid, why are you so hard with me?"

"I'm no harder than that member between your noble thighs seeking passage to mine, milord."

Keaton clapped his free hand over his mouth to keep from laughing at the top of his lungs. He didn't know what he was going to do with Francine. When she'd believed he was attempting to analyze her she reminded him of a cat arching its back before it sprang. But once she morphed into the serving girl character she appeared calmer, as if playing a role permitted her an escape from reality. Acting was as natural to her as breathing.

"Let's get out of here before I embarrass myself," he said.

"Did I embarrass you?" Francine asked innocently.

"No. But if you continue to talk about what's between my you know what, I will embarrass you."

Grabbing her jacket off the back of her chair, he held it out for her to slip her arms into it. Then he put on his own jacket. Holding her hand, he led Francine out of the coffeehouse and into the cool night.

The drive back to the island was accomplished in complete silence, and instead of taking the road leading to the Magnolias he turned off onto the one leading to beach parking. Putting the truck in park, he turned off the engine. A full moon lit up the sky, silvering the sand and the whitecaps as the waves came crashing onto the beach. He'd come to the beach instead of taking her home because he didn't want their time together to end.

"Do you ever walk along the beach?" he asked Francine as she stared through the windshield.

"I come here a lot."

"You game?"

Unbuckling her seat belt, Francine raised her knees and unzipped her booties. "Let's go."

Francine moved closer to Keaton as he wound his free arm around her waist. The sound of the incoming tide washing up on the beach was calming, hypnotic. They weren't the only ones on the sand. Two couples were huddled together amid light from lanterns on the sand, listening to the radio. She recognized a high school coed with two of her friends holding flashlights for her to see to read aloud from a book. Francine smiled when they attempted but failed to stifle nervous giggles. The eerie glow of the moon provided enough light for her to see a crab moving sideways as it floated on the crashing waves before disappearing into the water. There were large wire baskets with signs to pick up litter and deposit it in the baskets. There were also posted signs to douse all fires before discarding the wood.

"My mother and I would come down here every Halloween to see candles light up the sand like stars. They always begin at the ferry landing and end at Angels Landing. Some say it is a tradition dating back to when ship captains would place a single lantern on the sand as a signal to the runaways hiding in the swamp that they were sailing north that night. Others claim it was to keep away the evil spirits that come to life on All Hallows' Eve."

Keaton gave her fingers a gentle squeeze. "What do you believe?"

"I'd rather believe the former."

"So would I," he concurred.

She felt the muscles pulling in the backs of her calves when her toes sank into the sand. "Did Miss Hannah tell you that when you interviewed her?"

Keaton stopped, turning to face Francine, and took her face in his hands. "She did mention something about runaways stowing aboard ships of abolitionist sea captains. Most of what she told me I could find in history books or archival documents. I want to know about what wasn't written down."

"What's not written will probably make the hair stand up on the back of your neck *and* keep you awake at night."

"Why don't you let me be the judge of that?"

"One of these days I'll tell you what I've heard. Bear in mind I'm only repeating what has been passed down through generations."

"Now that I think of it," Keaton said after a pregnant pause, "Miss Hannah did mention something that reminded me of *Black Orpheus.*"

"Why that film?"

"Because it's an adaptation of the Greek legend of Orpheus and Eurydice set in a modern context. I could include it in the script but slavery is too painful an issue to romanticize on film. But then again, it would work in a flashback. What do you know about Shipley Patton?"

Francine circled his wrists with her fingers, pulling his hands away from her face. "I've heard his family was plagued with quite a few scandals. But you're going to have to ask Corrine Hamilton about one that involved some of her ancestors. Miss Corrine is Sheriff Hamilton's grandmother. She taught at the Cove's elementary school before becoming its principal. I'm certain she would be more than willing to talk to you. She has an appointment at the salon next Tuesday. If I see her before then I'll ask if she's open to letting you interview her."

They started to walk again. Walking the beach at night with a man like Keaton was something Francine had only fantasized about. Most kids in junior high school hung out on the beach in large groups until high school, when they began coupling off. But for Francine it had never happened. No boy had ever invited her to go to the beach with him. Right now she didn't know whether to laugh or cry. Why, she mused, had it taken her so long to find someone with whom to share her adolescent fantasy? And if she believed in the adage that good things happen to those who wait, then all of the waiting was more than worth it.

Threading her fingers through Keaton's, she pressed her head against his firm shoulder. Everything about him made her feel good. With Keaton she could be herself, and her vow not to become involved with another man after Aiden was now completely shattered. It was the first time in years she realized just how wrong she'd been when she told herself there was no room in her busy schedule for romance. Not only was there room, but also the possibility that she could learn to love again.

Keaton didn't know whether to kiss Francine or pick her up and swing her around until she pleaded with him to stop. He didn't know whether it was living in the Lowcountry or his fascination with Francine that fired his imagination. Normally it was a news story or something he'd overheard that got him to thinking about a particular idea. He'd mull it over for days before actually brainstorming. It'd begin with single words or phrases, then sentences and paragraphs. After that the characters would materialize, and he worked and reworked their physical and psychological characteristics until he was able to breathe life into them. The entire process from beginning to end usually took a month.

When he worked for a television daytime drama he'd become proficient in writing a script in less than a week. It hadn't mattered that he'd become a soap opera hack. The pay was good and he'd cranked them out in order to afford his fifth-floor walk-up in Manhattan.

Fortunately he knew how to cook, which cut down on eating out and ordering in. Whenever he announced he was cooking his friends would grumble about having to walk five flights of stairs with cases of beer and wine, but once he set out pots of chili and pans of buffalo wings, spareribs, pulled pork, and collard greens with smoked turkey the only sound heard was that of chewing and grunts of satisfaction. Word of his cooking ability went beyond his circle of friends and after a while Keaton found himself catering private dinner parties. The money he earned catering he deposited directly into the bank. Between cooking and writing scripts he'd saved enough to sustain him when he moved from New York to California to enroll in USC without taking out student loans. He continued to support himself writing scripts, this time for film and television.

His life changed completely when the

producer of a television police procedural fired the head writer and assigned Keaton to the position. Writing left him little or no time for a social life but the sacrifice paid off when he wrote and directed his first episode. The experience proved euphoric for him. He'd finally found his niche.

"It would be like writing for a daytime drama all over again. Thank you, Francine." The two words were so inadequate to what he was feeling.

Francine felt Keaton's excitement as surely as if it were her own. "Will you let me read the script when it's completed?"

Keaton palmed her head again, placing kisses at each corner of her mouth. "I'll let you read it *before* it's completed. If you don't mind, I'd like your input."

"What if I tell you something you don't like?"

"I'll take whatever you tell me under advisement. My ego isn't that fragile."

"But you do admit to being egotistical?"

Lowering his arms, Keaton fused his body to hers, sharing his heat. "Every artist has to be somewhat egotistical about their creations. With me it is scriptwriting and for you it's hair. This is not to say we can't improve, but for the most part we're satisfied with what we do."

"You're right." Francine hadn't thought that as a hairstylist she was also an artist, but after all, she was creating something that would enhance the person sitting in her chair. It was the same with a makeup artist. "Are you still planning to come for dinner tomorrow?"

"I wouldn't miss it for anything. Although I really like the food at Jack's, it's still different from a home-cooked meal."

"You're in for a treat because my grandma is cooking. By the way, I'm surprised she let you fix anything in her kitchen."

"I really like your grandmother," Keaton admitted.

"And she really must like you to let you prepare something in her kitchen even if only to make a drink. What on earth did you say to her?"

"I didn't say anything except that I'd wait in your apartment for you to come home. Maybe she didn't trust me to be there alone."

"I don't think it has anything to do with trust. What do you think it is?" Francine asked.

"Once I turned on the charm she just couldn't resist me."

Francine landed a soft punch to his shoulder. "You're incorrigible."

"No, I'm not, Francine. She likes me. At first I didn't do or say anything. She outright ordered me to follow her."

Placing both hands on his chest, she met his eyes. "My mother, whom my grandmother loves like a daughter, isn't allowed to boil water in that kitchen and I come home and find the two of you bonding like Pat and Gina Neely."

"What do you know about the Neelys?"

"I do watch television."

"You watch cooking shows, yet you don't cook." Dipping his head, he fastened his mouth to hers. "What am I going to do with you?"

"Teach me to cook," she whispered against his lips.

His mouth moved to the side of her neck. "There are other things I'd love to teach you, sweetie, but I promise that will happen only when we're ready to take things to the next level."

Francine knew if Keaton hadn't been holding her she would have sunk to the sand, dissolving into the grains like a drop of water. She'd admitted she hadn't had a date in more than six months and to him that probably translated into her not having sex for that period of time too, but it had been far longer. What he didn't know was that it'd been so long she'd forgotten what passion felt like. It was only in her erotic dreams that she was able to relive the sexual sensations that made her feel as if she were having an out-of-body experience.

Francine knew she had to be careful, very, very careful, not to fall into the same trap with Keaton as she had with Aiden. Her ex had used her for financial support to realize his goal, and she'd just offered to help Keaton brainstorm for a script yet to be written. The only difference was she didn't know where to start when it came to writing a script. He was the expert. But she and Aiden had been equals when they rehearsed parts with each other. Shaking her head as if to banish all thoughts of him from her memory, she bared her throat for Keaton's rapacious mouth.

Anchoring her arms under his shoulders, she held on to him as if he were a lifeline. Her mouth searched and found his, their lips parting and fusing like pieces of heated steel. Everything within Francine exploded, shattering her like colorful sparks from detonated fireworks.

He lifted her off her feet until her head was level with his, Francine's arms going around Keaton's neck in order to keep her balance. She drank from his mouth like a woman dying of thirst. All of her senses were heightened by his body's natural masculine scent mingling with his cologne, the smell of his leather jacket, and the taste of his tongue as it curled around hers.

She wanted him so badly that if they were not on a beach where anyone could come by and see them she would've begged Keaton to make love to her.

Francine couldn't fathom what it was that made her feel so wanton with Keaton. It couldn't only be prolonged celibacy, because it hadn't happened with the men she'd seen after she and Aiden broke up. And it certainly hadn't with David, who'd tried on several occasions to kiss her.

Somehow, before insanity replaced whatever common sense she had left, she floated back to reality. "Keaton, please. Let me go," she whispered.

Keaton's response was to hold her tighter. "Nothing's going to happen, sweetie. At least not here."

She managed to smile. "I know that."

The sound of their breathing competed with the sound of the tide washing up on the beach before it retreated back to its watery bed. Everything felt so right for Francine. Standing on the beach at the witching hour under a full moon with a man who stirred emotions she didn't want to feel. A man with whom she'd unknowingly connected years before when she appeared onstage while he'd watched from the audience.

"Why is it I don't trust myself around you?"

Keaton's query echoed her own thoughts. *Now, who's reading minds?* Francine mused as she lowered her arms. "Nothing's going to happen," she repeated.

He set Francine on her feet, while still holding her in a close embrace. "I know, because I'm going to take you home before I have a change of heart."

She didn't bother to put her shoes on once she was seated beside Keaton, preferring instead to hold them. It gave her something on which to concentrate instead of the man sitting less than a foot away. Francine had tried to figure out what it was about him that made her let her guard down, and not just emotionally, but physically. Each day she spent with Keaton, she found herself losing more control. Perhaps it was good that he was staying at the Cove Inn rather than in his house because that would've proven to be too much temptation. Although she had her own apartment with a private entrance, and her parents respected her privacy, she still couldn't get past the fact that she resided under their roof. It would've been vastly different if she and Keaton were married, but that wasn't even a remote possibility.

Francine did like Keaton. He was the epitome of masculinity, as evidenced by the number of women, regardless of their age, who gave him more than a passing glance. And she completely understood their reaction.

She was out of the SUV before Keaton could come around to assist her. With key in hand, she unlocked the door and would've escaped him completely if she'd been faster. He caught her upper arm, turning her around and pressing her back against the door.

Taking her shoes from her hands, he dropped them to the floor. Francine jumped at the thudding sound. Her hands curled into fists, nails biting into the tender flesh of her palms. She thought he was going to kiss her again but when he pressed his chest to her breasts, their breathing coming in a measured, syncopated rhythm, she smiled. The heat from his larger body warmed hers, spreading from her chest to her toes. She wasn't certain how long they stood together because time appeared to be standing still.

"I have to go up now."

Taking a step backward and dipping his head, Keaton kissed her cheek. "Good night, baby."

"Good night, Keaton."

"Don't forget to lock the door."

She nodded. "Okay."

The last thing she saw was the outline of Keaton's broad shoulders before she closed and locked the door. The image stayed with her as she washed her face, took a quick shower, got into bed, and pulled the sheet and blankets up and over her body. It faded only when she closed her eyes and fell asleep.

CHAPTER TEN

Francine waited for her grandmother to go inside the house, then maneuvered along the driveway, heading in the direction of Waccamaw Road. After the early service, she'd run into Jeff's grandmother, who told her Kara wanted her to come by and see the baby.

She waved to Miss Bernice through the driver's side window. Every morning she came out of her house to sweep the front porch whether it had debris or not. It was just an excuse for her to keep watch on her neighbors. The Tanners may have held the distinction of owning the largest private residence in the Cove but it still did not have enough acreage to provide complete privacy from their nearest neighbor. The former owners had sold off acre after acre of what had been more than twenty until less than a half acre remained. One by one other houses had been erected on half-acre lots along with countless magnolia trees that, when flowering, permeated the air with perfume from their blooms. Pulling into the driveway behind Miss Corrine's Camry, Francine parked the fire-engine-red Corvette. Kara stood in the doorway, holding her son to her chest. His tiny round head moved as he made grunting noises.

"Please come in," Kara said, smiling. "It's time for his feeding and if I'm one minute late he starts crying as if I hadn't fed him four hours ago."

Francine followed her into the sunroom with the framed artwork of renowned Southern painter Jonathan Green mounted on one wall. She peered closer at one painting. "Are these originals?"

"Yes. Gram is quite proud of her art collection." Kara sat on a rocker, unbuttoned her blouse, and within seconds her son had attacked her breast with such a vengeance that she made a hissing sound. "Slow it down, Austin, or you're going to choke." She gestured to a love seat covered with a sunny-yellow fabric with bright green leaves. "Sit down, Francine."

She complied, staring at the scene of a mother feeding her child that had been repeated since the beginning of time. Morgan was right. The newborn was his father's clone. "Your son is going to grow up to be quite the heartbreaker."

Attractive lines fanned out around Kara's large hazel eyes when she smiled. "Jeff keeps threatening to teach him how to be a player, but I told him my son will not grow up to mess over women as long as I have anything to do with his upbringing."

"How is Jeff adjusting to fatherhood?"

"It's like he was born to take care of a baby. He does everything but breast-feed. He and Gram fight constantly about who's going to hold him. I keep reminding them that they're spoiling him, but it's like talking to a wall."

"Babies are meant to be spoiled."

Kara rolled her eyes. "You say that because you don't have any. When Austin refuses to go sleep by himself because he wants to be held, I'll bring him right over to Magnolia Drive and hand him to you."

Throwing back her head, Francine laughed. "I'll take him. And don't expect to get him back."

Corrine and Jeff walked into the sunroom at the same time. Corrine handed Francine a cup of tea. "I heard your car when you drove up. I know you prefer tea to coffee."

Jeff was in uniform, which meant he was on duty or scheduled to go on duty. He'd resigned his commission as a captain with the U.S. Marine Corps to return to the island to care for his grandmother. He'd been recruited to fill in as sheriff when his predecessor resigned and no one, unless they'd taken leave of their senses, dared to challenge the former military policeman.

Francine nodded. "I do." She normally drank one cup of coffee a day, and that was decaf at night. Jeff came over and kissed Francine's cheek. "I just stopped by to check on my girls."

Corrine sat down next to Francine. "Your girls *and* your son, Jeffrey."

He gave his grandmother a sheepish look. "Why do you have to blow me up like that, Gram?"

She waved at him. "Go on and protect the good people of Cavanaugh Island from the rascals, scalawags, and perpetrators."

Jeff patted Corrine's silver hair. "They're not perps until they commit a crime."

"And it's your job to stop them from becoming perps, Jeffrey."

Kara, who'd finished feeding her son, handed Francine a diaper. "You can burp him. It doesn't hurt to get in a little practice for when you have your little one."

Francine jumped up. "I doubt if that's ever going to happen." And if it did it wouldn't be for a while, she mused. She hadn't planned on getting married again, but she was leaving her options open when it came to adoption. "Let me wash my hands first." She returned after washing her hands in the half bath off the kitchen, holding out her arms for the newborn. He opened his eyes and seemingly smiled at her. Morgan was right. He had inherited the Pattons' gray eyes. Placing the diaper over her shoulder, she supported his head in one hand, and gently rubbed his back. He had the new baby smell she loved. Austin let out a loud burp. "That was a good one." Francine cradled Austin in the crook of her arm, her features softening noticeably. "He's so adorable."

She couldn't help the direction her thoughts took as she stood holding the newborn. What would it feel like to watch her belly grow with a child she'd created with Keaton? To have their son or daughter feed at her breasts? To watch him cradle their baby in his large hands? In that instant she wanted what Kara and Jeff, and Morgan and Nate, had. Francine finally admitted to wanting a second chance to fall in love and marry, and this time get it right.

"He's a good baby," Corrine said proudly. "The only time he cries is when he wants to eat." She pushed to her feet. "Speaking of eating, can we offer you anything, Francine?"

"No thank you, Miss Corrine. I ate something before church."

Kara smoothed back the hair that had escaped the elastic band holding her ponytail in place. "Give me another three weeks and I'm going to redeem a part of your gift certificate with a haircut and hydrating facial. I'm going to save the full body massage for after I have my six-week checkup."

"Call me whenever you're ready and I'll be happy to schedule you. Remember, we're closed on Sunday and Monday."

Francine gave Austin to his mother, who placed him in the cradle Nate had made for him. She stayed another forty-five minutes with the Hamiltons, asking Corrine if she would be willing to talk to Keaton about the island's history for a movie script. Corrine said he could come by at any time. She seemed genuinely pleased that someone wanted to make a movie about the Lowcountry.

Her thoughts quickly turned to her pending chores once she reached her home. She had to put away several loads of laundry and planned to watch her favorite TV programs, her usual Sunday night routine.

Monday mornings were relegated to cleaning her apartment, leaving her the rest of day to relax and do things for herself.

When she walked into the main house, she headed straight for the kitchen, stopping short when she saw her mother sitting on a stool, hair covered with a colorful bandanna, at the cooking island rolling out piecrusts. "What are you doing here, Mama?" She expected her mother to be readying herself for the later service at church, not cooking.

Mavis's head came around and she smiled at Francine. "I live here."

"That's not what I mean and you know it," Francine teased. She closed the distance between them, kissed Mavis's cheek, and then sat opposite her mother. Francine noticed tightness around Mavis's mouth when she pressed her lips together.

"Where's Daddy?"

"He went over to that driving range in Goose Creek. He claims he's off his golf game and wants to get in some practice before he enters that fund-raising tournament next month."

"You're in pain, Mama."

"How do you know?"

"You're grimacing. It's your back again, isn't it?"

"It is a little tight."

"Why don't you go and lie down?"

"I can't. I promised Grandma Dinah I would make dessert for dinner."

Rising to her feet, Francine came around and eased Mavis up to a standing position. "I'm going to put you into bed where you're going to rest your back."

"Who's going to make dessert?" Mavis asked.

"I'll go out and buy something if Grandma decides she doesn't want to do it."

The Muffin Corner was closed on Sundays, which meant Francine would have to drive into Charleston. Curving an arm around Mavis's waist, she led her gently out of the kitchen and down the hallway leading to the master bedroom.

"Why don't you try to finish what I started," Mavis suggested. "All you have to do is roll out another crust."

"Please, Mama. You know I can't make a pie."

Mavis groaned under her breath. "We can't have dinner without dessert. There are melons, grapes, and berries in the fridge. You can make a fruit salad."

"Okay. I can cut up the fruit."

Francine managed to get her mother into bed without putting too much stress on her back. She'd tried to convince her mother to limit the number of hours she stood on her feet at the salon, but to no avail. "I'm going to bring you a couple of aspirins and a heating pad."

Mavis's high cheekbones were pronounced when she smiled. "Thank you."

Leaning over, Francine pressed a kiss to her forehead. "Don't run away," she teased. She went into the bathroom to get the aspirin, a glass of water, and the heating pad. "Does Daddy know about your back?" she asked when she returned to the bedroom to hand her the glass and the aspirin. She adjusted several pillows at the small of Mavis's back, then plugged in the heating pad.

Mavis peered at Francine over the rim of the glass. "No. It didn't start hurting until after he'd left this morning."

Sitting on the side of the mattress, Francine lightly touched the salt-and-pepper twists falling over the pillow. The familiar scent of coconut wafted to her nose. Mavis washed and conditioned her hair every week, painstakingly twisting her hair until it was smooth and smelling of coconut from the hairdressing she used to keep it from unwinding.

Francine crawled into bed and lay beside

her mother as she'd done when she was a child whenever her father went away on business. "I went to see Kara's baby after church."

Mavis closed her eyes. "How is he?"

"Delicious, Mama. He's a miniature Jeff right down to the slight cleft in his chin."

"Oh." She sighed. "This heat feels so good on my back."

"What you need to do is take a week off and go down to the Caribbean with Daddy and lie in the sun. Your pain may come from stress but it can also stem from you standing on your feet for hours without taking a break. It's time you think about cutting back your hours."

"And do what, boss?"

Francine laughed. "Relax."

Mavis opened her eyes, shifting slightly so she could look directly at Francine. "I'll relax when I can stay home and take care of my grandchild."

"Please don't go there again," Francine said under her breath.

"I will go there, Francine, because right now there's nothing to stay home for. Corrine raised Jeff when his mother died, and now I'm certain she'll look after her great-grandson if or when Kara decides she wants to go back to social work even if it's on a part-time basis."

"You don't have to babysit to stay home," she argued softly. "You can join the book discussion group Deborah hosts at her bookstore, or you can become more involved in the chamber activities. You can go with Grandma when she goes to the Creek for her quilting bee. Right now they're making personalized quilts for cancer patients in the children's hospital."

"That's all good, but some of those women gossip way too much. It's all right to talk sometimes, but that's *all* they do. Instead of talking about what's happening in the world it's about whose husband is sleeping with whom. Then it's about how much someone spends on shoes or a handbag. Who gives a flying fig if I decide to spend fifty dollars or five hundred dollars on a handbag? It's my money and I can do whatever I want with it. But you never hear them talk about how their badass kids get into trouble with drugs or if their boy was caught breaking into a store or even slapping his wife and kids around. That's when their jaws get so tight you wouldn't be able to pry them open with a crowbar."

"What else is there to talk about?" Francine asked.

"There are a lot of things. What do you

and Keaton talk about?"

She hesitated, wondering where the question had stemmed from. Her mother must have heard something about them. "We usually talk about ourselves and of course movies. He's new here so he wouldn't know too much about anyone."

"That's true, but there has been a lot of talk about him. A few of the folks staying at the boardinghouse claim he keeps to himself, and that he's quiet and very polite."

"I guess the word hasn't got out yet about his building the movie studio."

"That's where you're wrong," Mavis said. "Someone said Hannah let the cat out the bag when she mentioned it to Mayor White. This upcoming mayoral race is as nasty as the last presidential campaign, with people taking sides and hurling slurs at one another. Sanctuary Cove has only approximately eight hundred people, of which only half vote, yet you'd think it was the race for the White House."

"Remember, Mama, this is the first time Spencer has faced a serious challenger. Alice is the Cove's first female mayoral candidate and she's married to a man with deep pockets when it comes to campaign financing. She's young, attractive, a mother, and a nonpracticing attorney. Her husband has made certain Cavanaugh Island gets its fair share of federal government monies for the taxes we pay. Spencer is solely relying on his good looks and his bachelor status with the women voters."

"They're scheduled to have one debate a week before the March election and that's something I plan to witness in person even if we have to close the shop early. Now, back to you and Keaton," Mavis said without pausing to take a breath.

"What about us?"

"Do you like him?"

"Of course I like him," Francine said quickly. "If I didn't then I wouldn't go out with him."

"Your grandma told me she likes him too."

"That's because she knows he's going to give me cooking lessons. Did she tell you she allowed him to fix something in her kitchen?"

"No . . . no she didn't." She paused. "Your visions are bothering you, aren't they?"

Francine noticed her mother was slurring. Aspirin always made her sleepy. "Why would you say that, Mama?"

"Because you're in bed with me. Tell me about them."

Francine knew she couldn't get anything past her mother. As a child, whenever she had a disturbing vision she would crawl into bed with Mavis and they would discuss what she'd seen. She told her about the recurring one about the gaping mouths and shouting and that she knew the uproar had taken place in Sanctuary Cove because she recognized the town square.

"It's probably the election. Folks have become very vocal about who they want to see as their next mayor."

"That's what I keep thinking. I'm going to program the heating pad to go off in twenty minutes." Slipping out of bed, she folded the blankets under Mavis's shoulders. "I'll come and check on you as soon as I put up a load of laundry."

A tired smile parted Mavis's full lips. "Thanks for taking care of your mama."

"You're welcome." Francine wanted to tell Mavis she'd taken care of her for years and now it was her turn.

She took the elevator rather than the stairs to the second floor. The door to her grandmother's apartment was open, but she didn't go in.

Francine changed out of her slacks and blouse and into a pair of shorts and a T-shirt. She stripped her bed, gathered towels, and emptied the hamper, sorting everything by color. The washing machine, dryer, and collapsible ironing board were in an alcove off the kitchen. She put up a load of whites, then returned to the bedroom to make up her bed. As promised, she went downstairs to check on her mother and found her fast asleep. Rest and staying off her feet for a few hours usually lessened Mavis's back discomfort.

Francine's thoughts quickly returned to Kara and Austin. She knew her mother wanted a grandchild, but it wasn't as if she were a magician and could pull one out of a hat. A shiver swept over her like a cold wind when she thought about having Keaton's baby. Francine closed her eyes. What she couldn't wrap her head around was why he was the one who had her thinking about motherhood. Even when she was married the thought of becoming pregnant hadn't been a remote possibility. Maybe it was her intuition unknowingly coming into play.

Eight years had changed her. She had a new career and knew unequivocally that she didn't need anyone to convince her that she was worthy of being loved. She smiled inwardly. She had Keaton to thank for that.

Keaton was still transcribing the notes from his interview with the librarian when his cell phone vibrated. A slight frown appeared between his eyes when he saw the name of the caller. It was eleven on the East Coast and that made it eight o'clock in L.A. He couldn't imagine why his real estate broker would call him on a Sunday morning. Unless . . . he'd been out all night partying and had forgotten what day it was.

"What's up, Aaron?"

"I've got good news, my friend. I have a buyer for your house."

Keaton grinned like the Cheshire cat. He'd thought with the slow upswing in the housing market it would take months if not a year to sell his house. "That is good news."

His real estate agent's distinctive, horsey laugh came through the speaker. "I have even better news, my friend. I'm sitting here staring at a copy of an electronic transfer payable to you for twice the amount of the original asking price."

A knot formed in Keaton's chest, making it difficult for him to draw a normal breath. Aaron Cosgrove had earned a reputation for being a pimp and street hustler before straightening out his life to dabble in real estate. Men were usually won over by his smooth, persuasive demeanor, while most women were taken in by his incredible resemblance to the heartthrob actor Rob Lowe. "I hope you didn't sell my house to a drug dealer."

"Come on, my friend. I don't know people like that anymore."

"Who's the buyer, Aaron?"

"Some Middle East oil dude bought it for his twin sons who are here studying on student visas. It's apparent the boys have been running buck wild and their father decided if they live in a gated community with an American uncle sharing the house to monitor their actions they won't bring shame on the family name. The uncle told me they wanted to move in ASAP, but when I told him the owner had to arrange for someone to pack up the contents of the house and ship them across the country, he told me to name a price and he'd purchase the house and everything in it.

"I asked if he could wait twenty-four hours because I needed time to get in touch with the owner to see if you're willing to sell the furniture, because you'd employed the services of L.A.'s foremost interior decorator to the stars for your new home. I kinda stretched the truth a bit when I said you'd been on a wait list for three months. Meanwhile, I had someone, who will remain nameless, investigate this dude."

Smiling, Keaton shook his head. You could take the man out of the hustle, but with

Aaron you couldn't take the hustle out of the man. "What did he find out?"

"My friend, are you sitting down?"

"Yes."

"The uncle and his recalcitrant nephews are close cousins of a Saudi prince. It was like hitting the super trifecta in all of the Triple Crown races. I told him if he'd match the selling price, then he could move in within forty-eight hours of the transfer of his bank draft. The man paid you four point two million dollars for the house and its contents. I need you to fly out here like yesterday so we can close on the house."

Keaton couldn't believe Aaron had worked a deal where he would earn more than half a million in commission. "I'm going to call the airline and reserve a flight for some time tomorrow. I'll let you know when I'm scheduled to arrive so you can pick me up at the airport. Get in touch with Brian and tell him I need him to be at the closing."

Brian Appelbaum had handled the legal work when Keaton purchased the house in the exclusive enclave where the selling prices started at $1.5 million and went as high as $5 million. He'd bought the house on the one-acre lot for $1.8 million and had put it on the market for an even $2 million. But Aaron, hustler extraordinaire, had sold it for more than double what he'd paid for it. Keaton had arranged beforehand to let Mrs. Miller live in the house until it was sold, then she would move into a motel offering monthly room rates. Once the house in Sanctuary Cove was completed, she would relocate to the East Coast.

"He already knows about it," Aaron informed Keaton.

He had to give it to Aaron. The man was always one step ahead of him. He'd teased Aaron that if he'd gone to law school and passed the bar, then he could've become one of the most sought-after attorneys in the country. He was just that wily *and* intelligent.

"Good. I'll probably see you tomorrow." Keaton ended the call, then tapped the screen for Francine's cell. It went directly to voice mail. He left a message telling her he had to cancel eating with her family because he had to fly out to L.A. on business, and promised to call her while there.

His phone rang again. This call also had a Los Angeles area code. "Hey, Liana. How are you?" It'd been more than a month since he'd spoken to his sister. Their last call hadn't ended well — she'd abruptly hung up on him.

"I'm not doing too good right now."

"What's the matter?"

"Hollis and I had a blowup . . . I threatened to leave him."

All of Keaton's protective instincts were on full alert. "What did he do to you?" His brother-in-law had a hair-trigger temper and he didn't want to . . . His thoughts trailed off when he shook his head. "Talk to me, Liana."

"We had an argument."

"A lot of married couples argue."

"It was about you, Keaton."

He froze. "What about me?"

"He must have thought you were blowing smoke when you told him the two of you were through, but when he got the papers your lawyer sent dissolving your partnership agreement he went berserk. He wanted me to call and try to convince you to reconsider. I told him it was his fault because he should've known when to back off and then the proverbial shit hit the fan. He started screaming and throwing things, so I packed up the kids and checked into a hotel."

Pressing his fist to his mouth, Keaton counted slowly to five. "You should've called the police and they would've made him leave the house to ensure the safety of you and the kids. I'm coming out there tomorrow to take care of some business. I'll call you as soon as I get there. Meanwhile, I'm going to try and get in touch with Hollis."

"He was like a wild man, Keaton."

"He's nothing more than a spoiled brat who can't get his way. Don't worry, I'll take care of him."

Liana's sniffles came through the earpiece. "Daddy told me not to marry him."

This disclosure came as a shock to Keaton. He'd had no inkling that his father had disapproved of his future son-in-law. Liana had met Hollis when both attended Stanford University. They'd dated off and on for several years, lost touch with each other, and then were reunited at a party hosted by a mutual friend. Hollis Orman proposed four months after they reunited and they were married in a lavish wedding ceremony in one of Pittsburgh's oldest African American churches, followed by a reception on the lawn of an elegant country club boasting Japanese-inspired footbridges and ponds filled with water lilies.

"Why?"

"He witnessed Hollis yelling at his mother over the phone. He said if Hollis disrespected his mother, then he would disrespect his wife. I shrugged it off because his mother is such a witch. It's apparent Daddy's prediction came true."

Keaton attempted to process what his sister had just told him. If his father had mentioned the incident perhaps he, too, would've dissuaded Liana from marrying the banker. "Do you need money?"

Liana laughed. "I don't think so. Before I checked into the hotel I stopped by the bank and closed out our joint account, transferring the money to one I'd set up for the children. Hollis can pitch a fit but there's nothing he can do about it. This account is the only one we have that doesn't require two signatures. And if my husband decides to come after me, I will take out a restraining order."

"I know Kari and Jonathan are still in school, but if the house here was ready I'd tell you to come and live with me until you decide what you want to do."

"I spoke to Mom just before I called you and she's begging me to move back to Pittsburgh. I told her that I have to check with a lawyer to see if I can legally take the kids out of the state."

"They're your children, Liana. You and Hollis are co-parenting, so if he wanted to he could take the children and move out of the state and wouldn't be charged with kidnapping. That only applies where there is a custody ruling."

"I didn't think of that. I have to go back to the house to get their immunization papers and other documents I'll need if I want to enroll them in school in Pennsylvania."

"Don't go back until I get there. I'll go with you."

"No, Keaton. I don't want you involved in this. It will be like pouring gasoline on a fire."

"It's too late. I became involved the moment you called me. You're my baby sister. Haven't I always promised to take care of you?"

"Yes, you have," came Liana's plaintive reply.

"Then let me handle this my way."

Ten minutes later Keaton was still fuming while he paced the length of his bedroom in the boardinghouse. He'd always been one to turn the other cheek or walk away in a confrontation, but he drew the line when it came to his sister. Liana, three years his junior, had followed him everywhere as a child. She may have been an annoyance but he always made time for her.

Boys in their neighborhood learned quickly not to mess over the Grace girl or they would have to deal with her big brother.

The first time was when ten-year-old Liana came home crying because a neighbor's teenage son had touched her inappropriately. Keaton had faced down both father and son, who vehemently accused Liana of lying. It ended only when Scott Grace warned his neighbor to keep his son away from his daughter or he would have him arrested for attempted rape. Scott wasn't issuing an idle threat, because his brother-in-law happened to be the police commissioner. Several months later the fifteen-year-old was arrested and charged with sexual assault on another prepubescent girl. Within a month of the boy entering a juvenile detention center his parents sold their house and moved away.

Flopping down on the bed, Keaton stared up at the shadows on the ceiling. Every time he was confronted with a crisis in his life it involved a woman. First there was Jade and now it was Liana. He planned to talk to his brother-in-law and hopefully resolve the problem between him and his wife amicably. He'd witnessed the fallout of ugly divorces when a few of his friends' parents decided to end their marriages. There were no winners, but he always felt the children suffered the greatest loss.

He knew that was one of the reasons he'd

been so reluctant to marry. His mother had called him selfish, thinking that he just didn't want to share his life with a woman. Keaton wanted to tell Sophia Grace that she was wrong. If he found a woman who respected his solitary nature and understood his ambition to make movies, then he was willing to share his life and future with her. Making films for black actors was much harder. He wanted Grace Lowcountry to tear down the barriers, specifically those faced by actresses of color — some of whom had to wait years for a role to showcase their talent.

His gaze shifted to the three scripts on the table with his laptop and printer. There had been a time when he was tempted to send them out to major film companies. Each time he made the attempt something stopped him. He wasn't a superstitious person, but when he discussed the possibility of setting up his own production company with Devon she'd championed his idea. The more he thought about it the more it became a reality in his mind. Why work that hard for someone else when he could put in all of the effort for himself?

Keaton wasn't looking forward to flying to L.A. If he'd given Devon power of attorney to close on the L.A. property, then he would be able to remain on Cavanaugh Island. But there was also the problem with his sister and brother-in-law. Thankfully he would have to make only one trip to resolve both issues.

He didn't want to think about not seeing Francine. It was as if he'd stepped back in time when he sat in the audience transfixed by her riveting performance. When the curtain had come down for the last and final time he hadn't been able to tell himself it was over. That if he wanted to see her again, he would have to buy a ticket for another performance.

Meeting her in person and spending time with her forced him to understand it wasn't just her acting that had attracted him to her. It went deeper — as if they were connected or destined to meet in another lifetime.

Never one to question fate, Keaton decided to let destiny play out to see where it would lead him.

CHAPTER ELEVEN

Francine slept fitfully, and when she sat up the vision that had disturbed her twice before was back. The gaping mouths and unintelligible babble caused her to put her hands over her ears. But the noise persisted. "Go away," she shouted. Apparently the spirit had listened because the vision and the noise suddenly stopped. Combing her fingers through her hair she held it off her moist forehead.

Who, she mused, or what was the cause of all of the commotion in her vision? She didn't believe it had anything to do with the Beauty Box. Alice's campaign manager had set up a poster on an easel in the salon's plate-glass window and he'd left a basket with campaign buttons on the receptionist's desk for anyone wishing to take one. Mayor White's supporters grumbled under their breath or rolled their eyes but very little was said about Mavis and Francine throwing their support behind Alice's mayoral bid.

Francine felt a restlessness she hadn't experienced in a very long time. At first she thought it was because she missed going on her early morning bike rides with Morgan, so she resumed riding alone. She made certain to take her cell phone with her because she didn't know when Keaton would call her. She reminded herself that she was acting like a lovesick adolescent girl with a secret crush on a boy, hoping, wishing, and praying he would notice her.

She gave herself a stern pep talk, telling herself that he had noticed her enough to spend time with her. Francine wanted to believe he was dating her because he liked her and not to woo her into accepting a role in one of his movies. With Keaton there were no declarations of love or "I can't imagine my life without you" as Aiden had professed. He'd admitted he liked her, her red curls, freckles, and long legs — things that boys had teased her about in the past. He'd also revealed he didn't need her for sex because that was something he could get from any woman. That alone should've told her that Keaton was the complete opposite of the other men she'd known.

Perhaps it had something to do with his age. After all, he was forty-one and that made him older and more mature than the men she'd dated. He'd kissed her and each time she suspected he'd held back. He wasn't the only one holding back. She'd held back when she wanted to let her body communicate without words how much she wanted him. Each time she saw Keaton it had become more and more difficult to disguise her body's reaction to him.

Francine wondered how long she could continue to appear unaffected by his touch and kisses. When she'd returned to her bedroom after their stroll along the beach every nerve in her body screamed for release. The memory of Keaton's erection pressed against her bottom surfaced without warning and the pulsing sensations between her legs tortured her relentlessly, like icy pellets hitting her exposed skin. Francine had to wait for them to subside before she stripped off her clothes and stepped in the shower stall. She continued the torture when she stood under a spray of cold water for a full minute, then adjusted the temperature to a comfortable level, refusing to look at her reflection in a full-length mirror as she patted the moisture from her body.

Keaton had been gone for nearly three weeks and although he'd promised to call her he hadn't. Instead of calling he'd sent her one text message. What he had to take care of was taking longer than he'd anticipated. Francine didn't want to make too much of it for he could be one of those men who felt out of sight was out of mind.

Releasing her hair, she lay down and closed her eyes. She'd gone to bed earlier than usual. Her legs were aching. She'd been on her feet for most of the day with back-to-back customers. It was as if every man on the island had come in for a haircut. After the third one she discovered Joe Timmons had closed his shop because of a death in his family. This was the time when she welcomed the summer heat when all businesses closed down between the hours of noon and two. The two hours offered a reprieve when she could put her feet up and relax.

She'd almost drifted off to sleep when the cell phone on the bedside table vibrated. Picking up the tiny instrument she peered at the display. It was Keaton. Tapping a button, she crooned, "Hello stranger, it's been a long time."

His silken laugh caressed her ear. "How do you know that song? It was a hit before you were even a thought."

She affected a sexy moue even though he couldn't see her. "Are you kidding? I know all of the classic songs from back in the day. I even know who sang it."

"Who?"

"Barbara Lewis."

"Hey, you're real good."

"Don't forget I took musical theater for years, so I had to learn the lyrics of all the classic songs."

"I keep forgetting that you're an actress. Oops! Former actress."

Francine decided to ignore his reference to her former career. "How is L.A.?"

"Why don't you come downstairs and open the door and I'll tell you."

"You're downstairs?"

"Yes, waiting for you to open the door."

She turned on the lamp, scrambled out of bed, and walked on bare feet out of her bedroom, through the living/dining room, and down the staircase leading to the first floor. She opened the door and within seconds found herself lifted off her feet as Keaton smothered her mouth in an explosive kiss. Francine cradled the short beard covering his face as he tightened his hold around her waist. He smelled of soap and clean linen. It was obvious he'd showered before coming to her.

Somehow she managed to extricate her mouth, her breasts rising and falling as if she'd run a grueling race. "Come inside before you give my neighbors an eyeful."

Still holding her aloft, Keaton moved into the entryway and shouldered the door closed. He kicked off his running shoes. "If they're that nosy then we should give them a real good show."

"I don't think so."

Burying her face against the column of his strong neck, Francine inhaled his body's natural scent. He smelled delicious. Oh, how she'd missed him. He shifted, locked the door, and carried her up the staircase into her apartment. Again, he managed to shift her body as he closed the door behind them and locked it. Words of protest were tucked somewhere in the back of her throat when he carried her effortlessly into the bedroom and placed her on the bed, his body following hers down as he supported his weight on his forearms.

Being with Francine was enough to fill the emptiness he'd experienced during their separation. The hypnotic scent of her perfume clung to the sheets and blankets.

"What are you doing, Keaton?" she asked, her warm breath sweeping over his exposed throat.

"I'm holding my girlfriend."

"Am I really your girlfriend?" she whispered.

He raised his head, staring into her eyes. "Do you doubt it?"

"I . . . I . . . really don't know."

When he smiled at her his teeth shone whitely in a face made even darker by the short beard. "Why are you stuttering?"

"I didn't expect you to come here tonight. *And* get into bed with me."

His expression changed, sobering. "I didn't expect to come here either."

"Then why did you?" Francine asked.

Keaton closed his eyes for several seconds. "I don't know. When I got back my intent was to shower and go straight to bed. When I couldn't sleep I knew it was because you were on my mind. I'd promised to call you, but there were so many things happening at once. When I did find the time it was always too late here on the East Coast."

Her eyebrows flickered. "You managed to take care of all of your business?"

"Thankfully I did."

Rolling off Francine, he lay down beside her, took her hand, and laced their fingers together. Keaton told her he'd sold his house and about the volatile situation with his brother-in-law. "We were business partners for almost ten years. He put up the money to produce all my films. Things went sour when he wanted financial *and* creative control."

"Does he have any experience with movie-making?" Francine asked.

Keaton shook his head. "If he did, then I would've possibly considered relinquishing some control in lieu of his increased financing. Our business relationship ended once he refused to release the money I needed to complete my last film."

"What happened to it?"

"I had to scrap it. With the sale of my house I now have the money, but the principal actors are involved with other projects. I had my attorney send him a dissolution agreement and he took it badly. He retaliated by attacking my sister."

Francine's eyelids fluttered wildly. "Is she okay?"

"Physically, yes. Emotionally, however, she's a wreck. She's racked with guilt, blaming herself for staying in a marriage when she should've gotten out years ago."

"Why did she stay?"

"Liana kept saying it was because of her children. Personally I believe it's because she didn't want to be labeled a single mother. That is something that frightens her. But I told her being divorced doesn't necessarily mean their father won't be in their lives."

"That's silly, Keaton. Millions of women raise their children without a husband or man in their lives and the kids turn out okay. Look at Presidents Clinton and Obama. What she has to do is step up and become mother and father."

"You're preaching to the choir, Francine. My sister has always had a man's protection, so if it wasn't me or Dad, then it was Hollis. It's going to take a while before she's strong enough to realize she can make it through life without a husband. One thing she doesn't have to worry about is not having enough money to take care of my niece and nephew." Keaton told her about Liana's cleaning out their six-figure joint bank account.

Francine laughed uncontrollably. "At least she knew enough to secure her finances."

"She had to because she moved out of her home and into a hotel suite costing her two fifty a night. She delayed her plan to go to Pittsburgh because she'd left certain documents needed to register her children in a new school back at the house, so she asked me to get them for her."

"Did you?"

"Eventually I did, after leaving countless messages with Hollis's executive assistant that I wanted to meet with him but he kept putting me off for almost two weeks. He must have known I wasn't going away so he arranged for us to meet at a restaurant where I told him in no uncertain terms that if he ever raised his voice again or even breathed hard on my sister he would rue the day he woke up that morning."

"If her marriage was that bad why hadn't she considered marriage counseling?"

"I don't know. Liana can be very close-mouthed when she chooses to be, and I believe when she called me to say she and Hollis had had a terrible argument it wasn't the first time her husband had verbally abused her. My niece verified this when she told me her daddy yells at her mommy all the time."

"That's horrible."

Keaton nodded. "No child should grow up with parents verbally or physically abusing each other. I told him I wanted the file with the kids' birth certificates, school immunizations, and their Social Security cards, and after that he wouldn't have to worry about seeing me ever again."

"Did you get them?"

Keaton smiled. "Liana told me where I

could find them. When I went to the house I kept thinking Hollis had given in much too easily but he had to know it was over and his wife and children weren't coming back." He paused. "What have you been up to since I've been away?"

"Working."

"That's all?"

"That's enough, Keaton. I get up, go to the salon, cut, blow, perm, and relax hair, and then come home and chill out. Oh, I forgot. I've started biking between here and the Creek again."

"What time do you go biking?"

"I start out just before dawn. By the time I reach Angels Landing the sun is up."

"Aren't you afraid to be out at that time of morning by yourself?" he asked.

"No," she said, laughing.

"What if you get a flat?"

"I'd call my mother and tell her to pick me up."

"I want you to be careful, Francine."

Rising slightly on an elbow, she gave him a direct stare. "I am. Why the concern?"

Turning over, he flopped down on his belly. "I don't want anything to happen to you," he mumbled.

Going to her knees, Francine shook him when she realized he was falling asleep.

"Keaton, you're going to have to get up."
His response came in the form of a snore. Her gaze moved slowly over the white tee stretched over his broad back and down to a pair of khaki walking shorts, and then to his bare legs and feet. His physique was nothing short of perfection.

Her erotic dream had just manifested itself in the man sleeping in her bed. Slipping off the mattress, she turned the lamp to the lowest setting. Francine knew there would be another night and another time when Keaton would share her bed again. And it wouldn't be to sleep. She walked into the other bedroom and got into bed — alone.

Only her dramatic training kept Francine from reacting when Keaton walked into the Beauty Box for a much-needed haircut and shave. All conversations came to an abrupt halt when he sat in her chair, then quickly started up again as if there hadn't been a pause. Leaning closer, she draped the cape around his neck.

"Sleep well?" she whispered in his ear.

He smiled, his eyes meeting hers in the mirror's reflection. "Like a baby," he said sotto voce. "I'd expected to wake up to find you beside me," he continued, talking through clenched teeth.

She flashed a saccharine smile. "Win some, lose some."

Francine had slept later than she'd planned, rising to find Keaton gone. It wasn't until she walked into the kitchen to brew a cup of tea that she saw the note he'd left on the countertop. She'd read it once, and then again, unable to stop smiling. *Good morning, sleeping beauty. Will you go to the Happy Hour with me Saturday night? I hope you'll enjoy your day. XXXOOO—☺*

She planned to have a very good day. It was Tuesday, senior citizens' discount day, and she hoped to get the elderly men and women in and out quickly. Most of the women wanted roller sets and those wishing to hold back the hands of time had requested dyes and tints. The men were easier. She utilized either scissors or clippers to cut their short hair. Reaching into the pocket of her jeans, she handed Keaton the note, watching as he read it. She'd answered his invitation with *Yes,* enclosing the single word in a red heart.

She had made arrangements to meet Morgan at her shop. They'd made plans for Francine to select a kitten from the litter sired by Rasputin, Morgan's Russian Blue. The kittens were still too young to leave their mother, but Morgan had given her first choice of the pedigree felines. When Francine had mentioned Morgan's offer of a pedigree kitten to her grandmother, Dinah couldn't stop smiling. Dinah always had cats as pets. She'd had to give up her last one for adoption when she moved out of her home and into the condo, which had a no-pets rule.

Francine cut and shaved Keaton in record time because the chairs in the reception area were filled with customers with appointments and a few walk-ins. She gave him his bill, not meeting his eyes when he slipped a tip into the pocket of her smock. She didn't know why, but she felt as if every eye in the salon was trained on her and Keaton when he thanked her.

Francine couldn't believe she was becoming paranoid, but Miss Bernice was glaring at her. Brooke had wrapped her damp hair in a towel. "May I help you with something, Miss Bernice?" The woman mumbled something that sounded to her like "only the Lord can help you" under her breath. She froze. "Excuse me." Mavis returned to her station, unwrapping the towel from Miss Bernice's damp hair, preempting whatever she was about to say.

She'd learned since coming to work at the Beauty Box to ignore most of what was said or went on in the salon. Francine thought of herself as invisible when customers talked about one another without actually mentioning names. It was as if they were speaking in code. But she always knew exactly who they were talking about. Miss Bernice, who unfortunately lived on Magnolia Drive, had become the unofficial neighborhood watch. She could be seen peering through her curtains at any time of the day or night. What the Cove needed was a senior facility where retirees could play board games, dance, watch movies, or engage in age-appropriate exercises. It was something Francine planned to propose to Alice as the mayoral candidate touting change and progress for the town.

"I need you to attend the town hall meeting for me tonight," Mavis said to Francine, as she reached for the plastic rollers in a nearby tray.

"Are you okay, Mama?" It was a rare occasion when Mavis missed a monthly town hall or chamber of commerce meeting.

"I must have bent over the wrong way, because my back went out again. I have an appointment to see Dr. Monroe at five."

She saw her mother grimace each time she raised her arms. "Why don't you call him and ask if he can see you now."

Miss Bernice's head came around. "She gotta finish my head first."

Francine's temper flared. "My mother doesn't have to do anything but feel better," she said angrily. "Mama, go call Dr. Monroe and I'll finish setting Miss Bernice's hair." She engaged in a staredown, silently daring Miss Bernice to say something else.

Mavis put down her comb. "Thanks, baby." Resting a hand at the small of her back, she slowly made her way toward the lounge.

Francine moved over to finish what her mother had started. There were days when she could ignore the grumpy woman and days when she couldn't. Today was one of those days when she refused to put up with her backhanded innuendos.

Mavis had always had back problems, and standing on her feet for hours exacerbated them. After the last episode Francine had tried again to get her mother to reduce her workdays from five to four, but it was like talking to a brick wall. It was only when Mavis was down in her back that she was forced to stay at home and rest. Her mother knew Francine could run the shop as well as she did, but claimed she wasn't ready to give up doing what she so loved to do.

Francine finished rolling up Miss Bernice's hair, spritzing it with the setting lotion from a spray bottle. Covering the colorful rollers with a net, she inserted plastic ear covers under the net, making certain they were securely in place. Lifting the bonnet of a dryer, she waited until Miss Bernice sat down, then lowered the bonnet, programming the time and adjusting the temperature.

It'd become an assembly line when Francine slipped on a pair of latex gloves to apply a relaxer to a college student's new growth until it was straight. She directed her to the shampoo area where Brooke waited for her.

Francine retreated to the rear of the salon and mixed several colors to achieve a warm brown shade with golden highlights for her next client. The young woman had been warned not to put any chemicals in her hair during her pregnancy. Now that she'd given birth she wanted and needed a makeover.

"Do you want me to trim the ends?" she asked. The woman's hair hung halfway down her back.

Warm brown eyes met hers in the mirror. "I'd like you to cut it just above my shoulders. I don't have the time to blow it out."

"Are you sure?" It was the same question Francine asked every woman who requested she cut their hair. Once she picked up her scissors and began to cut there was no turning back.

"I've never been so sure of anything in my life. I know long hair is in style, but it's not practical for me."

Francine smiled. "Just double-checking. I'll cut it in layers so if you do decide to blow it out yourself, your hair will fall into a style."

There was a lull in activity midmorning and she slipped into the back to sit and put her feet up. Mavis had called to report that Dr. Monroe had given her a prescription for painkillers and that he wanted her to stay off her feet for a week. Hopefully her mother would take the doctor's advice and do just that.

Reaching for her cell, she sent her father a text about her mother's back problem. She had to wait only seconds for the reply. He was coming home. Francine knew if her mother wouldn't heed her advice, Mavis would listen to her husband.

Danita Yarrow approached her, pen and pad in hand. "I'm taking lunch orders. Do you want anything, Red?"

She nodded to the nail technician. "Where are you ordering from?"

"The supermarket deli."

Francine stared at the black-and-white air-brushed designs on Danita's nails. "I'll have the soup of the day and tuna on a bed of lettuce." Mavis paid for the coffee, sweet breads, and lunch for those employees who elected not to bring food from home. Surprisingly, no one abused the perk.

With the exception of the masseuse/aesthetician, all of the staff were paid a flat salary and at the end of the year received a generous bonus based on years of employment.

Candace, a stylist with short hair dyed a becoming platinum, a shade that complemented her golden-brown complexion, entered the lounge. "Red, your mama's eleven thirty is here."

She pushed to her feet. "Who does she have?"

"Miss Hannah. Good luck," she whispered as she turned on her heels and walked away.

Groaning to herself, Francine left to take care of one of Mavis's longtime customers. If the librarian wanted a dye job, then she was out of luck. There was no way she would be able to mix the tints and dyes to achieve the cotton-candy–pink shade. Then there was the teasing. It was a wonder the woman had any hair left after all these years of affecting that outdated style.

Hannah sat in Mavis's chair, her head swaddled in a towel. Francine rested her hands on the shoulders of the semiretired librarian. "Good afternoon, Miss Hannah. I'm going to do your hair today."

Hannah removed her glasses. "You know I like it teased. Do you know how to tease hair?"

"Yes, Miss Hannah." Removing the towel, Francine spritzed her hair, and then set it on large rollers.

"Your young man is as charming as he is handsome."

Her hands stilled. "Who are you talking about?"

"Keaton Grace, of course. I didn't want to believe it when he said he was building a movie studio in the Cove."

"Who's building a studio?" asked the woman sitting in Danita's chair.

Hannah, realizing she had a captive audience, revealed everything she'd discussed with Keaton. "Of course, I suggested he join the chamber if he's going to run a business here. It's going to put Cavanaugh Island on the map once it becomes known we have the only movie studio in the Lowcountry."

Bernice, who'd pushed up her dryer bonnet to hear the conversation, made a clucking sound with her tongue and teeth. "I don't understand, folks. First you want to vote for Alice Parker jest because she's a woman. Now y'all happy 'bout movie folks coming here with dey wicked ways. What's next? A topless bar?"

"You're wrong, Bernice," Hannah countered. "You underestimate folks. They're not going to vote for Alice just because she's a woman. They're going to examine the issues and vote for the candidate whom they believe will improve their quality of life."

Bernice refused to back down. "You say that 'cause you and her husband are blood."

Hannah's face turned a brilliant red. "It has nothing to do with —"

"Miss Bernice, you're going to have to stay under the dryer," Francine said, interrupting the librarian, while hoping to diffuse the volatile situation. Walking over to the dryer, she pulled the bonnet down over Bernice's head. She increased the time by an additional ten minutes. When the dryer stopped, she combed out Bernice, styling her hair as Mavis would've done. She tucked in a wayward strand.

Bernice patted the silver curls. "Nice job, Red."

She inclined her head. "Thank you, Miss Bernice."

Francine was certain she heard a collective sigh of relief when the door closed behind Bernice Wagner. If there had been another hair salon on the island Francine would've suggested the woman go there. The chatter continued as those who'd overheard Hannah mention a movie studio discussed the advantages and pitfalls of having actors and possible paparazzi invade their cloistered existence.

She still felt somewhat responsible that she hadn't warned Keaton in advance that his business would be all over the Cove and eventually the island because Hannah was a compulsive tattler.

Her practiced professional smile was in place when Hannah sat in her chair. She removed the rollers, brushing out her hair with a rubber-tipped brush. "I'm going to trim your ends before I tease you." Pulling up strands between her first two fingers, she showed Hannah the uneven split ends.

"Do whatever you think is best."

Hannah had given Francine the opening she needed to suggest that teasing was breaking and thinning the woman's hair. "I'd like to style your hair, giving you fullness without teasing it so much. Dying and teasing is weakening your hair follicles."

"But I like the color. It's my signature," Hannah said.

"The color is okay."

Hannah wagged a finger at her. "Just this once I'm going to let you do what you want, Red. If I don't like it, then I'm going to go back to my regular style."

Francine concentrated on cutting away the lifeless ends, then massaged a lightweight mousse into Hannah's hair before bending the ends with a barrel-type curling iron. Using a wide-tooth comb, she combed out the curls, achieving the height without her hair looking like tumbleweed. She counted out three drops of nongreasy polishing oil onto her palm, rubbed her hands together, and applied it to the smooth pink hair shimmering under the lights.

"Is it high enough?" she asked.

Hannah preened in the mirror. "Yes."

"Would you like a little holding spray?"

"Yes, please." Hannah touched her hair, smiling. "It's so soft and shiny. I like it, Red."

Francine returned her smile. "Good." *Two for two,* she mused. She'd managed to satisfy two of her mother's most critical customers.

Keaton drove out to see how the renovations on the farmhouse were progressing. All of the walls were up, and new windows, plumbing, and electrical wiring installed. The contracting crew had replaced the staircases in the living room and at the rear, including banisters and newel posts in keeping with the style of the historic structure.

He climbed the staircase to the second floor, walking in and out of the four bedrooms, each with a fireplace, sitting area, and adjoining bathroom. Wires hung from the ceiling where he planned to install ceiling fans. The construction crew had removed the old-style radiators, replacing them with baseboard heating. The house would be cooled using central air-conditioning, with each bedroom having its own thermostat to control the heating and cooling.

Keaton knew the house was much too large for one person, but he preferred spaciousness to being cramped. It was too much of a reminder of his New York City one-bedroom apartment that was only a little larger than the corrugated boxes used to ship refrigerator/freezers.

The contractor joined him in the smallest bedroom. "How does it look?"

He glanced at the ruddy potbellied man chewing on an unlit cigar. "Real good."

Harvey Rose rocked back on the heels of his worn construction boots. "The floors are next."

"How are the guesthouses coming?"

"I have a couple of men working on them full-time. The roofing, plumbing, and electrical work are done. Today we're putting in the windows." Harvey clamped his teeth on the cigar. "After we put in the floors and treat them, I estimate they should be ready about a week from now. You're going to have to let me know whether you want all white kitchen appliances or some other color."

The three guesthouses were less than one thousand square feet and that meant dark colors or bulky furniture would make them appear smaller. "White. By the way, do you have an extra set of floor plans?"

"Sure do. Come with me and I'll get them for you."

Keaton was anxious to move into his new home. Living at the boardinghouse had lost its appeal and he preferred entertaining and teaching Francine to cook in his kitchen rather than hers. He couldn't believe he'd fallen asleep in her bed. Whenever he'd stayed the night with another woman, it was usually after making love to her.

He'd consciously tried not to think about making love to Francine and failed. If she were any other woman, or if she didn't live on Cavanaugh Island, he would definitely consider seducing her. But she wasn't any other woman. She was someone he'd court, woo, or even romance before taking their relationship to the next level. She was different from the other women in his past because for Francine family was a priority. He still didn't know why she'd given up her acting career, but she'd come home instead of staying in New York. She was also committed to working at the salon with her mother, while looking after her grandmother, and for Keaton nothing in life was more important than family.

Although he'd planned to spend no more than a week in L.A., it had taken three. There was no way he could abandon his sister when she needed him most. Liana had exhibited mood swings that reminded him of Jade before the actress eventually took her own life. His sister would wake up crying, and after she'd dropped her children off at school, she would come back to the hotel and rant about what she wanted to do to her husband. Several times Keaton had to talk her off the proverbial ledge when she threatened to buy a gun and shoot Hollis.

However, there were intervals when she was calm and calculating. Liana had made certain to change her children's school emergency contact information, eliminating

Hollis as a person to contact in the event of an emergency. She didn't trust Hollis not to pick up her children and hide them from her.

Keaton knew his brother-in-law had sought to avoid him when he blocked his cell phone number and had his executive assistant answer his private line whenever he called. Hollis made him wait to agree to a sit-down until Keaton was forced to threaten him, leaving a final message with his assistant that if her boss didn't call him back she would have to look for a new boss and/or a new position. The ploy worked when Hollis returned his call an hour later. He recovered the documents Liana had requested, and got Hollis to agree to pack up his children's clothes and ship them to their grandparents' home in Pittsburgh. By the time he, Liana, and his niece and nephew boarded a flight to Pittsburgh, his sister had taken control of her life. Her children needed her and she had to be strong for them.

Keaton spent three days in the city of his birth, reuniting with relatives with whom he hadn't spoken since their last family reunion. His mother reminded him not to be a stranger. Phone calls were all right, but she wanted to see him more than a couple of times a year.

Francine had teased him, saying he was a frustrated actor, and she'd hit the nail on the head. When he'd joined his high school drama club it was because he enjoyed being onstage and pretending he was someone else. He was halfway into his junior year in college when he discovered the gift for writing scripts. One of his professors who mentored him had been a writer for daytime dramas. He taught Keaton all he needed to write for that medium. He'd been actor, writer, director, and now producer.

Life was good to Keaton. And now that he'd met Francine it was sweet.

Chapter Twelve

Keaton opened the door to Dane and Daniels Architecture and Interior Design. A bell chiming like Big Ben announced his arrival. He hadn't taken more than three steps when a young woman with inky-black, spiky hair and a nose piercing, dressed entirely in black, rose to her feet from where she'd been sitting behind the reception table.

"Keaton Grace?"

"Yes."

"I'm Patrice Watkins. You spoke to me when you made your appointment with Abram."

She extended her hand and he took it. "It's a pleasure to meet you, Ms. Watkins." Keaton noticed the diamond solitaire on the third finger of her left hand.

"It's Patrice. Since moving down here I discovered hardly anyone uses their last name. Please come with me. Abram is expecting you. May I get you something to drink?"

"No thank you."

Keaton followed her through the reception area, which was tastefully furnished with two side chairs upholstered in natural Haitian cotton flanking a low table topped with a vase of fresh flowers and succulents in small decorative pots. Twin Tiffany-style floor lamps matched the one on Patrice's table. Recessed lighting, recorded music flowing from speakers concealed in the ceiling, and the colors of blue, gray, and white created a calming effect.

A man he assumed was Abram Daniels came from around one of the two desks in a large open space with an armoire and drafting table on which sat a three-dimensional rendering of an antebellum mansion at the end of a live oak allée. Keaton was transfixed by the scaled-down detail of the model house with pale pink columns and tall, black-shuttered windows.

"This rendering is incredible." He was unable to disguise the awe in his voice.

Abram nodded, the skin around his brown eyes deepening when he smiled. He offered his hand. "Abram Daniels."

Keaton shook the proffered hand. "Keaton Grace." He smiled at the tall, thin interior decorator sporting a long, light brown ponytail. Tiny gold hoops in each ear, a reddish stubble, and a plaid shirt, jeans, and work boots rounded out his casual look.

"Please come and sit down, Keaton." Abram led him over to a table with a large computer monitor and two stools. Waiting until Keaton sat down, he touched the wireless mouse. "I'm responsible for decorating the interiors, while Morgan takes care of the architectural component of the partnership. That rendering is what Angels Landing Plantation should look like once it's restored."

"How long do you project the restoration will take?"

"Probably four years. Morgan's husband, Nate, still has to reconstruct the slave village and that won't be for at least another three years."

"It looks as if it's going to be phenomenal."

"It will. It's a daunting task, but once it's completed Angels Landing Plantation will become a smaller version of Williamsburg, Virginia." He pointed to the tube in Keaton's left hand. "May I see your floor plans?" Keaton watched as Abram scanned the floor plans into the computer, then pulled up another program. "Do you know the architectural style of the main house and guest cottages?"

"I believe it's a version of a Southern vernacular farmhouse. There's an open porch on the first floor and veranda on the second. The guesthouses are one-story, smaller versions of the main house."

"Siding or brick?" Abram asked.

"It's brick," Keaton confirmed.

"Now you're going to have to decide what style of furnishings you want — contemporary, traditional, American formal, European classic, or casual country."

"What do you consider casual country?" Keaton asked Abram.

"It's what I think of as simple charm or a vintage mix. Let me bring up each style and you can make your choice."

Keaton spent more than two hours with Abram; with a click of the mouse Abram was able to drop sofas, chairs, tables, and even paintings and photographs into each of the rooms on the floor plan. Keaton recalled the furnishings in the house on Magnolia Drive. The entryway and living room on the first floor were quintessential American formal. Dinah's apartment was definitely American eclectic, while Francine's claimed more of a Zen look. She'd created a home that projected harmony and balance.

"I'm leaning toward casual country that will include a few contemporary pieces," he told the decorator. "I prefer simplicity to fussy." For Keaton the more uncluttered the room the more freedom he had in which to move around.

"Let me work up some sketches and print them out for you. Once you narrow down which style you want, then we'll talk about color schemes."

"How soon after I decide what I want can I expect delivery?"

"I deal with several local furniture manufacturers that guarantee delivery within a month to six weeks. How does that fit into your schedule?"

"I met with the contractor and he predicts completing all the work by the first week of March."

Abram ran a hand over his hair. "If I submit your order let's say early next week, then you can expect delivery of all of the pieces by April fifteenth. Some may be delivered much sooner if they're in stock. I'll let you know about the availability once you give me the okay."

Keaton hadn't had to concern himself with decorating the house in L.A. because the style was predictable. The overall design of the house was Spanish contemporary and that made it easy to decorate. He would take Abram's suggestion and study the printouts until he was able to pinpoint which style would not only suit his taste but also his lifestyle.

And for the first time since coming to the island to live he felt as if he were a transient. The walls in the boardinghouse suite seemed to be closing in on him and Keaton found himself sitting out on the veranda just to offset the feeling of claustrophobia. Perhaps it had something to do with the three-week separation from what had become normal and familiar.

He was pleased with Liana's decision to move back to Pittsburgh, where she had the ongoing support of family members as she went through her impending divorce. Keaton was certain she would enjoy sitting out on her porch either early in the morning or at the end of the day. There was nothing and no one to keep her in L.A., and she'd said she was looking forward to moving away from a place that still held so many painful memories.

As Keaton left the architectural and design firm and made his way to the parking lot, he spied Francine's red Corvette parked in a space not far from the rear of the Parlor Bookstore. He scanned the lot, looking for her. He'd just gotten in behind the wheel of his vehicle when he spied her getting out of a gleaming white Cadillac Escalade along with Morgan. He paused, not turning on the engine as he watched her and Morgan as they stood talking to each other. Both were wearing sunglasses. The temperatures were now warm enough to go out during the day with a light jacket or sweater. He wasn't able to pull his gaze away from the curve of her hips in a pair of skinny jeans. A rising breeze blew her curls around her face. Staring numbly, he watched as she pushed the curls off her forehead, tucking them behind her ears.

Keaton felt like a voyeur as he watched the graceful movement of her hands when she gestured. His gaze lingered on the swell of her breasts under a pullover. In that instant he conjured up the image of making love to her, which triggered a violent reaction when he couldn't stop his growing erection.

He knew if he didn't pull out of the parking lot she would notice him and possibly come over and see the bulge in his jeans. All of his motions were slow, almost mechanical, as he started up the SUV, but as fate would have it she turned in his direction. Quickly, he pulled the hem of his shirt from his jeans, pulling it down over his waistband. He got out of the vehicle as she and Morgan approached him. Keaton tried thinking of anything else but his swollen manhood. He had to congratulate himself on a winning performance when he leaned down to kiss Francine's cheek before nodding to Morgan.

"Good afternoon, ladies."

Morgan smiled, dimples winking. "How was your meeting with Abram?"

"It went well. He gave me some printouts of different styles."

"That always works well because you get to see exactly what each room will look like." Morgan looked at Francine. "We just came back from looking at a litter of kittens."

Keaton's eyebrows lifted a fraction. "You're getting a kitten?" he asked Francine.

When she shook her head, red curls moved as if taking on a life of their own. "No. It would be for my grandmother. She's the cat person."

"You don't like cats?" he asked Francine.

"It's not that I don't like them. They don't like me."

"What breed are they, Morgan?"

"Patches is the queen and she is a Snowshoe. Rasputin is a Russian Blue."

Keaton smiled. "Very nice. Are you selling them?" he asked Morgan.

"Not to friends. If you want one, then I'll put it aside for you."

"I won't be able to come for it until my house is ready."

Morgan shook her head. "That won't be a problem." She smiled at Francine. "See, Fran, I told you I'm not going to get stuck taking care of five cats." She shifted her attention back to Keaton. "If Nate and I weren't putting an addition onto our house, I'd have you and Fran over for a little get-together. Right now I'm staying with my in-laws and their children."

"If you and Nate want some grown folks time you're always welcome to come and stay at my place for as long as you want," Francine offered. "You know I have the extra bedroom."

"Maybe we'll take you up on your invitation even if we stay over for a couple of days. And I'll even do the cooking," Morgan added.

Francine took a step, looping her arm through Keaton's. "That's not necessary. Keaton happens to be a wonderful cook."

Taking off her sunglasses, Morgan gave

him a long stare. "You cook?"

He nodded. "A little."

Francine tugged on his arm. "Stop being so modest, Keaton. This man comes from a family of chefs."

"That does it. Nate and I are coming." Morgan narrowed her eyes at Keaton. "What are you making?"

He smiled. "Anything you want."

"Can you make red rice and sausage?"

"Yes."

"How about mustard greens and cornmeal dumplings?"

"That, too," he confirmed.

Morgan placed a hand over her flat belly. "When are you cooking?"

Keaton looked at Francine. He didn't mind cooking for her friends, but it wouldn't be at his house, but hers. "When is it convenient for you, sweetie?" The endearment had slipped out unbidden.

Francine lowered her eyes, not wanting Morgan to see her uneasiness when Keaton addressed her as *sweetie.* She knew it would take a while before she was completely comfortable with their growing friendship. If he hadn't spent almost three weeks away from the island she was certain their relationship would've progressed from where it was now.

Reaching into the back pocket of her jeans, she retrieved her smartphone. Since the receptionist had double booked clients for that hectic week she'd begun keeping her own calendar. Tapping the icon for the calendar, she scrolled through the days. "I have a haircut at three tomorrow, and that should put me home at four."

Taking out his own phone, Keaton tapped several buttons. "Will your grandmother be home to let me in?"

She reached into another pocket and took out a set of house keys. "I'll give you the key so you can let yourself in."

Keaton took the single key when she slipped it off the ring. "How will you get in?"

"I'll use the front door."

"What time should Nate and I get there?" Morgan asked.

"Six," Francine and Keaton said in unison.

Morgan leaned into Keaton and kissed his cheek. "Thank you. I've had the weirdest craving for greens and cornmeal dumplings, and Nate's sister claims her dumplings either come out too dry or too soupy." She opened her tiny purse and took out a large bill. "This is to cover the cost of the food."

Francine groaned inwardly when she saw Keaton's expression and it didn't bode well for her best friend. "That's okay, Mo," she said quickly. "We've got this."

"Are you certain?" the architect asked.

A muscle in Keaton's face twitched noticeably as he clenched his jaw. "Very certain."

Morgan returned the money to her purse. "As soon as our house is finished, you and Fran must come for dinner. And unlike my BFF, I can cook." She glanced at her watch. "Gotta run. I was supposed to be at the restoration site fifteen minutes ago." She wiggled her fingers. "I'll see you guys tomorrow."

Francine waited until Morgan drove away, then turned to meet Keaton's eyes. "Are you certain you don't have another road trip scheduled for tonight or tomorrow?"

Wrapping his arms around her shoulders, he pulled her close. "Nothing that couldn't be avoided."

Burying her face against his shoulder, she laughed softly. "I was just teasing you."

"I take it Morgan's pregnant?"

"Yes. What gave her away?"

"She talked about cravings, and the only time I've known women to talk about them is when they're in the family way."

"I occasionally have cravings and I've

never been pregnant."

"We'll just have to wait and see, won't we?"

"What . . ." Her query was preempted by the chiming of her cell phone. It was an alert for her next scheduled appointment. "I'll talk to you later. I have to get back for my next customer." She tried to pull out of Keaton's embrace, but he held her fast.

"Wait, sweetie." Lowering his head, he pressed his mouth to hers. "I'll talk to you later. If you're not too tired I'd like you to join me on the beach. Maybe I'll bring a surprise."

"What surprise?"

He kissed her again. "If I told you then it wouldn't be a surprise, would it?"

"No." The alert chimed again and Francine smiled up at him through a sweep of brownish-gray lashes. "I'll see you later."

Two hours later and dressed in a pair of cropped jeans and a thick cotton pullover, Francine, clutching a quartet of lanterns, followed Keaton as he carried an oversize canvas bag in one hand and a smaller one in the other, her bare toes sinking into the soft, powdery sand with each step. There was only a slip of a moon in the dark sky littered with millions of stars. If it hadn't been for the lampposts in the parking area, the entire beach would've been pitch-black.

Keaton stopped and dropped the bags on the sand. "I think this is as good a spot as any."

She set down the lanterns at each corner of the blanket, then, resting her hands at her waist, she shook her head. "Anyplace on the beach tonight is a good spot." Unlike the night of the full moon, this time the beach was almost deserted.

She watched as he emptied the contents of the larger bag, spreading out a blanket on the sand, followed by a small hibachi and a bag of charcoal. It wasn't until he reached into the small bag and removed a plastic container with graham crackers and another with marshmallows and chocolate bars did it dawn on her he intended to roast s'mores.

Going to her knees, she knelt on the blanket. "How did you know I love s'mores?"

"Your grandmother mentioned it the night I waited in her apartment for you."

"You're just full of surprises, Keaton. And that's what I love about you." She couldn't see his expression but Francine did feel tension emanating from him. "What's the matter?"

"Don't ever tell me you love me unless you mean it."

"It was just a figure of speech."

"Not for me, Francine. Just . . . please don't say it again."

Francine wanted to stick her tongue out at him or make a face as she'd done as a child, but then reminded herself she'd left childhood behind years ago. "Is there anything you want me to do?"

"No, sweetie. I've got this."

She began to wonder if perhaps the man with whom she'd found herself so enthralled had a split personality — a Dr. Jekyll and Mr. Hyde. First he'd figuratively bitten her head off when she said she loved him, then within the next breath had called her sweetie. He had to be either one or the other, because she didn't do well with mercurial moods. And she had never bought into the temperamental artist stereotype. Her answer to that was to save it for the stage, the camera, or the canvas — mediums established for displays of genius and/or expression.

Keaton could've bitten off his tongue for barking at Francine. She didn't deserve to be the target of his increasing frustration about his growing feelings for her.

"I'm sorry, Francine. I shouldn't have spoken to you like that." The moment the apology left his mouth Keaton felt as if a weight had been lifted off him.

She'd uttered the word *love* so matter-of-factly he feared that his growing feelings for her wouldn't be reciprocated. He knew he was falling in love with her. Her face, voice, and body haunted him whether in wakefulness or sleep. It was as if she had cast a spell over him. At first he'd attributed it to immersing himself in the African American folk magic of the Gullah people, but whenever he came face-to-face with Francine he knew it had nothing to do with witchcraft. He was falling in love with a woman who made him think of a future, something he hadn't done in the past. Marriage, family, and a happily ever after. He'd always believed the sanction of marriage was forever, but knowing his sister's marriage would end in divorce was a blatant reminder that people fell in and out of love all the time.

"Apology accepted."

"I promise I will never use that tone with you again."

Keaton intended to keep his promise. Even when he suspected Francine was angry with him she usually gave him what he thought of as the stink-eye, but she never said anything that she had to apologize for.

He continued to empty the bags, removing an iPod, with a dock and speakers. "I thought we could use a little night music."

The brightness of her smile competed with the light from the lanterns. "My, my, my. You've thought of everything."

"Almost." He continued to empty the bags, handing her a bottle of Perrier. "It's not champagne, but you'll have to use your imagination."

Within the span of fifteen minutes they were holding tongs with a graham cracker, a piece of dark chocolate, and a marshmallow, topped with another cracker over the smoking coals, the sweet aroma redolent in the salty air. Francine held the paper plate while Keaton took one of the gooey treats.

"Let it cool before you burn your tongue," Francine warned him.

He took a bite, moaning softly. "Oh, man. That is good. I think it's cool enough for you to eat."

"You're right. It is good," she said after biting into the melted chocolate and marshmallow. They ate s'mores, washing them down with chilled sparkling water, and then lay together like spoons on the blanket listening to the eclectic playlist. "How come mine didn't come out like yours?" Francine asked after a comfortable silence.

"What's wrong with yours?"

"I don't know. They just taste different. Maybe I didn't use enough chocolate."

Keaton pressed his mouth to the nape of her neck. "Are you cold?"

"Not now. Your body's like a blast oven."

He laughed. "I don't know whether to take that as a compliment or an insult."

"It's a compliment. You're hot, Keaton, and I also want to thank you for offering to cook for my friends."

"It's no biggie, sweetie. I haven't cooked since moving here, and I don't want to lose my edge. I was supposed to cook for you, but flying out to California threw a monkey wrench in that plan."

"My grandmother waited for you to come and get the groceries you left at her place, but when I told her you had to go away she used them so they wouldn't go bad. As for you losing your edge, I don't think that's going to happen. You truly missed your calling when you decided not to become a chef."

"I don't think so," Keaton replied. "There are enough chefs in my family."

"Daddy told me he met your father when he played football."

Keaton nodded. "Dad used to tell me

stories about the players coming in after practice or a game. It was the only time when there were never any leftovers."

"My mother said when Daddy came after the season ended he'd eat her out of house and home. If he hadn't gone on a diet to lose his game weight he probably would tip the scales at three fifty. Right now he'd around two hundred."

"I weigh more than he does," Keaton admitted. "I'm two fifteen."

"How tall are you?" Francine asked.

"Six-three."

"You're three inches taller and twenty years younger than my father, so you're good."

"I have to work hard not to put on weight because I spend a lot of time sitting."

"You can come bike riding with me or you can walk the beach like a lot people do before the temperatures reach three digits. During June, July, and August all businesses shut down between noon and two."

"That's like siesta in Europe."

Francine laughed softly. "The tradition goes back more than a hundred years. Sometimes it's so brutal the mayor issues weather emergencies. Last year they mandated businesses close from noon to four in order to conserve energy."

"That's smart. What do you do during siesta?"

"I always go home, take a shower, and change my clothes. Right after the Memorial Day weekend we operate on a summer schedule. My mother and grandmother cook on Sundays for the entire week. They'll make a ham, roast several chickens, and occasionally a turkey. Then they make the sides: slaw, potato salad and greens, rice and sweet potatoes. All I have to do when I come home is heat up a plate in the microwave and I'm done."

"Does your father cook?"

Francine nodded. "Yep. Mama taught him."

"Who taught your mama?"

"Her mama. My maternal grandmother was employed as a cook by one of Charleston's wealthiest families. I believe it was my mother's cooking that prompted my father to propose to her. Then there's Grandma Dinah. A lot of folks here claim Grandma's dishes come as close to those at Jack's Fish House as anyone in the Lowcountry."

"I'm still pissed that I missed dinner at your house."

"Now that you're back you can expect another invitation. Grandma Dinah's first love wasn't cooking but the stage, but her mother was dead set against a career where in those days actresses were regarded as harlots, trollops, and prostitutes, so she threw all of her energy into learning how to cook. Home cooking is only one piece in our patchwork quilt of Gullah culture, but the kitchen is the most important room in the house."

"I notice people down here do eat a lot, but there aren't too many who are overweight."

"That's because there are no fast-food restaurants on the island. Even if you eat at Jack's every day you're getting locally grown produce without the additives and preservatives. Otis and Miss Vina buy their hogs from a local farmer and it's the same with their chickens. And most of the seafood comes from local waters."

"I guess you're out of luck if you're looking for sushi."

"Yuck! I don't like raw fish."

"Did you try it when you lived in New York?" Keaton asked Francine.

"Once and I swore never again. This Gullah prefers her fish fried, broiled, or baked."

"You can take the girl out of the South, but you can't take the South out of the girl."

"Do you have Southern roots, Keaton?"

"Yes. Why?"

"Then you should know the significance food plays in our heritage. How our ancestors were able to create scrumptious dishes from leftover scraps that now appear on gourmet restaurant menus. All you have to do is look at the number of cooking shows on network and cable TV. It's as if we've suddenly become obsessed with food. For years our kitchens have been the gathering place to catch up on what's going on in our lives and community. And don't forget about Sunday dinner with the table groaning with platters of fried chicken or baked ham along with all the sides. It made sitting in church and listening to the long-winded pastor extolling the wonders of heaven while warning us against the pitfalls that lead to hell and damnation worthwhile."

Keaton nodded in agreement. "I remember those sermons when I used to spend my summers with relatives in Tennessee. One day my aunt invited Pastor Evans to Sunday dinner. He was a big man with a big voice and an even bigger appetite. Every time he said, 'Bless you, Sister Thelma,' he would take another piece of fried chicken. My cousin, who was two years younger than me, started crying when the man reached for the last piece on the platter that had been piled high with two cut-up chickens. My aunt was so embarrassed when he cried out, 'Mama, please don't let him take the last piece.' The man had eaten a whole chicken by himself, unaware or not caring whether anyone else had had a piece."

Francine's giggles carried easily in the night. "What did your aunt do?"

Keaton's laughter joined hers as he remembered the look of terror on his cousin's face. "She punished my cousin. He couldn't leave his room for a week except to eat and use the bathroom. She never invited Pastor Evans back to her home no matter how much he publicly praised her cooking. And what we didn't know was that my aunt had been warned about the minister's prodigious appetite and she'd prepared a third chicken that she'd put away so none of us knew about it except my uncle. Normally two chickens would feed my aunt's family of six and she'd always end up with enough left over to turn into salad the next day."

"That is hilarious. I would've given anything to have seen your cousin's face when he said that. Better yet, the pastor's face."

"The good pastor either ignored my cousin or he was completely clueless as to what he'd done when he did take the last piece. It's something I tease my cousin about to this day whenever we have family reunions."

They fell silent again, and Keaton thought Francine had drifted off to sleep. He blew on her scalp and she shuddered visibly. "Now that I'm going to have houseguests for the next few days, do you still want to go to the Happy Hour on Saturday?"

"That's up to you. I made a reservation for the two of us. If Morgan and her husband are up to going, then I'll call and change it to four. Or I can cancel and we can stay home."

"Even though Nate's cousin is part owner of the club, he doesn't frequent it too much."

"Why don't I switch the reservation to the following weekend?" Even though he rarely went to clubs himself, Keaton thought it would be nice to take Francine to a place with live music and dancing.

Turning over to face Keaton, Francine rested her leg on his. "Thank you."

He kissed the end of her nose. "You're welcome." His left hand searched under her sweater, pressing his palm to her bare belly. "I'm not the only one who's hot." He felt the rush of her breath against his throat when she exhaled audibly. "You don't know how long I've wanted to touch you, baby.

And one of these days I'm going to kiss and taste every inch of your body until you either beg me to stop or I pass out from pleasure. It's going to be your choice, Francine." He felt her trembling and Keaton knew it wasn't from the wind coming off the ocean because her skin was warm to the touch. He withdrew his hand. "I'd better get you home before we end up doing something we'll both regret."

Keaton waited for Francine to put on her shoes before he rounded the vehicle to slip into his. He drove back to Magnolia Drive not wanting the night to end. Everything about his relationship with Francine was easy, uncomplicated. Once his bruised ego recovered from her refusal to accept a role in his film he realized his relationship with her had she accepted would've been vastly different than it was now. It would've been actor and director, the professional line indelibly drawn where he could not cross it.

It suddenly hit him when he maneuvered up close to the side of the house, only feet from her door. Francine was the first woman he'd met that he thought of as a friend before the possibility of becoming lovers. Guys had their guy friends and women their girlfriends. But it wasn't often a man could go out with a woman and count her as a friend. This is not to say he wasn't physically attracted to her because he was. However, the physical attraction didn't come with an all-encompassing need to sleep with her as it had with some of the women in his past.

Keaton waited until she'd unlocked the door leading to her apartment before pulling her close to his chest. "I had a wonderful time tonight." When she glanced up at him through lowered lashes he felt as if he was being seduced. Her mouth and body said one thing while her eyes sent out signals he had no problem interpreting.

"So did I," she admitted in a breathless, whispery voice. Francine put her arms around his neck, pulling his head down. "Thank you." She brushed her mouth over his. "Good night, Keaton."

He pulled her closer, one hand at the small of her back, molding their bodies from chest to thigh. The glow from the light fixture above the door turned her into a statue of gold as his gaze moved lazily over her face and down to her throat, longing to fasten his mouth to the spot. His gaze reversed itself, lingering on her mouth.

His lips brushed hers, the gentle kiss surprising Keaton with the amount of control it took for him not to devour her mouth. Raising his lips from hers, he buried his face along the column of her neck, breathing a kiss on the silken perfumed skin.

He kissed her neck again. "Good night, beautiful." Keaton waited for Francine to close and lock the door. It was as if he were paralyzed because he couldn't move. He didn't want to leave her. Not tonight. Only because he didn't want to spend the night alone.

Keaton didn't want to return to the Cove Inn and spend the night tossing restlessly because he'd spent more time denying his feelings for a slender woman with curly hair and freckles. When Francine told him that she loved him he feared blurting out the same. "I don't want to be alone tonight."

"You don't have to, Keaton." She held out her hand. "Come." She wasn't disappointed when he took it, threading their fingers together. "You can sleep in the spare bedroom."

Bringing her hand to his mouth, he dropped a kiss on her knuckles. "One of these days I'm going to return the favor, when the renovations on my home are completed."

"Is that a promise?"

He nodded. "It's a vow."

Chapter Thirteen

Francine climbed the staircase on shaking legs, Keaton following after he took off his shoes. She'd just invited a man to spend the night at her house. The first time Keaton had slept over it hadn't been planned. She told him he could sleep in the spare bedroom when she wanted him in her bed, their bodies joined in a sensual dance of desire.

"You'll have your own bathroom, and you can find a supply of toothbrushes and razors and other toiletries in a drawer under the vanity. If you want me to wash your clothes, then just leave them outside the door. I hope —"

Keaton caught her upper arm, turning her around. "Slow down, baby. You're talking a mile a minute."

Closing her eyes, she smiled. "I do that sometimes."

"Yes, when you're nervous. And there's no reason you should be nervous now. I'm not going to creep into your bedroom in the middle of the night to attack you. I don't have protection on me and I doubt you have any. Or do you?"

Francine opened her eyes. She struggled to control the momentary panic gripping her. It was the same emotion she experienced before each performance. It came and then disappeared the moment she stepped onstage. "No, Keaton. I don't happen to have any condoms on hand."

He smiled, bringing her gaze to linger on his mouth. "See. You're safe."

She wanted to ask him if she was really safe as his eyes seemed to undress her. "What time do you want me to wake you up?"

"I don't need a wake-up call. I get up with the sun."

"Then you can wake me up," she countered. "Tomorrow, we can start our discussion on Gullah folklore and a few of those scandals no one likes to talk about. No more talk about us or food."

"Agreed."

Francine patted his shoulder. "It's late, darling, I need to go to sleep."

"First you're my girlfriend and now I'm your darling."

"Go to bed, Keaton. Remember if you

want me to wash your clothes, leave them outside the door."

"Good night, sweetie."

Keaton walked into the bedroom and flipped a wall switch. The glow from bedside lamps reflected off jade-green walls, creating a calming effect. A platform bed, an armoire, and bedside tables were the only furniture in the room. He opened the doors to the Asian-inspired armoire to reveal a large flat-screen television and audio components. Stripping off his sweater, jeans, and underwear he left them outside the door. Walking on bare feet, he entered the bathroom. One entire wall was made up of mirrors.

Keaton stared at his reflection staring back at him. He was confused. Outwardly he looked the same as he had when he'd first checked into the Cove Inn, but he knew he wasn't the same person. He hadn't been the same since the day he saw Francine Tanner standing behind the receptionist desk at the Beauty Box. It was all he could do to keep it together when she leaned over to shave him. Her warmth and smell had lingered in his nostrils for days even when they were apart. Everything about her was stamped on his memory like a permanent tattoo.

Now he was electively sleeping under her roof with her in a bedroom across the hall. Either he was losing his mind or his edge. He was able to command the complete attention of every single person on a movie set, yet he couldn't garner the nerve to tell a slip of a woman with a sultry Southern drawl that he was falling in love with her.

Keaton brushed his teeth and took a hot shower, hoping it would help relax him enough to fall asleep without tossing and turning. It proved to be the antidote when he slipped between a set of crisp sheets, pulling several handmade quilts up over his shoulders. Within minutes of turning off the lamp he'd fallen asleep.

Keaton nuzzled Francine's ear until she stirred, then woke up. "What time is it?" Her voice was still heavy with sleep.

"Five forty-five."

She groaned. "You've got to be kidding, Keaton. It's too early to get up."

He ruffled her mussed hair. "I thought you told me to wake you up."

Francine buried her face in the pillow under her shoulders. "I did, but not this early."

"Don't tell me you're cranky in the morning."

She turned over on her back. "I'm never cranky in the morning. Come here." Raising her arms she waited for him to come into her embrace. "Good morning."

"Thanks for washing my clothes," Keaton said in her ear. "I'm going to let myself out. Remember you gave me your key."

"I have a spare."

"I'll see you later," he promised, kissing her hair.

"Later," Francine repeated, turning over and closing her eyes when Keaton moved off the bed. If she didn't have to get up early for work she would've been more than content to while away the hours in bed with him. Each time she sought to compare him to Aiden she realized there was no comparison.

One thing she did learn was that time had become her friend. It allowed her to step back and analyze her relationships with men. Those who'd had so little regard for her feelings that they blurted out whatever came to mind. And those who sought something from her whether it was money, or the chance to share in her success. And there were the few that had asked her out while she was awaiting the dissolution of a marriage that no one knew existed except for the parties involved.

All of them wanted something from Francine and she'd included Keaton in that group once he'd revealed that he wanted her for a film. However, when she'd declined his offer he'd accepted her declination without attempting to manipulate her into changing her mind. Perhaps he knew she would never change it and had become more accepting of her decision.

She respected him for not pressuring her to sleep with him. The physical attraction was apparent, yet he'd made it known that the final decision to take their relationship from friend to lover would be hers. Never had she felt as empowered as she did now. It was what she'd sought all of her life: to be able to balance her career with her personal life.

After a busy day at the salon Francine crept silently into the kitchen, smiling when she saw Keaton stirring something in a cast-iron pan on the cooktop. He'd sent her a text saying he'd finished shopping and was on his way to her place. Seeing him moving around the kitchen wearing a bibbed apron, humming along with a song coming from the radio on the countertop was an image she would remember for a long time.

"Something smells delicious."

His head popped up. "I didn't hear you come in." Wiping his hands on a terry-cloth towel tucked into the ties of his apron, Keaton closed the distance between them. Dipping his head, he kissed her cheek. "How was your day at the inimitable Beauty Box?"

"Believe it or not it was one of those magical days when everything fell into place." Her mother was still at home resting her back, so she did double-duty managing the shop and styling hair. "I'm going to go clean up. When I come back I'll set the table." She placed the bouquet of fresh flowers she'd picked up at the florist on a stool at the cooking island. "I'll take care of the flowers later."

Francine retreated to her bedroom, wondering if this was what she could look forward to *if* she'd married Keaton instead of Aiden. Coming home and finding him in the kitchen preparing dinner instead of picking up the telephone and ordering takeout or having to decide which of the many restaurants in their neighborhood they would frequent. Aiden claimed he couldn't cook, but after he was profiled in a soap opera magazine he claimed cooking was one of his hobbies, leading her to believe he'd lied about that, too.

Covering her hair with a large plastic cap, Francine stepped into the shower stall and turned on the water. She adjusted the water temperature, then picked up a bath sponge and a bottle of scented bath gel. This was her favorite time of the day, when she knew the rest of the evening was hers to do whatever she wanted. She would spend time with her grandmother, sit and read, watch television, or just listen to music. Her time was something she'd guarded jealously, not wishing to share it with anyone outside of her family or best friend.

Francine didn't linger in the shower as she normally would have. Patting the droplets of water from her body with a towel, she moisturized her arms and legs with the bath gel's matching scent and slipped into a pair of white, lace-trimmed bikini panties and matching bra. Sitting on the stool at the makeup table in a corner of the bathroom, she applied a light cover of makeup to her face: bronzer, mascara, and lip gloss. Using her fingers, she fluffed up her hair. When Brooke shampooed Francine's hair, she'd applied a solution that left her naturally curly hair in a mass of heavy waves. She'd taken her own advice — advice she told her customers: constant heat from blow-dryers and flat irons damaged hair.

She selected a white silk tailored blouse and a pair of black cropped slacks, pairing them with black leather flats. After checking her reflection in the mirror on the closet door, she walked out of the bedroom.

"What's on the menu?" Francine asked Keaton when she returned to the kitchen. "What?" she questioned when he looked at her as if she were a stranger.

His gaze softened. "You look beautiful."

"Thank you." Francine wanted to tell him that whenever she was with him she felt beautiful, feminine, and desirable. He had that much of an effect on her.

"Come here, baby."

She joined him at the stove. The aromas coming from a pot of red rice with sausage had her practically salivating. "Oh my goodness," she whispered reverently. "That smells incredible." He took off the top to another pot to reveal mustard greens with slivers of smoked meat.

"It's smoked turkey," Keaton said, answering her unsaid question. "I still have to make the cornmeal dumplings." He gestured to an envelope on the countertop. "I want you to look at some printouts and tell me what you think."

Francine glanced at the clock on the microwave. It would be another half hour before the Shaws arrived. "I'm going to set the table first, then I'll look at them."

She busied herself covering the dining room table with a tablecloth, matching napkins, china, and silver with place settings for four. After arranging the snow-white flowers in a crystal vase, she set it on the table as a centerpiece, then stepped back to admire her handiwork. The dining room needed an additional touch.

"Candles!"

"Did you say something?" Keaton asked.

"What do you think if I dim the chandelier and we eat by candlelight?"

Throwing back his head, Keaton roared in laughter. "So you want a romantic candlelit dinner? If you're not careful you'll end up like Morgan."

"Married or pregnant?"

Keaton sobered. "Both."

She shook her head. "That's not possible."

"Why not?"

"Because I don't want to get married."

Keaton gave her a direct stare. "I thought most women wanted to be married."

"I'm not most women."

Crossing his arms over the front of his apron, Keaton angled his head. "What do you want, Francine?"

She knew she had to choose her words

carefully because whatever she said could send Keaton running in the opposite direction. Something she definitely didn't want to happen. "I want a relationship free of commitment."

His eyebrows lifted. "In other words, you don't mind sleeping with a man but you don't want to marry him?"

"Haven't you slept with women you had no intention of marrying?"

"Yes, but —"

"But nothing, Keaton," she interrupted. "Why can't it be the same for a woman?"

"I'm under the impression that you don't sleep around."

"I don't," Francine confirmed. "The last man I slept with was eight years ago."

"But didn't you say you dated six months ago?"

"Dated, Keaton. Not slept with. I've dated men I never slept with."

Keaton came toward Francine in a motion that reminded her of a stalking big cat. "You're afraid of commitment." The query came out like a declaration.

"No, I'm not. I just don't want my life encumbered with a husband."

Keaton's hands came up to cradle her face. "A husband or a man?"

She stared up into large, deep-set eyes the

color of rich, dark coffee. "A husband."

"So you wouldn't be opposed to shacking up."

Her finger went around his strong wrists. "Please don't put words in my mouth, Keaton. I don't believe in shacking up."

"What *do* you believe in?"

"I believe in having a mature physical relationship with a man where I can respect him and vice versa. And it's not about putting pressure on the other to commit. I'm certain you've dealt with women who wanted marriage and children and you didn't."

Keaton slowly lowered his arms. "You're right. I've dealt with a woman who wanted what I wasn't able to give her."

"And that means you should know where I'm coming from?"

"I do."

Keaton knew exactly where Francine was coming from because he'd gone through that very scenario with Jade. What Francine didn't understand was that she wasn't Jade. Francine wasn't a clingy, needy woman craving constant attention in front of and behind the camera lens. She appeared mature beyond her years and secure about her place in the world. It was one of the reasons he was drawn to her, wanted to spend time with her.

Francine had endured a hellish childhood of teasing that no child should've had to endure because she didn't fit into the stereotype as Gullah. And like her ancestors she managed to survive to go on to have an illustrious, short-lived career as a stage actress. Whatever it was that had her returning to her roots, she'd embarked on a second career as a talented hairstylist. Her parents had given her the gift of her own apartment at a young age to foster independence and she'd become just that: an independent woman in control of her own destiny.

"You talk about marriage and children, Keaton. Why are you still a bachelor and fatherless at forty-one?"

Francine's question shattered his reverie. "I would've married if I'd met the right woman."

"Does she exist?"

Attractive slashes creased his jaw when he smiled. "Yes, she does."

"Who is she?"

Keaton knew what he was about to admit would either make or break his fragile friendship with Francine. "I'm looking at her."

Francine's jaw dropped, but no words came out of her mouth. Her eyes were reminiscent of a deer caught in the headlights. A beat passed, the silence shattered when Keaton's cell phone rang. He immediately recognized the ringtone.

"Excuse me, but I have to take this call." Picking up the phone, he entered his passcode. "Hello, Devon."

"Keaton . . . I . . . I have some good news, and as my best friend I want you to be the first to know."

He was surprised to find the normally unflappable attorney stammering. "What is it?"

"I'm pregnant."

It took several seconds for him to process the two words. "Congratulations. Are you happy?" he asked.

"I'm shocked *but* delirious. I didn't plan on becoming pregnant, but I'm quickly getting used to the fact that I'm going to be a mother."

Keaton smiled. "I'm happy for you, Devon."

"Thank you, Keaton. I'm going to hang up now because I need to get home and change because Gregory's flying up from Virginia. He still doesn't know that he's going to be a daddy. I thought it better to tell him in person rather than on the phone."

"Congratulations again and I'll call you in a couple of days to check on you. If you need anything, please remember that I'm always here for you."

"Thanks, Keaton."

He ended the call, turning off the ringer, his smile still in place. He couldn't believe Devon was going to be a mother; the career-oriented entertainment attorney had stated emphatically that she never wanted children because of her own dysfunctional childhood. It was apparent she'd changed her mind because she sounded happy and content. His gaze lingered on Francine as she set out candles on every flat surface in the living room. Taking long strides, Keaton eased the fire starter from her hand. "What were we talking about before Devon called?"

"I don't know," Francine replied.

"You're a horrible liar, darling. Don't you remember me telling you that I'd met my future wife?"

"Why do you sound so serious, Keaton?"

"Because I am. You really don't know just how serious I am."

Francine wanted so much to believe Keaton, but past insecurities had reared their ugly heads, making him suspect. *What do you want from me?* the silent voice in her head screamed. "You're not going anywhere and neither am I. I guess we'll just have to wait and see what happens."

"Who was he, Francine? And what the hell did he do to mess with your head?"

Keaton was asking the same question she'd asked herself over and over, and the only answer she could come up with was she didn't trust men. She wanted an honest relationship with Keaton but she knew that was possible only if she were honest with him.

Taking his hand, she led him over to the window seat. "Please sit down. I have to tell you something." Francine inhaled, held her breath, and then let it out slowly. "I was married, but only my parents, grandmother, and Morgan know that." She felt Keaton's fingers tighten momentarily on hers before he relaxed them. "It was when I lived in New York."

"Who was he?"

She shook her head. "I can't tell you."

"You can't or you won't, Francine?"

"I can't because we'd agreed to never disclose our marriage and divorce. I met him, slept with him on the second date, and married him six weeks later."

"Were you pregnant?"

"No. However, I did believe I was in love with him. I even kept my marriage a secret from my agent. Everything I wanted had fallen into place at the same time. I felt as if I'd climbed Mount Everest because I'd secured a part in a wonderful play that garnered rave reviews the night it premiered, and I was in love for the first time in my life. Then I fell back to earth a week after *Sisters* closed and my two-faced husband told me he'd fallen in love with someone else and wanted a quickie divorce so he could marry her. It was then that I realized he'd been using me all along. Once he uncovered I was Frank Tanner's daughter, he believed he'd hit the mother lode. It wasn't until we sat across the table from each other in my lawyer's office that it was his turn to be blindsided. The slug thought I had a lot of money, when it was my father who was supporting me. Daddy paid the rent on my brownstone apartment and sent me spending money. I may not have fit the stereotype of the struggling actress but I still had to rely on my father for support.

"I dated a few guys while I waited for my divorce to be finalized and discovered they'd asked me out because they either recognized my name and face from my performances or my father's fame. But this time I wasn't as gullible. My internal radar was on full alert and I realized they weren't taking me out because they liked me. They —"

"They wanted to use you," Keaton said, finishing her statement.

"Yes. So now you know the whole sordid story of my life in the Big Apple."

Releasing her hand, Keaton placed an arm around her shoulders. "You can't blame every man for what your ex did to you. The world is full of users lying in wait to take advantage of someone. But you know what they say about karma. What goes around comes around. He'll get his."

"I really don't care if he does or doesn't. What's important is that he's out of my life."

"If you really believe that then don't you think it's time for you to move on?"

"I have."

"I don't think so, Francine, because I've never had to work this hard to get as close to a woman as I have with you."

Shifting slightly, she moved over and sat on his lap, her arms going around his neck. "Would you like me as much if I were easy?"

Keaton stared at her mouth, only inches from his own. "Hell no."

"What you have to figure out is if I'm worth all of your hard work."

"I've already figured that out. You are

more than worth it."

Francine knew the day of reckoning couldn't be put off any longer. Fate was offering her a second chance for love and happiness with Keaton and she planned to grasp it before it flitted away. A deep feeling of peace swept over her as she pressed her lips to his, swallowing his breath.

"How about a do-over?"

"Do-over?"

Francine suppressed a giggle. "Let's pretend we're meeting for the first time."

A smile ruffled Keaton's mouth. "Okay. Ladies first."

"Hello, stranger," she whispered, her voice dropping an octave. "I'm Francine Tanner. Welcome to Cavanaugh Island's Magnolia Drive."

"It's a pleasure to meet you, Miss Tanner. I'm Keaton Grace, and because I'm new in town would it be possible for you to show me around?"

"I'd love to, Mr. Grace, but you'll have to call and let me know when you're ready."

"I'm always ready."

Francine schooled her expression not to react to the increasing hardness under her hips. Apparently her sitting on Keaton's lap had aroused him. He was ready to make love to her and she was more than ready to share her body with him.

"I think I'd better get off your lap before I forget we're having guests for dinner."

Keaton stood, bringing Francine up with him. "To be continued."

Chapter Fourteen

When she opened the refrigerator and saw shelves with a large covered glass bowl of endive and arugula salad, a tray of deviled eggs, a cheese platter with an assortment of fruit, and a bowl of cooked shrimp with what appeared to be cocktail sauce Francine wondered what time Keaton had come over to begin cooking. There were also bottles of wine on a lower shelf: white and rosé. She closed the door, and then walked over to peer through the glass of the double oven. Keaton had chosen game hens.

"When did you start cooking?"

"I got here around three."

Francine walked over to stand next to him. "You did all of this in a couple of hours?"

He gave her a smile parents usually reserve for their children. "It's all in the preparation. I put up the eggs to boil right after soaking the greens in cold water. Then I seasoned the game hens, washed and dried the salad leaves, and made the cocktail sauce while the eggs were cooling. The shrimp I bought from the supermarket deli, so that eliminated shelling, deveining, and cooking them. I cut up the cheese just before you walked in."

"It would probably take me all day just to make the appetizers."

"I doubt that, sweetie. Are you up to making the berry fizz?"

Her expression brightened like a child on Christmas Day who'd gotten everything on her wish list. "Yes!"

Keaton took off his apron and put it over her blouse, adjusting the length and looping the ties twice around her waist. He'd become the instructor and she the student when she did exactly as he'd asked. She smiled.

Francine stirred the concoction in a large pitcher filled with crushed ice with a wooden spoon. She poured a small amount in a glass, extending it to Keaton. "Tell me if I passed or failed." She watched his Adam's apple as he swallowed the berry-infused carbonated beverage with a hint of mint. "Well, Keaton?"

His impassive expression changed when he gave her a thumbs-up. "Perfect."

Buoyed by his compliment, Francine filled another glass and sampled her first attempt at making the chilled, refreshing drink. "You're right. That is good."

Keaton kissed her hair. "From now on you'll be responsible for making the drinks."

"Drink or drinks?"

"Drinks," he insisted. "I'm going to teach you how to make a peach sangria and a Bellini. They're a wonderful alternative to mimosas when serving brunch."

Francine wanted to remind Keaton that she wasn't much of a drinker, yet that wouldn't preclude her from making the cocktail for those who did drink. The soft chiming of a bell echoed throughout the apartment. "That must be Morgan and Nate."

She crossed the kitchen, making her way down the staircase to open the door for her friends. Morgan reminded her of a little girl with the leopard-print velvet headband holding her hair off her face. Nate stood behind his wife carrying a wooden crate filled with bottles of wine.

Francine and Morgan exchanged air kisses. "Come on up." She pressed her cheek to Nate's smooth one. "Welcome."

"Thank you again for inviting us."

Closing and locking the outer door, Francine waited for Morgan and Nate to climb the staircase, then followed close behind. Keaton met them in the entryway, taking the crate from Nate. Francine made the introductions, the two men exchanging handshakes and a rough embrace.

Keaton patted Nate's shoulder. "Thanks for the wine."

"You're welcome." A slight frown appeared between Nate's light brown eyes. "Why does your name sound familiar to me?"

Morgan slipped out of her high-heel, leopard-print booties, leaving them on the mat outside the door. "Keaton's a filmmaker."

"That's it!" Nate said excitedly. "I worked on a set for one of your films when I lived in L.A."

Francine's eyelids fluttered wildly. She couldn't believe how many connections Keaton had on Cavanaugh Island. Morgan had told her about the twenty years Nate had spent living on the West Coast. He'd worked building homes for a developer and after the collapse of the housing market he was employed as a carpenter building movie sets.

Keaton, appearing as shocked as Francine,

recovered quickly. "Wow. Talk about a small world."

Francine looped her arm through Morgan's, escorting her into the living room. "It keeps getting weirder," she whispered as they sank down on a love seat.

"This place looks fantastic. You should entertain more often. And what do you mean by weirder?" Morgan asked, her gaze following her husband as he and Keaton entered the kitchen together.

"What are the odds of Keaton moving to a Sea Island where he recognizes me from an off-Broadway play? Then I find out my father used to eat at his father's restaurant when he played for the Steelers. Now it's Nate. Who or what's next?"

"I don't know, Francine. You're the psychic. What do you see?"

"None of my visions are about Keaton. I can't believe I'm sitting here running off at the mouth and you probably need something to eat."

Morgan pressed a hand to her belly under a white poet blouse. "I'm always eating. What I'm trying to do is eat healthfully."

"Wait here and I'll bring you something to snack on until we sit down to eat."

Francine couldn't believe her first official dinner party was nothing short of perfection. Nate and Morgan raved about the appetizers and then dinner. Morgan ate slowly, savoring the mustard greens she'd been craving with fluffy cornmeal dumplings, red rice and sausage, and juicy, tender roasted hens. Keaton had added slivers of red onion, julienned carrots, grape tomatoes, and feta cheese to the endive and arugula, tossing them with a Greek-inspired vinaigrette. Morgan drank berry fizz, while Francine downed one glass of rosé.

Morgan dabbed her mouth with a napkin. "Nate and I will have to decline your offer to spend a couple of days with you, because earlier today I got a call from the wife of one of my former professors at the Savannah College of Art and Design. He decided to retire and she's hosting a surprise retirement/birthday party for him this coming weekend. Some of my classmates are meeting before the soiree, so Nate and I plan to drive up to Savannah tomorrow. I'm sorry to give you such short notice but —"

"Please don't apologize, Mo," Francine said. "There will be plenty of time for a grown folk sleepover before your addition is completed."

Nate leaned back in his chair. He'd removed his jacket and tie and unbuttoned the top button on his white shirt. "Keaton and I have some catching up to do. We probably know some of the same people from when we lived in Cali."

Keaton stared directly at Francine. "Some which I'd like to forget."

"Same here, brother," Nate drawled, extending his arm for a fist bump. "I know you told me about the renovations on the old Webber place. If you don't mind, I'd like to go by and take a look at it."

Crossing his arms over his chest, Keaton angled his head. "I'd like that. Just let me know when and we'll go together. What I'd really like to see is the Angels Landing restoration. I was floored when I saw the rendering at your wife's office."

Francine and Morgan exchanged a knowing look. It was apparent Keaton had found a buddy in Nate. She knew that since Nate's return he'd spent most of his time filling furniture orders for Shaw & Sons Woodworking, Inc., and working with a crew to add the second story to the house Morgan had inherited from her grandfather.

Nate sat up straight. "Once it's fully restored it will be a landmark masterpiece with the main house, gardens, and outbuildings."

"I agree," Morgan concurred. "Kara Hamilton is the sheriff's wife. She owns the property and I'm certain she would be willing to let you use Angels Landing Plantation for a set if you decide to do a period piece. As an architectural historian I loved the fact that Roland Emmerich, the director of *The Patriot,* used Middleton Place in the film."

Reaching for his wineglass, Keaton gave Francine a long, penetrating stare. "Francine has suggested I write a period piece."

"That's because my *bestest* friend is a history buff," Morgan teased. "She eats, breathes, and lives for historical dramas. There were a few occasions when I wanted her to go somewhere with me but she turned me down because she didn't want to miss her favorite cable program."

"What about DVR?" Keaton asked.

Francine gave him her death stare. "I rarely tape a show."

The topic of conversation segued from television and movies to the upcoming mayoral election, and finally sports. That's when Francine stood up to clear the table, Morgan joining her as the two men launched into a debate, becoming sports analysts when discussing the recent Super Bowl. They didn't seem to notice when she and Morgan retreated to the kitchen.

"I think my husband finally has someone

to bond with," Morgan whispered, as she scraped, rinsed, and stacked plates in the dishwasher.

Francine smiled. "All you have to do is mention sports and men who are complete strangers suddenly become best friends."

"You like him, don't you, Fran?"

"What's not to like?"

"That's not what I asked you. How well do you like him, Francine Dinah Tanner?"

She cut her eyes at Morgan. "There's no need to blurt out my government name, Mrs. Shaw. I like him a lot." Filling the sink with soap and hot water, Francine gently placed the crystal stemware into the soapy solution.

"Enough to give him *some*?"

"Morgan!"

"Stop blushing. Do you remember when you asked me the same question when I started going out with Nate?"

"Yes. When I asked you there was no one around to overhear us." Francine walked over to the radio and raised the volume enough so Keaton and Nate wouldn't be able to hear their conversation. She opened the refrigerator door for Morgan. "Yes. Enough to give him some."

Morgan's dimples deepened. "Good for you. It's about time you got that monkey named Aiden off your back."

Francine had to agree with her friend. Telling Keaton about her failed marriage was akin to sucking in a lungful of oxygen after being trapped in a room filled with noxious gas. She hadn't realized she'd been waiting for a man like Keaton to come into her life until their first night on the beach. She felt as if she'd known him for years instead of days.

"I told Keaton about him without mentioning his name or that he's an actor."

Morgan hugged her. "Good for you. Keaton is the whole package. He has a good face, he's not a player, and he cooks well enough to give any woman an orgasm."

Francine laughed at Morgan's assessment of Keaton. He was good for her. So good that she knew she was more than ready for the next chapter in her life. A shadow fell over her and her head popped up. "Yes, Keaton?"

He pointed to the sink. "I would've done that."

"It's all right. You cooked, so I don't mind cleaning."

Keaton clapped his hands. "Ladies, I want you out of my kitchen pronto."

Francine and Morgan executed a snappy salute as if they'd rehearsed it. "Yes, sir,"

Francine drawled.

"Aye, aye, sir," Morgan added.

"Oh, that's how you get women to obey you," Nate drawled, as he strolled into the kitchen."

"Obey!" Morgan and Francine chorused.

Keaton put up his hands. "I'm not touching that one."

Morgan poked a finger into Nate's ribs. "You'll pay for that once I get you home."

"Run, Nate! Run!" Keaton said, laughing loudly.

Nate gave Keaton a rough hug, pounding his back. "It's been good, Grace. We have to do this again. Next time it's at our place."

"I'm looking forward to it."

Nate extended his arms to Francine. "Red, thanks for inviting us."

She walked into his embrace. "Anytime. I know you're busy, but you know you and Mo don't have to wait for an invitation. And thanks again for the wine."

Francine and Keaton walked with the Shaws as they descended the stairs, waiting with arms around each other's waists as they drove off. She leaned into his tall frame. "Thank you, Keaton."

"For what?"

She smiled up at him. "For making tonight very, very special."

"It doesn't have to end now."

"I don't want it to end."

His expression changed, becoming serious. "You know what this means, don't you?" Francine nodded. "It's got to be all or nothing. The choice is yours."

Francine took a step, pressing her breasts to his chest, knowing she could no longer deny his touch, his kisses. "All."

Keaton cradled her face. "I want you to go upstairs and pack an overnight bag."

"Where are we going?"

"Do you trust me, Francine?"

"Yes, I do, but I'd like to know where you're taking me. And don't forget I have to work tomorrow."

He kissed the bridge of her nose. "I know you have to work. Please, baby, go upstairs and pack. I'll be back in less than half an hour to pick you up."

Francine normally didn't like surprises yet she'd told Keaton she trusted him. "Okay. I'll be ready by the time you get back."

Driving slowly toward the Cove Inn, Keaton knew what he'd planned for himself and Francine would impact their lives. It would become the opening act to a play yet to be written. It would be a one-act production with two characters and no intermission or closing act.

He didn't view sleeping with Francine as a conquest or triumph. Quite the contrary. Keaton saw it as a connection with a woman who in the span of a very short time had gotten to know him better than any woman from his past. He knew it was impossible, yet he felt as if she could read his mind. She would say something and it was like activating sensors in his brain where images appeared and he felt compelled to jot down what he saw.

Keaton knew he had to rewire his brain to come up with a concept for a period piece because the essence of the Gullah culture was steeped in history — a history filled with pain and untold stories of survival against the greatest odds. He'd spent countless hours reading and researching Gullah history and culture online, eliciting scenes that would become a part of his script. His ability to write scripts that translated well to film came from a talent for character development. Keaton thought of dialogue as words on a page until the actor understood his character well enough to make it believable to everyone watching the actor. It'd been that way when he watched Francine's performance in the off-Broadway play.

Francine's portrayal of Abigail had everyone in the theater riveted to their seats each time she took the stage. Not only could he hear her anguish when she pleaded for acceptance from her half sisters, it had become palpable. When she offered to give them enough money to allow them to move out of public housing and they'd torn up the checks, throwing the pieces in her face, the image of the silent tears rolling down Francine's face elicited sobbing from theatergoers, and Keaton was no exception. He'd felt her character's pain.

Fast-forward nearly a decade and although Francine looked the same he knew she wasn't. A marriage founded on deceit and avarice had made her wary of marriage and relationships, and Keaton suspected she'd been married to someone in the business, otherwise she would've disclosed his name.

He slowed when entering the Cove's downtown business district. All of the shops were closed and as he passed Jack's Fish House he saw they'd dimmed their lights. Many of the benches in the town square were unoccupied, unlike on weekends when scores of high school students gathered there. He'd overheard the boardinghouse staff talk about the number of teenagers from the mainland who came to the island to meet at the fountain in the square before going down to the beach. Sheriff Hamilton and his deputies kept up regular patrols in and around the Cove to limit underage drinking and drug use.

When he maneuvered into a parking space behind the Cove Inn, Keaton thought about the tarot card reader's prediction. He had moved, taken the steps to control his career, and tonight he'd unconsciously let go of his past so he could have a normal relationship with a woman. He knew Francine would never agree to living with him, and that meant he had only one option: continue to date her without committing to a future.

Keaton loved Francine, wanted to marry her, but he was afraid of getting his hopes up since she was so clearly against marriage. There were occasions when she appeared so indifferent he doubted whether she actually wanted to date him. Then she would literally and figuratively flip the script when he believed her feelings for him went beyond liking. She was an enigma, a chameleon, changing in front of his eyes, or was she a more adept actress than what she'd projected onstage?

The questions continued to taunt Keaton as he swiped his keycard in the slot at the boardinghouse's rear door. He mounted the staircase without encountering anyone. His steps slowed when he saw an envelope taped to the door to his suite. He'd just removed it when the door across the hall opened.

"The editor of the newspaper left that for you."

Keaton smiled at the elderly woman with blue hair and close-set brown eyes that'd made it her responsibility to monitor his comings and goings. The night he'd stayed over at Francine's Mrs. Benjamin had announced to those sitting around the breakfast table that he hadn't come back to his room the night before. He'd been tempted to ask her if she had X-ray vision or if she sat by her door listening for his footsteps. If he hadn't been raised to respect his elders Keaton definitely would've told her what he did was none of her business.

"Thank you, Mrs. Benjamin."

"Do you know what he wants, Mr. Grace?"

Turning his back, he rolled his eyes upward. "No, I don't, Mrs. Benjamin."

"Aren't you going to read it?"

"Harriet, close that door and leave that young man alone!"

Keaton smiled. Mrs. Benjamin's husband had caught her snooping again. *Thank you,* he mused as he swiped his keycard, opening and closing the door and shutting out the image of his meddlesome neighbor.

It took him several seconds to read the note from the editor of the *Sanctuary Chronicle.* Eddie Wilkes wanted to interview him about his proposed movie studio. He tossed the note on the table doubling as his desk. His reply to Eddie would have to wait. Opening the closet, Keaton took out a bag, filling it with underwear, T-shirts, jeans, sweats, and a leather case filled with toiletries.

Picking up the house phone, he dialed information, asking the operator to connect him to an inn on King Street, and when he was connected, he made a room reservation for Mr. and Mrs. Keaton Grace. Keaton had decided against spending the night at the Charleston Place Hotel, where he was on a first-name basis with the hotel staff. Staying at the historical residences that were converted into boutique hotels was more private and intimate.

Francine was ready when he drove up; he took her bag and stored it with his behind the rear seats, then assisted her up into the SUV. Her Corvette was nowhere to be seen, and he surmised she'd parked it in one of the three garages. She handed him his cell phone, which he'd left at her apartment.

He slipped behind the wheel beside her.

"Are you ready?"

Francine flashed a bright smile, scrunching up her nose. "Are *you* ready?"

Keaton slumped back in his seat. "Oh, it's like that."

"Aye, milord," she drawled, slipping into the character he'd come to look for.

He drove away from the house, grinning from ear to ear. "I know it sounds clichéd, but with you I was born ready."

Chapter Fifteen

Francine waited for Keaton to unlock the door to the suite before stepping inside. "I decided on this place because of its history. It belonged to former plantation owners," he added when she smiled at him.

"It's charming, Keaton."

When she saw the king-size, four-poster bed with a crocheted canopy, some of the bravado she'd exhibited back in the Cove had dissipated. It wouldn't be the first time she and Keaton would sleep together but she had a feeling it would be the first time she made love.

She knew he'd called ahead because there were lighted candles lining a buffet and dining room table. The scent from a vase of blood-red roses permeated the living/dining and kitchen areas.

"I'm going to check out the bathroom," she told Keaton as he turned and walked back to the bedroom.

"Okay."

She entered the bathroom and again there were more candles, along with an assortment of bath gels and salts lining the shelf above a sunken tub with a Jacuzzi. Turning on the faucet, she emptied a capful of foaming gel under the running water. Within seconds the spell of lavender wafted to her nose.

Francine returned to the bedroom where she found Keaton sprawled on the bed watching television. "I'm going to take a bath."

He sat up. "Would you like some company?"

She hesitated. She'd never shared a bath with a man. "It's lavender bubble bath."

Keaton swung his legs over the side of the bed. "I don't care, because I'm going to enjoy washing every inch of your gorgeous body."

Francine opened her bag, which Keaton had placed on a luggage rack, and removed her cosmetic case and a bathrobe. She hadn't brought any birth control, so she was going to rely on Keaton to protect her. Suddenly it hit her! Why did sleeping with Keaton appear to be scripted?

It was as if she were playing a role in a daytime drama and the writers had agreed it was time for one of their lead couples to sleep together. But she had to push those thoughts aside. Francine knew she never would've agreed to permit Keaton to make love to her if she hadn't had feelings for him. At first she thought it was because of the recurring erotic dreams that had left her shaken, while craving the feel of a man's hands on her body. But then something inside her changed once she realized he hadn't put any pressure on her to sleep with him. He'd come to her in the middle of the night, lain beside her, and all the while hadn't made an overture to seduce her.

The thought that perhaps he was gay never crossed her mind. She'd dealt with enough actors on and off the stage to identify a man who preferred a same-sex relationship. There were some with whom she'd even had love scenes, knowing in the back of her mind that they were only acting.

Whatever inhibitions she may have had vanished when rehearsing scenes that called for her to be partially clothed or completely nude under a sheet or blanket. Her instructors had shown Francine the proper technique for kissing a man, and how to use her body to convey without words the extent of her desire for her partner. The first time she'd had a kissing scene she was nauseated because the actor had sought to put his tongue down her throat. When he continued and she finally gagged she'd slapped him so hard there was stunned silence in the theater. The director was so impressed with her rage he decided to change the scene to include her slapping the man who attempted to force her to sleep with him. Then he directed her how to slap another actor without causing injury.

Her feelings for Keaton grew deeper because of respect and the realization he was a protector of women. He'd stayed in L.A. longer than he'd planned to help his sister resolve her volatile situation. And now it was his attorney who'd called him. Francine hadn't wanted to eavesdrop on his conversation but he hadn't attempted to walk away. She'd felt her heart turn over when he'd told Devon, "Remember that I'm here for you." In that instant she knew Keaton was a keeper.

She gave him a sensual smile. "I'll see you inside."

Francine brushed her teeth, following up with a peppermint mouthwash. Stripping off her clothes, she left them on a chair and stepped into the warm bubbles, which floated up and tickled her nose. She'd rested her head on a bath pillow, luxuriating in the pulsing waters, and closed her eyes when she heard Keaton moving around the bathroom. He'd turned on the radio and the familiar voice of Faith Hill singing "Back to You" filled the bathroom.

All of Francine's senses were heightened when she heard him brushing his teeth, and then gargling. She opened her eyes, sitting up straighter. Keaton had placed a low table next to the tub and she tried not to gawk at his nude body in the flickering candlelight. He moved out of her line of sight and then returned, carrying two flutes of a sparkling liquid and setting them on the table. It was apparent he'd raided the minibar. Her eyes widened when he stepped into the tub, his semierect penis swaying heavily between muscled thighs. His eyes met hers and she was certain he could see the rapidly beating pulse in her throat as he lowered his body, sitting opposite her. There was a dusting of hair on his chest and a tattoo covering his entire right shoulder.

"Is it too hot for you?" she asked. Francine said the first thing that came to mind.

Keaton stared at her under lowered lids. "No. It's perfect. Just like you." Reaching for a flute, he handed one to her, then took the remaining one. His eyes never left hers when he touched his glass to hers. "Here's to being all in."

She blinked once. "All in," she repeated, then took a sip. Francine replaced the flute on the table and sank lower, until the bubbles concealed the tops of her breasts. She watched Keaton drain his glass. He moved closer, and without warning anchored his hands under her shoulders, shifting her effortlessly until she sat between his outstretched legs.

"This is better," he whispered in her ear.

Francine lay with her back against his solid chest, his arms around her waist, unable to believe she felt so comfortable with a man she'd known only a few weeks. She knew he made films, his parents were chefs, his sister was undergoing a divorce, and his lawyer was pregnant. He'd admitted not having married or fathered any children, but he'd never spoken of the women in his past. Was there one he'd loved unconditionally and she'd not returned his love? Or was he incapable of loving?

"You're not drinking your sparkling cider. I ordered it because you said you're not much of a drinker."

Keaton's voice broke into her musings. Reaching for the flute, she took another sip. "I really appreciate that. I'm certain you don't want to make love to a drunk woman."

He chuckled softly. "No, I don't."

"There was a time when Cavanaugh Island had quite a few drunks. Kids in school used to whisper about their fathers sneaking off to buy moonshine from an illegal still that had been set up in the Creek. Some would be so tanked up they'd never make it home and when they did their wives forced them to sleep outdoors because they didn't want their children seeing their daddies in that condition."

"Do they still sell moonshine?"

"No. Someone decided to snitch and agents from the ATF came over from Columbia, destroyed the still, and arrested the family operating the illegal enterprise."

"How long ago did this happen?"

"It was during my first year in high school. The bad thing about living in a small town is that nothing is sacred. If a man is cheating, then it's only a matter of time before his wife will find out. If she doesn't discover his indiscretion on her own, then someone would be sure to let the cat out of the bag. Some women seek out root workers to either stop their husband's philandering or chase away the other woman."

"That's unbelievable."

Peering up over her shoulder, Francine

tried reading Keaton's expression in the flickering candlelight. "Not to the Gullah. Prominent among the culture is the belief in herbalism, spiritualism, and black magic."

Keaton brushed his mouth over the nape of her neck. She gasped when his hands covered her breasts, gently kneading them until her nipples were hard as pebbles.

He kissed her again. "Tell me about it tomorrow because I don't want to end up with nightmares tonight after talking about spooks and mojo."

Francine managed to slip out of his loose embrace and straddled him. She touched her mouth to the tattoo on his shoulder. It was Melpomene and Thalia: the masks depicting tragedy and comedy.

"Will you wash my back?"

"Is that all you want me to wash?"

She kissed Keaton under his ear. "Use your imagination."

Francine closed her eyes, reveling in the magic of her soon-to-be lover's hands on her mouth, throat, and breasts. The water cooled, the bubbles disappeared, and Keaton turned off the jets swirling the water around their writhing bodies, then opened the drain for the tub to empty out.

Her mouth was just as busy as she caught Keaton's earlobe between her teeth, worrying it and eliciting gasps from him. They'd become sculptors, fingers stroking muscle, sinew, curves, dips, and her sex. Francine closed her knees, sandwiching Keaton's hand between her thighs.

"Don't baby," he whispered. "Please let me touch you."

Her knees slowly parted as if pulled apart by an invisible wire, and she inhaled as his finger gently stroked the swollen flesh at the apex of her thighs. The sensations she'd dreamed about came back, and this time it was no fantasy. It was very real.

Keaton stared directly at Francine, watching a myriad of emotions cross her features as he continued to slowly caress her clitoris. She was beautiful, magnificent. The darkening of her eyes, heightened color in her face, and skin stretched taut over her high cheekbones revealed her rising passion. Resting his forehead on hers, he kissed her with all of the passion that was coursing throughout his body. He devoured her mouth as if he'd been denied food for days. He increased the pressure until her lips parted, permitting him the access he sought when his tongue touched hers.

He'd never related to other women as he had to Francine. With her he could be himself. She was beautiful, charming, seductive, sexy, witty, and she made him laugh. In the past he'd taken himself and life much too seriously. Before relocating to Cavanaugh Island he'd spent more time alone than with people, writing and revising scripts.

Living in the Lowcountry had changed him — for the better. He'd learned to kick back and relax. He now took time to enjoy the sunrise and sunset. Seeing Francine and walking the beach had become the highlights of his day. Keaton had watched her interaction with Morgan. Their closeness was more than obvious when he saw them in the kitchen together giggling like teenage girls. Her demeanor at the dinner table was less effusive, more reserved, and several times he'd caught her staring off into space. Initially he thought her bored or that her mind had drifted but within seconds she picked up on the conversation as if she hadn't missed a word.

Combing his fingers through her curling hair, he held it off her face. "You are so beautiful," he whispered reverently. "Everywhere."

Francine lowered her eyes, unaware of the effect of the demure gesture on Keaton. "Whenever I'm with you I feel beautiful."

"You're beautiful all the time, Francine. You're even beautiful when you're sleeping, awake, bumping, blowing, and cutting hair at the Beauty Box."

She affected a sexy moue. "You were watching me sleep?"

He nodded. "Sleeping Beauty has nothing on you. You're much sexier."

"Stop, Keaton, before you give me a big head."

"No, sweetie. Right now I'm the one with the big head." As if to verify what he'd just disclosed, he reached between his thighs and rubbed his swollen penis against her mound. "You don't have to be afraid."

A slight frown appeared between Francine's eyes. "I'm not afraid, Keaton."

"I'm not talking about hurting you physically," he said correcting himself. "What I don't want is to hurt you the way your ex-husband did. I love you too much to do that. I don't know what's going to happen between us, but I'm willing to wait and see where it leads."

"I don't either," Francine whispered, "but you have to know that I love you, too."

Keaton lingered in the tub longer than he'd planned. Releasing Francine, he stood up and stepped out of the tub, and reached for a nearby bath sheet. His gaze met and fused with hers as he dried his body. He picked up another bath sheet, holding it out when she stood and stepped out. Slowly, gently, he blotted the moisture from her face, chest, arms, and legs. Her thighs trembled slightly when he drew the terry-cloth fabric between her legs.

Tossing the towels in the tub, Keaton bent slightly, scooping Francine up in his arms. Her hands went around his neck at the same time she rested her head on his shoulder. It wasn't until he placed her on the crisp sheets, his body following hers, that it finally hit Keaton that he'd waited more than eight years for this moment. When he'd walked into the small theater that seated fewer than three hundred theatergoers and he saw Francine Tanner walk onto the stage, he hadn't known their lives would be inexorably linked. He'd gone back again to see her perform and would've gone back to see every performance if his schedule and wallet had permitted it.

Reaching under a pillow, Keaton held a condom between his thumb and forefinger, smiling when Francine nodded her approval. Her gaze was fixated on his hands when he opened the packet and slipped the latex sheath over his erection.

"You can breathe now, sweetie." Francine

had held her breath while he'd put on the condom, and he suspected she'd been apprehensive about a possible unplanned pregnancy.

His hand splayed over her cheek, his fingers entwining the curls framing her face. Keaton's head came down slowly, inch by inch, until his mouth hovered over hers, capturing her breath as she exhaled.

Angling for a better position, he slanted his mouth over hers, slowly increasing the pressure until her lips parted slightly. Feeling the tension in her limbs, he knew he had to go slowly. Her mouth opened wider and it was what he needed to stake his claim, his tongue meeting hers in a heated joining that raced through his body like the rush of molten lava.

The heat from Keaton's mouth swept from Francine's mouth to her core. Waves of passion shook her until she could not stop her legs from shaking. He suckled her breasts, worshipping them, and the moans she sought to suppress escaped her parted lips.

His tongue circled her nipples, leaving them hard, erect, and throbbing painfully. His teeth tightened on the turgid tips, and she felt a violent spasm grip her womb. Her fingers were entwined in the cotton sheet, tightening and ripping them from their fastenings at the same time she arched up off the mattress.

"Keaton!"

His name was torn from the back of her throat as he inched his way down her body and held her hips to still their thrashing. Francine dissolved into a maelstrom of ecstasy when he buried his face between her legs. His hot breath seared the tangled curls between her thighs and she went limp, unable to move, unable to protest or think of anything except the pleasure her lover offered her.

Francine registered a series of breathless sighs, unaware they were her own moans of sexual satisfaction. Eyes closed, head thrown back, lips parted, back arched, she drowned in the sensations taking her beyond herself and any passion she'd ever experienced. Then it began, rippling little tremors increasing and shaking her uncontrollably and becoming more explosive when they sought escape.

Keaton heard her breath come in long, surrendering moans. He moved quickly up her trembling limbs and eased his erection into her body. He was met with resistance. How had he forgotten that it'd been years since she'd slept with a man? Knowing she had waited filled Keaton with immeasurable pride, and he prayed he would never do anything to make her regret her decision to permit him to make love to her. Gritting his teeth, he drew back and with a strong, sure thrust of his hips, buried his sex in the hot, moist, tight flesh pulsing around his.

Sliding his hands under her hips, Keaton lifted her higher, permitting him deeper penetration, then quickened his movements. Francine assisted him when she wound her legs around his waist. There was only the sound of their labored breathing as both strained, tendons bulging in their necks, to get even closer. Then without warning, like lightning streaking across a summer sky, their passions peaked simultaneously, moans and groans harmonizing in a cacophony of explosive ecstasy.

He held back, refusing to ejaculate because he didn't want it to end. He'd waited much too long to make love to Francine to have it end now. He reversed their position, bringing Francine with him until she lay sprawled over his body. Pushing into a sitting position, he caressed her damp back and trailed kisses along the column of her perfumed neck. "Are you okay, sweetie?"

"I'm more than okay. I'm wonderful,"

Francine drawled, placing soft kisses on his throat and shoulder.

"I —"

She stopped his words when she placed her fingertips over his mouth. "Please don't say anything, darling."

Keaton realized Francine was one of those women who didn't like to talk when making love, while he wanted to tell her how much he wanted and needed her in his life. His right hand moved over her bare hip, caressing the silken flesh. He drew in a deep breath, luxuriating in the intoxicating fragrance of the lavender mingling with the lingering scent of their lovemaking.

His eyes went to her breasts when she braced her hands against the headboard on either side of his head. They shared a smile as Francine began to move again, grinding her hips against his erection in a slow, measured rhythm. Up and down. Around and around. Cupping her hips, Keaton let her set the cadence as he visually feasted on the motion of her firm bouncing breasts, the rush of color suffusing her face and chest, the sound of her labored breathing as her passions rose higher and higher.

Lowering her head, Francine lightly touched her lips to Keaton's, the tip of her tongue tracing the outline of his full, sensuous lower lip. Her body told him what her lips couldn't: She loved him. She loved Keaton more than she'd ever believed possible for her to love a man, and sharing her body with him wasn't enough. She wanted more, as in sharing a future with him. She closed her eyes against his intense stare, gritting her teeth when she felt the familiar flutters of her impending climax. She squeezed her thighs together to stop the pulsing, but it continued.

"No, Keaton!" His hands held her waist as he moved her up and down the length of his manhood. "Please let me go."

"I can't, baby. It feels so good."

Francine wanted to tell him it was better than good. "Love me, Keaton. Please love me," she chanted over and over until it became a litany. She closed her eyes, gasping at the sweet agony tearing her asunder. It eased slightly before she was hurled higher, climaxing, her orgasms overlapping one another until she collapsed on Keaton, while struggling to catch her breath. She sighed when his deep moans of satisfaction reverberated throughout the bedroom. They lay together, joined, losing track of time. She emitted a small cry of protest when he changed their position again, pulling out of her warmth. "I have to get rid of the condom," he said in her ear.

Moving off the bed, Keaton pulled the sheet and lightweight blanket over her naked body. He'd paused for several seconds to stare at the sexy curve of her hips and incredibly long legs as twin emotions of pride and awe swept over him. He'd spent years fantasizing about Francine, never believing the fantasy would become a reality.

He walked into the bathroom, discarding the condom and extinguishing the candles. Francine was snoring softly when he joined her in bed. Pulling her close to his chest, Keaton buried his face in her hair, and minutes later fell into a deep, dreamless sleep.

Francine opened her eyes. The warm body pressed against hers and the overhead canopy reminded her that she wasn't in her own bedroom. Heat followed by a chill gripped her as the images of two hands, one atop the other, flashed into her head. The darker hand belonged to a man and the smaller one to a woman. At first she thought the hands belonged to her and Keaton, but she'd glimpsed the glint of a ring on one of the man's fingers, and the woman's fingers were not quite as fair in coloring as hers. Who, she thought, did the hands belong to?

She turned her head, meeting Keaton's eyes. It was apparent he'd awakened before she had. "Good morning." The numbers on the clock on the bedside table read 5:40.

Shifting onto his left side, he swept her mussed hair off her cheek. "Good morning. How do you feel?"

Francine knew he was asking about the area between her legs. "It's a little sore, but I should be all right in a couple of days. Were you hoping for seconds this morning?"

His gaze went to her mouth as he twisted a curl around his finger. "No. All you have to do is show up at the salon walking as if on eggshells and everyone will know what you were doing."

She rested her hand along his jaw, grazing the emerging stubble with a fingernail. It was as if she were seeing Keaton for the first time, although she'd shaved him twice. The skin on his face was soft and firm to the touch, his thick, dark eyebrows silky and his eyes — his eyes appeared to see inside her to uncover her true feelings for him. Francine had openly admitted to Keaton and Morgan that she liked him. But if she were truly honest she would've told them she was falling in love. It'd begun so quietly, without fanfare, that she wasn't aware of it until she'd agreed to make love with Keaton.

He was everything the men of her past wouldn't or couldn't be. First, he hadn't pressured her to sleep with him — something she'd encountered much too often, and because he was obviously solvent he didn't need her to support him.

"They can surmise what I've been doing, but I doubt if they'll be able to prove it, especially if some of the more inquisitive ones in the Magnolias don't see your truck parked outside my house all night."

"There *were* a couple of nights when I *did* park outside your home."

A slight frown appeared between her eyes. "I forgot about that."

"I didn't. That's why we're here instead of in the Cove."

"Listen to you," Francine crooned. "You sound like us locals who shorten the names of our towns to the Cove, the Landing, and the Creek."

Keaton nuzzled her neck. "I am a local, or I will be when I move into my house."

"As long as you don't forget to register as soon as you can so you can vote in the next local election. As a supporter of Alice Parker's candidacy I have an invitation to attend a Valentine's Day fund-raiser at her home. I'd like you to be my plus one."

"Are you asking me out?"

"Yes, I am."

"Okay. I'm honored you asked me to be your plus one." Rolling over on his back, Keaton stared up at the ceiling. "I notice folks on the island take their elections quite seriously."

Francine assumed a similar position. "You just don't know the half." She told him about Alice Parker challenging the incumbent and how townspeople had taken sides. Those loyal to Spencer thought he was doing a good job, while his former supporters believed he hadn't done enough to stop the developers that were still attempting to get longtime residents to sell their homes so they could put up condos, hotels, and golf courses, and overpriced gated communities.

"That definitely would spoil the ambience and natural beauty of the island."

"What will the design of your studio look like?"

"I was thinking a four-thousand-square-foot Charleston Single House with a two-story porch overlooking a garden. It will be protected by closed-circuit cameras, a wrought-iron fence, and an electronic gate."

Francine frowned. "Isn't that excessive?"

"Not if I want to insure the building."

Her frown disappeared. "I didn't think of that." She turned over again. "By the way, I had a chance to look at the floor plans."

"Which style do you like?"

"Even though I had Morgan decorate my apartment in a Zen style, I prefer the ones labeled simple country charm because your home is a farmhouse. The tables and chairs have a country look with a subtle contemporary side."

"I like it simple," Keaton confirmed. "Maybe one of these days you'll come with me to see the house."

"I'd love to. I think it's time I get up and take a shower."

Keaton rested a leg over hers, stopping her when she moved to sit up. "What time do you have to be at the shop?"

"I'm usually there around eight thirty, but I need to go in earlier because my mother will be home for the rest of the week."

"I'll call downstairs and make a reservation for breakfast before we head back."

Francine tried to move his leg off hers but it was like attempting to lift a log. When it appeared he wasn't going to let her get up she tried another approach. Smiling, she reached between his legs, holding fast to his flaccid penis.

"No!" Keaton bellowed when she began

to stroke him.

She increased the motion. "Move your leg, baby."

Jerking as if he'd been hit by a jolt of electricity, Keaton fell off the bed onto his back, bringing Francine with him as she lay sprawled over his chest. He glared up at her. "That's a low blow."

Pressing her fist to her mouth, Francine smothered the giggles threatening to escape. "I did not blow you, milord," she said in a clipped British accent.

Keaton's shoulders shook as he struggled not to laugh. "What am I going to do with you, wench?"

"That is for you to find out, milord." She got up and walked into the bathroom, feeling the heat of Keaton's gaze on her naked body.

Chapter Sixteen

Keaton paced the length of his bedroom suite much like a caged cat. The restlessness had come from his wanting to begin drafting the script from beginning to end. He'd finished digesting a voluminous amount of research. He'd spent what felt like hundreds of hours studying the Gullah culture and his brain was quickly approaching overload. He'd met with the archivist and together they'd poured over diaries, letters, journals, census reports, bills of sale for slaves, and household accounts for landowners. He'd also interviewed Corrine Hamilton, recording hours of the oral history of Cavanaugh Island. The scenes and characters had come alive in his head, eliciting an excitement he hadn't felt in a very long time.

It'd been more than a week since he'd seen Francine, although she called him every night to repeat some of the stories she'd overheard when eavesdropping on her mother and grandmother when they gathered in the kitchen with their friends when she'd been warned to "stay out of grown folks' bizness."

Keaton could hear the fatigue in her voice and limited their conversations to ten to fifteen minutes. Her mother had been instructed by an orthopedist to take several weeks off from work in order to rest her back, which had left Francine with the responsibility of running the salon, while taking on Mavis's clients as well as her own, and looking in on her grandmother before and after work.

The memory of the night they'd stayed over in Charleston still lingered around the fringes of his mind, occasionally eliciting erotic dreams. He knew if he worked himself to the point of exhaustion it would keep him from thinking about Francine. Keaton missed her more than he'd thought possible — her smile, her laugh, listening to her when she morphed into the Cockney tavern maid. He also missed the demure blushes she wasn't able to control and her passion when they'd shared an intimacy that left him wanting more. He was tempted to stop by the Beauty Box to see her, but decided to wait until his scheduled appointment.

After breakfast at the inn they'd returned

to the Cove, where he left her at her front door. However, he wasn't able to escape the eagle-eyed women sitting on their porches or the few who were sweeping or hosing down porch steps. They'd stopped whatever they were doing to stare directly at him when he drove past. The Magnolias' neighborhood watch was on patrol.

Keaton had waited two days before calling Eddie Wilkes and when the editor returned the call Keaton had turned off the ringer on his phone; he'd been up for more than twenty-four hours, reading and transcribing the archival notes. They played phone tag for days until Keaton finally connected with the man, confirming a date and time to meet.

Keaton sat on a worn leather chair staring at the editor of the *Sanctuary Chronicle* as he moved a stack of old newspapers from one corner of his desk to another. Each time Keaton shifted the springs on the chair groaned as if in pain. Eddie had asked if he would come to the newspaper office because he wanted to talk to him, while Keaton surmised that meant an interview. Keaton also assumed he and the newspaper reporter were about the same age. The date on the degree hanging on the wall behind the desk was the same year Keaton graduated from college.

Eddie looked as if he'd been in a rush to get dressed because he hadn't bothered to tuck the hem of his shirt into the waistband of his slacks. His sandy-brown hair complemented his redbone complexion. "I'm sorry you had to wait for me, Mr. Grace."

Keaton waved a hand. Eddie's secretary had directed him to sit in the newspaper's waiting room because her boss was running late. "Please call me Keaton."

When Eddie sat down on his chair it, too, squeaked under his weight. He managed to look sheepish. "One of these days I'm going to get some new office furniture." Patting the desk, he pulled a pair of glasses from under several pieces of paper and put them on. "This morning is not going too well for me. I got a call from the principal at the high school that my son was placed on an in-school suspension for pushing another kid who'd gotten in his face. Do you have children, Keaton?"

"No, I don't."

"The only thing I'm going to say is to think long and hard before you decide if you want to become a parent. Do you know what's wrong with these kids nowadays? They have more rights than their parents," he said, answering his own question. "You can't talk hard to them or they'll accuse you of verbally abusing your child. You can't hit them, because then it's physical abuse. I remember my grandmother used to tell me to go outside and get a switch so she could light up my behind. She didn't have to do it too often because I was a quick study. Just do the right thing and you don't get whipped."

"Some of what you're saying is true but I believe the breakdown in the family unit has to take the most blame."

Eddie nodded. "You're right about that. There was a time when fathers were in ninety-nine percent of the homes here on the island. The exception was if he'd died. Today that average would be closer to eighty-seven percent. It's still better than the national average for women heading single-parent homes, but for us on Cavanaugh Island it's still not good enough." He shifted another stack of paper. "I know you didn't come here to listen to me bitch and moan about my kid."

Keaton crossed one denim-covered leg over the opposite knee. "I'm curious as to why you wanted me to meet with you."

"I'd like to interview you for my 'What's New?' column. Cavanaugh Island is a small barrier island when compared to Hilton Head, and the Cove is even smaller, so there's always a lot of talk when someone new decides to put down roots."

"Do you know who I am?"

Eddie ducked his head. "I must admit I did research you online."

Keaton knew there was plenty of information on him on the Internet for the editor to glean enough to fill up a column. "What else do you want to know?"

"Why did you decide to move here?"

Leaning back in the creaky chair, Keaton crossed his arms over his chest. "I suppose it's the same reason anyone would want to live here. I wanted a slower pace, someplace where I'm not jolted awake by the sirens of first responders or gunshots. I want to live where, if I do decide to marry and raise a family, my children could grow up as children. I know I wouldn't be able to shield them from some of the problems plaguing our youth in larger cities, but at least I would have some control over their environment."

Eddie smiled and nodded. "That's the reason I didn't move away. Once the kids leave here to go to high school on the mainland some of them just act the fool because they believe no one's watching them. What they forget is that they have to come back home and when they do there's hell to pay. They get the business from every member of their families." He patted his shirt's breast pocket. "It starts with me, because I took my boy's driver's license. He's going to have to work hard to get this baby back."

Keaton's relaxed stance belied his impatience. He wanted to get back to his room at the Cove Inn and his research project. And the talk about parenthood was a constant reminder that he had to decide whether he wanted to marry and father children. After all, he was forty-one and not getting any younger. And he didn't want to be one of those fathers who were too physically challenged to play with their young children. He remembered the tarot card reader's prediction that he would never marry or father children if he didn't let go of his past.

Keaton had let go of his past once he realized he was in love with Francine. But even if he wanted her as his wife he knew it would never become a reality. She'd been emphatic when she said she did not want her life encumbered with a husband. Her ex had blindsided her with his duplicity, making it difficult for Francine to trust a man to love her for herself.

"What else do you want to know, Eddie?" he asked, using the man's name for the first time.

"You're a producer, director, and screenwriter. Is there any truth in the rumor that you're planning to build a movie studio on the old Webber property?"

"The rumor is true."

Eddie picked up a pencil, and using shorthand symbols, jotted down Keaton's response on a white legal pad. "Why Sanctuary Cove when you could've chosen Charleston?"

"Why not Sanctuary Cove? Having a movie studio here will help the town's economy. Even before I begin filming I will have hired camerapeople, set designers, carpenters, painters, animal trainers, set dressers, and still photographers. Then there will be people responsible for costumes and makeup, stunt people, those responsible for props, lighting cameramen, a gaffer, key grip, and best boy. Don't forget the cinematographer, caterers, visual, sound, and special effects. All of that translates into employing professionals and interns looking to break into moviemaking. I hope that answers your question."

Eddie rolled the pencil between his thumb

and forefinger. "I guess I didn't think of it that way. All I thought about was hordes camping out here just to get a glimpse of some movie star."

"That's not going to happen because there will be security and because the studio sits on private property and trespassers will be subject to arrest."

The journalist pinched the bridge of his nose above his glasses with his free hand. "And I don't think they'd want to have to deal with the sheriff and his deputies. They have a no-tolerance rule with outsiders starting trouble on the island."

Keaton had met the taciturn lawman when he introduced himself during a foot patrol in the Cove's downtown business district. They'd chatted briefly after he told Sheriff Hamilton he was now the new owner of the Webber property. Jeffrey had reassured him his studio would be off-limits to any unauthorized visitors.

"Is there anything else you want to know?" he asked Eddie.

"Not right now. I think you gave me what I needed to fill in the blanks. Once I complete the article I'll let you see it before we go to press. That way if there are any inconsistencies, you can correct them. By the way, have you attended any of the open town council meetings?"

"No."

Eddie removed his glasses. "There's one tonight that should be quite interesting. The mayor and his town council meet the second Tuesday of each month to bring residents up to date on proposed new ordinances, budget items, and reports from department heads, including but not limited to transportation, engineering, housing, fire, police, and the school board. After the regular meeting the candidates running for mayor are scheduled to debate each other before next month's election. Tonight's meeting will be at the library because they're expecting a larger than usual turnout. I believe you might be interested in what they have to say about the future of the Cove. It begins at eight, but you should get there a little earlier so you won't have to stand up."

"I'll try and make it."

Keaton left the newspaper office and walked back to the boardinghouse. He'd known about the town council meetings from the local townsfolk. After a meeting it was all they would talk about for days. Seemingly the upcoming mayoral election had most riveted to their televisions when Charleston's local news aired, or they bought up copies of the *Sanctuary Chronicle* as soon as it was delivered to the supermarket, Muffin Corner, and the Parlor Bookstore, forcing the editor to increase its circulation. The biweekly's circulation had been in slow decline over the years and if it hadn't been for the ads Cavanaugh Island's only paper would've gone out of circulation.

Keaton read the paper every two weeks from the front to the last page. The *Chronicle*'s headlines were more provocative than the articles, while he did manage to discover something about the island and its citizens he found interesting. It was truly a hometown paper, highlighting the accomplishments of schoolchildren, graduations, births, deaths, weddings, and the milestone birthdays of longtime residents and of those serving in the military.

However, it was the folktales Francine recounted when he spoke to her at night that Keaton found most fascinating and frightening at the same time. He felt like a voyeur, peering into a window to the past. She spoke of forbidden love between the wives of plantation owners and male slaves. And how the mixed-race newborns that could never pass into the white race were suffocated at birth, or the black midwives would concoct excuses for the babies' darker complexions, such as the lack of oxygen from the umbilical cord being wrapped about an infant's neck. One plantation mistress solved this dilemma by taking only mulatto men to her bed. The result was a baby she was able to raise as her own. Fortunately, her cuckolded husband was too busy drinking, gambling, and visiting the slave quarters to satisfy his taste for darker women to notice his wife's similar predilection.

Whenever she spoke of roots and spells he'd felt the hair rise on the back of his neck. Keaton had found himself transfixed when Francine told actual stories she'd heard or read involving hexes, and she'd suggested he research the infamous Dr. Buzzard, a professional root doctor rumored to dispense charms to help find love, bring money, or cure whatever ailed one. There were a number of root doctors who, if you paid them enough, would curse your enemy. She'd given him the name of another conjurer. The legendary High Sheriff of the Lowcountry was rumored to have been made bulletproof by magic. These conjurers were known to visit cemeteries to work their spells as determined by the phases of the moon.

Keaton was particularly fascinated by her

account of Angels Landing's most prominent family. The Pattons were synonymous with scandal, beginning with the nineteenth-century patriarch, Shipley Patton, and continuing into the twenty-first century with Taylor Patton. If he wanted to know more about the Pattons she suggested he contact Corrine Hamilton, grandmother of the island's sheriff. It had been Corrine's great-great-great-grandmother who'd hidden the son of Oakes Patton after Oakes's wife had placed a hit on her husband's mistress and children. The Patton line would've ended with Oakes if Corrine's ancestors hadn't saved his son's life.

His notes made for fascinating reading and once he began drafting the script he was confident he'd be able to bring the characters to life on the screen.

Keaton spied Francine with her mother and grandmother the moment he walked into the library's largest meeting room for the scheduled town council meeting. It was like seeing her for the first time. Her hair was pinned atop her head in sensual disarray, and when their eyes met he saw the dark shadows under her brilliant eyes. His heart stopped for a beat, and then started up again. She appeared thinner, exhausted, and he wondered whether she was eating and sleeping enough.

Mumbling apologies as he wended his way down the row where she was seated, Keaton nodded to Mavis and Dinah. "Miss Dinah. Miss Mavis, how are you feeling?"

Mavis smiled. "I'm feeling much better. Thank you for asking. You know you owe us a visit. My husband still has to give you that jersey for your father."

"Let me know when it's convenient for me to come by."

Dinah patted his shoulder. "You know you don't need an invitation. Our doors are always open to you."

Keaton saw curious stares directed his way. *Let them look and let them talk,* he thought. He was past caring who saw him with Francine, and had tired of pretending they were nothing more than barber and customer. He hunkered down in front her, taking her hands and pressing a kiss to her knuckles.

"Wait for me in the parking lot and I'll follow you home."

Leaning closer, Francine kissed Keaton's cheek. "Okay. Love you, sweetie."

He focused his gaze on her mouth. "Love you back."

■ ■ ■ ■

Francine ignored the audible gasp from the woman sitting on her left who hadn't bothered to pretend she wasn't eavesdropping on her and Keaton's conversation. She wanted to tell Keaton that she missed him, that she needed him. The gossip and bickering at the Beauty Box had escalated during her mother's absence, and because Francine didn't have her mother's personality it had gone on unchecked. She'd found it virtually impossible to keep order and openly reprimand some of the clients who'd watched her grow up. Like all of the children on the island, she'd been raised to respect her elders. Screaming at them wasn't an option and she was left to endure the uproar whenever the topic of the upcoming election was mentioned.

Francine slumped in her chair and closed her eyes. She wasn't as physically exhausted as she was mentally. Managing the shop without the assistance of her mother made her aware of how difficult it was for Mavis to run a successful business. However, Mavis made it look so easy.

Whenever she spoke to Keaton she made certain not to disclose her dilemma. Talking about the narratives she'd overheard whispered took her mind off the drama in the Beauty Box. However, Francine knew she had to decide what action to take to restore order before her mother returned. The doctor still hadn't cleared Mavis to return to work. Whatever solution she came up with had to be handled without impinging on the first amendment right of free speech. The shop's no-gossiping rule pertained to the salon's employees and not its customers.

Talking with Keaton every night had kept her calm and for that she loved him. It helped to take her mind off what she would have to encounter the next day whenever Alice Parker's or Spencer White's name was mentioned. Inasmuch as Francine wanted Alice as the Cove's first woman mayor, she hated that it'd polarized the townspeople. In another five weeks it would be over and folks would be forced to resign themselves to the outcome of the election.

Those who were standing around talking scrambled to find a chair when the members of the council filed into the room, followed by the mayor. Spencer took his seat at the table in the front of the room, rapping a gavel and calling the meeting to order at exactly eight o'clock. A murmur went up from the assembly. It was the first time since becoming mayor that Spencer had begun a meeting on time.

Keaton got his first look at the dapper mayor with movie-star looks. He'd never been one to closely follow politics, yet he always voted in national and occasionally local elections. If someone were to ask about his first impression of Mayor White, Keaton would've said "slick." Every issue of the *Chronicle* included a profile of both mayoral candidates up to and including a special issue the weekend before the election.

Spencer had earned the distinction of becoming a third-generation mayor of the Cove. His grandfather had been the Cove's first black mayor, serving six four-year terms. Spencer's father then ran for the vacated office and won. Spencer had married a model-turned-actress, who'd spent more than half of their brief, two-year marriage in Los Angeles. They'd parted amicably, and he'd joined the ranks of a small number of single men on Cavanaugh Island who were in their early forties.

Spencer straightened his tie as he cleared his throat, garnering the attention of all in the room. "I'd like to thank everyone for coming out tonight. Before we start our official meeting I'd like to acknowledge a few new faces." His tone and words, along with his cropped hair, tailored suit, flawless brown skin, and even features, made him the consummate politician. He gestured to Keaton. "Sir, do you mind telling us who you are and what brought you to Sanctuary Cove?"

Keaton felt dozens of eyes directed at him. He paused, choosing his words carefully. "I'm Keaton Grace, and I'm currently living at the Cove Inn until my house is renovated. I bought the old Webber property."

Spencer smiled, showing everyone his porcelain veneers. "Congratulations, Mr. Grace. I, along with everyone on the town council, had hoped someone would purchase that property because not only had it become an eyesore but we're always looking to increase our tax rolls." A smatter of laughter followed his statement. "Is there anything else you'd like to tell your fellow citizens?"

Stretching out his legs, Keaton crossed his booted feet at the ankles. He was ready for the esteemed politician. Hannah had warned him Spencer would be less than happy that he hadn't been apprised of his intent to build a movie studio in his town.

Affecting an expression of indifference, he shook his head.

"No, Mayor White."

"Are you certain?" Spencer insisted, his toothpaste-ad smile slipping.

"Very certain," Keaton said.

Lacing his fingers together, Spencer shot Keaton a long, penetrating stare that was more a glare. "Aren't you in the movie business, Mr. Grace?"

Keaton nodded. "I am."

"If that's the case, then perhaps everyone would like to hear about your future plans as it pertains to your livelihood."

A shadow of annoyance crossed Keaton's face. If the mayor believed he was putting him on the spot, then he was delusional. The years he'd spent working in Hollywood were like swimming with blood-crazed sharks. He'd learned to remain completely still, not moving until he was certain of a means of escape.

"Everyone can read about it in the *Chronicle.*"

"Are you certain you don't want to give us a hint?"

Keaton nodded. "I'm very certain. I don't think Eddie Wilkes would appreciate it if I cut into his circulation with a spoiler." It was his turn to flash a saccharine smile.

"Everyone will just have to pick up a copy of the *Chronicle* to find out about my plans for the Cove."

"Let's move it along, Spencer," someone called out from the back of the room. "I didn't come out here tonight to listen to you get into folks' business."

Spencer's eyes narrowed as he banged the gavel. "You're out of order, Henry."

"And you're looking to lose my vote," shouted the locksmith, refusing to back down from the reprimand.

The threat was not lost on Spencer as he continued with the introductions of first-time attendees. Keaton had come up with another adjective for the man: *bully.* The mayor's bravado appeared to take its leave when Alice entered the room and sat in the back.

Keaton met Francine's gaze when she turned and smiled at him. Both had noticed the incumbent's expression when his challenger walked into the meeting room. It was uncertainty.

The official meeting went quickly, most of the department heads giving condensed reports to allot time for the hour-long debate. During the first half hour Spencer and Alice answered questions from the moderator, who worked for a local

Charleston-based television station. During the second half hour the questions came from the floor.

Although ineligible to vote, Keaton knew he would vote for Alice if he could. She was intelligent and insightful, and gained the approval of everyone in the room when she announced she would work as a full-time mayor for a dollar a year. Unfortunately for Spencer, he did not offer the same. The office of mayor was a part-time position, and despite having a lucrative Charleston-based practice, he hadn't declined the five-figure salary from the town relying on the revenue from snowbirds and tourists to keep it out of the red.

The night ended with the candidates shaking hands with those in attendance, as Keaton made his way to the parking lot to wait for Francine. He was really beginning to feel like a part of the town.

Chapter Seventeen

Francine sat in her parents' family room watching the man with whom she'd fallen in love interact with the man she loved. Keaton and her father had hit it off as if they'd known each other for years instead of twenty minutes. Her mother and grandmother had retired for bed and it was becoming more difficult to conceal her yawns when compressing her lips. Finally, she gave up pretending.

Pushing to her feet, she crossed the room. "Don't get up," she said when the two men attempted to stand. "This is when I have to make my exit, because some of us have to get up and go to work in the morning," she teased. She kissed her father's cheek. "Good night, Daddy."

Keaton stood up. "I'll be up to check on you before I leave."

She blew him a kiss. "If I'm asleep when you come up, just close the door. You can tuck me in if I'm still awake." She went upstairs to her apartment, kicking off her shoes and heading to the bathroom. Francine turned on the radio, then the water in the bathtub as she brushed her teeth and cleaned her face. She stared at her reflection in the bathroom mirror. She knew she loved Keaton and didn't care who on Cavanaugh Island knew it. She was certain if they married her life with him would be nothing like the one she'd had with Aiden. He would actually love her for who she was, not for her money.

She climbed into the bathtub, moaning when she sank down into the warm water. A slight smile tilted the corners of her mouth upward. "Mrs. Francine Dinah Grace." My, my, she mused, it did sound as if she were a society matron, hosting dinner parties or afternoon tea. She sobered quickly. Is that what she would be resigned to? Becoming Keaton's hostess when he entertained movie studio executives or entertainment reporters who came to the island to interview him? Becoming his wife would thrust her back into the spotlight and she had to decide if that was what she wanted.

Francine lay in the tub, listening to the beating of her heart. It thumped uncontrollably at the thought of giving Keaton up. Though she may not have wanted the attention, she was not willing to give Keaton up. She loved him that much. Marrying him meant sharing his life as he would share hers. And it would be only a matter of time before those who did remember the actress she once was would come to know her again — this time as the wife of independent filmmaker Keaton Grace.

If Keaton wanted her to become his wife and the mother of their children, then she was ready to accept his proposal.

Keaton didn't sit down again until Francine disappeared from sight. Frank Tanner had welcomed him with a rough embrace, then ushered him into the family room, where they launched into a lively discussion about the Steelers. He'd noticed Francine's eyelids drooping as she tried vainly to stay alert.

"You like her a lot, don't you son?"

He nodded. "Yes, I do." Keaton wasn't going to pretend he didn't know what Francine's father was talking about because he did not want to insult the man's intelligence.

"That's good."

Keaton smiled at the man who'd been his father's football hero. "So you approve?"

"I do. It's been a while since my Frannie found someone who could make her smile. What I'm about to say stays between you and me." Frank pointed at Keaton and then tapped his own chest. "Do I have your word it will go no further than this room?"

Silence swelled until it was deafening. Keaton didn't know what Frank was going to reveal and he wasn't certain whether he truly wanted to know. He nodded. "You have my word."

"My daughter married someone who nearly destroyed her. He took advantage of her naïveté, and once he got what he wanted, he walked away. When the delivery room doctor placed Frannie in my arms I vowed I would always protect her. However, I failed because I couldn't protect her from a son of a bitch who used her to his own advantage. I seriously thought about killing him, but had second thoughts once I realized how going to prison would impact my family."

Keaton stared, complete surprise freezing his features. "Are you threatening me, Frank?"

"No, Keaton. I just want you to be aware of what she's been through."

"Point taken. The distinct difference between me and Francine's ex is that I don't believe in using women."

Frank nodded. "I'm happy to hear that. Now go on up and see her before she goes to sleep. Go on," he insisted when Keaton hesitated. "Come by tomorrow after Frannie gets off and we'll hang out outside, grill a few steaks, watch some basketball, and shoot the breeze."

Keaton wasn't certain what Francine had revealed to her father about their relationship. However, that no longer mattered. The Tanners knew how he felt about her, and it would just be a matter of time before all of Cavanaugh Island would know once he accompanied her to the Valentine's Day party hosted by Alice Parker.

He walked out of the family room, down a long hallway, and to a staircase leading to the second floor. The door to Dinah's apartment was closed, while Francine's at the far end of the hallway stood ajar.

A lamp on the table in the entryway, turned to the lowest setting, illuminated the space. Keaton closed the self-locking door. He sat on a chair and removed his boots, leaving them on a mat beside the drop-leaf table. His footsteps were silent as he walked on sock-covered feet through the living/dining room and down a hall to Francine's bedroom. The sound of music coming from a radio in the adjoining bathroom pulled him in that direction.

Standing under the entrance, he leaned against the doorframe, watching Francine. She was reclining in the tub, eyes closed, her head cradled on a bath pillow, moisture from the hot water beading up her bare face. The Oscar-winning instrumental version of "You Must Love Me," from the *Evita* motion picture soundtrack, filled the space. As she sang the lyrics to the poignant song written by Tim Rice and Andrew Lloyd Webber the emotion in her theatrically trained voice stirred emotions in Keaton that were completely foreign to him.

It was as if she were singing directly to him: *Deep in my heart I'm concealing. Things that I'm longing to say.* What was she feeling? he mused. What was she longing to say? That he could become more to her than just her lover?

Without warning her eyes opened and she stared at him as if he were a stranger. She sank lower in the tub. Her shocked expression changed when a mysterious smile softened her mouth. "I thought you would still be with my father."

Keaton entered the bathroom and sat on the chair to the makeup table. "He sent me up here."

"Why would he do that?"

"I suppose he felt we should have some alone time."

Her smile grew wider. "I never figured Daddy for a matchmaker."

Leaning forward, he braced his elbows on his knees. "He's a little late for that."

She nodded. "I guess you're right."

"I know I'm right." Standing, he positioned the chair closer to the bathtub, and sat down again. "What's going on with you, Francine?" Keaton knew he'd struck a nerve when her spiked lashes fluttered. He'd caught her off guard and all of her theatrical training proved futile.

"I don't know what you're talking about."

Not wanting to accuse her of lying outright, he said, "I believe you do know what I'm talking about. I haven't seen you in a week." He caressed her face. "Are you all right? You look exhausted."

Francine went completely still. "Thank you for the compliment."

"I didn't mean for it to be a compliment and you know it. You've lost weight, you have dark circles under your eyes, and whenever you call me at night you sound as if you're on drugs. What is it?"

"I've never taken drugs!"

Keaton bit back a smile when she displayed a flash of anger. "That's good to know, because I don't want to have to deal with a weed-smoking, pill-popping, coke-snorting girlfriend."

"You forgot about meth and crack," she drawled sarcastically.

"That's not funny, Francine."

"I didn't mean for it to be funny, Keaton."

"Now back to the issue."

"Which is?"

"What's going on with you?"

"I'm worried about my mother."

Keaton leaned over and kissed her temple. "Is she okay?"

Tears filled Francine's eyes, but she blinked them back before they fell. "She pretends she's okay, but I know she's in a lot of pain. So much so that her doctor told her she has to stay off her feet and rest her back."

"How long does he want her to rest?"

"At first he told her a month, but when she pitched a fit he compromised and said at least three weeks. He prescribed muscle relaxers, and they really make her sleepy. She can't drive, so that forces her to stay home. Daddy has cancelled his business trips to make certain she doesn't do anything strenuous. Grandma spends most the day with her —"

"It looks as if your family is taking good care of your mother," Keaton interrupted.
"They are."
"If they are, then why are you falling apart?"

Francine knew Keaton was a little too perceptive for her to hide much from him. She was truthful when admitting she was concerned with her mother's health but that wasn't the entire story. Her disturbing vision had manifested. The gaping mouths and the sound of angry voices belonged to those that frequented the Beauty Box.
"It's the Beauty Box."
"What about it?" he asked.
She told him everything, except her vision about the arguments that sprang between customers whenever someone mentioned the name of one of the mayoral candidates. "I can't stop them from talking but the arguments over the race are causing problems. My mother has an in-house rule for our employees that they are not permitted to repeat gossip with the customers, but that rule can't be enforced on people who pay for our services."
"It's that bad?"
Francine nodded. "You come in every two weeks, so you might overhear snippets, but

I have to put up with the bickering five days a week. I can't tell them what I really feel because I'd undo all of the sacrifices my mother has had to endure to build her business."

"So it's just the election that's turning neighbor against neighbor?"

"Yes. And what I don't understand is, whoever wins, their lives will not change that drastically. For Spencer it will be business as usual, and if Alice wins we may see some positive changes because Cavanaugh Island is within her husband's legislative district. For years there wasn't a road between the Cove and the Landing, and Jason managed to get Congress to appropriate monies to build the road. That happened before he and Alice decided to move here from Charleston. Having Jason live here is a win-win for everyone living on the island because he's always touted that charity begins at home."

"I know it may sound trivial, but you'll only have to put up with the nonsense for another month."

Francine flashed a wry smile. "I hope I last a month without getting arrested for assault. You don't know how many times I've been tempted to pull some woman's hair out by the roots. Or better yet, leave a relaxer on too long."

Throwing back his head, Keaton roared in laughter. "Please, baby. I'm a very visual person. They probably would look like the old woman character in *Shutter Island.*"

Despite the seriousness of her dilemma Francine laughed along with him. "I'm willing to bet that if some of them could read minds they would be very, very afraid to sit in my chair."

Keaton sobered quickly. "Don't let them get to you, otherwise you'll become as nasty and narrow-minded as they are. I think of them as people who have much too much time on their hands or don't have enough going on in their lives so they have to get into other folks' business."

"That's a good way to look at it, but I still want to strangle a few of them. By the way, you held your own tonight with our esteemed incumbent mayor."

"That's because he crossed the line, Francine. First, I wasn't on trial, and if he refused to respect my decision not to disclose information about my business, then he left himself open to take whatever came at him."

"Spencer is a blowhard."

"Spencer is a bully, sweetie, and I don't give bullies any energy." Reaching out, he ran a finger down the length of Francine's nose. "Have you been eating?"

"Yes. Why?"

"You look thinner."

Picking up a bath sponge, she trickled water over her shoulder. "I wouldn't know, because I haven't weighed myself lately."

Keaton took the sponge from her loose grip, making circular motions over her chest. "You're thinner and you haven't been eating. At least not three meals a day. Please don't tell me I'm wrong."

Francine closed her eyes against his intense stare. How, she thought, did he know her that well? She'd lived with Aiden for nearly a year and he'd never taken the time to get to know her. "You're not wrong, Keaton. I usually have a sweet bread and coffee in the morning. Lunches are hit-and-miss because I'm covering for my mother. When I come home I'm usually too tired to eat."

"That's going to stop, Francine. I'm going to come here early enough to make breakfast for you. Then I'll bring you lunch, and when you get off I'll make certain you have something for dinner."

"That's not necessary, Keaton."

"Yes, it is, because if you continue the way you have you won't last another month."

"You're being melodramatic," she countered, unable to ignore the sensations coursing through her body when Keaton drew the sponge over her breasts.

"I'm being realistic and you know it."

Her hand covered his, stopping the pleasurable sensations as her nipples tightened and her breasts grew heavy. "Why are you doing this?"

He gave her a wolfish grin. "Feeling you up?"

"No! Why are you volunteering to bring me meals?"

His grin slipped. "Don't you know, Francine? Don't you know that I love you?"

"I do know."

Moving off the chair and going to his knees, Keaton cradled her face. "Then let me take care of you. If the renovations on my house were completed, I'd asked you to move in with me —"

"You can ask but I told you before I don't shack up with men."

"I'm not men. I am one man, Francine."

"My parents married within a week of their high school graduation because my father didn't want my mother to live with the stigma of being a *kept* woman. He had too much respect for her to subject her to that type of ridicule. All I heard growing up is why would a man buy the cow when he can get the milk for free. If I hadn't believed that, then I never would've married my ex. I would've shacked up with him."

"That still wouldn't have stopped him from using you," Keaton argued quietly. "Even though you had a bad marriage, that's not to say all marriages are that way. All you have to do is look at your parents. I'm certain they've had their ups and downs, but they've stayed together because they love each other. It's the same with my folks."

"True." She took a deep breath. "I said all of that to let you know I wouldn't shack up with you if you were the only man left on earth. That's not who I am. That's not how I was raised. However, I have a confession to make."

"What's that?"

"I'm not as anti-marriage as I used to be. I suppose I can thank you for that."

He smiled. "Are you saying I should start looking at engagement rings?"

She paled. "Umm, no . . . not exactly."

"What about children?"

"What about them, Keaton?"

"Do you want them?"

She nodded. "Yes. Growing up an only child is not much fun."

"Did your parents plan to have one child?"

"No. Mama said she became pregnant two years after she had me, but unfortunately she lost it in the third month. She waited three years before trying again, and again she miscarried, this time in her fifth month. That's when the doctor cautioned her about trying again. She took his advice and underwent a hysterectomy. I've only heard you talk about your sister. Do you have any more siblings?"

"Nope. There's just the two of us. My father wanted a son and my mother a daughter. Apparently they both got their wish."

Francine knew it was time to get out of the tub. The water was beginning to cool. She held out her hand for the sponge. "How did they come up with the name Keaton?"

"Keaton is my mother's maiden name. There's a tradition in my family that the firstborn male child is given his mother's maiden name. My grandmother was Sadie Scott before she married my grandfather. Therefore, my father is Scott Grace."

Francine nodded. "It's a lot easier for us. We select a name and that's it." She paused. "Do you mind giving me a little privacy so I can finish bathing?"

"It's a little late for modesty, sweetie. I've seen parts of your body you'll never get to see unless you're a contortionist."

Pinpoints of heat stung Francine's cheeks. Blushing was the only holdover from her childhood she still was unable to control. "Give me ten minutes. Please."

The attractive slashes in Keaton's lean jaw appeared when he smiled. "Okay."

Waiting until he'd left the bathroom, she scrambled out of the tub and wrapped her body in a towel. Removing the pins from her hair, she ran a wide-tooth comb through the damp strands. She applied a moisturizer to her face and a lightly scented cream to her body. Pulling on a silk robe, she walked out of the bathroom and into the bedroom, stopping abruptly when she saw Keaton in bed.

He patted the mattress. "Come get into bed."

"I . . . I have to get a nightgown." Francine chided herself for stuttering like a frightened virgin.

Keaton whipped back the sheet. "You don't need a nightgown. I'll keep you warm."

Untying the belt to the robe, she shrugged out of it, leaving it on the foot of the bed. Her gaze met and fused with Keaton's. He extended his arms and she ran and jumped on the bed and into his embrace. Burying her face against the column of his neck, Francine breathed a kiss there. "I've missed you so much."

Keaton flipped her on her back as if she were a small child. "That's all going to change."

"What are you talking about?"

"Remember what I said about making certain you eat?" She nodded. "I'm going to the supermarket tomorrow to buy enough food to stock your refrigerator and your pantry. I'll come over every morning to make breakfast for you until your mother returns to work."

"I won't let you in."

"Too late, sexy. Have you forgotten that you gave me a key?"

"You were supposed to use it that one time."

"Oops, I forgot to give it back," he teased with a wide grin. "As I was saying. I'll make a nutritious breakfast for you, then I'll stop by the shop, say around one, and bring you lunch. Then when you come home at night you'll have just enough time to take a shower before we sit down for dinner *together.* After dinner we'll unwind by watching your favorite historical dramas, taking walks on the beach, or just talking. Then I'll tuck you into bed before it gets too late so you can get enough sleep to get rid of those dark circles under your beautiful eyes."

"You're taking on a lot of responsibility."

"You don't think you're worth it?"

"It's not about whether I'm worth it, Keaton."

Supporting his weight on his forearms, he pressed her down into the mattress, not permitting her to escape. "What do you think it's about?" Keaton angled his head. "Please don't tell me you think I want something from you."

Francine felt as if a hand had closed around her throat, not permitting her to speak as old fears and insecurities crashed down on her like storm clouds. Every man she'd become involved with wanted something from her. It'd begun in high school and ended with her failed marriage.

"It has crossed my mind."

He ran his hand over her face. "I want you to erase that thought. There's nothing I want more than *you.*"

Francine felt like crying, because she so wanted to believe him. Her hands moved slowly up his biceps, the muscles under his skin tightening and flexing. "I believe and trust you," she whispered against his warm throat. "You talk about feeding me, taking walks along the beach, and watching television with me. What about your work?"

"I'm still doing research. It'll be a while before I begin my first draft."

"How many drafts do you do?"

"As many as it takes for me to feel comfortable with it." Keaton palmed her face. "I'll stay with you until you fall asleep."

"Okay." Francine moaned softly when he kissed the corners of her mouth. "What are you doing?" she asked when his hand went from her face to her inner thigh.

A chuckle rumbled in his chest. "I'm going to help you sleep."

She wasn't certain what Keaton was talking about until he rained down light kisses over her throat, chest, belly, and even lower to her thighs. Francine wasn't given time to react when he anchored her legs over his shoulders, his rapacious tongue searching the moist folds concealing her vagina until he found the opening he sought. Keaton's mouth demanded and her body answered, his tongue plunging inside her quivering flesh, branding her as his own.

Francine tried concentrating on any- and everything to stave off the telling ripples shaking her from head to toe. She didn't want to climax just yet. Not only did she want it to last but to go on and on and on. However, passion was not to be denied. Her body stilled for several seconds, then shook as if she were experiencing a seizure.

She screamed, not recognizing her own voice. The screams continued as multiple orgasms overlapped one another, leaving her spent. She lay with her chest rising and falling heavily as she tried catching her breath. Francine didn't know when Keaton lowered her legs, drew the sheet over her moist body, and reached over to turn off the lamp. What she did remember was that he'd kissed her, permitting her to taste herself on her lips, and held her to his chest until her world went dark.

Chapter Eighteen

Francine did not have to look to see who'd come into the Beauty Box when all conversations faded away before there was complete silence. As promised, Keaton arrived at the salon every day at one with lunch in an insulated bag. With little or no fanfare he left the bag with the receptionist and then walked out.

What he'd selected to prepare came as a pleasant surprise. One day it was shrimp salad on a bed of lettuce with sliced hard-boiled eggs, sliced avocado, and carrot sticks. On another he would prepare a broiled chicken breast with wilted spinach and couscous. He would alternate — one day hot and the next cold. Dessert was either sliced fruit or homemade oatmeal raisin nut cookies.

She'd come to look forward to him sharing an early breakfast with her. Most mornings she would leave him in her apartment.

He'd admitted to spending more time at Magnolia Drive than at the Cove Inn. He made it a practice to leave her house to return to the boardinghouse in time to watch the late-night news.

Mavis claimed she was feeling much better and looking forward to returning to work, but Francine told her if she came back too soon she would probably experience a setback and then she would have to stay out even longer.

The campaign for mayor and two other positions on the town council escalated to a fever pitch as it grew closer to election day. Candidates and campaign workers were out in force, handing out literature and making personal appearances, and Francine couldn't remember a time in the Cove's history when an election mirrored one with national overtones. The positions of mayor and town council member were part-time positions and the salaries were commensurate, so it wasn't the money the various candidates sought. It was the status of being an elected official in their hometown.

Francine had always suspected Spencer was using his position as mayor as an entrée into politics because he'd set his sights on representing the state of South Carolina either as a state senator or as a member of

Congress. And despite his vocal protests about developers coming to Cavanaugh Island to purchase tracts of land that would eventually squeeze out locals with reassessed real estate taxes they would never be able to afford, he had yet to work with the members of the council to draft a resolution that would bar them from doing business in the Cove. Francine knew she wasn't the only one who believed that a few developers had Spencer in their pockets, and were counting on him to win reelection so they could use another ruse to gain the confidence of those willing to sell their land for more money than they could otherwise ever hope to earn in their lifetime.

Kara said a few had come to her with a blank check hoping to purchase the antebellum mansion and the two thousand acres that made up Angels Landing Plantation, but she had no intention of selling out to developers that planned to turn the historic property into another millionaire's paradise as they'd done on many of the other Lowcountry Sea Islands.

Francine turned off the dryer of a man who'd gotten a special conditioner made with avocado and olive oil. She beckoned to Brooke. "You can wash him out now." He'd come into the shop for a haircut, and when she checked his scalp she found it dotted with dry patches.

She decided she wasn't going to let anything or anyone bother her today. Later on that evening she and Keaton would join a select group of invitees to Alice and Jason Parker's home for the pre–Valentine's Day party. All of the invitations were hand delivered with a warning not to tell anyone they'd received it. Not knowing who else was invited added to the overall mystique of what promised to be a wonderfully festive gathering.

Mavis had put in a rare appearance earlier that morning to pick up employee time sheets so she could write out paychecks. When asked when she was coming back her reply was "any day now," although Francine knew her mother was being overly optimistic. She still had another full week before the doctor would medically clear her to return to work.

Francine had searched her closet for something to wear, then decided she wanted a new dress. The invitation indicated semiformal attire, and she drove to Charleston and spent hours in several boutiques until she found a dress she liked. Luckily she was able to find a pair of stilettos in a color that was a perfect match for the dress. She hadn't worn a pair of heels since the night of Kara's baby shower and that now seemed so long ago. Kara and Jeff had sent out invitations to friends and family to witness the christening of their son the third week in March. When Kara called Francine to make an appointment for a haircut and facial because this would be the first Valentine's Day she would celebrate as Mrs. Jeffrey Hamilton, Francine suspected the Hamiltons were also invited to the Parkers.

Patience, the salon's receptionist, moved from behind her desk, carrying the bag Keaton left with her into the lounge. "I'm taking bets that it's beef today," she announced loudly.

Francine had just washed and dried her hands when she overheard the receptionist. She and Mavis had staggered lunch hours so half the employees ate at twelve and the other half at one. Patience was instructed not to schedule anyone during a designated lunch break.

She rolled her eyes at Patience. "Mind your business and put my lunch down."

"Miss Patience is hatin' 'cause her man don't bring her lunch," Danita teased.

Patience glared at the nail technician. "No, I'm not. Besides, my man can't bring me lunch because he works over in Goose Creek."

"That's not that far," Danita countered.

"It's far enough," Patience mumbled.

Francine unzipped the bag. Then she noticed everyone staring at her. "It would serve y'all right if I ate in my car."

Brooke moved closer. "Come on, Francine, show us what he brought you today."

If it hadn't been for the salon staff, Francine knew she wouldn't have kept it together during her mother's convalescence. They'd helped with walk-ins, shampoos, and deep conditions.

She felt the heat from their gazes on her when she took out a glass container with meat loaf, oven fries, green beans with slivered almonds, and a smaller container with sliced strawberries, kiwi, and pink grapefruit sections. Keaton had also included a note: *Your first cooking lesson is scheduled for Monday.*

Patience jumped up and down. "I told you it would be beef today." She pressed two fingers to her forehead. "I told y'all I was psychic."

Candace emitted an unladylike snort. "Yeah, you psychic all right. What happened to your psychic powers when you booked all those customers on the wrong week?"

Only the receptionist's dark complexion concealed the rush of heat in her face. "Even psychics can be wrong sometimes."

The masseuse, Taryn Brown, walked in at the same time she overheard Patience's excuse. "That's because you're no psychic. And stop telling folks you're one, because one of these days you're going to run into a real one who will put a root on you and shrink your head like they do in New Guinea."

Francine waved her hand. "That's enough talk about roots and spells." Their conversation led her thoughts to Keaton. After their many conversations and interviews, he was now well versed in the various types of incense, oils, and brews, and the color of candles used to cast a spell for good or evil. He'd become so immersed in the Gullah culture that he'd begun keeping a journal of Gullah words and phrases. She'd wrestled with the idea of whether to confide in Keaton about her own psychic abilities, because she knew if they were going to have a truly honest and open relationship he deserved to know she could discern the future.

They continued to make love and the encounters were always spontaneous and passionate. One Sunday after she'd returned from church Francine accompanied him to see his house. The walls, windows, and floors were completed, and the contractor was awaiting the arrival of the kitchen cabinets and appliances to complete the renovation. She loved the idea of having ceiling fans in every room, including the front and back porches. Abram had ordered the furniture Keaton had chosen, with her input, and the anticipated date of delivery was less than six weeks away — April Fool's Day, which had made them laugh uncontrollably.

The confrontations at the salon had deescalated after the town hall debate. Skeptics who'd believed Alice didn't have a chance of defeating Spencer were silenced, those who'd supported Spencer were reevaluating their decision, and those who'd supported Alice when she'd first announced her candidacy were buoyed by the success of the lopsided debate.

Francine retrieved a fork from a drawer in the utility kitchen and sat at the table to enjoy her lunch. She felt a little smug, having a personal chef. Though she'd tried to downplay it by saying it was only temporary, that Keaton would stop delivering lunch once her mother returned to the salon.

When she reassessed her relationship with

Keaton, Francine knew she'd hit the jackpot. He was everything she'd looked for in a man, with a little extra thrown in for good measure. He was a wonderful cook and an exquisite lover.

Keaton had just turned down the collar of his shirt when his cell phone rang. He recognized the ringtone immediately. Picking up the instrument, he activated the speaker feature. "Hey, Devon. How are you?" It'd been weeks since he'd last heard from his attorney. As promised, he'd called her and left a voice mail on her cell phone. Three days later he called again — this time leaving a message with her secretary, who told him Devon was out of town.

"You should be asking where I am."

His hands stilled, tightening the tie under the collar. "Where are you?"

"I'm in Charleston. I just checked into the Francis Marion Hotel on Upper King Street. As soon as I settle in I'll drive over to see you."

"We can't meet until tomorrow. I have a prior engagement tonight."

"How about tomorrow?"

"What time tomorrow?" he asked.

There came a pause, then Devon said, "I'm willing to work around your schedule."

"How's three in the afternoon?"

"Three works for me."

"You don't have to come to the island. I'll drive to Charleston."

There was another pause, this one longer than the one before it. "Okay. Have fun, Keaton."

"Thank you."

Disconnecting the call, he slipped the phone into the inside breast pocket of his suit jacket. Keaton didn't want to think about Devon, but about Francine and their upcoming date. Francine informed him that the names on the guest list were known only to Alice and her husband. She'd timed the event to coincide with the House's recess. Adjusting his shirt's cuffs, he picked up his jacket, keycard, and key fob before walking out of the suite and into the mild February night.

He drove slowly, the scent of salt water coming in through the open windows. When he'd first checked into the Cove Inn the days seemed to move as slowly as a sloth. That changed when he sat across the table from Francine at the Charleston Grill, where he once again found himself enthralled by her presence. That had been six weeks ago. Now there didn't seem to be enough hours in the day. He saw her for breakfast, delivered lunch to the salon, and spent a few more hours with her over dinner. They talked about anything and everything but themselves.

Not only had he fallen in love with her, he also loved her enough to propose marriage. He'd heard women complain constantly about a man's inability to commit. However, with him the tables were turned because it was Francine who'd refused. Maybe he was being paid back for his refusal to marry Jade.

He arrived at the Tanner house, parking alongside the door to Francine's apartment. Tapping a button for the Bluetooth, he scrolled through the directory for her number. It rang twice.

"I'm on my way down."

"Wait there. I'm on my way up."

The only time he didn't call to let her know he was on his way up was when he knew she wouldn't be home. She may have given him a key, but he still respected her right to privacy. Keaton was out of his truck and up the staircase in less than a minute. He entered the apartment, coming to a complete stop when he saw her standing in the middle of the living room. Recessed lights had become a spotlight as they shimmered on her burnished hair, which was swept up in an elegant twist. His gaze moved from her subtle makeup highlighting her eyes and mouth and down to the lacy electric-blue, body-hugging, long-sleeved dress with a matching underslip ending at her knees. His gaze moved even lower to her long, smooth bare legs in a pair of matching silk sling backs. His body reacted violently and he folded his hands over his fly so she wouldn't detect his erection.

He blinked. "I didn't believe you could get any more beautiful." The admission was torn from his heart.

Smiling, Francine laced her fingers together to stop their trembling. "Thank you."

She'd admitted to Keaton that whenever she was with him she felt beautiful, as if she were the only woman in the world. There wasn't anything she didn't love about him, and if she had created a wish list with five qualities she wanted in a man Keaton would've gotten five out of five.

He was generous, even tempered, laid-back, funny, and sexy as hell. He wasn't blessed with Spencer's too-pretty-to-be-a-man's good looks but a classic attractiveness that wouldn't fade with age. Her heart beat a double-time rhythm when Keaton half turned, reached into the pocket of his trousers, and handed her a small black velvet box.

Please no! the voice in her head screamed. It was Valentine's Day and she prayed he hadn't planned to propose marriage. She'd known him six weeks, and couldn't help but think about Aiden whom she'd married after knowing him six weeks. But Keaton wasn't Aiden and he had made it so easy for Francine to love him.

Reaching for her hand, Keaton placed the box on her palm. "I think these will go very nicely with your hair styled like that."

It took two attempts before Francine opened the box to reveal a pair of heart-shaped diamond studs. Her free hand covered her throat. "Omigosh! They're beautiful." Her eyes shimmered with happy tears. She handed him the box and removed the pearl studs from her ears, replacing them with the diamond hearts.

Keaton nodded his approval. "They're perfect." Dipping his head, he kissed the side of her neck.

Her hand grazed his smooth cheek. "Thank you, milord."

"Did I not say you were born to wear silk and fancy baubles, my fair maiden?"

Francine giggled. She loved their playacting. "Aye, milord."

"A most fetching maiden, who has the power to make me give up my nomadic wandering and settle down and become a gentleman farmer."

Francine's smile did not reach her eyes. Keaton had used their playacting to issue a backhanded marriage proposal. If there was one man who could get her to change her stance when it came to marriage it would be Keaton. But not now. It was their first Valentine's Day and she hadn't expected him to give her jewelry. Her normally smooth relationship with Keaton had just become a little more complicated.

"This maiden is ready to leave whenever you are," she said in response. She knew from Keaton's expression that he wasn't pleased with her comeback. Picking up a black cashmere shawl, small silk evening bag, and house keys off a chair she walked to the door.

U.S. Congressman Jason Parker opened the door, inviting his wife's guests into their home with an open smile and a handshake. Francine introduced Keaton to their representative, the two men exchanging strong handshakes.

Jason kissed Francine's cheek. "I'm glad you could come, Red. Alice really appreciates your family's support. We're sorry your mother couldn't make it. Please send her my best for a speedy recovery."

"I'll definitely tell her."

"I hope you don't mind if I borrow your boyfriend for a few minutes, because I want to introduce him to some of the other guys."

Francine met Keaton's eyes. "No, I don't mind." Her gaze lingered on Keaton's broad shoulders under a dark blue tailored suit jacket when Jason led him out of the living room.

"Don't worry about your man, Francine. He's not going anywhere."

She turned to find Kara standing behind her. "You got an invitation, too?"

The new mother was stunning in a short, flared black dress with a revealing neckline. Motherhood agreed with her. Everything about her, including her body, was lush. Kara nodded. "Jeff's the one who got the invitation. I just came along for the ride."

"How's Austin?"

A dreamy look flitted across Kara's face. "He's getting so big." Her hazel eyes sparkled like precious jewels. "I wake up in the middle of the night just to go and stare at him. I still can't believe I gave birth to such an incredibly lovable little person."

"Is he sleeping throughout the night?"

"Not yet. If I feed him just before putting him down for the night he'll usually sleep between four and five hours without waking up."

"I assume Miss Corrine is babysitting tonight."

"She's in heaven because this is her first time babysitting."

"How is Oliver adjusting to sharing Miss Corrine with the baby?"

"Not well. He growls at Gram whenever she picks up Austin. I suppose it's going to take a while before he realizes Gram has enough love to give him and her great-grandson." Kara rested a hand on her chest. "I told Jeff that we can't stay too long because I'll embarrass myself if my milk starts leaking through my nursing pads."

Alice swept into the living room wearing a thigh-high, revealing black tank dress and four-inch-heeled booties. She'd brushed her hair off her face. The hairstyle and clothes were the complete opposite of her side-swept bangs, conservative suits, blouses, and shoes she wore when campaigning. She took Francine's hands, exchanging air kisses with her. "Well, look at you," she crooned. "You look absolutely gorgeous. And your earrings are exquisite."

Francine smiled, touching a diamond in

her lobe. "Thank you. And you've made quite a transformation, Miss Soon-to-be-Mayor of Sanctuary Cove." She glanced around the living room. "You've also done wonders with this house."

Two years before, the Parkers had down-sized their lives when they sold their six-bedroom, palatial home overlooking Charleston Harbor to move into a three-bedroom Lowcountry-style fixer-upper in the Cove. The Parker name wasn't new on the island. It went back more than two hundred years, when Cyrus Parker established a rice plantation on Haven Creek.

"Thank you. I love this house and the Cove. When Jason suggested moving back here I was ready to divorce him because I'd already established a lifestyle that I'd become accustomed to. But he was adamant when he said he was moving with or without me. I fought too hard to get Jason to marry me to give it up over a house. I think we were here a month when I realized I was born to live in a small town. The kids know everyone in their school and every weekend there're kids running in and out of the house. Instead of becoming a soccer mom wearing designer clothes, I'm now baking cookies and chaperoning sleepovers."

"What made you decide to run for

mayor?" Kara asked Alice.

"Despite what he professes, Spencer is soft on developers. When I hear him talk about them there's no passion in his voice. The reason Jason fought so hard to get money to build the road between the Cove and Landing was to counter the argument that Cavanaugh Island's infrastructure was eroding. And the Angels Landing Plantation's restoration couldn't come at a better time." She paused. "Excuse me, ladies, but Hannah and the caterers just arrived."

Kara gave Francine a sidelong glance. "Are they a gift from someone special?"

"What?"

"Your earrings."

"Yes."

"Keaton?"

"Yes," Francine repeated.

"You're next, Francine."

Her brow furrowed. "Next for what?"

"You're the next one to get married. I started it, then Morgan followed, and now you're next. The man looks at you as if you were a decadent dessert," Kara continued. "I've heard talk about how he brings you lunch every day. A man who looks after his woman like that is someone you should hold on to. I can assure you that if you let him get away some woman will reel him in before you bat an eye. I thought there were some hungry women in New York, but they've got nothing on these barracudas down here." She leaned in close to Francine. "Jeff told me about a woman, whose name I will not mention, who opened the door for him wearing nothing but a pair of red panties. When he threatened to arrest her for lewdness, she went back into the house and put on a dress."

"Damn," Francine drawled.

Kara laughed. "That's what he said. I think I see our men now."

Francine was reunited with Keaton when he reappeared with Jeff, both men carrying highball glasses filled with an amber liquid. Within another fifteen minutes the living room was filled with Alice's supporters as the caterers' waitstaff offered her guests hot and cold hors d'oeuvres that included jumbo prawns and sushi before everyone filed into the dining room for a buffet dinner.

She found herself hovering close to Keaton after a man she'd never seen before tried hitting on her. At first he'd complimented her on her dress, then it was her legs and feet. When she tried to appear gracious he deliberately pressed his groin against her hips. It was apparent Keaton saw what was happening when he stalked across the room.

"You can look at her, but I'm warning you not to touch her again."

The man with an oily comb-over held up both hands. "It's not what you think."

"I know it's not what I think but what I saw. Stay the hell away from my *wife*."

Gurgling sounds came from the throat of Alice's press secretary. "I'm . . . I'm sorry, man. I didn't know she was your wife."

My wife. The two words caused Francine's breath to stop in her chest. It wasn't only what Keaton said, but *how* he'd said it. The passion and possessiveness was so obvious that she felt as if she truly were his wife.

She and Keaton departed soon after Kara and Jeff did, their ride back to Magnolia Drive accomplished in complete silence. She unlocked the door, and he followed her up the staircase. It was only a matter of time before word got out that she and Keaton were married, while nothing could be further from the truth.

"Tonight was nice," Francine said over her shoulder as she opened the apartment door and walked in.

Keaton closed the door behind them. "It was until that cretin lost his mind and decided to hump you."

She turned to face Keaton. "He had one more hump before I inflicted some serious pain that would've had him cradling his family jewels. I had enough of humping whenever I rode the subways in New York to last me for the rest of my life."

"How often does that happen to you?" Keaton asked.

"What, someone humping me?"

He shook his head. "No. Men coming onto you when you're dressed like this."

"What's that supposed to mean, Keaton? You think I dress to get attention?"

He took a step, anchoring his hands against the wall next to her head. "No. I think it's because you don't realize just how sexy you are." He tucked in a curl that had escaped the pins holding her hair in place. "Just looking at you makes me hard." He grasped her hand, holding it against the solid bulge in the front of his suit trousers.

Knowing she had that effect on Keaton elicited an erotic hunger in Francine she hadn't known she possessed. Her hands were busy when she unzipped his fly, her fingers closing around the hardness pulsing against the fabric of his briefs. Her mouth was as busy as her hands as she covered his mouth with hers. She wanted to get closer, absorb everything about Keaton inside her.

He picked her up, one arm holding her aloft while the other found the waistband of her thong panties, pulling the scrap of silk off her hips, and tossing it to the floor. Common sense fled, insanity taking over when Francine freed his erection. They stood in the dimly lit entryway, her legs around his waist, arms holding onto his neck. She was in heat and all she wanted was his hardness sliding in and out of her wet, quivering flesh.

Chapter Nineteen

The sounds of heavy breathing, punctuated with the slip-slap of flesh meeting flooded Keaton's senses. The raw passion Francine offered him made him forget every woman he had ever known. She'd suspected he wanted something from her and if he were honest he would've told her he wanted her to love him as much as he'd come to love her. He wanted to go to sleep with her every night and wake up with her beside him every morning. He wanted to watch her belly swell with the children he hoped to have with her. There were so many things he wanted to share with her.

Keaton felt the tingling sensation at the base of his spine, the tightening of his scrotum, and knew he was close to ejaculating. He knew he should pull out, yet he didn't want it to end. He knew the possibility of getting Francine pregnant would complicate everything. Keaton wasn't certain where he summoned the strength to pull out, while he continued to pump his hips against her mound. Together they climbed the peak of passion, poising at the precipice before floating back down to earth and reality.

It ended when he slid down to the floor, taking Francine with him. She straddled his thighs, her head resting on his shoulder. "I love you, Keaton. I love you so much it pains me to even say it."

Keaton kissed her forehead. The night was filled with surprises. He hadn't expected Francine to look as if she'd just stepped off the pages of a glossy fashion magazine. He hadn't expected to spend his time at the Parkers watching her every move, hanging on to her every word when she introduced him to those she'd known for years. Despite there being more than two dozen people there, it could've been only the two of them, because he'd blocked out everyone except himself and Francine.

He cradled her face, his heart turning over when he saw her tears. "I love you, too."

She let out a long shudder. "Thank you, Keaton."

"There's no need to thank me for loving you."

She closed her eyes, spiked lashes resting

on the ridge of high cheekbones. "Not about that. It could've ended in disaster if you hadn't pulled out. I picked the wrong time of the month to get reckless."

"It's okay, baby." Dipping his head, he brushed a kiss over her parted lips. "I like spontaneity."

Her expression changed, becoming somber. "We can't do this again. It's too risky."

His eyebrows lifted. "Making love?"

"Making love without using protection," Francine corrected. She anchored her arms under his shoulders. "I want children, but . . ."

Keaton stopped her words when he placed his fingers over her mouth. He knew what she wanted, because he wanted the same. "I know what you want."

"What do I want besides children?" she asked.

"You want a husband you can trust to love, protect, and provide for you and the children you hope to have together. And you want a stable life filled with people you love."

She giggled, the sound reminiscent of Keaton's sister when she was a little girl. "You really think you know me that well?"

"Not as well as I've come to know your delectable body, sweetie."

Francine nuzzled his ear. "It looks as if I'm going to need some extra tutoring before I get to know yours," she said teasingly.

Keaton played with the curls grazing the nape of her neck. "I don't mind staying after class to help you out."

Francine kissed the bridge of his nose. "Sorry, darling, but I'm going to have to postpone that lesson for another time. Help me up, please. My legs are going to sleep."

Keaton zipped his fly, massaged her calves and thighs, and then helped Francine to her feet. He stared at her intently as she smoothed down her dress. Bending down, he picked up her panties, dangling them from his forefinger. "I think these belong to you."

She flashed a sexy smile. "I do believe they do." She kissed him. "Go home, Keaton."

She wanted him to go home when it was the last thing he wanted to do.

"Is that what you want?" he asked with deceptive calm.

Francine nodded. "I need to be alone to think about everything that's happened between us tonight."

"Everything that happened tonight was supposed to happen." That said, he turned on his heel and walked out.

She loved him.

He loved her.

But was it enough to commit to a future together? The question nagged at him when he stood under the spray of the shower, and it continued to plague him when he lay on the bed staring into darkness. It was sometime before the sky brightened with the dawn of a new day that he finally fell asleep.

Sunday afternoon Keaton sat across from Devon at a table in a restaurant within walking distance of her hotel. Peering at her over the rim of his cup of coffee, he met her eyes. Her face had changed. It was thinner and it was the first time he'd seen her without makeup and her hair pulled off her face.

"What's the matter, Devon?"

She avoided his eyes. "Everything."

Reaching across the table, he held one of her hands. "Is something wrong with your baby?"

Devon's hazel eyes filled with tears. "No, it's not the baby. It's me."

Keaton released her hand and leaned back in his chair. "I'll understand if you don't want to talk about it —"

"I have to talk about it," she said, interrupting him, "or I'll lose my mind."

He couldn't figure out what it could be,

but he knew it had to be serious to make his friend and attorney leave New York to seek him out. The most obvious thing would be that Gregory wasn't thrilled that she was carrying his child.

"Remember what I said before, Devon. Whatever the outcome, I'm here for you."

"He doesn't want this baby, Keaton."

"Has he told you that?"

Devon picked up a napkin and touched it to the corners of her eyes. "Remember when I told you he was flying up from Virginia to see me?" Keaton nodded. "Well, it never happened."

"Did he at least call you to tell you he wouldn't be coming?"

"No. And when I called him, it went directly to voice mail. I waited a day and called again and that's when I found out that he'd blocked my calls."

"Did he suspect you were pregnant with his child?"

"I think so, because I'd mentioned to him that I was late and my period always comes on time."

"So, the bastard bails on you because he believes you're going to tell him that he's going to be a father?"

Devon sniffled audibly. "It's more than that, Keaton."

"How much more?"

"I did something that I told myself I would never do, and that was chase a man. I drove down to Newport News to confront him. When I rang his doorbell a woman who identified herself as his aunt told me that Gregory was staying with his parents, because his father had just had open heart surgery. She also told me that Gregory and his fiancée had postponed their wedding until his father's health improved. When I asked about his fiancée, his aunt told me she was the daughter of the junior senator from Mississippi."

"You believed her?" Keaton asked.

"At first I didn't, but when I Googled the senator's name I saw photographs of him with his wife and daughter. There was also one with Gregory cuddling with the daughter at a fund-raising event."

Now he realized why Devon hadn't returned his calls. She had to have been devastated by the news that the man she'd been sleeping with was engaged to another woman. Rising to his feet, Keaton moved his chair until he was sitting next to her, his arm going around her shoulders.

"Do you still plan to tell him about the baby?"

She shook her head. "No."

Dropping his arm, he stared at her strained profile. "What are you going to do? I know you intend to have the baby," he interjected quickly, "but what are your future plans?"

"I don't know. New York City is a wonderful place to live and socialize, but I can't see myself raising a child there. And as an entertainment attorney, I have the advantage of having a small number of select clients who pay quite well for my services. That means I can live anywhere."

"What does *he* do for a living?"

"Gregory is also an attorney. We met in law school."

"Oh shit!" Keaton swore under his breath. "You're playing with fire," he warned his attorney. "What if he finds out that you had his baby? Do you think he's not going to put two and two together and possibly sue you for joint custody?"

"I doubt that, Keaton. Gregory didn't have to buy the cow because he got the milk for free. His engagement isn't a new thing. He's been with her for a while. Oh, I didn't mention that the fund-raising photo of them was taken more than three years ago. When Gregory and I ran into each other in New York he didn't tell me at the time that his girlfriend was in Japan studying for a graduate degree in Asian studies."

Keaton knew he had to be there for Devon — at least emotionally, because she'd been estranged from her brother and parents for more than a decade. "When do you plan to go back to New York?"

"I'm leaving tonight, but I'm going to stop in Chicago first to tell my mother and father that they're going to be grandparents before the end of the year."

He smiled for the first time. "That's good."

Putting her arms around his neck, Devon pulled his head down and kissed his cheek. "Thank you for hearing me out. You're an incredible friend," she said as a single tear escaped her eye.

Keaton patted her hair. "Friends are supposed to take care of one another. Now, I want you to promise that you'll call me with updates."

"I will."

"Say it like you mean it, Devon."

"I will call you so much you'll get sick of hearing my voice."

"I doubt that. And when you want a change of scenery let me know and I'll put you up."

Her smile was dazzling. "I like the sound of that."

He settled the bill, and then walked her back to her hotel, waiting until she disappeared into the elevator before returning to the lot where he'd left his car. Seeing his friend in tears had affected Keaton more than he wanted, and it was a blatant reminder that it didn't matter that Devon was smart, attractive, and successful. She was going to join the growing number of single mothers — something she'd told him she never wanted to become.

Concern for his friend plagued Keaton until he returned to his suite at the Cove Inn, changed into a pair of shorts and a T-shirt, booted up his laptop, and began working on his script.

Keaton walked into Francine's apartment Monday afternoon carrying a large canvas tote and was greeted by the sound of show tunes coming through various speakers and the smell of lemons. He knew it came from the wax she used to dust the tables and wood surfaces. "Honey, I'm home," he called out in his best Ricky Ricardo imitation. Francine met him in the dining room, where she'd set the table for two. She wore a bibbed apron stamped with red and green apples over a pair of cutoffs and a tee, and had pushed her bare feet into a pair of flip-flops.

Holding her arms out at her sides, she smiled. Going on tiptoe, she touched her mouth to his. "I'm ready for my lesson."

Dipping his head, Keaton brushed a kiss over her parted lips. "Where did you get the cute apron? It makes you look like a domestic goddess," he added, teasing her.

Francine executed a graceful curtsy. "I ordered it and several others online." She peered into the tote. "What did you bring?"

"Let's go in the kitchen and I'll show you." Turning on her heels, Francine led the way into the kitchen, Keaton following.

"I have a little surprise for you," she said, peering over her shoulder.

Keaton stopped short at the entrance to the kitchen when he spied the glass bowl filled with ingredients for a Greek salad. "You made that?"

Francine curtsied again. "Yes, I did. I went online early this morning and found a site featuring easy recipes. I figured I'd start with a salad because it doesn't require cooking. I even made the dressing. I want you to be honest with me when you taste it."

Resting the tote on the floor, Keaton pulled her into a close embrace, burying his face in her hair. "If you followed the directions, then I'm certain it's going to be delicious."

"One of these days I'm going to prepare an entire meal for you."

He closed his eyes. "I'm certain you will." He wanted to tell Francine that cooking together in the kitchen of his new home was something he wanted more than anything. He also wanted to go to bed with her and wake up beside her as a husband and the father of the children he hoped to have with her.

Francine pushed against his chest and he released her. "What's my first lesson?"

Reaching into the bag, he removed a package with a large roasting chicken, and plastic bags of asparagus, tiny red potatoes, carrots, celery, and onions. "This is also an easy recipe because you're going to make an entire meal in one pot."

"How long will it take to cook?"

"That all depends on when you want to eat," he explained. "A roaster this size cooked at three hundred seventy-five degrees should take about ninety minutes. But I prefer cooking it at around three hundred twenty-five for at least three hours to ensure it will be moist and juicy. The lower temperature and slower cooking always makes for a moist dish. That's why slow cookers are so popular."

"My mother makes her pulled pork in a slow cooker."

"Do you have one?"

Francine shook her head. "No. But I'm definitely going to buy one, along with a cookbook with Crock-Pot recipes."

Keaton felt her excitement. "Come on, Iron Chef, let's get you started on this chicken. Once you put it in the oven I want you to come with me to see the house. The construction crew just finished installing the floors." Harvey Rose had called him earlier that morning to inform him that the renovations on the main house were close to completion. All that remained was painting. As requested by Keaton, he'd hired a night crew to finish the project a month earlier than projected. He still had to wait for the furniture delivery, but he planned to buy a blow-up mattress and a folding table and chairs to use in the interim. He was even willing to sleep on the floor if it meant living under his own roof.

He took out a white box stamped with the Muffin Corner's logo. "Red velvet cake."

Francine moaned softly. "No one can make red velvet cake like Lester Kelly."

Keaton removed the last item from the tote, placing it on the countertop. "This is the first draft of my script."

She picked up the bound pages. "You finished it!?"

"It's only a draft. It will go through a number of revisions before I'm completely satisfied with it."

Francine pressed it to her chest. "I can't wait to begin reading it."

"You're going to have to wait until after you put the chicken up and we see the house." Francine placed the script on the table in a corner of the kitchen, then picked up a pair of latex gloves and put them on.

"You don't need the gloves, sweetie. You're going to prep a chicken, not dye it," he teased.

Francine wiggled her fingers. "I get creeped out if I touch raw meat."

He wanted to laugh, but didn't. Maybe, he mused, Francine's aversion to cooking came from her loathing of touching the flesh of animals. However, he wasn't going to challenge her, because he was more interested in the results rather than the method it took to achieve the meal. He knew they were going to have fun cooking together.

Francine held on to Keaton's hand when he led her up the porch to the house he would eventually call home. She'd followed his instructions when he told her how to prepare the roasted chicken with vegetables. She experienced a measure of satisfaction when she finally placed the one-pot meal in the oven, while carefully adjusting the temperature so it wouldn't cook too quickly.

The last time she'd accompanied him to the house the floors were covered with drop cloths, boxes of appliances were lined up along a wall in the living room, banisters and newel posts on the staircase leading to the second floor were unfinished, and workers were still installing Sheetrock in some of the spaces to create rooms and alcoves.

"How did they finish so quickly?" she asked, peering out a window of a second-floor bedroom that overlooked what would eventually become a garden. The landscaper had sectioned off parcels of earth for what she predicted would be a flower garden.

"I had the contractor hire a night crew, because I was seriously thinking of checking out of the Cove Inn and moving back to the Charleston Place. At least at the hotel I wouldn't necessarily have to eat in a communal dining room."

Francine turned to stare at the man she loved beyond description. "You know you could always come over and eat with my family whenever you want."

Resting his hands at her waist, Keaton pulled her close. "You know what I want, Francine."

She nodded, then said, "I do know. But I need time to think about it. Are you willing to wait?" Francine knew Keaton was referring to marriage. She knew she was being unfair to Keaton because she continued to compare him to Aiden.

Keaton's hands moved up to cradle her face. "Take all the time you need. I'm not going anywhere and neither are you."

She smiled. "Does this mean we're stuck with each other?"

Keaton returned her smile, his gaze lingering on her mouth. "As if we were joined at the hip," he teased.

Resting her head on his shoulder, Francine breathed in his masculine smell mingling with the familiar scent of his cologne. "I love your house."

"Our house," he corrected. "I want you to think of it as your house, too."

Francine pulled her lower lip between her teeth rather than tell Keaton that she didn't want him to put pressure on her about their future. "I asked for time, Keaton," she said instead.

"My bad," he apologized.

They continued touring the house, and

she attempted to imagine what the rooms would look like when fully furnished. She was partial to the front and back porches, the latter screened in, because of the ceiling fans resembling banana leaves. It was so easy to fantasize about hosting dinner parties and celebrating holidays in the expansive farmhouse with family and friends. A secret smile curved her mouth when she thought about the sound of tiny feet running over the polished wood floors. Everything she wanted, and had talked about with Morgan when they were young girls, was right in front of her. All she had to do was open her mouth and tell Keaton she would marry him. But an unforeseen uneasiness held her captive and she wasn't able to say what lay in her heart.

"They've finished but you still can't move in until the furniture is delivered."

"Yes, I can. I'm going to Charleston tomorrow to pick up an inflatable mattress and a table and chairs. Then I'm going to shop for pots and housewares. I plan to move out of the boardinghouse before the end of the week."

"Will you have a housewarming?"

"Eventually . . . don't worry. We'll have plenty of time for that."

Francine noticed he'd said "we" instead

of "I." What good was her gift for seeing into the future of others when she couldn't see into her own? Even when she'd tried concentrating on Keaton she couldn't discern anything. Was it, she wondered, because their futures were truly linked that they'd become one?

"I think it's time we get back so I can check on my chicken."

Keaton kissed her forehead. "Spoken like a true chef."

When they returned to her apartment Francine gasped when she opened the oven to find the chicken had turned a beautiful golden brown. The meat thermometer she'd inserted into the thickest part of the thigh registered 180° F. "How do I test it for doneness?" she asked Keaton as he stood behind her.

"You can pierce the thigh with a long fork to see if the juices run clear or you can wiggle the leg and if it comes away from the breast, then it's done."

"It's done!" Francine couldn't disguise her excitement when she realized she had actually cooked something.

"Turn off the oven and leave it in there for another five minutes. Then you can take it out to let it rest so the juices will distribute evenly while you grill the asparagus."

"How long will it take for the asparagus to cook?"

"It won't take more than ten minutes. I'll heat the grill while you drain the asparagus and pat them dry with a paper towel before you season them."

Francine opened the fully stocked refrigerator and took out the asparagus she'd placed in a bowl of ice water to keep them from wilting. Keaton, in preparing lunch for her, had stocked the refrigerator and pantry. There were jars of exotic spices she'd never heard of on a revolving rack. He'd even stocked the wine rack with bottles of merlot, rosé, and dry and fruity whites. In honor of preparing her first meal she'd decided to serve a blush to accompany the chicken.

She sprinkled salt, fresh pepper, garlic powder, and grated Parmesan cheese on the asparagus spears before drizzling them with olive oil. Using a pair of tongs, she placed them on the surface of the heated grill, searing them on one side before turning. The mouthwatering aromas filling the kitchen reminded Francine that she'd had only a cup of tea and a slice of toast for breakfast.

She plated the asparagus, while Keaton expertly carved the chicken before he placed it on a platter and took it into the dining room. Francine had to admit they worked well together. Within minutes the bowl of salad and the cruet with the dressing she'd made from vinegar, garlic, dill, oregano, salt, pepper, and olive oil were set out on the table.

She handed Keaton the bottle of chilled wine and a corkscrew. "Will you do the honor of opening it?"

His eyebrows lifted a fraction. "I suppose wine is in order today because we must toast this momentous occasion." Keaton seated Francine before rounding the table to sit opposite her. He uncorked the bottle, filling the wineglasses with white zinfandel. Smiling, he raised his glass in a toast. "Here's to a wonderful dinner prepared by a woman who one day will become legendary when it comes to hosting Cavanaugh Island dinner parties."

"Hear, hear," she intoned.

Francine had to admit she'd done very well with her first meal. The chicken was moist and flavorful, as were the accompanying vegetables. The asparagus, Greek salad, and dressing elicited effusive compliments from Keaton that made her blush. He cleared the table, while she brewed coffee to go along with the slices of red velvet cake.

A half hour later she sat on the window

seat reading the first draft of Keaton's script while he lay dozing on a recliner. Francine couldn't believe he'd captured the essence of Lowcountry culture so expertly. How, she wondered, had he picked up the vernacular so quickly? The two most riveting characters were the mother and daughter conjurers who were willing to do whatever someone wanted if they were paid what they'd requested from their prospective clients. Their deviance caused the hair on her arms to stand up.

She was only pages from the end of the script when Keaton opened his eyes.

"What do you think?"

Francine shivered noticeably. "Lottie and her mother are witches." It wasn't a question but a statement.

He nodded. "Witches who are also time travelers. This is my first attempt at writing a paranormal script."

"Have you thought of who you would cast for Lottie and Annie Mae?"

Sitting up and swinging his legs over the side of the recliner, Keaton placed his feet firmly on the floor. "I respect how much you like doing hair, but I really believe you would be perfect in the role of Lottie. I've made her a redhead because Montague

Summers's translation of *Malleus Maleficarum* indicated red hair and green eyes as traits of a witch, werewolf, or a vampire during the Middle Ages."

Francine set the script on the cushioned seat. "You developed this character in the hope I would accept the role even though I told you I'd given up acting?"

"Yes." He didn't want to lie to her.

Rising to her feet, Francine's hands went to her hips. "When I asked what you wanted from me and you told me nothing I believed you, Aiden. But, it's apparent I've been too trusting."

Keaton sprang up as if pulled up by a powerful wire. "What did you call me?"

"Keaton."

"No, Francine. You called me Aiden. Was he your ex?" The seconds ticked off. "The fact that you're not saying anything says he was. And was he an actor? Is that why you decided to leave the business, because you didn't want to run into him or be reminded of what you once had?"

"You're the one who seems to have all of the answers, Keaton."

Shaking his head, he approached her. "I may have answers, but not the ones I want."

"What the hell do you want to know?" she screamed. "Yes, I was married to Aiden Fox, and yes, he's the reason I gave up acting. And do you want to know something else about me? I'm psychic. I see visions."

"What? I can't believe you, Francine. I specifically asked you if you were a psychic and you lied and said no. You talk about not being able to trust me, when I can't trust you to be honest with me. You talk about needing time to figure out whether we'll be together. Well, baby, you're not the only one."

Turning on his heel, Keaton walked out of the living room. He wanted to punch something, if only to release the frustration making it hard for him to think clearly. He loved Francine, and because he did he found it impossible to turn his emotions off and on like a faucet.

Minutes later, he sat in his truck, staring out the windshield. Aiden Fox. The name was vaguely familiar. He did recall Fox had begun his acting career starring in a daytime soap opera, but the fact that he hadn't popped up onto the big screen told Keaton his career must have gone stagnant. Running a hand over his head, he exhaled an audible breath. He wanted to walk away from Francine the way he had with the other women in his life, but he couldn't because he loved her too much. He had no idea what he was going to do now.

Chapter Twenty

"You look like crap."

Francine affected a wry smile. "Thanks, Mo, for the compliment."

Morgan gave her a direct stare. "Well, you do. In fact, you look like something the cat dragged in. Speaking of cats, you can pick up the kitten for your grandmother any time you want. Now tell me. What's the matter?"

Francine had spent the past three nights tossing, turning, crying, and racked with guilt. Keaton was right. She *was* a hypocrite. She talked about not being able to trust Aiden when she hadn't trusted Keaton enough to confide in him about the identity of her ex-husband. She'd taken a chance and stopped by Morgan's office in the hope that her friend would be there.

"Keaton and I had a disagreement."

Morgan waved her hand. "What makes you think you're exempt from disagreeing with your partner? Nate and I agree on most things but not everything."

"It's different with me and Keaton."

"What makes it different, Fran?" Morgan asked.

"I insisted on honesty from him when I wasn't able to give him the same."

Morgan picked up the phone and tapped the extension of the design firm's receptionist/office manager. "Patrice, please hold my calls. I'm going to be in the lounge." She hung up. "Come in the back with me so we can talk in private."

She followed her friend into the lounge and sat next to her on the leather love seat. It was as if time stood still when Francine confided in Morgan as she'd done when they were in high school. "I've lost him, Mo, because I can't seem to let go of what I had with Aiden. I haven't been fair to Keaton or myself."

"Does he love you, Fran?"

A sensual smile parted her lips. "Yes. He loves me and I love him."

"Has he asked you to marry him?" Francine nodded. Morgan compressed her lips in frustration, dimples deepening in her cheeks. "What did you tell him?"

"I told him I need time."

Morgan's right hand came down hard on the leather seat cushion. "Time for what,

Francine Tanner! You're a grown-ass woman who doesn't need anyone's permission or approval to marry this man. A lot of women on Cavanaugh Island are just waiting for you to kick him to the curb so they can have a shot. And trust me, he won't stay available when they start tossing their panties in his direction. After all, he is a man."

Francine narrowed her eyes. "What's that supposed to mean?"

"Don't play dumb, Fran. You know exactly what I mean. Men have needs just like we have needs. You may have divorced Aiden on paper, but emotionally you're still connected to him when I'm certain he's not letting losing you affect his life."

"He didn't lose me. He left me."

"Big whoop! He may have left you because as a parasite he moved onto another host. Please don't let Keaton get away or you'll regret it for the rest of your life. Don't be stubborn, Fran. Go after your man."

Francine stared at her folded hands in her lap. She knew Morgan was right. For the past eight years she'd allowed Aiden to dictate her life and if she didn't let him go she would never be able to rid herself of his invisible hold. "You're right, Mo. I can't lose him. Not when I've been given a second chance at love."

"That's my girl. I happen to know where he is at this very moment."

Her gaze met Morgan's. "Where is he?"

Morgan grinned like a Cheshire cat. "He called Abram, because he's expecting a furniture delivery. He needs Abram's assistance with where things should be placed."

Leaning over, Francine hugged Morgan. "Thanks, Mo. I'm going to get my man."

"That's my girl!"

Francine was practically running when she went to retrieve her car from the lot behind the row of shops along Main Street. She slipped into the low-slung sports car. Within seconds the engine roared to life and she shifted and maneuvered out of the lot with the skill of a NASCAR driver. It was the first time since she'd begun driving that she didn't heed the island's unofficial speed limit. Francine ignored the curious stares as she shifted into a higher gear, increasing her speed. She drove past her house in a red blur, slowing only when she turned off onto the road leading to Keaton's. It was as if she were seeing it for the first time. The coat of white paint shimmered in the bright early afternoon sunlight. Parking alongside Keaton's BMW, Francine got out of the Corvette and walked up the porch steps, finding the front door unlocked. She saw Keaton and Abram sitting on folding chairs in the empty living room. Abram noticed her first.

"Hey, Francine. What's up?"

She smiled at the interior decorator. "Hi, Abram. How's it going?"

"Good. Real good. You need to see me?"

"No, Abram. I came to see, Keaton." Keaton stood up as if in slow motion. It was obvious he hadn't expected to see her. "I'm sorry to interrupt you, but we need to talk. Out on the porch, please," she added when he glanced over at Abram.

Keaton had been wondering what it would feel like to be sentenced to live out his days in complete isolation, because that was what he'd been experiencing since he walked out of Francine's apartment three days ago. He got up and went through the motions of showering and changing his clothes because he'd been conditioned to start his day that way. But he hadn't shaved in two days and the stubble was beginning to itch, yet he welcomed the discomfort. He hadn't realized how much a part of his existence she'd become until he discovered he couldn't just pick up the phone and talk to her as he'd done before. She needed time and he'd given it to her. He'd told her he also needed time but within an hour of driving back to the Cove Inn he knew he still wanted to marry her.

"Are you sleeping okay?" It was the first thing he could think of to say to Francine. Her green eyes appeared lighter because of the dark circles that indicated that she was either not sleeping or she wasn't feeling well.

"No," she replied. "I've been doing a lot of thinking."

Leaning against a column holding up the porch, Keaton gave her a long, penetrating stare. "What about?"

Tilting her chin in a defiant gesture, she smiled. "Us."

His impassive expression did not change when he held his breath. If she was going to walk away from him he was determined to never let her see his pain. "What about us, Francine?"

"I love you, Keaton, and I want to spend the rest of my life with you. As your wife and the mother of our children."

Keaton took a step, bringing them inches apart. "When?"

"June. I've always wanted to be a June bride."

He extended his hands and wasn't disappointed when Francine took them. Folding her to his chest, Keaton closed his eyes and whispered a prayer of gratitude. "I was hoping you'd say next week."

Leaning back in his embrace, Francine smiled through the tears turning her eyes into pools of fluorescent green. "There's no way my parents will be able to plan a wedding in a week. And what about your family, Keaton? They will need time —"

Keaton's explosive kiss stopped her protest. He wasn't disappointed when she pressed her breasts to his chest as she deepened the kiss. He was willing to marry Francine tomorrow but knew it wouldn't be fair to her, or to their families. He'd waited more than forty years for a woman like Francine to come into his life and three months would come and go quickly.

"When do you want to announce our engagement?" he whispered against her slightly swollen lips.

"On my birthday."

"When's your birthday, sweetie?"

"St. Patrick's Day."

"Don't tell me my serving wench has a bit of Irish in her?"

Throwing back her head, Francine laughed. "Aye, milord. Do you have a problem with that?"

"No, milady." He kissed her again, pulling back when he heard the approach of a truck with the living room and kitchen furniture. "To be continued," he whispered in her ear.

Francine sat opposite Keaton at the table in the Tanners' formal dining room. It was St. Patrick's Day and everyone had worn green to celebrate the festive holiday. Mavis and Dinah had outdone themselves when they cooked all of her favorite dishes. Morgan, Nate, Kara, Jeff, and David had been invited to help her celebrate her thirty-fourth birthday. Keaton had also invited Devon to join them.

Frank tapped his water glass with a knife. "I'd like to thank everyone for coming to help celebrate my baby's birthday." He ignored Francine when she pushed out her lips. "I know she doesn't like it when I refer to her as my baby, but that's who she'll always be to me. This birthday is very special not only because I'm sitting here with the women who've made me the happiest man on Cavanaugh Island, but also because there's a man sitting at my table whom I'm honored to think of as a son." He raised his glass in Keaton's direction. "Keaton. Welcome to the family."

Morgan looked at Francine, then Keaton. She'd taken to wearing oversize blouses to conceal her expanding waistline. "Are we missing something?"

Reaching into the pocket of her blouse, Francine took out the ring Keaton had slipped on her finger earlier that morning. She held it up for everyone to see as Keaton came around the table. He took it from her and dropped to one knee. "Milady," he said in a dead-on aristocratic British accent, "I knew when I entered the tavern and saw you for the first time what I had been missing. Your beauty, your wit, and a well-turned ankle caused me many sleepless nights. I must admit you were quite a challenge, but as someone used to giving and not taking orders I am willing to offer you my title and protection if you would become my wife."

Francine felt everyone staring at her and Keaton. She knew she was about to give the performance of her lifetime: accepting Keaton's proposal with her family and friends as witnesses. "Milord, I did not reject your advances outright but I had to make certain you were not toying with my affections. Although a serving wench, me mum and father raised me to be a lady despite our lowly station. You have proven yourself noble; therefore, I will marry thee." Keaton slipped the ring on her finger. A chorus of gasps and applause went up from those seated at the table.

"Bravo!" Dinah yelled loudly.

"I knew it, I knew it," Kara crowed loudly.

Morgan hugged Francine, as tears streamed down her face. "Fran, I told you you'd find someone worthy of your love."

One by one she received hugs and kisses from those sitting around the table. She and Keaton had planned to take a few days off to fly up to Pittsburgh to meet his family. They decided not to set a wedding date until they conferred with the Graces. Francine knew for certain it would take place on Cavanaugh Island, because there was nothing more spectacular than a Lowcountry beach wedding. She and Keaton posed for photos as everyone took out their cell phones.

"I love you, milord," she whispered.

"Fancy that, maiden, because I love you, too," Keaton said in her ear.

Francine had left the stage but her greatest performance was yet to be seen. The day she became Mrs. Keaton Grace she would give an award-winning performance spectators would talk about for years to come. "Do you see what I see?" she said under her breath.

"What is that?" Keaton questioned.

"Devon and David seem to be hitting it off well." The very pretty lawyer was laughing at something David had said to her.

He gave his fiancée a mischievous smile. "I hope you're not thinking of playing matchmaker."

Francine rested her head on Keaton's shoulder. "I just want everyone to be as happy as we are."

Keaton dropped a kiss on her hair. "There are different degrees of happy and we haven't even begun."

She knew Keaton was right. Not only was she happy, but she was also grateful to share her birthday and engagement with people who loved her. The rooms in the house she would share with Keaton were filling up with furniture and when she finally moved in to live with her husband Francine knew they would begin traditions that would be passed down to another generation of Gullah Tanners. Keaton had revised his script, and although he realized she would never step in front of a camera again, she'd agreed to become a technical advisor for the first film to be released by Grace Low-country Productions.

A mysterious smile flitted over her mouth as she closed her eyes. She'd had another vision. This one showed Mavis cradling a baby. Her mother was going to get her wish. Francine would make her a grandmother.

The employees of Thorndike Press hope you have enjoyed this Large Print book. All our Thorndike, Wheeler, and Kennebec Large Print titles are designed for easy reading, and all our books are made to last. Other Thorndike Press Large Print books are available at your library, through selected bookstores, or directly from us.